SPINDOWN
Andy Crawford

Other titles by Andy Crawford:
Sailor of the Skysea
The Pen is Mightier
Untethered (short story)

For Nina

2240, Earth Calendar

~3 Earth years since departure of colony ship Aotea *from Earth system*

~63 cycles (52 Earth years) until arrival at destination, Samwise, a habitable moon of Abhoth, a gas giant planet orbiting the red dwarf star Gliese 876.

CHAPTER 1

Constable Lo spotted the man he was hunting with his head poking out around the corner passageway. "Hey!" he shouted. "Stop!"

The constable was alone, and this passageway of the colony spaceship *Aotea* was empty, aside for a lone whirring DustBot. The fugitive made a snap decision and charged. Surprised, Lo shifted his stance and braced himself.

Too late. The fugitive led with his shoulder and sent Lo bouncing off a bulkhead at the end of the passageway. *Earth-bred strength beats these low-gravvers every time.*

"You're down," said the fugitive as he scooped up a dropped wearable, eyeing the constable, who remained motionless on the deck. It wasn't just the difference in gravity from their upbringing — so many Aoteans, even among the constabulary, seemed constitutionally incapable of violence. He stifled a laugh as the little DustBot scooted along and purposefully gave the prone constable a wide berth, obeying its programming — to always stay out of the way of humans — to the letter. Hearing footsteps, the fugitive made a quick scan of the neighboring passageways, located a supply closet, hefted the limp constable, less than half the weight he'd be on Earth, and manhandled him into the cramped space. "You're still down," he added before shutting the hatch.

3

Peering around the next corner of the passageway, the hunted man finally had a moment to breathe. He used the moment to hate. He hated this ship. He hated the low gravity, simulated by rotation, which left him disoriented every morning, his waking body expecting Earth-normal gravity as he rose to his feet. He hated the windowless views, and the endless and featureless passageways, kilometers and kilometers winding underneath the massive cylindrical inner "surface" on which most Aoteans lived. He hated the surface itself — bland structures, a few stories tall, divided by regular and identical walking lanes, and a mirror-like reflection on the other side of the interior cylindrical surface overhead. He hated the false "suns," massive, fusion-fired lights at each end of the kilometers-long cylinder, progressively lit and dimmed for the progression of every Aotean "day" and "night." He hated nearly every one of the twenty thousand souls onboard, and he found that, with the barest effort, even those Aoteans he found tolerable could be rather easily swept into that hated pool. And most of all, he hated himself for making the decision to leave Earth and join the crew, and this endless, hellish voyage, in the first place.

The hunted man waited for a bit, watching the sparse foot traffic of the passageway from his corner vantage point, one level below *Aotea's* interior surface. A shift change was approaching, with an accompanying increase in traffic, down to the scattered watch stations of the machinery spaces below, and back up to the living and recreation spaces on the interior surface. He shook his head at his own luck, for the carelessness of the constable — if the man had just called in his observation, instead of standing there gaping, the hunted man would be cornered by now. He clipped the stolen wearable to his collar, practiced fingers flicking the hard-reset, allowing voice and eye control. With a flick of his eyes he linked it to to his own earpiece, setting the volume low, wondering if they knew he could be listening in.

"…witness reported the fugitive seen near Hab 13…"

"… another witness who saw him by aft food service 7…"

"…description put out is too vague; adult male, just under two meters, brown skin, tear in the jumpsuit leg…"

"Lo, report?"

After a pause, the order was repeated.

The fugitive silenced it and chuckled to himself, looking down at his leg. *They handicap themselves.* He had already replaced the torn jumpsuit — thievery was trivial among these people, and in such a culture. A few centuries ago, Aoteans would have been called hippies, or peaceniks, or some other forgotten slur … no weapons, no surveillance cams, no currency, everything running on mutual trust. Doors and hatches could be locked, but few bothered.

And a single nonconformist could blow up the whole thing. *How can they hope to survive like this?* There would be more noncomformists, undoubtedly. More who cared more for their own whims and desires than the mandates and structures of the routine onboard. And these dupes had no idea how to handle it. They'd learn or die.

It was time to move — dumb as they were, they'd figure out Lo's last known location soon enough. The fugitive easily flowed into the growing traffic of the passageway, exchanging pleasantries with a few Aoteans he recognized just getting off watch. Did they even suspect anything? Why would they? They were on a giant spaceship trillions of kilometers from Earth, with twenty thousand hand-picked pacifists onboard. There hadn't been a single crime worse than petty theft or assault since they departed three Earth-years before. They queued up cordially and climbed the ladderwell to the surface.

And he had another decision to make. Hide or strike?

Not much of a choice to make. Checking his mental topography while he weaved between the structures on the surface of the aft Can, as the cylindrical interior of *Aotea* was commonly known, the hunted man considered his targets. Engineering was too far and would require a pass through the dangerous bottleneck of the Ring at the aft end of the Can. So was Operations, at the forward end. He cringed when he realized the nearest.

Medical. Not his first choice, but it was the most logical. Just a few "blocks" away, easily accessible from the surface, and with numerous entrances and exits.

The wide automatic doors of the infirmary, a clean-lined white structure larger than most onboard, were unguarded. A yawning admin tech perked up at the front desk, but the hunted man strode confidently as if he knew exactly where he was going. He rounded the desk, took a lift to the second deck, and headed down the passageway.

He stepped silently, turning away to examine a display when a doctor passed by. The long-term-patient wing was mostly empty, except for a constable seated at the end of the hall at a corner juncture.

Damn. There were a dozen doors along the passageway, but it wasn't clear which one the officer, a junior constable named Khan, was watching over. He ducked back behind the corner before she turned toward him. He took the long way around the perimeter of the level — the other passageway leading to the corner was much busier with a handful of outpatient appointments. An idea came to him, and he looked at the time, then turned and headed for the cafeteria.

He carried the tray haphazardly as he strode down the outpatient passageway once again. He passed a laundry cart and grabbed a small towel, tucking it into his belt to look more like an orderly. He looked down and angled the tray to obscure his face, but the constable wasn't paying much attention anyway. *Idiots.* Finally, she perked up when he stopped in front of her, a quizzical expression on her face.

"Which room?"

She looked down at a projection from her wearable. "Isn't it early for lunch?"

He shrugged his shoulders. "Can't I do a favor for a friend?"

"He's in room seven, but—"

He didn't let her finish, lashing out with a free hand and striking her neck.

"Stay down," he said as she went limp in her seat.

Idiots. He put the tray down on her desk, and checking that there was no one else in the long-term passageway, sprinted to room seven.

"That you, Khan?" came the voice as he pushed open the door.

"No, not Khan," answered the hunted man. The infirmary room was small — barely big enough for the bed and the medical device, snaked with tubes, that surrounded it.

The patient chuckled when he saw who it was. "Did you even break a sweat?"

"I'm afraid not."

The reclining man sighed. "That's a shame. I expected better."

"Sometimes we can't tell the difference between what we hope for and what we expect."

The hunted man reached out and took hold of the cluster of fluid lines. "Ready?"

Another sigh and then a nod.

The hunted man pulled abruptly, setting off a cacophony of electronic complaints. He shook his head to himself and snorted. He had also been expecting more from *Aotea*'s constabulary.

Then the alarms started — not the machines, but in the overhead. If he had a lens, the wearable could display directly onto his eyeball. But he didn't, so he projected the wearable's display onto the back of his hand — it had an alarm too, just a red pulse, silent since the hunted man had muted it earlier. *Huh.* Maybe they weren't quite so bad as he thought. He couldn't help but grin as he sprinted into the

7

passageway. At the next turn he almost crashed into an orderly, who let out an exhausted exclamation.

They were waiting for him at the lift bank. Three constables, two armed with stun sticks. *Finally brought those out...* For a moment he considered fleeing the other way — he was pretty sure there was a ladderwell in the corner of the structure, but he heard footsteps.

So he made another snap decision and charged, at the same time wrapping the towel around his left fist. Once again the constables were caught off guard, almost bumping into each other in their confusion. The first gave an awkward thrust of the stun stick, which he absorbed with his towel-hand, punching sharply with his right into the constable's ribs. As that one went to the deck with a grunt, the second waded in, swinging the stunner with more vigor. *Not enough.* The fugitive blocked it at the handle with his forearm, turning and striking with an elbow to the chin, and wrenched the stunner free of his grasp as the constable collapsed. The last constable had wisely backed away, yelling into her wearable. *Not far enough.* The hunted man leapt forward, pressed the trigger, and thrust the stunner into her belly, sending her to the deck.

And then the lift doors opened, six constables charged forward, and upon feeling the unfamiliar shock to his skin, the hunted man went limp and was hauled away.

He sat in an uncomfortable chair in the constabulary briefing room, meeting the eyes of each of more than a dozen constables and inspectors. They shook their heads, and a few looked down at their feet.

He stood up. The hatred, at least some of which had been deliberately manufactured in his head, morphed into disapproval.

"That was pathetic. If that was a real VIP instead of DCI Gregorian, he'd be dead by now, thanks to you." He eyed the deputy chief inspector, Kiro Gregorian, who just a half-hour before had been the "patient" in the infirmary room, and appeared to be hiding a smirk. Constable Khan met his eyes with a sheepish expression and then looked at the deck.

He wanted to rail against the culture of *Aotea*, the idea that non-violence disapproval and discussion could solve everything, that all conflict could be avoided, and the listlessness that resulted from such ideological devotion. But he held that in. "You'll have my report by tomorrow, and I expect a written report from each and every one of you as well, on what you observed, and the mistakes you made, and how they can be prevented."

They were silent.

There were positives, but he kept silent about them. There were other targets aside from Kiro and the two he'd "killed" earlier, and after stumbling for the first few hours, at least they had reacted quickly enough to subdue him following the attack in the hospital. But there shouldn't have been more than one successful attack.

"Is that clear?"

They responded in unison. "Yes, Chief Inspector!"

Cyrus Konami knew there was more to say. But the chief inspector suspected he was already on thin ice from the higher ups — he'd had to beg and plead and finagle for months before they agreed to his plan for such a large-scale, ship-wide security drill.

"Very well," said Konami. "Back to your duties."

He didn't hate these people, and this ship, and this culture, frustrating as they all were, he decided. *It's not hate,* he told himself, *just boredom.* And perhaps just a slower adjustment than he thought it would be.

I'm not a hateful man, he thought to himself. He even managed to smile and nod to one of the few constables who had demonstrated some aptitude and ingenuity in the drill.

Just bored. And tired.

As he left his office for the day, he yawned, even though he wasn't tired.

CHAPTER 2

Trillions of miles from Earth, on the largest and most advanced spacecraft ever constructed, a shit filter was clogged. Not "evacuate the people spaces and don HazMat suits!" clogged, but "might cause a slight stench once-in-a-while" clogged.

Data Technician 1st Class Theo Muahe sighed as he scanned the display monitors and past the abnormal readings on the console in the cramped Sewage and Water Control station. If he had been claustrophobic, this particular watch would have been a nightmare, but First Muahe was used to the tight quarters in many of *Aotea*'s watch stations and machinery spaces. Numbers for gas partial pressures, particulates, acidity, bacteria, and dozens of other details of the complexities of maintaining the potable water systems for every shower, kitchen, and head for the twenty thousand souls onboard the colony ship *Aotea* danced cleanly over the crystalline display. *Technically, everything's green.* But Muahe wasn't the type to pass off a problem, however minor it might be, to the next watchstander. He looked again at the first few log readings, confirming his suspicions. All the numbers were in the normal ranges, but bacterial and particulate logs had jumped a few ticks, after several hours of nearly identical values.

"Damn shit filters…" he mumbled.

A chirping interrupted his log reading, and Muahe turned his attention to his wearable, projecting it onto his lens. The multi-purpose device displayed a simple alert from the NetBug tracer he had started before reporting for his proficiency Sewage and Water Systems watch. *Shouldn't be full yet*, he thought as he read the alert. The tracer had noted that hard drive 271w, one of thousands of identical data storage drives, was prematurely full. A black spot took his attention for a moment. *Gonna have to re-lens the damn thing.* His heart sped up when he realized there were no spare lenses in the watch station; he'd have to wait until he was back in his quarters. *S'okay, Theo, you can still see it just fine. A little speck is no big deal...* He took a deep breath, recognizing that he sometimes had trouble differentiating between trivial issues and major problems. A half minute of concentration told him that this one was the former.

He shifted his attention back to the Tracer he had started immediately before he took the sewage watch. The data sponge he was tracking down was just the latest nuisance in his primary duty as part of the team that managed the data systems and automated programming of the massive colony ship *Aotea*.

With practiced fingers dancing in the air, DT1 Muahe quickly navigated to the hard drive in question, and found to his surprise that it was mostly empty. "Huh," he grunted. He queried the NetBug again, and after a few seconds, the tracer returned with the same result as before — hard drive 271w was full. Commands through his wearable simply queried the hard drive's own logs. But the NetBug tracer was much more thorough, actually trawling the quantum-molecular data net itself. *So who's lying? My tracer or the hard drive?* He groaned as he realized he wouldn't be able to go right to sleep when he got off watch; his own nagging sense of duty would compel him to solve this little mystery. His primary responsibility would have to wait, though; as a fully qualified crewmember of *Aotea*, DT1 Muahe was required to periodically stand watch at most of the major ship's systems to maintain proficiency. He returned to the sewage system logs.

"Damn filter clogs," he grunted. Accumulating debris in the water would occasionally gum up the works of the chemical cleaners that maintained bacterial levels near zero.

"Where's the RoverBot?" he muttered to himself as he scrolled through menus on the console as fast as the eye could follow. The sewage station shared a roving maintenance robot with some of the neighboring systems; minor maintenance like cleaning filters was usually left to the Rover. *Atmospherics plant? Damn it!*

"Voice: get me the Atmo watch." Unlike most Aoteans, Muahe routinely switched between voice, ocular, and tactile control of his wearable, finding each method to be more useful for different tasks.

"Atmo, MT2 Taki," answered a musical, feminine voice.

Taki? Oh yeah, that little MedTech. I like the way her hips move... DT1 Muahe cleared his throat. "Atmo, Sewage. Where do you have the Rover?"

"With a TechBot. Joint servo broke."

Jacks-of-all-trades in electronics and delicate machinery, TechBots served as general practitioners and surgeons for other Bots, though it was unusual for a RoverBot to require unscheduled repairs. "How much longer?"

"Hour or two."

Goddamnit. He tried not to let his frustration show through the comms system. "Thanks, Atmo, Sewage out." Muahe closed the connection and shut his eyes, for some reason feeling a tad more energized. *At least we get off watch at the same time. Maybe she'd like to get a drink or a dip in the Pond...* Then he recalled the anomaly the NetBug found. *Damn.*

The bacterial and particulate readings were still technically within specification, so he was not bound by the regulations to do anything but note it in the logs and mention it to the next person on duty. But nothing was more irritating then relieving a watch only to have to solve a problem the last guy was too lazy to fix. *If only I had a UI today...* Periodically all watchstanders would be accompanied by an Under Instruction watch, usually a youngster still working on their ship's qualification. And this would be an excellent job for a UI — he vaguely recalled that the Sewage qualification card had a Practical Factor requirement for manual clearance of a filter clog. He shook his head unconsciously. *Guess it's all on me, damn it.* He didn't look forward to squeezing his bulky frame into the maintenance crawlway, and dreaded even more the too-snug feeling of the thinsuit and breather he would need to wear to open up the purifiers.

"Might as well get it over with," he mumbled as he made his way through the cramped passageways, instinctively ducking his head under various pipes and other obstacles for the tall. He was so busy minding the head-level obstructions that he nearly tripped on an insectile DustBot, and cursed at the indignant squeal from the little fist-sized cleaning robot, ubiquitous throughout *Aotea*.

The thinsuit locker was unhelpfully placed next to a bulky suction pump, leaving him little room to actually don it. And to add insult to injury, the breather seal was broken, eliciting an involuntary growl of frustration. He projected onto a bulkhead and navigated to the logs for this locker. It was signed by MRT2 Gustafson, dating about three weeks ago. *Gustafson, damn it!* Every time a breather was used, the regulations said the user had to replace the filter, recharge the tank, and apply a new tamper seal. The seal helpfully turned red if there was any leakage. Cursing, DT1 Muahe hooked the breather up to the pressure test device, only calming slightly when the readout came up clean. *Okay Gustafson, you charged it and put the filter in, so that earns you a reprieve... but if you forget the fucking seal again, the brotherhood of the watch be damned, you're getting reported!*

The maintenance crawlway was even more confined than he remembered; he hadn't had to traverse it for several months. Every step required a contortion — around a pipe, or an electrical box, or a data conduit, or one of hundreds of other components. By the time he reached the purifier lockout space, he was massaging a cramp in his hamstring. As soon as he shut the hatch behind him, he spent a full, luxurious minute stretching his muscles. He pawed through a few choices on the tiny display and temporarily shut off the flow through these filters. It took another minute for the purifier bank to drain with a telltale *glug-glug*. He took a deep breath and thumbed the release for the purifier bank entryway. Under the thinsuit hood, he barely heard the hiss of equalizing pressure as the narrow hatch opened.

He had to get on his knees once again to access the filters, with nothing but a porous grate between him and the innards of each device. *At least this damn breather takes away the stink.* The hatch shut automatically behind him. A small click from somewhere nearby took his attention, but nothing seemed out of place when he glanced around. He disconnected the power for the first machine in the bank and removed the grate, then reached in with a snake-like brush, guiding it through to scour every surface of the interior filter, carefully feeling for any lumps or snags. There was only a hint of dust on the brush head when he pulled it back. *No clog here.* He paused, for barely an instant smelling the fetid odor of the sludge that passed through these filters by the gallon. He took a deep breath as he replaced the grate, but all of a sudden his lungs were on fire. He jerked back involuntarily, slamming his head into the back panel of the next bank of purifiers. Dazed, he tried to stand, gulping the air in great gasps despite the burn. Hand over hand, he tried to pull himself back into the lockout space. *The seal… the fucking seal…* His left arm began to shake uncontrollably. He awkwardly slurred the voice control for an emergency call. "Sewage… purification bank 7. Can't… breathe…" he managed to croak, vision blurring. And the blackness took over.

CHAPTER 3

Chief Inspector Cyrus Konami prayed for a murder. He shook his head, admonishing himself — perhaps not a murder, but maybe an assault — even a bar-fight, unheard of for Aoteans — or a burglary, a theft... even just some disorderly conduct. From his small, folding bunk he stared at the wearable, still clipped to his shirt, willing it to produce the report of some interesting emergency. Anything to break the monotony of life aboard *Aotea*, especially life as the chief inspector. *Top cop on a ship of twenty thousand souls... and more than three years outside of Earth, just one crime of note.* Only one crime more serious than vandalism. *The Case of the Poisoned Cigar.*

Well, it hadn't really been poisoned; a jilted lover from the Bio lab spiked a batch of fobacco with a fungal strain to which his rival was allergic. The next time the poor guy puffed up on a fresh cigar, his throat started to close up. Luckily, emergency response was lightning fast when all the living space inside *Aotea* consisted of just a few square kilometers. *It wasn't even that hard to solve.* The suspect had confessed after being left alone in the interview room for just an hour.

Maybe the SNH guys really were onto something, getting rid of Earth media. Decades before the expedition left the lazy orbit around a medium sized asteroid in the belt, the Society for a New Humanity had laid down specifications for the media that was allowed onboard, even if they couldn't actually enforce those rules until they left the system. Chief among those restricted were those vids and texts believed to glorify aggression or dishonesty. Even the occasional bored teenage vandal couldn't seem to dissemble their way past a rookie cop. But that nagging concern remained — Aoteans might be pretty damn agreeable folks... but what happened when someone misbehaved? Humans were the same everywhere, he was

15

convinced — Lagos and Singapore might be two of the most different cities on Earth, but his time working as a cop in both cities had taught him that people did the same awful shit to each other everywhere. Agreeable and honest as they were, and as technically skilled, he was sure that Aoteans were not ready for the real shit that people could do to each other. Especially with the boredom of a decades-long journey.

A whine shifted his attention. His brindle dog Kostya ambled over and licked his fingers. "You want a treat, I guess," said Konami. "Well, tough. You can't always get what you want." He knew he'd give in later, even though the jenji breed, the only dogs onboard, were famously even-tempered; Kostya's single whine was the extent of her begging. Konami scratched behind her ears and she closed her eyes contentedly, finally strolling over to the waste tray in the corner. He wondered if the amiable canine was his biggest reason to live these days.

"How much can a man sleep?" he muttered to himself and yawned as he rose to his feet. Lately he had been averaging more than ten hours per day; aside from the latest drill, there was rarely more than an hour of work to do at the Constabulary, and he only stood a proficiency watch at a system station once or twice a month. He had taken to volunteering for extra duty shifts, even at the most hated watch-stations like Sewage and Reclamation, just to pass the time. Since he covered someone's watch the previous day his waking time was reversed, and he felt discombobulated — well rested but awake during the ship's night. *Nights, days, months, years...what do those words even mean to us out here?* The only intrinsic rhythm aboard *Aotea* was the rotation amidships to simulate gravity, and this was just about once per minute. The four-kilometer-long, six-hundred-some-odd-meters-in-diameter cylindrical living space, divided in two pieces commonly called the Cans, steadily rotated to produce the centrifugal force that held everything tethered to its inner surface at a little over a third of Earth's gravity. Day and night were simulated by bright lights, a faux sun and moon, at the ends of the Cans. *Will we even stay awake all "day" and sleep all "night" when we arrive?* The length of the day would very slowly increase, throughout their long journey, in order to match the multiple Earth-day-long periods of light and darkness on their new home, the moon called Samwise, which revolved around a gas-giant called Abhoth, orbiting a star more than a dozen light years from earth.

Konami had been ecstatic when he got the call five years ago that *Aotea* had reconsidered his application. That excitement was only tamped down when he learned the reason they reconsidered: the first chief inspector had hung herself. There was no explanation, just a terse farewell note. It had certainly seemed suspicious at first, but after five Earth-years on the job, Konami was starting to sympathize. And she had been on the job for ten years during construction and initial settlement. *Though if she really couldn't take it anymore, why not just bow out of the mission?*

The excitement was gone. At the beginning, just the concept of being the first humans to leave the solar system – real pioneers, like no one since the first settlers on Mars – was enough to set his heart beating. Just a few thousand souls in deep space, with nothing but the blackness around them, and if the ship had had windows, nothing to see but the stars. And the dream of a wholly new society, even a wholly new people, to be created at their destination.

But after five years onboard, he still felt like an outsider. Most Aoteans younger than thirty Earth years had spent almost all their lives onboard, and at forty-one, Konami was older than nearly everyone else besides the most senior officers, technicians, and the SNH bigwigs. And now he had fifty-five more years in deep space to look forward to before they reached Samwise. There was a culture here that he still didn't fully understand. It was more than just the tenets and history of the Society for a

17

New Humanity – it was an earnest optimism and belief in not just a better future, but a wholly new future, unlike any society humanity had ever conceived. Try as he might, Konami had never been able to silent his inner cynic; he believed that people were people, and tended to have the same flaws no matter where they were or how they lived.

He tried to look on the bright side. *Ninety-six isn't so old... a few organ replacements, a month of gene therapy, and plenty of time to raise a few kids, play with the grandkids, maybe spend a few decades in retirement.*

It didn't work. *Fifty-five Earth years is a goddamn lifetime — even more than a lifetime, if we go back far enough.* He shook off that train of thought as he showered and put on the roomy blue jumpsuit that served as the working uniform for most of the men and women onboard — only the badge on his breast served to distinguish the Constabulary's uniform from those of his crewmates.

The lack of sky no longer felt disorienting, but looking up and seeing ground, dim as it was in the low lighting of the simulated night, still felt awkward when he was "outside." On a whim he donned his low-light lenses — feeling a bit silly, since they were fashioned to look just like stylish sun-shades — souvenirs from an Earth stakeout-gone-wrong, years ago. His captain had awarded the goggles to him as compensation for the chronic problems a flash grenade had caused his night vision ever since.

Tiny shapes of ant-like children played ball on a green hundreds of meters above him, defying one's instinctual sense of up and down. Their minuscule shadows, cast by the dimming fusion-fired lights from along the dividing Ring kilometers aft, danced and merged like inkblots. A spider-like presence on the corner of the green could only be a robot, though Konami could not recall the colloquial used for the handful of landscaping robots onboard to maintain the surface fields and parks. *GreenBots? GardenBots?*

Even stranger, at least when he first arrived, was the arcing curve of the surface. There was ground "above" him, but also where the horizon should be in the spinward and anti-spinward directions, gracefully curving "upwards" and around. Forward and aft were the massive bulkheads and arches of the Ring dividers, separating the forward Can from the forward Operations section of the ship, and the forward Can from the aft Can. He lowered his gaze and meandered onward, taking a circuitous route to loosen his legs.

He stopped for a minute at the wide windows of a kindergarten, one of the few classes with similarly reversed days and nights to accommodate the handful of parents who routinely worked the night shift. Thirty youngsters, no more than five or six years old, played among the padded furniture of the playroom far more gently than Konami's memories of the children in Lagos and Singapore, or his own childhood in New Orleans. Two seized the same toy, and after just seconds of a bewildered tug-of-war, a MOMbot was between them. The furry, vaguely humanoid robot distracted one with tickles and the other with a dexterous one-handed juggling act, the toy in question promptly forgotten. The Bot's cartoon-like countenance gave Konami the willies, but every Aotean who grew up on the huge vessel, including Konami's youngest deputy, adored the MOMbots. Constable Ginsberg even had a habit of periodically visiting one of the older units — Konami had learned that the robots, a decades-old Mercurian model designed to supervise children while their parents were core-mining, were programmed to form deep attachments to children that could last for decades.

He couldn't help but have some pity for the children – all their lives, into their middle age, would be spent on *Aotea*. Was it possible to fully mature in such a limited environment? In such a structured society? They would certainly face challenges, whether on this long journey or on their alien destination. How could a few square kilometers of metal and habitat, and the cult-like strictness of the SNH culture, prepare them for that unknown?

At the cafeteria, Konami tried to respond with more than a grunt to the greetings from others in line; pursed lips and raised eyebrows told him once again that his acting was sub-par. *At least it's pasta day.* He doubled up on carbonara, smiled at the faceless ServiceBot, and took a seat at an empty table. He closed his eyes and tried to clear his mind of everything but anticipation of the food when his wearable chirped to life.

"...purification bank 7... can't breathe..." was all Konami could make out as he grimaced and dropped his fork, and he sprang to his feet, dashing out of the cafeteria and redonning his goggles.

Who's on Emer this morning? He voiced a non-emergency call to the watch station. The Emergency dispatch station responded just as he stepped outside, shielding his eyes against the bright white light from the aft end of the ship; his goggles enhanced the gentle moon-like glow of the lighting during ship's night into a blazing beacon.

"Emer, Loesser." *Good, Maria's quick on her feet.* Inspector Maria Loesser was, for all intents and purposes, third in command of the Constabulary after Konami and Deputy Chief Inspector Kiroshi Gregorian.

"Maria, Cy. MedTechs on their way?"

"Affirmative," answered Maria. "Call was from Purification Bank 7."

"Roger, Emer. On my way." *Wait a minute...* Konami tried to recall some of the details of his, frankly, slightly less-than-intensive ship's qualification process. Because of his senior position even as soon as he arrived onboard, he had the distinct impression that his qual watches and qual boards were made easier for him. Nonetheless, he had felt the same distinct surge of pride on being presented with his "star canoe" qualification pin that he imagined all Aoteans felt. For Konami, however, that pride had been short lived, quickly overwhelmed by the boredom and resentment of the long journey.

Nevertheless, he was pleased to find that he actually remembered some technical details of the Sewage and Water systems. "Maria, the Purification banks use hazmat, right?"

"Affirmative. The MedTechs have breathers and thinsuits."

"Roger. Cy out." *Guess I'll have to stop by one of the lockers.* He made his way through narrow alleys to a maintenance hatch, doffing his low-light goggles once inside the neutrally lit machinery spaces, and climbed down to the moveway level. As big as *Aotea* was, even the most far-flung watch stations on the Cans were within walking distance. But for emergencies and convenience, rapid fore-aft moving walkways were maintained every hundred meters or so at a lower level. Konami stepped onto one of these and was zipped along to the aft Ring. He nodded a greeting to a technician taking apart an electrical relay next to the moveway.

The moveways were useful for travel along the longitudinal axis, but not around the polar axis. The Rings were ten-meter-long cylinders, one in between the Cans, and one at each end, between the living spaces and the free-floating null-g operations and engineering spaces forward and aft of the Cans — but separated such that they could rotate freely. Aoteans used the Rings to travel both in the spinward/anti-spinward directions, and between the living space and Operations and Engineering, as well as between the two Cans. Konami thumbed his emergency authorization into the Ring callbox and listened to the whirring rumble as it spun up to match the aft Can's rotation speed. Anyone else currently needing or riding the aft Ring would have to wait, but everyone onboard was long accustomed to such occasional inconveniences. He felt

21

antsy as he stood there waiting — his instincts were telling him he had to *move*.

The Ring locked to the Can with a thunderous *ka-chunk* and the doors slid open. A cheery female automated voice announced "Moveway one two," and Konami stepped onto the Ring car and took a seat on an overstuffed sofa opposite a sleepy but irritated looking young couple in khaki jumpsuits. *Probably just got relieved from reactor watch.*

Konami shrugged, pointing sheepishly to the badge emblem at his breast. "Sorry folks, got an emergency in Sewage. I'll just be a moment." The young woman scowled at the interrupted journey.

"Please strap in now," directed the automated voice, and Konami snapped the padded straps over his chest. The Ring disengaged loudly and reduced speed, then sped up again and re-engaged to the Can. The rapidly changing "gravity" made Konami's guts churn, but less so than his last time on a Ring. *Maybe I'm finally an Aotean...* "Moveway zero four" said the voice.

After another short jaunt on the moveway, Konami climbed down two more levels and followed the sound of anxious MedTechs, stopping at a thinsuit locker on the way. Agitated MedTechs were not a good sign. He voiced another call.

"Emer, Loesser." There was an edge to Maria's voice.

"Maria, it's Cy. Report."

"The purifier lockout space inner hatch — it's stuck. It won't budge."

22

CHAPTER 4

Fuck! In thinsuit and breather, Konami squeezed himself into the corner of the purifier lockout space, staying out of the way of the weld tech cutting through the inner hatch. *Goddamnit... how long 'til brain death starts again?* He decided not to interrupt the doctor, who was awkwardly huddled with the MedTechs, and Konami recalled that more than five minutes was pushing it. The hiss of five breathers, plus the whine of the welding torch, were loud enough that the doc and MTs were nearly shouting back and forth. Konami projected the time from his wearable. *Seven minutes, almost eight. Heads are gonna roll when we figure out what caused this damn hatch to stick.* Even the hatch-cut had to be delayed; with the inner lockout hatch cut open, there would be no way to clear any potential toxic gases from the purification bank, so they had to rig the length of crawlway outside the space as a sort of extra airlock. Just in case, they stayed in their breathers until they could get a second verification that it was safe.

Konami inhaled sharply through his mask. *If he doesn't make it...* Since his predecessor's suicide, there had not been a single death onboard *Aotea*. There were occasional crises like choking on food, gestational difficulties, some industrial accidents, and even a short-lived fire, but everyone had been reached by the MedTechs and damage control techs within three or four minutes. *Until now. Shit — I might have to tell the family.*

He suddenly had a realization — he was enjoying himself. Somehow this was what he had missed. Konami knew he should feel some sort of shame at this, but the elation remained. He knew it wouldn't last.

"I'm through!" announced the weld tech as he stood up with the big hunk of alloy that used to be the inner hatch. Before he left Earth, Konami would have marveled that the tech lifted it so easily. On Earth, that hatch probably would

23

have been more than fifty kilos; in the reduced "gravity" of *Aotea*, it was more like fifteen. Konami took the hatch from the weld tech so he could clear out the welding gear, and the MedTechs dove through to pull the prone man into the larger space of the lockout.

Konami informed Emer that they had the patient as he watched the practiced hands of the MedTechs. One stripped off the patient's breather and replaced it with a forced oxygen system, while the other checked vital signs and cut open the thinsuit. Konami tapped into the medical voice circuits, and while he didn't understand all the medical jargon, he got the gist that, right now, they were dealing with a dead man. *Just how dead are we talking about?* Some ancient Earth vid flashed in his memory. *"Mostly dead, or all dead?"* Konami understood that their primary focus was to get oxygenated blood to the brain. The MTs had attached a bag of super-oxygenated neutral fluid, while the doctor made a small incision in the chest and connected the defibrillator.

Moments stretched to an eternity, and finally the doctor nodded. "Pulse present," he reported. "Slow but steady."

If only restarting the brain was that easy... While the MTs set up their collapsible gurney, Konami called Emer. "Maria, are the constables in position?"

"Affirmative, Chief." Standard procedure would place constables at every junction from Sewage to the infirmary to keep the path clear for the MedTechs and the patient.

Well done, Maria. He hadn't even needed to tell her to call the reserve constables.

Konami watched as the medical team maneuvered the casualty out the lockout space and down the cramped passageway. He almost chuckled at the absurdity of a clumsy TrashBot trying to contort itself out of the way of the team, but stifled himself and turned his attention to the scene. *The crime scene. Maybe.* He scowled as he realized part of him wanted this to be a crime, rather than just an

24

accident. But it was more than that, and Konami recognized another feeling in his gut he hadn't experienced in years. *This was not an accident.* He couldn't place why he had that feeling.

He began to survey the deck where the man had lain but a loud *whoosh* took his attention. *Must be the fans; flushing out the space to clean the air.* He bent down to inspect the inner hatch, but stood up abruptly. "Oh shit!" *Goddamnit, the air itself could be evidence!* He looked around wildly and found a sample flask laying in a corner. Konami quickly snatched it up and unscrewed it, shaking it vigorously before re-screwing it shut. He frowned at the absurdity, holding the flask up to the light, as if toxins could be visible.

"Inspector?"

Konami turned around. He must not have heard the lockout hatch open over the fans. A tall, lean figure in thinsuit and breather stood in the hatchway, wearing the khaki cap of one of *Aotea*'s line officer corps. A smaller figure, also with a khaki cap, stood to the side of the first. Most of the men and women onboard wore the working uniform of the staff and support crew, but the officers in charge of the navigation, power, and propulsion systems of the colony ship maintained their own chain of command and wore khaki uniforms when on duty.

"Uh, good morning, Commander." Konami had to pick his brain for a moment to translate the rank insignia, a pair of crossed silver pine boughs.

The officer spoke softly into his wearable and promptly removed his thinsuit and breather. "It's safe now, Inspector."

"Shouldn't we get an analysis first?" Konami responded, momentarily distracted by the feminine shape as the other officer slid out of her thinsuit. *Is that uniform...* he pulled his eyes away when she met his gaze.

The first officer's name and position were now readily visible on the khaki uniform jumpsuit: CRISWELL on his

25

left breast, XO on his right. Criswell waved his hand dismissively. "The fans. It's safe now."

"And Atmo's sample results are clean," added the other officer, a Lieutenant Mattoso.

Konami frowned at his sample flask. *Probably not much left of whatever it was in here.* Konami wanted to tell the XO that they should have waited to flush the space, but he held his tongue. In the formal chain of command, the executive officer only had authority over civil section department heads like Konami in matters concerning operation of *Aotea*'s systems, but he thought prudence would be wise in this case. *At least, at first.* Konami had exchanged only a few words with the colony ship's XO in his five years onboard — he recalled a short meeting in his first few months, and he would see him at the periodic department head meetings, but the chief inspector realized that most of what he knew of the ship's second-in-command fell in the category of gossip and rumor. Popular opinion held that the XO was a stern, humorless man who commanded more than a little fear in his subordinates.

Konami shrugged and took off the breather and thinsuit. There was the barest chemical tinge to the scent of the air.

"Bag up Muahe's suit and breather and get them to the lab," ordered CDR Criswell as he bent to examine the partially melted hatchway. Lieutenant Mattoso acknowledged, and Konami realized they were ignoring him.

"XO?" Konami offered, and after a moment, repeated it louder.

"Yes, Inspector?" responded Criswell from a crouch, almost growling.

Konami ignored the tone of the XO's voice and tried not to smirk. "I'd like to go over the scene before we move anything else." *This ought to be good.*

"Inspector, you'll have plenty of time in a few minutes. There were at least two system failures here — the breather and the hatch — and I mean to find out what went wrong."

"Of course. So do I, XO. But please, don't touch anything until my constables and I have looked everything over."

The XO stood up straight, crowding Konami without even taking a step. "I don't think you understand, Inspector…"

"No, XO. You don't understand," Konami cut in quietly. CDR Criswell pulled back in surprise. "Section 5.27.3.a.1 of the Charter: the Chief Inspector will have authority over any possible crime scene unless the location or equipment within must be utilized for vital operations as determined by the Commanding Officer." Konami was far from an expert on the *Aotea*'s systems, but no one knew the law enforcement procedures of the Charter for a New Humanity Beyond Earth better than him. He studied it for the year-long lead up to his interviews and selection as first alternate, and even in the years afterwards, before he was called up to take the place of the deceased, he recalled most of it. No one but the commanding officer could override Konami at a crime scene.

"'Possible' crime scene?" echoed the XO. "What makes you think this was a crime?"

Konami refrained from explaining the feelings a cop might get sometimes. *And as out of practice as I am, I'm not sure if I even trust my gut.* "Like you said, two unprecedented system failures at the same time?"

The XO remained stone-faced and silent for several seconds. "Very well, Chief Inspector. But I expect to be notified of your progress, and the minute you're done with the scene."

Konami tried to quash the little schoolboy surge of delight he felt when the XO instructed Lieutenant Mattoso to stay behind as liaison between ship's force and the Constabulary before he departed. Luckily, the chief

27

inspector was saved from awkward banter by the arrival of two constables.

"The casualty is through to the Ring, Chief," one reported.

Konami nodded and called Emer, instructing her to have a constable stationed at the Infirmary to wait for news. Konami doubted a single one of his forty-six constables was not awake and busy right now. *Probably for the first time in years.*

Konami turned back to the two nervous-looking constables. "Take it easy, guys. Just remember procedure. Like the drills." He left out his opinion on their performance in the most recent. On Earth, Konami had despised drills. Now he spent weeks making them as perfect as a murder mystery novel, just to have something to do. "First thing's first. Moby: logs. Peter: images and prints. Especially in the purifier space. What was he doing in there?" The two constables snapped into action, and Konami made a short call to Emer to make sure more were on their way to, among other things, bag up every loose object in the vicinity for analysis. With the first potential crime scene in years, Konami was sure every one of his constables would be eager to assist.

He found himself awkwardly alone with Lieutenant Mattoso once again; he nervously looked at his shoes for a moment after their eyes met.

"So what now, Inspector?" The officer's question snapped him back into the present.

Gotta think like a cop again. It would be just like exercising a long-dormant muscle. "Now we recreate his steps. Follow me."

CHAPTER 5

Beatriz Mattoso followed the chief inspector as he made his way stiffly down the crawlway, looking over his hunched shoulders every few moments to ensure that she was still behind him. *Steel yourself, Bea. You didn't minor in investigation for nothing.* Maybe he was just as nervous at the prospect of death as she was, despite the cycles (she recalled they counted by *years* on Earth, rather than the three hundred-day cycles on *Aotea*) of experience he had. So she had heard, anyway.

But it couldn't be anything but an accident. This wasn't Earth. This was *Aotea,* and everyone onboard was a member of the Society for a New Humanity. It wasn't just the genetic screening – psych tests, background checks, interviews... surely any hints of a capacity for violence would have been finagled out and sent packing.

She had to tamp down her sense of excitement. This was a tragedy, of course, but she felt exhilarated – which led to a wave of shame. It wasn't the way of the SNH to find any positive feeling in death, even in the death of one's enemies. Per the SNH, *there were no enemies,* at least no human ones. The real enemies were those aspects of culture that glorified violence and conflict – the parts the Society had purged.

This exhilaration she felt must be a remnant of that culture – even on Ceres, and with parents that had subscribed to the Society's tenets, she couldn't help but be influenced by the wider culture. It wasn't her fault, she decided. The important thing was that she recognized that it was wrong, and did the right thing. She knew how to do the right thing; that sometimes she had feelings otherwise was merely an obstacle to be overcome.

The sewage control space was already manned by a junior HabTech, who greeted Mattoso and Chief Inspector Konami with a nervous nod. The department chief arrived moments later. HTM Wells was a lanky, angular woman in a rumpled jumpsuit. *XO would send her back to change.* Or maybe not — he didn't seem as stuck on appearance with the bluesuits as he was with her fellow khakis. Inspector Konami started to brief the HTM on the incident, but she interrupted him.

"I already heard the scuttlebutt," said Wells. "DT1 on watch, non-responsive in the purifier lockout space."

"Right," answered Konami. "So what would he be doing there?"

"Purification Bank clean and inspect, which is a periodic task, or clearance of a filter clog." Wells projected a field of numbers on the bulkhead. "Bacterial was a bit high with the last log, so he must have decided to clear it himself. Wish all my watchstanders were as conscientious…"

"Can't the rover clean a filter clog?" asked Mattoso. Konami raised his eyebrows minutely.

"Of course," replied Wells. She reached over the HabTech's shoulder and swiped one of the screens. "RoverBot is in recharge." The HTM tapped the Voice unit.

"Atmo, MT2 Taki."

"Atmo, this is HTM Wells. Did you have the RoverBot busy earlier?"

"Uh, yes it was. Some emergent repair with the TechBot." Mattoso could still hear the machinery white-noise through the Voice channel. "Did something happen to the Sewage watch?"

Konami spoke before Wells could answer. "Atmo, this is the CI. We're conducting an investigation right now, so we can't answer any questions. Thanks for your assistance." He gestured and the HabTech closed the Voice channel. "So the RoverBot was occupied…"

HTM Wells talked them through some technical background for the purification filters as they walked back toward the scene. The discussion went silent at the sounds of an argument in the crawlways around the corner.

"Just tell me what's going on…" said a short, balding master technician. "I heard that one of my guys was hurt in there."

"I'm sorry, Master Tech, but the CI ordered us—"

The chief inspector cut in. "That's okay, Constable." He thrust out his hand to the master technician. "Chief Inspector Konami."

"I know who you are," grunted the master tech, but he took the proffered hand. "Master Data Tech Lopez. Muahe's one of mine."

"DT1 Muahe is in Medical right now," said Konami. "But you can join us, if you like — we're trying to recreate his most recent activities."

Mattoso felt an opening. "Master Tech, can you tell us about Muahe's duties?"

He turned to her with raised eyebrows, as if he didn't even realize she had been there. "Data systems maintenance, for the most part. There are dozens of possible—"

"Can you pull up his work log?" she interrupted.

DTM Lopez blinked and scowled. "Yes, of course." He projected a blank screen onto the bulkhead and navigated through it with casual skill. He stared at the screen for a few moments before showing it to the CI and Mattoso. "Just before his watch he was running a NetBug tracer." Mattoso noted some technical jargon along with references to the NetBug, slang for a class of particularly creative problem-solving programs. "That's no big deal — a task to track down any anomalies in the data storage systems. Every thirty days."

"And before that?" she asked.

Fingers danced and swiped through a few more screens. "He was off duty. Before that, a weekly consolidation, a virus drill, a clean—"

"That's okay, DTM," said Konami, to Mattoso's annoyance. But she stayed silent. "Let's get back to Muahe's last few minutes before the incident."

"Incident?" said Lopez. "Don't you mean accident?"

Konami ignored the question. "So now he would have donned the thinsuit."

"Right," said HTM Wells. "Then he would have entered—"

"Shouldn't we go through the thinsuit procedure?" asked Mattoso. She wasn't quite sure how it might help, but she recalled the emphasis on thoroughness during her classes on criminal investigation. She hoped her nervousness wasn't visible; she was wracking her brain for every little detail she could recall from those classes that might give her a veneer of the competence she didn't feel.

"I don't think—"

The CI interrupted Wells. "No, that's a good point. Let's go through the thinsuit procedure." He called over a deputy and sent him to the clinic to retrieve Muahe's thinsuit.

The silence of waiting frazzled Mattoso. "So who was the last one before Muahe to wear the suit?" she asked HTM Wells.

She scanned the logs. "MRT2 Gustafson."

Mattoso made a note and pretended to lose herself perusing a projection while they waited. It didn't take long — the CI's deputy returned after just a few minutes with the thinsuit, bagged as evidence. Konami and his deputy dutifully donned plastic gloves, thumbprinted the evidence log, and opened the bag. HTM Wells reluctantly put on the gloves, and Mattoso stopped herself from grinning as the HTM performed the thinsuit donning procedure, ignoring the gaping holes the MedTechs had cut into the suit to treat the data technician.

Just as Mattoso started to worry that she had insisted on this delay for nothing, HTM Wells paused, frowned, checked a projection, and frowned again.

"What is it?" asked the CI.

"It's the breather mask," she answered. "It failed the pressure test." HTM Wells demonstrated, closing the test device over the mask, activating it, and pointing to the telltale red "failure" light.

They looked at the locker logs again — MRT2 Gustafson had fully annotated the thinsuit logs, including the pressure test, as did DT1 Muahe.

"So that was it..." said Konami. "The mask couldn't protect him from the toxic gas."

"Wait a second — the filter's in, right?" asked Mattoso. "Because Muahe was wearing it, and already installed it. But wouldn't he test the mask before he puts in the filter? According to procedure?"

DTM Lopez nodded vigorously. "Muahe would follow procedure. Definitely."

"Actually, you're right," answered Wells, pointing out the steps on the posted procedural guide. She removed the breather filter and tested it again, and this time it passed.

"But that doesn't make sense." Wells scratched her head. "The filter shouldn't make a difference — it's entirely inside the mask."

The CI was about to speak when he got a call and stepped aside. He returned a moment later with a grim expression. "I'm sorry, Master Tech," he said, hand on Lopez's shoulder. "DT1 Muahe is dead."

CHAPTER 6

Aotea's Commanding Officer, Captain Lillin Horovitz, was annoyed. The solidly built veteran spacer didn't try to hide it — she drummed her fingers, cleared her throat, and stared down each of the department heads, including Konami, who flinched from her gaze just like everyone else. Her silver hair was unusual onboard — most rejuvenated their follicle cells periodically. He wondered what that said about her personality — the chief inspector did not know the captain very well, despite the recurring department head meetings. When the ship's operational command structure interacted with the civil command structure, in which the constabulary was included, it was usually through the mayor. The few times he'd spoken to her she'd been curt, professional, and entirely unflappable. And notably, she was one of the few onboard in a senior position who didn't make a point to rhetorically kowtow to the Society. Ship scuttlebutt suggested that there were no veteran spacers within the Society when crew decisions were made, and the Captain was one of those few outsiders, just like Konami, brought in to fill experience gaps.

The captain's orange cat, Halifax, echoed her owner's mood, gracefully marching across the meeting table and giving every department head a good stare. The jenji cat's gaze was a bit easier to meet then Captain Horovitz's, and she deigned to let Konami rub her belly.

In contrast to Captain Horovitz's visible vexation, Director-Superintendent Harry Akunle was as positive as ever. The man most Aoteans called "mayor," or "CE" for civil executive, reminded Konami of career politicians on Earth — always smiling, quick to shake hands, quick with a laugh (and with Society pablum), and reluctant as hell to say anything substantive. Konami knew him well — Mayor Akunle held weekly meetings with each of his department heads, and asked probing questions, even when the

Constabulary had little of note to do. And at the end of each meeting, the mayor would slap Konami on the shoulder, praise his work as chief inspector, and say "just remember who we're doing this for, Cy." Konami knew it wasn't sincere, but couldn't help but like the mayor anyway.

They had been waiting long enough that various side conversations, held in whispered tones lest they incur the captain's intimidating gaze, had broken out. Medical Director Madani tapped Konami on the shoulder.

"Did you see the ironball game yesterday?" the lanky doctor asked, louder than Konami would have risked.

He said he saw the highlights.

"I was at the Arena," she bragged with a grin. "Great game — it went to double overtime. You should come with me to the next one."

Konami raised an eyebrow, recalling distantly, now that he thought about it, that she might have flirted with him at the last meeting. He hadn't had a date in months, not that he had put much effort into it. He met the medical department head's eyes for a moment, wondering if he had missed other signals as well. Konami decided that she was attractive, and the decision brought a long-absent feeling of adventurousness. "That sounds nice, doctor."

"Please, call me Ilsa."

"Ilsa." He blinked. "And call me Cy. What time?"

"Two days, evening. I'll send you an invite."

He did his best to smile, and she let out a breathy laugh. Konami cut short his grin when he recalled why they were gathered. *Ah, crap.* Theo Muahe had no family onboard, but according to DTM Lopez, his best friend was a mechanical technician, MCT2 Don Olivier. Second Olivier had been shocked to his core when Konami told him, even trying to call Muahe on his wearable, before breaking down in tears. But Konami tried to let himself feel good for a moment — "If you don't learn how to compartmentalize the bad shit you see, you won't be a cop for long," his first partner had told him.

35

Madani furrowed her brow at Konami's expression.

"Sorry," he said. "Rough day."

She nodded. "I know. Our first loss…"

They were interrupted by the arrival of the three popularly called the "Bigwigs." Well into their fifties, the three Sponsors from the Society for a New Humanity were the oldest people onboard, and the only adults actually outside the formal command structure. Nominally, each of them had a day job — Wilson Paramis was a demographer, Mara Ngayabo was a geneticist, and Hamad Maltin was an agro-biotechnologist. But they never stood proficiency watches, and Konami seriously doubted that their department heads gave them any real assignments without their express permission. The fact that Captain Horovitz and Mayor Akunle waited for them to start the meeting was the real proof of their influence onboard *Aotea*. Even Halifax tended to stay away from them, finally lying down imperiously next to the commanding officer.

The Bigwigs made Konami nervous. They had no formal role — in contrast to all other positions onboard, "bigwig" wasn't called out in the Charter. Unlike the director-superintendent, they were not elected by the civil section department heads, and unlike the commanding officer, they didn't serve as one of the operational section department heads and executive officer prior to ascending to command. Each had a formal title of "professor," but nearly everyone just called them the "Bigwigs." They had been onboard since the start of construction, and thanks to gene therapies and organ replacements, the Bigwigs would probably be onboard when *Aotea* reached Samwise. *Nobility.* That's the word that the Bigwigs conjured up — unelected nobility, outside of the struggles and challenges of the rest of society, *outside of the law*. Well, perhaps they were — Konami was thankful he hadn't had to test that. But it was just another thing about the *Aotea* that turned his stomach… he wondered if he could ever feel truly comfortable in such a society.

"Inspector?"

It took Konami a second to realize he was being addressed. Harry usually called him "Cy."

"Inspector?" repeated Mayor Akunle. "The latest with the investigation?"

"Sorry," Konami cleared his throat. "With the help of the Habitability master tech, we're looking into the thinsuit breather and filter." He explained the odd results of the pressure test device.

"So it passed without the filter in, but failed with the filter?" asked the chief engineer, a fussy, wiry commander named Ishi Papka.

Konami answered in the affirmative. "That's what the test device at the scene told us. One of my deputies is confirming the result with the lab guys as we speak."

"Now that we've determined that there was an equipment malfunction," said the XO, "I think we can consider this an operational issue, Captain."

Konami frowned. *A fucking jurisdictional argument...* God, it had been years since he'd had one of those. He almost felt nostalgic.

"No, we're not ready to conclude that yet," answered Captain Horovitz. "We don't know what caused the malfunction."

She paused and Konami jumped in. "And we are coordinating closely with one of the XO's officers, Captain. Lieutenant Mattoso will be involved in every step."

CDR Criswell looked annoyed, but he stayed silent.

The skipper nodded agreement. "Very well. Any other issues before we adjourn?"

A nasal voice spoke up. "It's the signal thing, Captain." Lieutenant Commander Lara Olin, the Comms/Signals officer, spoke nervously.

"Oh no, it's the Klingons!" mumbled the navigator, Commander Rusk, to nervous laughter around the table. The captain's cat jumped at someone's high pitched bark of amusement.

37

"I know I've mentioned it before—"

"Many times before," was the reply under someone's breath.

"But my techs aren't imagining it. We have almost a cycle of these UHF transmissions, and we can't make—"

Captain Horovitz cut her off with a raised hand. "Keep logging the signals. Report any patterns your team notices."

Klingons... Konami snorted. He wondered if he envied Lieutenant Commander Olin for having a mystery, until he recalled that he had a mystery of his own. *A mystery and a dead man.*

"No one's been inside, right?" the chief inspector asked the deputy guarding the door to DT1 Muahe's quarters, inside one of the standard four-story habitation structures on the surface of the aft Can. Konami was perturbed since the data master technician had given him the wrong directions to the deceased's quarters — aft Can, 3rd Rib, *forward* third, when it was aft Can, 3rd Rib, *aft* third. He could have easily looked it up himself, of course.

"Right, CI," answered Junior Inspector Dillon. "I relieved Lee, who reported no one tried to go in since she arrived."

"Very good. Let's take a look." Konami removed the bright yellow vidcam from its case and cleared his throat. Just as he was about to turn it on, the junior inspector's eyes went wide. "Nothing to worry about, Deputy. Just a vidcam."

"But... personal vidcams are banned, right?"

This wasn't the first time Konami had encountered anxiety over recording devices onboard. "No, just nanocams. And unmanned surveillance cams. But vidcams are allowed as long as they're not hidden, and they conform to specs." He tapped the casing above the lens, explaining the minimum size and marking requirements.

Imagine being scared of a vidcam. On Earth, of course, they were ubiquitous. Every gadget doubled as a camera, and nigh-invisible nanocams could be purchased by the bucketful, attached to every surface, and continuously upload to the cloud. A restoration of privacy was one of the primary drivers, aside from the desire to eliminate violence, behind the creation of the Society for a New Humanity.

"You okay with this, Deputy? We can get someone else."

"Yeah, I'm okay. It's no problem."

"Good, because you'll be recording." Konami handed the fist-sized camera to the junior deputy and showed him how to turn it on. "Get everything, and touch nothing." Once the red light was blinking, he looked into the lens. "5 May 2240," he said, and paused. He still thought by the Earth calendar, even though most onboard tracked the three hundred-day cycles since departing from the solar system. "Cycle three, day 261," he continued, "approximately eight hours since the Emer call for the incident leading to the death of Data Technician First Class Theodore Muahe. We can verify that no one has entered the quarters of the deceased since about one hour after the Emer call."

Konami opened the door with DT1 Muahe's key. It was a standard two-room single quarters, and rather than the more common living or sitting area, it was apparent that DT1 Muahe had arranged his front room as a small workshop. *Cluttered would be an understatement.* Muahe had his very own desk computer, something he'd never seen in someone's quarters before — with a dozen modifications and additions, it was almost as big as those ancient units he recalled from an old 21st-century vid. The computer desk took up a quarter of the workshop, with the rest of the space taken up by computer gear and bot parts in various states of repair. One bot was operating — it looked like a DustBot at first, but it was larger, with a few extra appendages. It ignored the two inspectors while it fussed over a pile of small parts in a corner.

Konami carefully made his way through the mess, gesturing toward various details for Dillon to record. The bedroom was Spartan, the bunk unmade and slightly sour-smelling. *Antisocial tinkerer? Lonely nerd? Quirky inventor?* Konami tried to tamp down on his own speculation before everything could be analyzed. Satisfied that the vidcam had captured anything in the quarters that might possibly be useful, he had Dillon shut it off and made a call to Emer.

"Emer, Floros."

"Floros, it's Cy. We finished recording in Muahe's quarters. Detail the baggers — apprentices are fine. Dillon will stay behind and supervise." Konami noted a grin passing on the junior inspector's face. "You okay with that, Inspector?"

"Absolutely, CI. We'll bag and tag everything, clean as the black."

Konami nodded as he departed. He knew "the black" referred to the clean vacuum of space, but for some reason, the reference made Konami think of a different kind of darkness.

CHAPTER 7

Mattoso used to hate waiting, but cycles into a half-lifetime-long journey had cured her of her impatience. At least, that's what she thought — now that she was actually waiting for something as important as this, her predilections returned with a vengeance. The diagnostic techs were positively gleeful — she reckoned this was probably the first time they had to investigate a malfunction more severe than a squeaky hinge. At least their enthusiasm was a tiny bit infectious; they explained the workings of the molecular scanner with real zeal, even while waiting for the minute lenses to complete their nigh-undetectable, and seemingly endless, movements across the surface of the faulty breather filter.

She realized she was nigh-buzzing with energy. *An actual murder!* It should be terrible – and she recognized intellectually that it was terrible – but she was as excited as she'd been in cycles. *Well, maybe a murder.* Maybe it would just be an accident. That felt disappointing to contemplate, which made her feel a momentary wave of shame.

Mattoso checked a message on her wearable – her girlfriend/boyfriend (Pat alternated which term they preferred) complained about their kids and promised fresh vat-grown duck breasts for dinner. She smiled, well aware that they adored teaching, and especially adored the children in their class.

A bell rang, setting the lab techs back in motion. Chief Chari frowned as she passed — Mattoso had had to pull rank in order to remain in the little diagnostics lab while the techs worked, and the DGT chief had not been pleased. After a two-minute huddle, Chari approached her.

"It was the edge of the filter, Lieutenant," she said gruffly. "There was enough scoring along one side that it didn't seal properly when fully installed." Chari pointed out the scoring on an imager. "Normally it wouldn't matter, but this one stuck out a few extra microns — enough to sort of stick between the connection."

She asked about possible causes.

The diagnostics chief shrugged. "Normal wear and tear, a fab error, who knows?"

Mattoso subvocalized, making a note, and saving the images from the scanner. *Can't be a fab error, can it, if this filter was used before?* But she recalled that, according to procedure (and according to the breather unit logs), breather filters were only used once and replaced. *Then that might argue against wear and tear, right?*

Her wearable vibrated — a call from the chief inspector. The department head meeting had completed. She updated him on the results from the lab. "What's the next step, CI?" she added.

"Cy, please. Next step is interviews."

Konami beat her to MRT2 Gustafson's hab, one of a sixteen identical units in a standard Hab near the central Ring. She was pleased to find him waiting in the passageway, examining the ministrations of the blocky TrashBot as it cleaned the edges of the walkway — she had been worried he would go ahead and start the interview without her.

She wasn't quite sure what to make of the Chief Inspector. Earthers made her feel just a bit nervous, but she knew that wasn't quite fair. Yes, the problem of violence and aggression throughout the solar system was inherited from Earth's history, but all the teachings of the SNH abhorred any sort of bigotries based on categories like place of origin. He struck her as competent, and his reasoning for the recent drills made logical sense... but just the knowledge that someone onboard was capable of the assaults, even in a drill, she'd read about in the aftermath reports, gave her the willies. Now why would that creep her out, but the prospect of investigating a murder did the opposite?

She asked about the autopsy – there was nothing surprising, just asphyxiation and toxicity from the gas mixture.

She was annoyed that she had to ask, and he apologized and promised to keep her informed.

Gustafson turned out to be a prematurely balding young man in a sleeveless shirt and shorts. "Uh, who are you?" he grunted while a shirtless youth gestured in the air, a cluster of wearables arranged around his head. A yellow jenji dog sniffed the visitors' feet before returning to the food dispenser.

Gustafson's eyes went wide when Konami introduced them. They ignored the triumphant shout from the vidgame player.

Konami met Mattoso's eyes and tilted his head toward the young tech, suppressing a yawn. She swallowed her surprise. *He's telling me to lead the interview!* "According to the breather logs, Second Gustafson, you were the last one to use the thinsuit and breather before the deceased."

"Breather?" The tech scratched his neck. "Guess I was on watch, and had to go into a hazspace."

A pause, and Konami broke the silence. "Mr. Gustafson. Try to think back. We can pull up your watch records if it would help."

Damn it, Bea. She was annoyed at herself for waiting too long and allowing Konami to take the lead again.

"No, that's okay," the tech answered Konami. "Let me think for a minute… Sewage, right? Yeah, I have to stand Sewage every quarter-cycle, I think, for proficiency — yeah, I remember. Purifier clean and inspect — a bi-cyclical, or tri-cyclical, or something. Big pain in the ass — nearly took all watch… the offgoing should've started it, but—"

"Please, Second, the breather?" interrupted Mattoso. She chided herself for checking to see if Konami approved. *Doesn't matter, Bea. It's not like he's your boss.*

"Yeah, the breather. What's to tell? I followed procedure, donned the thinsuit and breather, scrubbed down the crap on the purifier, and doffed it."

"Can you remember donning it?" asked Konami.

"I don't know, I just put it on."

"Do you remember any problems with the breather?"

"No, it worked fine."

"How about doffing it?"

The second just grunted. "I just took it off. What's—"

Konami scrolled down a projection. "Did you replace the filter?"

"Uh… yeah, of course. That's procedure."

"And then…?"

"Then? Oh, then I put on a new seal. No wait — the seal is last. I recharged the tank, then the new seal. Then I thumbsigned the logs, of course."

Mattoso was impressed — she wasn't sure if she could recite the procedure from memory without consulting the posted info plate. *But then, I don't have to stand Sewage watch.* As an Operational officer, the closest she might come would be the Machinery Control watch, supervising all of the various non-vital machinery systems watches onboard from the Machinery Control Room.

"Okay, Second. Thank you for your cooperation." He turned to her, but she didn't have any more questions. "We'll let you know if we have any more questions, Mr. Gustafson. Don't leave town."

They left the young tech with a confused look on his face.

"'Don't leave town'?" she asked Konami.

"Sorry," he chuckled. "Earth joke."

They made their way to the Central Ring in silence. "Do you miss it?" she asked while they waited for the Ring. "Earth?"

Konami looked at the deck. "I miss the sky. I miss seeing... nothing." He pointed upwards. "You look up on *Aotea*, you just see the other side of the Can. On earth, you look up — you might see clouds, or the moon, or the sun... But every so often, and especially at night, you see nothing. Emptiness. Not even stars, unless you're outside the city, though I miss those too. In Lagos, it was like a grey blanket over the city." He laughed. "A warm, grey, reeking blanket." *Doesn't sound like something worth missing.*

Mattoso considered this. "I've never seen sky before, except through a window." She honestly wasn't even sure if the empty black vacuum of Ceres' surface counted as "sky."

Konami raised his eyebrows. "Really? Where are you from?"

"Ceres City. One of the exurbs, actually. We took a tube into town for school."

"Exurbs?" chuckled Konami. "I thought Ceres City was all there was."

She was too far from home to be offended. Few that hadn't grown up in the asteroid belt knew much about the solar system's largest asteroid. "There's New Hawking, on the south pole, and Mahatma, on the equator, and—" She stopped herself as felt a twinge of homesickness. "It's as big as India, you know. Ceres, I mean. It's not so small." She knew nothing about India aside from its status as a large land region on Earth, but ever Cerean student learned that their home was approximately the same size. "So just the sky? Anything else?"

"The dogs. Maybe I miss the dogs."

"The dogs?"

"Yeah. On *Aotea* all the dogs look alike. Jenji dogs and cats are all the same, except for the colors, and they all have the same personality. They're great, but in Lagos

45

there were dogs that looked like wolves, and dogs that looked like rats, and everything in between. My neighbor had a big yard and a dozen dogs, and I used to watch them play with her children. And not just dogs — monkeys, antelope, squirrels, and birds — oh, the birds are beautiful—"

They were interrupted by a chirp from Konami's wearable as they stepped onto the Ring. With effort, Mattoso managed to refrain from eavesdropping. The conversation was short.

"They found the hatch malfunction," said Konami.

"Really? What was it."

"Just an interlock short. You know, the inner door can't open unless the outer door was shut, with both doors failing shut. Truly ancient technology, say the techs."

"Tried and true, the engineers often say," she replied. "The fewer moving parts, the fewer things that can go wrong."

"Maybe that wasn't the best philosophy in this case."

Considering the result, she couldn't argue with that.

CHAPTER 8

The funeral was brief and surprisingly moving. DT1 Muahe's closest friends and colleagues gave speeches, mostly improvised, it seemed, praising his unfailing loyalty and commitment to his duties, as well as his sense of humor. A young data technician, weeping softly, was gently urged by his compatriots to make a speech, but refused. They were gathered at the small park next to the reclamatorium, recorded dutifully by the colony ship's lone journalist, Elena Conneer.

The park was overflowing — Konami doubted more than a few dozen of the mourners knew Muahe particularly well, but the shock or novelty of the first funeral onboard since departure proved to be a draw for many Aoteans. His eyes roved the crowd, looking for some sort of unusual reaction or clue, but the only faces without expressions of sadness or shock were those of the Bigwigs. The stout, jovial Wilson Paramis had managed to tamp down his typically broad smile to a tight-lipped grin, occasionally mopping his brow, while Hamad Maltin and Mara Ngayabo were as expressionless as Bots.

A senior solacer by the name of Lumbee gave a warm eulogy, placing extra emphasis on the importance of a positive attitude for the survivors, and all Aoteans in general. "Mourn well," she said. "But do not only mourn. Celebrate Theo's life, and emulate his dutifulness and compassion. And remember that he, or someone with identical DNA, will live again among us someday soon." Among the many provisions of the Charter was a promise that, should one pass away during the journey by any cause other than genetic illness, one's DNA will move to the "top of the line" of the reproduction queue. The next time an Aotean couple was authorized to have a child, Muahe's genetic code would have a high likelihood of being selected over the millions of genetic contributions from people all

47

over the Solar System that were stored in *Aotea*'s genebanks.

A genetics technician took a ceremonial last sample — in actuality unnecessary, since the banks already had frozen tissue samples from every Aotean — and Muahe's remains were placed gently in the reclamator pod. A hymn was sung — something about the peace a New Humanity would bring — and the crowd broke up.

As he made his way back to his quarters, Konami subvocalized, "News." He was wearing a lens, so hovering in front of him, the top headline read "HIDDEN SPACES OF AOTEA REVEALED." He chuckled as he swiped through the latest article on *Aotea Today*, Conneer's daily periodical. Her piece was complete with images and vids of empty storage and machinery compartments, with ominously low lighting, as though it wasn't trivially easy to bring a sack of fist-sized lamps that could illuminate the largest spaces onboard. *Poor Conneer*. If his job was boring, Conneer had to manufacture something interesting to write about every single day.

A chirp signaled an incoming call.

"CI Konami," he answered.

There was a pause. "Uh, sorry to bother you sir," said a wobbly male voice. "It's MRT2 Gustafson; you were by my place earlier."

"What can I do for you, Second?"

"Um... I'm sending you these texts I got. I, uh, don't think it's right. I didn't do anything wrong."

Gustafson tersely ended the call and Konami slid through several screens, idly scratching Kostya's belly. There were seven messages forwarded from the 2nd class tech, all from anonymous accounts. *You've failed us.* read the first. The second read *His death is on you*. The other five were all variations on the same sentiment.

He shook his head. *How did this get out so goddamn quick?* He thought back to his time in Lagos and Singapore

— no one cared about the petty crime of the day, but if a celebrity was involved or if it was a sex-related crime then there was always a leak. *People are people everywhere, I guess, on Earth or in interstellar space.* And it made sense that, onboard *Aotea,* any possible murderer would be a celebrity.

But the voice messages... they were so tame to be laughable. On Earth, it would have been death threats. On *Aotea,* you get shamed. And the funniest, or saddest, part, is that *it worked.* Shame rolled through the wearable speakers, clear as if the tech had been in the room. *Only on Aotea!*

A whine distracted him for a moment — Kostya realized Konami was apparently occupied with other thoughts, and stood by the food tray which remained frustratingly empty.

Konami thought back to Earth procedures as he filled Kostya's tray with kibble. *What did we do when a rumor gets out, and someone starts getting threats?*

The ball came in low and Konami just barely caught it on his racket with a backhand swing.

"What's the latest?" asked Konami's deputy chief inspector, making an improbable leap to return the racketball. Kiroshi Gregorian was short, wiry, and a few years older than Konami. He had more experience in law enforcement than the chief inspector, but all of it was in the smaller settlements of Mars. Konami had learned that the captain and mayor both had wanted a big city cop to head up the constabulary, and the only truly big cities were on Earth. The affable deputy CI didn't seem to mind — a big part of the reason Konami counted him as his best friend onboard. And Konami planned on supporting Gregorian at the six-cycle point for the next department head rotation — per the Charter, departments could rotate their leaders every six cycles between the senior members of each department to balance experience and reward service.

49

Konami figured that by then he would be happy to take a break from leadership. When he really thought about it, he'd happily relinquish his position much sooner than that.

"What do you care, you damn layabout?" replied Konami, trying to manufacture the camaraderie that seemed so hard to find lately. Just before the recent drill, Gregorian had returned from a week-long respite at the Beach, as the walled-off leisure zone, tucked against the aft Ring, was known.

The older man chuckled as he hit a winner into the bottom corner of the back wall. "You know the key to vacation on this tub, Cy?" Gregorian's next serve was a surprise — high and wide.

"What's that?" Konami grunted as he backpedaled to return the ball. Even with a less elastic ball, *Aotea*'s racketball courts had to be a bit longer than on Earth due to the substantially lower gravity.

"Don't go very often. There's not much at the Beach — just the jet-pools, the widescreens, the games, and the top-shelf food and booze. Keep it to once every cycle or two, and it's a nice break. More often than that, and it'll bore you out of your skull."

Konami took advantage of a gift serve from Gregorian and won the point. He lined up a solid serve to the back corner. "How about the other vacationers?"

His best friend returned it easily, sending Konami diving to keep the ball in play. "I'll just say the timing was lucky, my friend. Even though I had to cut it short."

"No details?"

"You know what they say, Cy. What happens at the Beach..."

...stays at the Beach. Konami realized that he hadn't actually taken a break for over a year. In fact, if it hadn't been for Muahe, he might be packing up for a break as soon as Gregorian got back.

"You gonna serve, boss?"

"Yeah, sorry." Konami gave a half-hearted serve which was promptly drilled into the corner. *Crap again.* He almost never beat Gregorian at racketball — despite Konami's relative youth and longer reach, his second-in-command had some special sense of where the ball would be at any given moment. *Maybe 'cause the gravity on Mars is almost identical to Aotea's, and I grew up playing racketball on Earth.* If he wanted any chance to win now, he'd have to stay more focused. *Or maybe I can distract him.* "What have you heard so far?"

"Maria gave me an outline. Dead data tech, hatch malfunction, mask malfunction, etc. An MRT2 screwed up the suit records. What else you got?"

Cursing, Konami missed an easy shot. "How'd you hear about Gustafson?"

"The MRT2? Wasn't he in the report?"

Konami thought that was in the detailed report that hadn't been finalized, not the initial bare-bones report, but he couldn't recall exactly.

He missed another shot. He needed something to turn the game around, so he told the story of Muahe's death but kept the details vague at first, timing his shots as he answered Gregorian's questions. It earned him two points.

But his opponent caught on quickly, apparently, and stopped before taking the next serve. "Okay, Cy, nice try," he chuckled. "Two minute break. Just lay it on me."

Damn... I was just about to take the lead. He finished the story.

"Two malfunctions at the same time?" Gregorian shook his head. "Sounds like quite a coincidence."

Konami grunted his agreement.

"So what do you think about Gustafson? Did he botch the procedure?" Gregorian lined up his next serve.

Konami had been pondering this since the unfortunate Second called him. "I don't know. Maybe by accident. I don't get any... you know, *squicky* feeling from him." The serve whizzed by his head. *My turn to be distracted.*

51

"Yeah, yeah," answered Gregorian. "Simplest answer's usually the best, right? But I dunno. Shit, it's like exercising a dormant muscle."

Konami chuckled, surprised for a moment that it came naturally. "Maybe we oughta watch those old cop vids — the ones with the murder and the bang-bang and the explosions and the misogyny? They always talked about instinct and gut feeling."

Gregorian pursed his lips. "Watch out, Cy. We all signed the Charter."

"Of course. Only joking." And as soon as it came, the amusement was gone. On Earth Konami had never been particularly attached to the sorts of mindless, bloody entertainment that the Society for a New Humanity banned as both a cause and symptom of Earth culture's inherent violence, but after a few years of nature documentaries and the all-smiles pseudo-propaganda vids the Aotea Players produced, he missed it. "Never liked that crap anyway."

Gregorian laughed. "Right, Cy. Right."

Konami tried to focus on the game, but it didn't matter — Gregorian was just a step above him in skill, or at least in familiarity with low-g racketball. He matched Konami's hardest shots and returned them even harder. Maybe when he was younger, Konami's athletic ability and long legs would keep him in the game, but not today. With one more serve just out of his reach, it was over.

"I want you to supervise something a little unusual," said Konami as they walked to the changing room.

"What's that? Punishment for kicking your ass?" Gregorian laughed.

Ha ha. "Call it that if you like. Activate the reserves — alpha-level — for now." It was a relief to give the order — like calling in the cavalry. Normally, the Constabulary only had two personnel on watch at any given time — one on patrol, and one at the Emer station. The reserve watchbill consisted of multiple constables that could be at leisure, as long as they were awake and dressed and wearing their wearables. 'Alpha' was the lowest activation level, bumping two reserve constables up to the active watchbill. "One more on patrol, and one watching the hab building of Second Gustafson."

"Roger, Chief," replied the Deputy Chief Inspector. "General surveillance?"

"Yeah. He's been getting messages. Nothing that serious so far, but I want to catch any property vandals in the act."

"Wow," said Gregorian as he toweled off. "I'll get right on it." The deputy chief inspector changed the subject. "You know what the talk was at the Beach?"

"What's that?"

"Those ghost signals. There was this comms tech — CM1 Dor..." Gregorian cut himself off with a grin. "Well, you don't need to know her name. But she said these UHF signals were all over the place. They'd be there one second and gone the next, but there were just a few patterns of the burst, all related."

Konami recalled the mockery of Lieutenant Commander Olin over the signals at the department head meeting. "Odd stuff. What do they think is causing it?"

"They have no idea, but a couple of the techs think it's aliens. That we're being followed, or shadowed — the signal source vector changes over time."

"Have we responded?"

Gregorian lowered his voice. "She wouldn't say for sure, but she hinted that the comms techs have free reign to send any signals they want."

"Nothing in the Charter about aliens, after all," answered Konami. His memory of the non-law-enforcement parts of the Charter was less than perfect, but he was confident it didn't discuss extraterrestrials.

He was far less confident that it was wise for bored comms techs to be sending signals out to possible non-human lifeforms, however.

CHAPTER 9

"It was a one-in-a-million fluke, according to the electronics techs," Mattoso explained to the executive officer, holding up a small and shiny sliver of metal. Commander Criswell's office, beneath the command bridge, was Spartan and functional, like the XO himself. He even had his own DustBot clinging magnetically to the wall, programmed to remain in his office and keep it spotless, unlike most of the thousands of little robots that could roam nearly everywhere onboard there might be dirt. In the operational and engineering spaces forward and aft of the ever-rotating Cans, gravity was not quite null due to the constant small acceleration of the *Aotea*'s propulsion drive, but it was close enough to feel like zero-g. She pushed gently against the fixed desk with her feet to prevent herself from drifting to meet the executive officer, explaining the source of the metallic shard. She handed the XO the culprit. "So that's quite a coincidence — this shard shorts the circuit at the same time—"

Commander Criswell cut her off, somehow appearing to be standing steady despite the lack of gravity. "Sometimes coincidences actually happen. And maybe not that much of a coincidence, if the rumors about Second Gustafson are true."

You should know better than to listen to rumors, XO. But she kept her mouth shut.

After a couple of years onboard, she was finally used to the XO's personality. But it had taken a while. The Societans on Ceres had won her over with their warmth and kindness – the promise that a new humanity wouldn't just be free from violence, but free from conflict of any kind. That freed from the shackles of Earth culture, by our very nature humans would want nothing more than to love, be loved, create, and recreate.

That might have been a childish hope, but it was effective. And while her joy in joining the crew of the *Aotea* was still as high as it ever was, she understood now that it was much broader than that childish sales pitch. She'd come to understand and respect that there was indeed more to natural human inclinations than love and pleasure and joy, and that communities needed more rigid personalities like the XO just as much as it needed those like the neo-hedonists of the Cerean Societans.

"The chief inspector is still conducting his investigation," was all she said.

"Now we know the cause. Tell that to the chief inspector — he can wrap up his investigation, but it should be soon."

But what caused it to fall and short the circuit? "Aye, sir," was all she said, and she was dismissed.

Someone was waiting for her in the passageway outside her quarters. The woman's face was familiar, but it took Mattoso a few seconds to place it — the face at the bottom of every issue of *Aotea Today*.

"Elena Conneer," she said.

The journalist oozed energy, even as she stood. The muscular little woman thrust a vidcam forward, a pulsing red light signaling that the device was recording. "Lieutenant Mattoso, what's the latest on the investigation into First Muahe's death? Did Second Gustafson's negligence lead to his death?"

Mattoso took a deep breath. *Damn cameras.* Escaping the near constant video surveillance of Earth, whether by public or private forces, was a significant part of the Society for a New Humanity's Charter. The ubiquitous wearables didn't even have the capacity to record video without modification.

"I can't comment on an ongoing investigation." *You know that, Elena, even if you're out of practice.*

The journalist switched off the camera and smiled, the tense energy in her gymnast's build seeming to evaporate. "I know, Lieutenant. Just need to have some sort of vid in the article — 'no comment' is par for the course for a murder investigation."

Mattoso chuckled. "Okay... wait, murder? Who told you this was a murder investigation?"

Conneer just widened her crocodile grin.

"It's not," Mattoso added. "Well, maybe... no comment. Just no comment." *Guess I'm out of practice too.*

"Thank you very much, Lieutenant. You've been very helpful." The journalist finally stopped smiling and walked away.

Mattoso shook her head to herself. *Nice going.* At least Conneer hadn't recorded Mattoso's verbal misstep.

She was startled upon entering her quarters to be wrapped up in wiry, strong arms. "I've been waiting for this all day..." Mattoso silenced Pat's husky voice with her own lips.

"How long've you been waiting?" said Mattoso, finally pulling away.

"Hours. Cycles." Mattoso's companion pulled her in for another kiss. "But I have a qual watch in an hour."

"Then we gotta be quick..."

She signed contentedly after Pat left. She had that urge to lie in bed forever, but motivated herself to arise and change into off-duty duds. Her door chimed — it was Konami. She caught his eyes darting for the barest moment to her chest.

"I just wanted to give you the latest news."

She invited him in and offered him a drink.

"No, thank you," he responded, clearing his throat. "Let me get to the point — Second Gustafson called me. Rumors have already spread. Nothing major, but he's been getting anonymous emails."

For a moment she was shocked. Not by the rumors, but by the emails. Aoteans were the cream of the human crop in terms of rational thinking and emotional control, based on the geneset requirements for potential colonists. The millions of individual genomes submitted alongside the submission fees — a substantial part of the funding of *Aotea*'s construction in the decades prior to launch — were weeded down to the twenty thousand applicants with the right combination of skills, experience, diversity, personality, and genetic tendencies toward health, advantageous behaviors, and other concerns. The ones that didn't make the cut, but were close, were saved for the sake of genetic diversity — new generations would be largely built off these saved genesets. *And all it takes for network vandalism and threats is the death of a crewmate?*

"We should assign someone to look out for him. Can your watchbill support?" she asked, finally.

"Taken care of."

"How about the messages? Can we track down who sent them?"

Konami shook his head. "Maybe, though we'd need the cooperation of the data techs. But none of the messages were direct threats — they wouldn't violate the Charter, even if we knew who sent them."

"So what's the latest from the labs?" he asked.

She filled him in on the shard of metal that short circuited the hatch interlock. And she forced herself to tell him about Conneer's "interview" — she didn't want it to be a surprise if he saw the vid on the next issue.

At the mention of the XO's request, Konami laughed. "You can't rush an investigation. Didn't you learn that in class?"

"Of course," she replied. *Please don't lecture me, CI.*

"Tell the XO next time you see him, that it'll be done when it's done."

57

CHAPTER 10

A cheer rippled through the Arena, loud enough to interrupt their conversation despite the sparse attendance. Not that the attendance was surprising, considering that the Arena had nearly enough seating for the entire population of *Aotea*.

"Did you see that?" asked Medical Director Ilsa Madani. "Smooth!"

"Smooth indeed!" said Konami with genuine wonder. He was enjoying himself far more than he'd expected. It had been a while since he'd done anything that could credibly be described as "fun".

"Shame that Eng is so far ahead that it probably won't matter," responded Madani.

He agreed. The engineering department's team dominated the ship's ironball league most seasons, and this one seemed no different. Most departments, like Konami's constabulary, were too small to form their own team, so they joined up with another department or two. Engineer's current opponent, Fab-Supp, was made up of players from the fabrication and supply departments. Only two of Konami's constables were interested and talented enough to play ironball, so they joined the human resources and administration departments' team. Konami recalled that it was rare for them to win a single game. He thought he ought to try and attend more games — or at least the games in which Maria and Owen played. *Gotta support my deputies, even if they barely see the field.*

He asked her about Medical's team.

Madani gave the so-so gesture with her hand, explaining that they joined with the Science department, with middling success.

The buzzer sounded for the final break between periods.

He thanked her for inviting him.

58

"It's my pleasure," she replied. Madani spoke again just before Konami worried the silence was becoming awkward. "What do you think it's going to be like? Samwise? I mean, a whole new world. And the first world we've seen, besides Earth, with an atmosphere to support life. At least some sort of life."

"We'll need oxygen masks, right?"

She explained that the gas mixture on Samwise wasn't quite right, but that the geneticists were working on modifying the human genome to better adapt.

Konami successfully kept his eyes from glazing over at the technical details and nodded. "As to what it will be like, I suppose that will depend on what we make of it," said Konami. He thought for a minute. "It will be big."

"Big?"

"Yeah, big. Where are you from, if you don't mind my asking?"

"The Jovian moons. My parents were frontier doctors."

"Frontier? But they've been settled for a century!"

"Sure, but they're big too." She laughed. "Like Samwise. Every time some ice prospector finds a new cache of volatiles, there's a run to set up a new settlement."

"Volatiles? What is this, the 20th century? Why not fusion?"

"Earthers..." She shook her head. "Sorry. Fusion reactors are tough to build, and they take time. Years — Jove-years, I mean. Volatiles are easy. I must've seen a dozen new towns on Callisto and Ganymede with my moms. It was always the same — get there first, burn the volatiles while you dig tunnels, plant the bloom farms in the melt, and charge the mineral prospectors for the right to dig in your claim."

"What happens when the volatiles run out?"

"That's only a worry if prospectors find some valuable mineral. It goes two ways — if no one finds a thing, everything is abandoned long before the volatiles run out. Or someone finds something. If it's a big enough vein, then some investor will cough up the cash to build a fusion plant."

"Exciting stuff."

"How about you? Tell me about Earth."

"Have you ever been?"

She shook her head. "Expensive journey, even for doctors. Plus, all those open spaces…" She shivered.

Konami raised his eyebrows. "Samwise is gonna have those big open spaces."

"Yeah, I know," she replied. "By then, I'll be accustomed to it."

"Accustomed? On a spaceship?"

She laughed, gesturing up and around the cylinder of *Aotea*. "There's not a single chamber on Ganymede as big as one of the Cans."

Konami hadn't thought of it that way. "Did you ever go to the surface?"

"Occasionally. Just for fun, really… but it's such a pain, suiting up. Kind of a rite of passage, unless you're a prospector."

The way she looked at him brought him back. Way back – he hadn't been in a serious relationship since Earth, and not even recent Earth. More like a decade before. He felt an overwhelming longing, and it was gone in an instant.

"It will be different on Samwise," he said. "Real sky — blue and violet, I think — not just black and stars."

She smiled and put her hand on top of his. "I'm looking forward to seeing it."

CHAPTER 11

"Fuck!"

For the third time in the last fifteen minutes, Konami bumped his head on some overhanging object. Mattoso didn't remember him being clumsy at the scene of Muahe's death — in fact, he had been rather adroit in navigating through the passageways. *Maybe he's distracted?* Or maybe he just wasn't used to this part of the ship. Mattoso could count on one hand the number of trips she'd made to the Fabrication shops, deep as they were beneath *Aotea's* living spaces. The curses were a little much, though. *Did aggression count if it was against inanimate objects?* She didn't recall anything specific on the subject from various SNH tomes. But his scowl certainly seemed un-Aotean.

She tried to focus her mind on the task at hand. She'd had a little blow up with Pat that morning and her mind always seemed to go into overdrive after their rare fights – *what if they leave me? What if they've had enough?* She knew it wasn't logical. They'd had these little fights before, usually about something trivial like conflicts on their calendars, and it always blew over. Usually in less than a day. Another bump and a curse from Konami brought her attention back, and she suggested they slow down, but he waved dismissively and blamed himself.

They passed a shop and stopped to watch. A narrow hatch opened up into a very crowded workshop. Along a short conveyor belt, robotic arms moved so quickly as to blur together, building up what looked to be the main casing for one of the ubiquitous DustBots, molecule by molecule.

Mattoso asked if he'd been in these spaces before.

He turned and furrowed his brow. "Of course. Ship's quals. Gotta tour every space on this tub."

"And since then?"

61

Konami scratched his temple. "Maybe once or twice. I'm not sure, though — why would anyone need to come down here? Anything I need, I just make an order."

"Sometimes folks just don't want to wait." They both turned toward a little passageway to their left — the speaker was a little bald man, almost as small as a child.

"Chief Inspector, I presume?" said the man. He was accompanied by a round-domed TaskBot, child-sized and vaguely human shaped, which the little man occasionally patted on its "head." Probably the most common type of robot onboard aside from the cleaning Bots, TaskBots were utilized for assistance and general manual labor throughout the ship.

"Yes," answered Konami. "And you must be Fabrication Engineer Zubiri."

The engineer came forward and stuck his hand out. "A pleasure," he said as he shook Konami's hand.

He looked at Mattoso and smiled, and she introduced herself. His hand was dry and papery.

"Enjoying our handiwork?" he asked, idly scratching the TaskBot where its ears would be, if it had any.

"Yes, very impressive," replied Mattoso. "Is it all automated?"

"Come, I'll show you." Zubiri led them past a few more shops of varying sizes and functionality. They seemed to differ based on the material and size of the objects produced — one small shop was making household sundries out of polymers, while the largest shop was putting together an enormous alloy object that could be destined for a fusion reactor.

They arrived at the fabrication control room, manned by a single fabrication tech presiding over a jumble of monitors and touchscreens. Two additional stations were unmanned.

"I remember, from my quals," said Mattoso. "Only one fab tech on duty at a time."

"Normally, that's correct," replied Zubiri. "For unusual orders, or particularly high-volume times, we might assign a second tech on watch."

"And these extra stations..." started Konami.

"...Are for special orders, usually," Zubiri finished for him. "Not everything is in the main catalogue. And some Aoteans enjoy designing their own products, even down to the molecule." He laughed. "A few weeks ago, a youngster came in for a new set of polymer dishes. He demanded a strict molecular count — powers of the number two!"

"We had fun with that one," the fab tech added.

"Fascinating," said Mattoso, though it wasn't. But maybe she could come back later and finally get a blanket that wasn't too warm and wasn't too cold.

"So what is it I can help you with?" inquired the fabrication engineer.

"You've heard about the incident with DT1 Muahe?" Zubiri answered affirmatively, and Konami summarized their findings so far with regards to the mask and filter. "We'd like to see one produced, soup to nuts."

"That shouldn't be a problem." Konami gave him the fab number and the fab tech entered a string of commands.

Zubiri ordered his tech to wait, and led them to one of the smaller fabrication shops. "Go ahead," he said into his wearable, and the automated shop sprang into action. "As you can see," narrated the fabrication engineer. "The first step is for the printer to build the 'draft,' as we call it." Mattoso watched closely as a small, oblong machine glided back and forth over the beginning of the conveyor belt, accelerating to a blur. It was finished in less than a minute, a soft polymer object in the rough shape of a breather mask filter. The engineer's pride in his work was evident on the man's face. "The draft advances forward to the shapers." Insectile arms skimmed over the surface of the draft, cutting and trimming the details of the filter into the draft. "Then, the cladders." Another set of little automated arms, this time attaching generic tags and clips used for countless applications. "And finally, the scan." The filter slid into a transparent box and was lifted and spun. "The green light tells us the scan was satisfactory, so it's packaged and sorted."

So they're scanned... Mattoso thought back to the lab analysis. "Would the scoring on Muahe's filter be picked up by the scanner?"

"May I see it?" asked Zubiri.

Mattoso projected on a bulkhead and showed the engineer close-up images of the defective filter.

Zubiri sent his TaskBot to pick up the just-produced filter, removed the packaging, and they compared it to the images on her projection.

"Absolutely. The scanners would pick this up in seconds. Their resolution goes down to the nanometer scale, and this would be well out of tolerance. My friends, this was no fabrication error."

Konami crossed his arms. "So the scanner never makes mistakes?"

The engineer's brow furrowed. "Impossible. Each box has three scanners, and they all have to agree to go green."

"Can the scanner be disabled?" asked Mattoso. She noted that the chief inspector did not look satisfied.

Zubiri scratched the top of his head. "I suppose, but only from the control station. And it's not a standard procedure — I don't think anyone but one of my Techs could do it."

A shadow of a grin crept into the corner of Konami's mouth. "How good are your logs?"

The engineer tilted his head. "As good as any, I suppose. All fabs are logged automatically, by date, fab number, and quantity."

"And originator?" Mattoso chimed in.

"Yes, originator too. At least for outside orders. Manual on-site orders, like this filter, wouldn't record an originator."

"Thank you, Engineer." Konami had apparently heard enough. "We'll need to see all logs for these filter fabs, going back six months."

"Six months?"

Konami did the math in his head. *Not everyone's from Earth.* "One hundred eighty days. To start with. And I want your watch logs too, cross referenced with the filter fab times."

"That might take a while. We're just about to start a refurb of—"

"I'd be very grateful if you could have them to me by tomorrow morning."

"Tomor..." Zubiri met Konami's eyes and his expression hardened. "Yes, tomorrow. Understood, Chief Inspector."

CHAPTER 12

Konami yawned as he scrolled through the logs from fabrication. He was tired, but it was almost a welcome tiredness. Tired from honest police work for change, rather than from extreme boredom.

For the first time in at least a year, he considered that perhaps it wasn't a mistake to join the crew. Maybe they did really need him.

The breather filters were ubiquitous onboard *Aotea*, stored in bulk anywhere breathers were found — and considering that, in emergencies, specifications called for the ability for every single soul onboard to be able to don a breather at once, that meant that they were stored all over the ship. *But why do we use so damn many filters, when there hasn't even been smoke, much less a fire, in months?* A quick query revealed all the various events that could result in someone putting on a breather — training, various practical factors for qualifications, hazmat and hazspace evolutions, and more. And every time someone used one, they ordered a replacement, to keep the stocks full. *All breathers shall have no less than three clean and unopened filters stored with them at all times,* according to the specs. Practically speaking, this meant that most breathers had five or six filters stored alongside them to account for any delay in ordering new filters when one was used.

So that added up to a few dozen filters ordered each month. So far almost all of them were ordered through the Supply system, which meant that the individual making the order was recorded. And the department that the filter was ordered for — which often didn't match the rate of the ordering individual — was recorded as well. But there were a handful that were ordered in person, at the fab controls, with no delivery recorded — they must have been delivered and replaced by the ordering crewmember.

Fingers dancing in the air, Konami started two lists — one of all the filters that were delivered to the Sewage department, and one of all the fabrication techs on duty when the anonymous orders were made. Thinking about it further, and considering how easily filters could be swapped out, he made a third list of all the filters that were ordered by habitability techs, since the defective filter was in a Hab space. He sighed when he realized how many records he'd have to pore through to account for each and every one of these filters. Maybe someone could make a NetBug that could do it for him. He promised himself that at the next personnel review, he'd request that a Data Tech be permanently assigned to the Constabulary.

He was well into the records when the door to his office chimed. "Sorry, Cy, but he insisted," announced the Constabulary's duty secretary, Administrative Technician Second Class Yok-Sing, sticking his head in the door.

MRT2 Gustafson was pouring sweat, wiping it from his head with a rag. The young second's lip quivered before he spoke.

"Maybe… maybe it was my fault," said Gustafson, looking at the deck. "I just don't remember." The young tech physically deflated, but somehow looked relieved, despite the tears in his eyes.

Konami's guts twisted. *He's being honest,* he decided. But something still didn't feel right. He put his hand on Gustafson's shoulder, directing him down the passageway. "Let's take a short walk, Second," he directed, and the young man meekly followed.

The disciplinary process could be very fast, it turned out, contrary to the glacial place Konami recalled from past crewmember misbehavior. He made two calls — a brief one to Lieutenant Mattoso, and then to Gustafson's department master tech. Within a quarter-hour the master tech met them at the Constabulary. Mattoso and the XO arrived shortly afterwards.

67

Gustafson listened silently as he was taken off duty, after the XO and master tech made sure that Maintenance and Repair Department had enough manning to make up for his absence. The master tech walked the young man out, quietly consoling him; Gustafson would be confined to his quarters until a requalification plan was developed.

Commander Criswell turned to Konami, with an expression as close to a smile as he had ever seen on the executive officer. "Our mystery is solved, Chief Inspector," said the lean commander. "Not two random malfunctions, but one — the solder shard in the hatch circuitry. The breather filter mishap was caused by personnel error — a failure to follow procedure."

"We don't know that for certain," answered Konami, well aware of how weak his protests would sound. "Second Gustafson said he doesn't remember—"

The XO cut him off with a swipe of his hand. "I think that's enough grasping at straws, CI. I'll have a writeup tomorrow for you to sign. You can feel free to add any objections you may have. But officially, this case will be considered solved once the captain signs it." Criswell nodded to Lieutenant Mattoso, who had been sharing a sympathetic glance with Konami. "Your dedication is commendable," he said with what Konami took as a sneer, and walked out, with Mattoso close behind.

Konami sat and put his head on his desk. He wasn't even sure if it was worth going to Mayor Akunle to protest. He should be happy, he thought, with the case solved. *So why does it turn my stomach?*

CHAPTER 13

"Can you feel it?" Madani asked Konami. "The rotation?" She took his hand in hers.

They walked along one of the garden paths on the surface, winding from park to park, allowing idle Aoteans to walk in pleasant greenery for hours without backtracking. Konami ignored the occasional odd looks from passers-by — he knew that his sunshade-like low-light goggles were out of place during the artificial moonlit "nights" of the ship — but when he was with Madani, he didn't seem to care.

He had to shake off the feeling of disappointment from the ignominious ending to his investigation. It had been going so well – he felt it in that old investigative muscle that they were on the right track. But he couldn't think of a logical reason to continue, beyond this gut feeling.

He reached down to pet Kostya, leaning against his shins, as she tended to do. Genetically engineered to form strong attachments and with little desire to explore, jenji dogs didn't need leashes when taken on walks.

"When I stand still," continued Madani. "Especially on the edge of one of the Cans, I imagine I can feel the spin."

Konami stood still and tried to *feel*, through his feet. He vaguely recalled an exercise like this when he first joined the crew, and feeling the barest tremor.

"Close your eyes," said Madani. He obeyed. "Anything?"

He tried his hardest, but couldn't feel a thing, aside from the pitter-patter of activity at the little 'park' on the edge of the Can, and the vibration of Kostya's heart next to his ankle. It was hard to avoid the obvious conclusion, that the mind created this kind of feeling out of hope and excitement. He tried to recapture some of that excitement, of being in a select group accomplishing something incredible.

69

"Fact or treat, fact or treat!" He opened his eyes, thankful for the interruption, and was presented with a tiny elephant. And not just an elephant — there was a little bear, a shark, and some sort of spotted feline. A few meters back, their MOMbot chaperone lurked, ignoring all the park's activity except for the children under its care. The permanent smile on its cartoonish, teddy-bear face never failed to unsettle the chief inspector. Kostya inched forward and sniffed cautiously.

Konami crouched down and mustered up a smile. "You first," he said, pointing to the shark. He thought he recalled some shark facts from old Earth documentaries.

"What's a shark's skeleton made from?" The voice was almost unbearably cute, high pitched and complete with a minor speech impediment.

Konami took a pose and scratched his chin. "Hmm, that's a tough one. It's not bone..." He raised his finger exaggeratedly. "I've got it! Cartilage, right?"

The shark seemed disappointed. "That's correct."

Konami crouched down again. "You know what else is made of cartilage?"

The shark was silent.

He reached carefully under the costume and tweaked the child's nose. "Your nose! And now I've got it!" He put his thumb between his fingers and showed the child.

"No you don't, it's right here!" the youngster laughed.

Konami reached into his pocket and offered a candy to the child. "Who wants to be next?"

Each child took a turn, asking Konami and Madani a question about the animal they chose. Nominally, they didn't have to provide a treat if they answered the question correctly, but most Aoteans ignored that rule and gave out something regardless. The delighted children moved on, and the MOMbot gave Konami a curious nod before following.

Madani clapped her hands together. "Beast's Eve always makes me smile."

"Me too," he responded, trying to match her enthusiasm. "I look forward to it every year."

"Not year, silly. Cycle."

Konami cringed. "Yeah, cycle, of course." It was one of many little mistakes that marked him as an Earther. *Aotea*'s destination, Samwise, which orbited a planet that was much closer to its small sun than Earth, only had a "year" of about thirty Earth days. For holidays, birthdays, and similar events, Aoteans followed "cycles" consisting of ten Samwise years, adding up to three hundred days. Konami still couldn't help thinking in Earth months and years instead of Samwise-years and cycles.

"Did you have Halloween, on the Jovian moons?" asked Konami.

"Halloween?"

"Old Earth holiday. Not everywhere, but it's real big in North America. Beast's Eve rips it off." He started to explain the differences in the two holidays before being interrupted by a chirp.

Konami excused himself and stepped aside, answering the call. It was Emer – missing person: female, seventeen cycles, Fiona Vasquez. Her parents reported that she'd been missing and out of contact for several hours. The duty constable also sent him the interview transcripts.

Seventeen cycles — that's about fourteen or fifteen Earth years.

"What's going on?" asked Madani.

"Missing person. I'm afraid I'm going to have to cut short our walk." He tamped down the embarrassment he felt just for being excited by the chance to be useful.

"Can I help? Maybe they'll need a doctor."

Konami almost smiled at this. *Maybe she really likes me.* "As long as you can keep up."

He crouched down for a moment, petting Kostya, and gave her the order "Go home." She took one last look and dutifully set out for his quarters, obedient as always. After

71

that he set out immediately, barking orders into his wearable, to inform watchstanders and assign searchers.

Beta reserves might be a bit much, he thought, but it couldn't hurt the department to get a little extra action, considering how habitually underworked they were. Once again, he felt that rush of pleasure — his mind and body were telling him that this was *great*. He decided not to feel bad about it — after all, there was a missing child. Maybe enthusiasm could help find her.

Madani asked where they were going.

"Not sure yet." After scanning the interview, Konami called Emer once again. "Lee, it's Cy. Vasquez's parents mention a boyfriend, someone they don't seem to approve of. Javier Khama."

"Already on it. Calling him every few minutes, but no answer. Gregorian's talking to Khama's father."

Konami ended the call and buzzed Gregorian – his Deputy had talked to Will Khama, a GravTran Engineer, but he had no idea where his son was.

He considered the information so far. *Where would a young couple go…?*

Madani asked how she could help. He considered asking her to call up her reserve MedTechs and nurses, just for extra bodies for the search, but decided it wasn't necessary yet.

They were heading for the arena — he guessed that, when no events were being held, it would have a plethora of cozy hiding spots for a young couple. Bystanders and other Aoteans gave way, sensing the official purpose in Konami and Madani's stride. His wearable beeped — Emer had ordered all stations to report any recent anomalies, and he scrolled through the list, hazy in the air in front of him, uncertain of how it might help. Most were extremely minor malfunctions and log corrections, but one triggered something in Konami's mind, recalling the duties of the boyfriend's father, as they cut across a basketball court, and he thumbed a call to Gravity and Transportation Central.

A GT2 Udval answered. "Second, this is CI Konami. You got the message about the search?"

"Affirmative, CI. My rover is searching the machinery spaces as we speak."

"What was this Ring malfunction you reported?"

"It was in the aft Ring — car four is having hatch problems. I've taken it offline. No big deal — the other cars will pick up any passengers until we get it fixed."

Konami ended the call, turned around abruptly and, despite her long legs, Madani had to jog to follow his strides. They descended the nearest ladderwell and a moveway quickly zipped them to the central Ring. The Ring was still, sparing him the need of calling it, and they crossed through to the aft Can. Another moveway took them to the aft Ring, and Konami entered his override code to call car four.

He was about to force the door open when Madani grabbed his arm.

"Wait, Cy. They're kids. They'll be in enough trouble... do we really need to embarrass them too?"

He put his ear to the door and stifled a laugh — nothing but heavy breathing and moaning.

Madani listened as well and frowned at him. "Come on, Cy — we were all young once. Give them a break."

He put in a call to Emer, directing them to cancel the search and send deputies.

The chief inspector unhooked his belt buckle, the only metal he had on him, and used it to bang on the door.

After a moment of scuffling sounds and muffled voices, the young lovers emerged sheepishly, but at least they were fully clothed. Konami hid his amusement and looked sternly at the skinny, lanky youth. He asked what he'd done to the door.

The boy looked at the deck and mumbled something. Konami took a step forward. "Speak up! This ship is our home, Mr. Khama. Damaging a system could hurt someone, and it's a serious crime."

"There's no damage!" cried the boy, rushing inside of the car and lifting a plate off the bulkhead, gesturing that Konami should come and see. "Look here — I just put it in local maintenance mode and locked the door shut. It's Dad's system — doesn't do anything bad." He flipped a switch. "It's back now, it's fine. No damage at all!"

"Okay. That's a warning, Mr. Khama. I'm making a note with your name. No more tricks. If you want some alone time, then you'll just have to find another way."

"Yes, Chief Inspector."

"That goes for you too, Ms. Vasquez. No more going missing. You ruined a dozen family dinners tonight."

The young girl was crying, and Konami had to resist the urge to comfort her. "I'm sorry, Chief Inspector. We just…"

His deputies arrived, and Konami told them to escort the teens back to their parents.

Madani gave a throaty laugh after the deputies left with their charges. "So how often does that happen?"

"Missing person? Well, not too—"

"Kind of gives me an idea…" She took his hand and led him into the Ring car.

"Wait… what are you – oh. Yeah."

CHAPTER 14

Mattoso waited in Data Central, a crowded space near the forward Ring, buzzing with computer terminals. A jenji cat roamed the terminals, meowing in front of each tech until she got the scratch or pat she desired. The XO had said that the murder investigation was complete. *But XO isn't here.* Days before, Lieutenant Mattoso had made an appointment with the Data Systems department chief, Master Tech Lopez, to go over DT1 Muahe's routine and duties. She had no other duties at the moment, so she decided not to cancel the appointment. She knew the XO might tell her that the investigation was over. But something still went wrong. Even if it was just a gear malfunction, the engineer in her wanted to know. Even more than that, whe wanted to make sure it didn't happen again and hurt one of her shipmates.

Lopez was scowling. "I'm rather busy at the moment, Lieutenant, but DT3 Wren here would be happy to take you through Theo's basic routine." He immediately left for some other task.

Wren was short, slight, and round-hipped, and so bursting with youth that Mattoso wondered if he had finished growing. "Well, Lieutenant, I'm here to help in any way I can." The smarmy tone of the technician's high-pitched voice did not lend confidence to his words.

Mattoso asked to go through Muahe's routine. The young tech scowled for an instant before demonstrating his department's most common duties, one of which appeared to be affectionately nuzzling the department cat.

The tasks of data technicians were somehow both endlessly convoluted and endlessly tedious, but then perhaps her Operations tasks, balancing in real time the oft-conflicting power and system needs of the myriad of departments on board *Aotea*, would be equally unpleasant to data technicians.

Mattoso's mind drifted during Wren's droning. In her off time she had been compiling sources on an interest of hers, the history of the formation of the Society for a New Humanity, and the organization's ultimate goal, the construction and launch of the colony ship that she and twenty thousand others called home. There were gigs and gigs of data on most cycles in the decades prior to launch, but there were frustrating gaps, coinciding with apparent dips in SNH influence and wealth. *Maybe I'll ask Elena Conneer.* The journalist seemed to have access to information ranging from the obscure to the forgotten. She surprised herself by realizing that just a few cycles ago, the idea of bypassing the ship's records onboard for an unofficial source of information would have struck her as dubious, if not sacrilegious.

Something DT3 Wren said snapped Mattoso back to the present, and she asked him to repeat it.

"I said that the NetBug tracer is a cyclical task, but Theo must have wanted to get it out of the way since it wasn't due for a quarter-cycle or so."

"Hold on a minute," responded Mattoso, reading her notes on her lens. She scrolled to what she'd noted the first time she and Konami talked to DTM Lopez. "You said it's every cycle?"

"Yeah," yawned Wren. "It's a pain in the ass — needs a deep trawl of the net, and it can be disruptive to users while it's in progress." Mattoso located the line in her notes — *DTM notes that Muahe's tracer task was every thirty days.* She shook her head to herself. *Thirty days ain't the three hundred-day cycle, Master Tech!*

Wren sniffed. "But Theo, he was special..." The young tech cleared his throat. "He had a great work ethic, is what I'm saying. He would always help you, no matter what, and always wanted to stay ahead of things." Mattoso hesitated, and added a note that DT3 Wren seemed to have some very fond feelings for the deceased. She double-checked the security settings for her notes to make sure they were private.

"Master Tech?" Mattoso called out gently, repeating herself until Lopez turned around from the monitor he and another tech were hunched over.

"Yes, Lieutenant?" grunted the scowling man.

"What's the periodicity to run a NetBug tracer?"

Lopez's mouth hung open for a fraction of a second. "Why, every cycle, of course. It's a very demanding task."

"Are you sure? After the incident, you said it was every thirty days."

"I don't think so, Lieutenant. I'm quite sure I wouldn't make that mistake."

She wanted to respond, but couldn't come up with anything before he spoke again.

"If you'll excuse me, Lieutenant, we've been a bit short-handed since the tragic death of one of my best men, so I need to get back to work." The master tech turned and proceeded to a terminal at the other end of Data Central.

"Whoa, that's cold," said DT3 Wren.

Could my memory be off? As Wren brought her to another task, she reviewed the notes for a third time. *No. No fucking way I hear "cyclical" and enter "every thirty days."*

If she wasn't wrong, then she wasn't sure what that actually meant.

CHAPTER 15

Despite his complaining, Konami could tell that Agro-Engineer Fitzkelly loved his job. His enjoyment was so infectious that he actually felt a bit jealous.

"No one wants to see the Sausage Factory," said the mousy engineer. "Three quarters of the calories consumed onboard are produced here, but all anyone wants to see around here is the Garden."

"Why do you call it the Sausage Factory?" asked Madani. She and Konami had spent most of their non-duty hours of the past few days together. "'Cause of the vat-meat?"

Konami was pleased that he already knew the answer — Engineer Fitzkelly was one of the handful of other Aoteans onboard that used Earth idioms.

The wiry man shook his head vigorously. "No, no, it's not just vat-meat. That's just a fraction of what we do." He led them to a massive tank, with clear tubes pulling off a greenish liquid. "Cyanobacteria — that's the real staple onboard. Everything you eat — well, everything but a salad, fresh from the garden, I suppose — has cybac in it. They don't have much taste, but in protein and carbs they make up most of our calories."

Konami wrinkled his nose and a few Agro techs chuckled at Fitzkelly's complaints.

The engineer sighed. "But I suppose I can show you the meat tubes, if vat-meat is your thing. Right this way—"

"I think that's enough manufactured calories for now," said Konami with a slight grimace. "Ilsa?"

She cleared her throat. "Yes, of course. Thanks so much, Engineer. To the Garden?"

Konami agreed.

Fitzkelly scowled and stomped away, and Konami and Madani made their way, hand-in-hand, a few compartments over to Aeroponics, also known as the Garden. Between rows and layers of fruits and vegetables and even a few decorative flowers, they walked. The walkways were so narrow that they were nearly joined at the hip, and Konami felt like a teenager again, walking with a date between the skyscrapers of Singapore.

At an alley they stopped and kissed. Since Beast's Eve they had spent most of their free time together; Konami found he had far more of this precious resource than his girlfriend. *Girlfriend... doesn't seem so strange, all of a sudden.* The glimmer of happiness and optimism, that was strange. He let himself be lost in the moment, focusing on the softness of Madani's lips.

"Oh, I'm sorry..."

Konami looked up abruptly. His eyes widened for a moment when he realized who it was — the SNH Bigwig, Hamad Maltin.

"It's Professor Maltin. So sorry to interrupt."

"No problem at all," said Madani, grinning at Konami. "The Garden is yours, right?"

Maltin smiled — the effect was somewhat remarkable: with the smile, his coarse, leathery features softened into a warm grandfather's face. "Yes. I designed the Aeroponics compartment, years ago. Decades, ago, in fact — even before construction started."

Madani said that it was beautiful.

"Yes, beautiful. And functional, too." The pride was clear in Maltin's voice. "It requires barely any power to distribute the water and nutrients into the air. Even with no power, the passive misting will keep everything alive for weeks, or more."

"Very impressive," said Konami, trying to involve himself once he figured out that Madani was interested. "Will this be how we grow food on Samwise?"

"To start with, yes — probably from *Aotea* itself, in orbit. Along with the cybac reactors and such. But hopefully, one day, we'll be able to grow food on the surface of Samwise — without harming the native life, of course."

"But how?" asked Madani. "We can't know how the native vegetation will react."

"Of course. But we'll spend many years studying the properties and genetics of the native life forms, and before we do anything on a large scale we'll perform quarantined experiments and tests." He smiled. "I know many Aoteans look forward to landfall, assuming that we'll have a bounty of fruits and vegetables... but unfortunately it will be many years before we're eating anything different from what we eat now. The green rationing will be in effect long past the first day of settlement."

Konami's attention wandered while Madani and the Bigwig discussed the future of Aoteans' agriculture in more detail, but it got him thinking. When he first arrived onboard, he had thought that everyone's focus would be on their destination: the lush moon Samwise, which revolved around the gas giant planet called Abhoth, a dozen light years from Earth. But Samwise almost seemed to be an afterthought, at least in many conversations he'd had. He recalled one Aotean responding to his question on Samwise with "Right now we're on *Aotea*. In many cycles we'll be on Samwise. But it doesn't matter where we are — we're already the New Humanity. Our new society travels with us." SNH dogma, one of the many things that kept Konami from feeling like an Aotean, seemed to consider distance from Earth, both physical and philosophical, as far more important than one's actual location. Considering his status as one of the SNH Bigwigs, Konami would have thought Maltin would be the last person onboard to be so interested in Samwise.

He wasn't sure why this struck him as so odd.

"So what else on this tub should we see?" asked Madani with a smirk, leaning back in the booth of one of the cafes that dotted the surface of *Aotea*.

Konami asked what else there was.

"The Theatre," she answered. "And the Repro Lab. And Engineering and Nav/Ops, of course, but we'll need special permission."

"I don't know, zero-g makes me queasy."

"It's not quite zero — we're still accelerating, so you'll have a little weight. A few grams, maybe."

"Oh joy," laughed Konami.

A server brought their coffee, foaming the top of Madani's order with a flourish.

"That's quite a coffee mug," said Konami, impressed at the bowl-like mug she drank from.

"The infirmary goes through three cups per day, per person," replied Madani. "That's the most of any department onboard. I checked. Supply's threatened to cut our ration."

Konami looked at his own cup — indistinguishable from all the other cups in the café, and all the others he recalled ever seeing onboard. "Where'd you get it? Did you design it yourself at the Fab shop?"

"Oh, it was cycles ago. I was going to, but they told me at the shop that there were tons of designs in the archives that no one ever used, and it was true — there were hundreds of dishes and mugs, and it was much easier just to pick one."

"Interesting," said Konami, before something fizzed in his brain. "Wait, did you say there are unused designs in the Fab archives?"

"Oh yeah. I had to scroll past hundreds, and look at dozens of designs."

He stood up in a hurry and grabbed Madani's hand, apologizing for having to leave in a hurry and promising to call.

He made the call to Mattoso as he was leaving, asking her to meet him at Fabrication.

"So you want to see filters, but not in the catalogue? Whatever for?" asked Engineer Zubiri. Konami couldn't recall ever seeing him outside of the Fabrication shops, and he wondered if he ever left.

Mattoso asked if they could search by physical dimensions. Konami had filled her in on his coffee mug revelation as they arrived.

"We can search by any parameter you can think of."

"But down to the nanometer?"

Zubiri smiled. "We can go to the picometer, my dear."

Konami read off the dimensions from his projection, and the Fab tech on watch punched it into his console.

Something tingled in Konami's head during the seconds it took for the terminal to report back its findings. Out of billions of product designs, there was a single match.

Zubiri bended to look more closely at the screen. "That's funny… why would there be design for a defective breathing filter?"

Konami ignored the question, his head throbbing. It had been years since he felt this way. "The scanners wouldn't pick this up, would they, Engineer?"

"No, it fits the design perfectly, so it would pass," answered the Fabrication department head. His eyes went wide. "Chief Inspector, does this mean that poor Mr. Muahe—"

"When was this item ordered and produced?" interrupted Mattoso.

The Fab tech read the date off the screen. "It was done in person, here, so no names were recorded."

Konami shared a look with Mattoso. "Just a few days before Muahe died," she said softly.

Konami beckoned her to the passageway, taking off at a fast walk.

"So we go to the XO?" asked Mattoso, almost jogging to keep up with Konami's long strides.

"Screw the XO," said Konami. "We're going straight to the captain."

"Shouldn't we test the filter first, just to make sure?" she asked.

He paused in his tracks. "Yes, that's a good idea. We should have all the data to share. Can you take care of that? I'll go straight to the captain and the mayor, but while I'm waiting—" His wearable buzzed. He almost ignored it, but recognized the characteristic trill of a call from Emer. He answered it.

CHAPTER 16

Goddamn it goddamn it goddamn it... Sulemon Nicolescu's guts tossed and roiled so much that he groaned. *It was supposed to be smooth, easy. Painless.* But DT1 Muahe's death didn't sound painless. What was the right thing to do?

"It's bigger than us, bigger than anyone," the coordinator had said, after word got out about Muahe. "We all knew these times would come — they're just coming a bit sooner than we expected."

A bit sooner? More like fucking Earth-years sooner. Decades, even. Dozens of cycles more onboard... He knew in his gut things weren't going to get smoother, and easier. They never did. His thumb hovered over the "send" command on his wearable's projection. One message could end it all. Or would it just make things worse?

He didn't hit send. Instead, he reached for a bottle of medication next to his bunk. Thanks to his duties at the Chem Lab, Senior Chemist Nicolescu never had trouble acquiring the meds he needed.

It shouldn't have been this way. He didn't sign up for violence – even impersonal violence. Quite the opposite, in fact.

His quarters' front door chimed. "Go away," he whispered. He didn't have another watch until the following day. He didn't need to decide today. He could still think about it, maybe even talk to the Solacer.

It chimed again. After a third chime, he finally roused himself and stumbled over to the door.

He thumbed it open, sighing when he saw who was there. "Didn't we already finish—"

The needle jabbed his neck before he could see it. A cry of surprise came out as a croak, and his legs turned to jelly. As he hit the floor he reached for his wearable, but everything was numb.

CHAPTER 17

"An injection wound was found on Chemist Nicolescu's neck," explained Konami, gesturing to the wide projection in the conference room. Captain Horovitz and Mayor Akunle had called an emergency department head meeting after Konami reported the senior chemist's death and the breakthrough in DT1 Muahe's case. "Preliminary analysis suggests that Nicolescu's body reacted the same way that it would to certain types of neurotoxic venom, produced by some Earth animals."

The shocked reactions – gasps, hands clapped over mouths, even department heads abruptly getting to their feet – in the room when the Chem Tech's murder was revealed had almost brought a smile to Konami's lips, even while he felt a bit guilty about the impulse. *Finally, they'll see what people are actually capable of. Even in this little fantasy world they've created.* But he had to admit to himself that it wasn't just a fantasy, at least not entirely. Aoteans were an agreeable folk, on the whole, and the rational part of his brain knew that he ought to be both pleased and honored to be a part of them. Even when the other part of his brain insisted on mockery and derision.

"Venom?" asked one of the Bigwigs, Wilson Paramis. "There are no snakes onboard *Aotea*." The heavily built demographer chuckled openly, defying the tense atmosphere of the meeting.

"No snakes," said Madani. "But I don't think we'd have much trouble mixing up a synthetic venom."

Another Bigwig, geneticist Mara Ngayabo, agreed.

Konami added that they hadn't found a syringe.

After a pause, Captain Horovitz spoke up. "Director-Superintendent Akunle and I are treating Nicolescu's death as a murder."

Konami fought to hide the urge to snort after a clichéd round of gasps from the department heads, briefly waking

86

up the cat Halifax from his slumber on the table next to the commanding officer. He collected himself, mentioning that this was not the first murder.

The captain agreed, and he took an incline of her head as license to speak. Konami had noticed no more reaction than the barest purse of her lips when he first explained the breakthrough in Muahe's death to her and the mayor. On the other hand, Harry Akunle did nothing to hide his surprise.

Konami went through his findings from Fabrication, displaying the recordings and data for everyone to see. He made sure to make note of the contributions of Lieutenant Mattoso, who was undoubtedly fuming in the passageway for being kept out of the meeting. He explained, in detail, the proof that the anomalous filter was fabricated as defective on purpose.

The navigator, Commander Rusk, asked when the filter was ordered.

"It's been only ordered a single time on record," answered Konami, displaying the Fab order. "Days before Muahe's murder." Too late he realized Criswell might see this as baiting him, but the XO seemed to be as interested and attentive as everyone else present. Another asked who ordered it, and Konami explained that they were still trying to find out.

That prompted the captain to order that, going forward, there would be no more anonymous fabrication orders onboard.

A glance from the captain silenced a budding side conversation. "Taking all this into account," said Konami. "We can conclude that the death was not accidental."

"But the filter wasn't replaced properly," interjected Commander Argosi, the head of the Habitability Department. "Second Gustafson confessed, right?"

Konami was prepared for this, and displayed the signed statement of the Second-Class Maintenance and Repair technician. "It wasn't a confession," said Konami.

"He just stated that he couldn't remember if he followed procedure, and that it was possible that he failed to do so. But his record is otherwise exemplary, with no disciplinary actions at all. In my professional opinion, Second Gustafson was succumbing to a mixture of guilt and sadness over a colleague's death, along with external pressure."

"And it turns out to be immaterial in any case," added the captain. "The filter that killed First Muahe was not the filter that Second Gustafson may or may not have replaced." She turned to Commander Criswell and directed him to return Second Gustafson to duty. "A lesson from this," she continued. "There will be no more rushing to judgment about junior crewpersons. Any disciplinary action going forward will go through the mayor and I. This ship and our mission will not survive without good morale for the crew, and morale will not survive if the crew believes the leadership is not on their side." She met the eyes of every department head in turn. "Careers have been ruined, and lives have been lost, all because leaders no longer had the confidence of their team. That must not happen onboard. Is that clear?"

"Yes, captain," came the unified response.

There were a few more questions about details of the case, but Konami was surprised to see that no one, including the XO, appeared skeptical of his conclusions.

"We are all agreed," said the mayor, his characteristic smile absent. "We will be investigating two murders onboard. Correct?" He looked around the room, but no one dissented. "The chief inspector will continue his investigation, of course, which the captain and I agree is our highest priority, aside from continuing safe operations of *Aotea*. But there's a larger question here. A murder requires a murderer. A killer among us. Perhaps even killers. Word will get out, if it hasn't already, and people will be afraid."

"Cameras," suggested Lieutenant Commander Olin, the Comms/Signals officer. "For surveillance. We can put a nanocam above every door, at every junction—"

Chief Engineer Papka interjected, citing the charter and arguing that excessive invasion of privacy was one of the reasons for *Aotea*'s journey.

The meeting descended into a jumble of arguments until Captain Horovitz brought her palm down hard on the table. "Enough bickering."

Konami jumped at the opening and read off his projection. "Section 5.13.2.b of the Charter: In response to shipwide emergencies, restrictions from subsection b.1 may be waived if both the Civil Executive and Operational Commanding Officer agree and declare Martial Alert." Department heads scrambled to follow along on their own. Konami continued: "To continue Martial Alert beyond any thirty-day period, a majority vote of confidence from the Department heads is required for both the CE and the CO, and every thirty days thereafter, with the threshold to continue increasing by an additional single-vote supermajority each thirty day period." He scrolled down, slightly confused by the arithmetic. "The restriction on unmanned cameras is one of the restrictions from subsection b.1. So according to the Charter, Captain and Mayor, if both of you agree, you may invoke this waiver." *For thirty days, at least.*

The captain and mayor huddled together briefly, whispering. The three Bigwigs did the same. Hamad Maltin approached the captain and mayor, and after another minute, Captain Horovitz spoke, asking for more options.

Konami suggested more roving watches.

"The Constabulary won't be enough," cut in the XO. "Not even for a single Can. To cover both Cans, much less Ops and Engineering, we'll need more deputies."

Konami was surprised by Commander Criswell's suggestion. A few department heads immediately offered their own personnel — they could go on three or four-section rotation for their own watch stations and would have several personnel left over to deputize.

"And they could carry cameras," said Lieutenant Commander Olin. "No, seriously—" she added after Commander Papka groaned. "The Charter only bans unmanned or hidden cameras. It doesn't say a thing about manned, visible cameras."

"That's true," Konami agreed. "We can put a camera on every rover, and even every stationary watchstander. No special votes or waivers required, per the Charter."

The captain and mayor huddled together again. This time the Bigwigs stayed away. "Very well," announced Mayor Akunle. "Commander Chulanont, Fabrication will work with the Constabulary on the necessary camera specs. And the following departments will provide approximately one sixth of their fully qualified manning to the Constabulary to deputize: Propulsion and Power, Navigation/Operations, and Repair. Every other department will provide a list of personnel they can spare in case more are needed."

Konami was dumbfounded — that would more than double his strength, if not triple. Maybe even more.

"Other business?" asked the mayor.

Konami's mind wandered to the challenge of covering the entire ship with roving watches while the mundane business of *Aotea* was discussed. He had no stomach for "other business" when there was a double-murderer, or two murderers, onboard.

CHAPTER 18

HUMANS GO HOME!
Comms Techs have detected alien signals.
Two Aoteans dead.
Coincidence? Or a sign that we should never have left?
Maybe we should take the hint! We were never meant
to leave.
Maybe the universe sees humanity for what we are,
and will never let us settle anywhere else!

Mattoso's concern grew as she saw this and similar
sentiments posted anonymously in the comment forums
and discussions, sometimes even in topics totally unrelated
to the deaths. She ended the projection when she reached
the Constabulary.

"How are the assignments and deputizations going?"
she asked, taking the offered seat across from the chief
inspector's desk.

"Ugh... this is what I get for requesting more people,"
Konami shook his head. "This tub's layout is damn
complicated. Even with the two hundred and something
deputies I'm about to have, it's going to be hard to cover it
all."

Mattoso nodded agreement. "I have a thought on that,
and it's tied to what I'm here for."

"What you're here for?"

"It didn't seem so important at the time, but now that
we know we have two murders..." Mattoso explained the
scheduling discrepancy between her notes and what Master
Tech Lopez told her a few days prior. "I wouldn't have
written down 'thirty' if he had said 'every cycle' or 'every
three hundred days.' I'm sure of it."

Konami leaned back and scratched his head. "So he
got it wrong... maybe just a brain fart?"

"Maybe," she agreed. "But he wouldn't admit it at the time. He said I must be mistaken."

"Big ego?"

"Perhaps." Mattoso leaned forward, lowering her voice. "But I think it's something else. I remember some old 'Investigator's Handbook' — it was really old... a scan in Ceres' educational archives, not even searchable until I ran it through the text-identifier! But it talked about instinct, and gut feel — an investigator would inevitably have to rely on her gut. And I think this was that, Cy. It didn't feel right when Lopez said it. Something wasn't right. I could *feel* it."

Konami looked straight at her for a long time. "So you said you had a thought." A blood vessel in his jaw pulsed.

She took a deep breath. "We need our own data tech."

He nodded very slowly.

She wasn't sure if he understood. "We need someone we can, uh, trust, just in case—"

"I understand," he cut her off. "We need to get into Muahe's logs, personal and otherwise."

"And not just his logs. With our own data tech, we can get into, well, any concerns we have about—"

He cut her off again. "Right. Don't say it. But who? And how?"

She had no answer.

Theo Muahe's best friend, Mechanical Technician Second Class Trung Olivier, looked worried just answering the door.

Konami nodded to her, and she asked about friends of Muahe in the Data department.

Olivier frowned. "I thought I told you before. He didn't really get along with any of the other data techs."

"Are you absolutely sure? He never talked about any of them in a, well, nice way?" she asked.

The mechanical tech shook his head but stopped abruptly. "Well, he was mentoring one. I guess he kind of liked her — him. I think he liked him okay."

Mattoso ignored the misgendering, unsure whether it was deliberate bigotry or just carelessness.

The tech continued. "DT3 Wren. I met him once — strange kid, kind of a sarcastic prick, I thought. Didn't have any friends at all. But Theo said he was a natural data miner, and programmer, and a hard worker. That's the highest praise he ever had for any of the DTs. I guess that's as close as it got to a friend in Data."

"So, Third Wren," said Konami, after they returned to his office. "Know anything about him?"

She checked her notes to her memory. "Yeah, he showed me around the DT spaces and their routine. I got the real impression he was fond of Muahe — maybe very fond of him."

Konami pulled up Wren's bio on his monitor. "Huh," said the chief inspector, looking at Wren's boyish countenance on the screen. "I remember him at the funeral. He took it hard. Very hard."

"So is this our guy?" she asked. "Our ally?"

"I don't know," responded Konami. "But this has got to be gentle. Soft, even. Careful. Jesus." Konami shook his head, his brow furrowed. "'Allies' implies 'enemies.' And we're years — cycles, that is — away from Earth."

"Or Axis," she added.

"Axis?"

"Sorry. Just one of the few snips I remember about Earth history. Axis versus Allies. The bad guys and the good. Genocide and all that... you know, what we're trying to get away from." Her cheeks bloomed and she felt foolish.

He looked at her oddly. "Anway, I was saying we need to be careful with this." He fiddled for a minute, then projected on the bulkhead. "DT3 Wren was on watch in

Data Central when the defective filter was fabbed and picked up, and on an Under Instruction watch in Navigation for ship's quals when Nicolescu was killed."

"So we can rule him out?" she asked.

"I don't know if we can rule out anyone this early. But if we have to trust someone, I think this is as good as we're going to find right now." He scratched the back of his head. "I don't think we should go together to recruit him. Too intimidating, for a young Third, I think."

She nodded in agreement. "I'll do it. I've already spent the better part of a day with him."

"Use that gut feel. Your instincts. This is still a risk."

She nodded and turned to go.

"Wait," he said. "You said this would help with my deputies?"

"Oh yeah. A mapping algorithm. Engineering has the 3D layouts — it should be a snap to put together roving routes that cover everything. I could probably spend a half-day reading up and do it myself, but I bet a DT could do it in five minutes."

Konami slapped his forehead. "Of course! Why didn't I think of that?"

She grinned and left.

CHAPTER 19

"When can I see you?" he asked Madani.

"Oh, you just want to see me, do you?" she responded through her wearable. Konami imagined her eyelashes batting. "What do you want to see me for?"

"I want—" *Damn,* but the way she flirted turned him on, even while it made him blush and lower his voice. "I want you to show me around the Repro lab."

"Is that what they're calling it these days?"

He coughed as some saliva went down his air passageway. A text alert came up. Konami caught his breath. "I gotta go, Ilsa. I want to see — I want you." *Weak.*

"You'll have me, Cy. Soon." She ended the call and Konami stepped into the passageway.

Mattoso stood at the junction of the passageway, leaning against the bulkhead. "So he's in?" Konami asked her, his voice low.

"Oh I'm in," answered Wren, stepping out from around the corner. "Nothing better to do. And besides, someone killed Theo. I wanna help you find that *hijo de puta.*"

Mattoso chuckled. Wren's exuberance reminded Konami of the youth of Lagos, and gave him a distinct feeling of nostalgia — which didn't make much sense at all, since the data technician was born and raised Aotean. He was probably one of the oldest 'natives,' as those youngsters born on *Aotea* called themselves, onboard. It was possible he had never stood in natural gravity — Konami recalled someone telling him that, before departure, Aoteans were strongly encouraged not to leave the ship. Like most that were born onboard the colony ship, this meant his parents probably went through the genebank lottery — they would have been selected randomly from the Aotean couples who were interested in a child, and his genes would similarly have been selected randomly from the hundreds of thousands gene samples provided by applicants who just barely missed the final cut of crew selection for *Aotea*.

"So how do I help?"

Konami started to explain his problem with the roving watches.

Wren snorted. "You kidding?"

"It's not an easy problem, I think you'll find. With the number of temporary constable deputies assigned, about 50 rovers at a time should work. But the lower levels of the Cans are like a maze — every passageway needs to have coverage about once every hour or two, and that includes lockout spaces, trunks, and—" Konami went on for a full minute about the logistical difficulties.

"Done," said Wren, grinning.

"What?"

"It's done. Well, it will be in a few minutes. DustBots already do this — it's built into their programming." He projected onto the bulkhead. "They work together to cover the whole ship, for cleaning. I just modified a DustBot roving plan — changed the roving speed to 5 kph, the coverage parameter to 'entire ship', the sweep-size to line-of-sight, and the number of rovers to fifty."

"But we don't know how fast—"

"Oh don't worry. I'm already running simulations — a tough cleaning spot for a bot might be like something interesting a rover sees and wants to look more closely at — we'll see what areas don't get enough coverage. I'll have a few million sims done in a half-hour or so."

"Huh," grunted Konami. Just like in Lagos, the youths onboard *Aotea* could apparently still leave him confused and speechless. He'd have to praise Mattoso for her instincts later. "Thanks, Third."

"So how do we find the killer?" asked the young data technician.

Konami led them from the passageway into his office. "Bea?"

She told them that they wanted to know more about the NetBut Tracer run by Muahe.

"I'd guess he was just trying to get ahead," said Wren. "I mean, it wasn't due for more than a quarter-cycle, I think. That's early, but maybe he was bored. He was weird that way."

"We don't want to guess," added Mattoso. "We want to know the real reason."

Wren snorted. "Well how should I know? Maybe he made a note in his personal logs or something, but private logs are restricted—" The young Third's eyes went wide for a moment. "Wait. The logs... you guys want me to..."

Konami waited, but he didn't finish his sentence. "Yes, we want to see those logs."

The data technician furrowed his brow, somehow looking even younger. "We're going to need to schedule that with the master tech, then. Maybe the director, too. It'll take a lot of bandwidth to get in."

Konami was confused. "Bandwidth? Can't you just guess the password?"

Wren's laughter was high pitched and girlish. "Are you kidding? Theo's a DT. Not just a DT, but the best DT onboard. You think he has a password that a person could just *guess*?"

Mattoso stroked her chin and nodded. "So the bandwidth is for a brute-force hack," she added.

"Right. Guess the password, with a gigawhale of guesses per second," he said, recognizing Konami's confusion. "Uses up a ton of bandwidth. That's the only way. Private logs are supposed to stay private. No back door and no data-net trawling. Hell, you can't even delete private logs without logging in — they go straight to the solid-state drives!" He began tutting his fingers in the air. "So do you want me to send in a request—"

"No!" Konami almost shouted, worried at the speed at which Wren operated his wearables. "No request. This needs to be..."

"...discreet," finished Mattoso. Konami nodded his thanks.

"Right, discreet," said Konami. "If we're not discreet, and the wrong person knows, then those logs could disappear forever — wiped from the drives before we take a look. That's why we came to you personally, Third, and not to Master Tech Lopez, or anyone else."

Wren scratched his head and played with his hands for a half-minute. When he spoke, his voice was softer, and pitched higher. "So that means, you think — well, you're worried that the Master Tech might be... the killer."

"We have no idea who the killer is," Konami replied. "We're pretty sure it's not me, and it's not Lieutenant Mattoso, and it's not you. We need you to think, Third. How can we look at Muahe's logs? Discreetly?"

"It's the bandwidth that's the problem," responded the Third, his voice a little stronger than before. "If we can get thirty percent spared, we could get into the logs in less than a day, I bet. Maybe hours. But there's no way we could get a spike that big, or even close to that big, without someone noticing. The data tech on watch will probably notice anything bigger than zero point one percent or so, especially if it's ongoing. At point one percent, it could take weeks to get in. Maybe more."

Shit. Konami only half-way followed as Wren expounded on the details.

"Could there be some way to mask it?" asked Mattoso. "Some way to make it look like it was just maintenance?"

The data technician shook his head vigorously, then stopped. "We can't mask it, but maybe we could time it right." His fingers danced again. "DT2 Kunayak. He's lazy as shit. And he's a big gamer. We could boost it up for his watch — it'll be about once, for six hours, every day or two. I bet we could get away with one percent or so. Maybe a couple decimals more. If he notices, I think he'll call me first — it'll come from my account, and I'll just tell him to shut up about it 'cause I'm gaming. I don't think he'll rat me out… he'll want me to do him the same favor. Man, with a whole percent of bandwidth, we could game *smooth*…"

Konami looked at Mattoso, but she just shrugged her shoulders. "How long will it take?" asked Mattoso.

"With a percent? I'll do the calc later, but I'd guess a few days of computational time. Maybe more, or less if we're lucky."

Damn. Konami did some quick math on his wearable — that could still be ten watches at least — it could take weeks for DT2 Kunayak to stand ten watches. But they'd run it at the lower rate for the rest of the time, so hopefully a lot sooner.

"Alright Third. When can you set it up?"

The young man fiddled in the air again. "It'll be ready by tomorrow when Kunayak takes the watch."

Konami wished him luck and Wren left.

"So we have an ally…" he said to Mattoso.

"Three against a killer," she responded. "We have the odds."

He shook his head, pursing his lips. "I don't think we're facing just one."

CHAPTER 20

I don't think we're facing just one... Lieutenant Mattoso had asked him to explain, but Konami just said he had a feeling. That didn't help her anxiety, especially when she realized she had the same feeling. The CO and XO kept urging that everyone continue about their lives. They said there was no reason to believe anyone was in immediate danger.

She wanted to believe it. *And I wanted to believe in Santa and his clones delivering presents to obedient children from his workshop on Pluto when I was little.*

She was still struggling to accept that there could be killers aboard. That was why they left in the first place! Was this whole journey – the entire purpose of the Society for a New Humanity – for naught?

She refused to accept that. They weren't perfect, but that doesn't mean it wasn't a worthy goal. For all they knew, one or two killers managed to get past the *Aotea's* character screenings, but everyone else was still as worthy as she'd believed from the beginning.

That had to be it. Anything else was unthinkable.

She had a little time before she was supposed to meet Pat at the Repro Lab, so she checked her network feed. The latest article on *Aotea Today* featured a text interview with the user of the handle Pol Revear who, apparently, originated the 'HUMANS GO HOME' forum posts:

Aotea Today: What drove you to make these alarming posts?

Revear: It's not just me. There are many of us, and our numbers are growing.

Aotea Today: So what are your goals?

Revear: Simply put, our goal is to survive and protect all Aoteans. We are the first humans to leave Earth's solar system. We all know why we left — endless conflict, endless violence, the toxic culture inherited from humanity's birth and social evolution. But maybe we're not the only ones who noticed. Maybe they — and by 'they' I mean whoever is sending these signals — think that we're just going to bring that conflict with us.

Aotea Today: Do you think they're right?

Revear: I don't know. It doesn't even matter; what matters is what they believe. We're only just able to travel to other solar systems — anyone out there is going to be far more advanced than we are. If they want us to stay home, all that matters is what they believe.

Aotea Today: Is anonymous advocacy, and what some are calling vandalism, really consistent with the values of the Society for a New Humanity?

Revear: Telling the truth isn't vandalism, and there's nothing in the Society texts about anonymous advocacy. In fact, if I remember my history, one of Paula's biggest advocates before the Society was created was an anonymous writer.

Aotea Today: Why do you believe that these strange signals are related to the two recent deaths onboard?

Revear: Simple — it's too much of a coincidence. Two murders at the same time as unexplainable signals?

Aotea Today: This sounds far-fetched. Do you really believe Aoteans will accept that we're being warned to return home by aliens?

Revear: I'm not positive myself. But I'm worried. If my concerns are borne out, then we better turn around before we all end up dead.

Aotea Today: What do you think we should do?

Revear: If I were captain, I'd slow us down. If the signals continue, even as we turn around, then maybe it's nothing — just a comet reflecting a pulsar or something. But if it stops, or if they change, and especially if the deaths cease, then maybe that means they approve of our course change.

Mattoso scanned the rest of the interview, and it was just more of the same — wild hypotheses and accusations and doomsaying. She shook her head and ceased the projection. *We were supposed to be the cream of the crop — the best twenty thousand of all of humanity, or at least the very best out of the billion applicants.* Her Earth-born grandmother used to say "when it rains, it pours" — an idiom unfamiliar to most Cereans, since the domes and tunnels on the asteroid had no weather patterns — but she had a feeling that it fit here.

"This is a weird time to be getting a pet, you know," said Pat, smirking.

Mattoso and her lover stood in front of the Repro facilities while they waited for a Genetic Engineer to be free.

"We live on a spaceship, babe," replied Mattoso. "Doesn't get much weirder than that."

"I'm glad we're doing it here," said Pat. "It'll be a lot more fun to order in person than just through the net." Mattoso squeezed her companion's hand in agreement.

An older woman in a lab coat emerged from an office inside the Repro space and greeted them. She looked awfully familiar.

Pat whispered in her ear, wondering if it was one of the Bigwigs

Holy shit! It was. "Miss — Professor Ngayabo," mumbled Mattoso. "There must be some mistake. We're here—"

"You're here to choose a pet, correct?"

"Yes," said Mattoso.

"Then there is no mistake," said Mara Ngayabo. Mattoso flinched at her stare. She knew that each the Bigwigs had a professional specialty, and performed duties outside of their unofficial advisory role, but she had never actually interacted with any of them other than in passing. Certainly not in any professional capacity. Mara Ngayabo was a Genetic Engineer, she recalled, while Hamad Maltin was an Agricultural Biotechnologist, and Wilson Paramis

102

was a Demographer. "Let's begin," said Ngaybo, finally, leading them down a passageway.

In a small laboratory, a pair of genetic technicians worked from holographic displays, twisting and splicing and mixing DNA strands from dozens of lifeforms, each one marked by a digital image as it looked on Earth. Ngayabo pointed to a pair of heavy doors, set far apart on the opposite bulkhead. "Behind these doors are the most valuable treasures we are bringing with us." For the first time she could remember, Mattoso sensed a flicker of feeling behind Ngayabo's stone face. *This is what she cares about.* The Bigwig pointed to the larger door. "Simply put, we have brought with us the genetic legacy of Earth. Everyone knows about the millions of human genetic samples — the future populations of our colony on Samwise — specifically chosen for their hardiness and diversity, as well as positive neural traits." Ngayabo pointed to the other door. "But that's just half of our treasure. Joining them in the secondary bank are samples of thousands of non-human species from Earth — from microscopic creatures to marine behemoths; any creature that might possibly be useful or desirable."

She led them to a dark room, handing out low-light goggles. "And here is the nursery." Mattoso knew that Repro had the capability to incubate non-human animals in artificial wombs, but it was quite another thing to actually see these wombs — rows of translucent poly structures, a few actually occupied by alien-looking, wriggling zygotes, ranging from infinitesimal and magnified on displays, to "giants" the size of her big toe. A spindly, long-limbed TenderBot moved from womb to womb, taking fluid samples and administering nutrients, while a young apprentice veterinary tech looked on and took notes.

"Where do they all go?" asked Mattoso.

"If they're not pets, then the vet lab," replied Ngayabo. "For practice. Or other labs, for research. Skills need to be maintained, even if we won't need them for decades."

103

"You said you could recreate whales," said Pat. "How is that possible? None of these wombs are big enough for a human, much less a whale."

"We have other nurseries," answered the genetic engineer. "With artificial wombs large enough for humans, and even for small cetaceans. Theoretically, once we establish a coastal colony on Samwise, we can use larger and larger adult cetaceans to bear the next generation of a slightly larger species, if we wish."

"Why would we need whales?" asked Mattoso.

"Ask the ecology department," said the older woman. She reminded Mattoso of a particularly harsh schoolteacher from her childhood on Ceres. "With the samples in the genebank and our nurseries, we will create a new biosphere on Samwise, with whatever Earth life we deem necessary or pleasing."

"What about Samwise's native life?" inquired Mattoso. The question burst out before she could hold it back.

"Ask the bioethicists," responded the genetic engineer, leading them to a bank of monitors. "Now, your pet. Dog, cat, or other?"

Mattoso looked at Pat. "A dog," she said.

Ngayabo led her through a series of choices — coat color, size, energy level, attachment level, affection, and more, showing signs of impatience any time they took more than a few seconds to choose. When it was complete, Ngayabo departed without so much as a goodbye, leaving them with a third class genetic technician.

"Your pet will be ready in approximately eight weeks," said the Third. "You may come visit any time after week two to view its development." The technician lowered her voice. "But I don't think you'll want to see it until week four or five. Before that it's pretty much gooey-tadpole territory. And don't worry about Engineer Ngayabo — you just had the bad luck to catch her on her once-per-month proficiency watch."

"Not as much fun as you hoped, huh?" asked Pat as they strolled back to Mattoso's quarters.

"It's so strange, seeing one of them at work, on watch," Mattoso replied.

"You're not kidding," chuckled Pat. "You should see our curriculum... I'm not sure who you learned about growing up on Ceres, but on Earth we grew up learning about Nzinga, Yoshimune, and Charlemagne, among others. Now, on *Aotea*, I teach kids about Edda Ngayabo, one of the founders of the Society for a New Humanity, and her granddaughter, our very own Mara Ngayabo. And before they graduate fifth cycle, every student conducts an interview with one of the Bigwigs." Pat gave her a wry look. "Guess which Bigwig is everyone's last choice?"

CHAPTER 21

Konami waited in the passageway outside the Solacer's office, checking his feed for the text of his constables' interviews of Senior Chemist Nicolescu's colleagues. The chemists and chem techs were effusive in their praise for the deceased, offering to help in any way they could, but had no information that jumped off the projection as immediately useful. He'd been so busy lately that he hadn't felt bitter in days. When it occurred to him that, upon solving these crimes, everything would go back to normal, he felt a momentary panic.

As he waited for Mattoso to arrive, he found himself thumbing through Inspector Loesser's electronic interview notes — she had the habit of scrawling anything that caught her eye in the margins. Chemistry Director George was "smooth and polished, and overly verbose, but nervous as hell under the surface," while the "hulking" Second Class Chem Tech Singh was "shaken and barely verbal."

The search of Nicolescu's quarters had been a bit more helpful — an anachronistic handwritten dry-erase calendar, with the chemist's daily appointments scrawled in, led Konami to the passageway outside the office of Solacer Assunta Patil. Just as he checked the time, Mattoso arrived.

As if she could sense their presence, Solacer Patil appeared and beckoned them through an open doorway. The solace therapist had the grace and loveliness of a dancer, and wrinkles at the corners of her eyes and mouth did nothing to lessen her beauty. Her sleek, silken dress, and the exotic, colorful décor of her office completed the illusion that this was a very different sort of place, with a different sort of people, then the rest of *Aotea*. "Please, sit," she offered, her voice low and melodic. "You're here about Sulemon."

"Yes," said Konami. He recalled his own most recent visit to a solacer, several months prior. Saara Angelini was short and curvy where Solacer Patil was tall and slender, but they had the same voice — confident, mature, and musical. He wondered if this was from solacer training. A look from Mattoso snapped him out of thoughts of his last visit. "His colleagues did not know of any close friends," he said to the solacer. "Do you know if Nicolescu was close to anyone outside of Chemistry?"

Patil pursed her lips. "I'm in a very difficult position, chief inspector. I want to help your investigation in any way I can, but the Oath of Solace prevents me from sharing any details of my time with Sulemon."

Konami anticipated this. "Voicenet: Charter doc eighteen." He projected to show the Solacer. He realized, a bit uncomfortably, that he was getting very skilled at citing regulations to serve his investigations. It was a necessary skill, but it made him feel like a bullying bureaucrat. "Captain Horovitz and Director-Superintendent Akunle have both invoked this section of the Charter — that the needs of this investigation override any internal guidelines and regulations of individual departments." He traced the applicable parts with his finger, explaining that the Therapy Director agreed that this includes the Oath of Solace.

Eyes scanning nothingness in front of her, the Solacer read for several minutes. She sighed and shook her head as she finished. "Very well. Even putting aside the Oath, there's not a whole lot I can tell you about Sulemon's acquaintances. He rarely spoke of others, and no one close."

Konami asked how long she had been meeting with Nicolescu, and she said more than five cycles, since before the departure.

"So why did he come to see you?" asked Mattoso. "Intimacy?"

"Well, yes, I suppose. But not just intimacy. He had — a weight. That's what we called it — 'the Weight'. He wouldn't say what it was — long ago I learned to stop asking. But it was always there, and it was always on his mind, and figuratively pulling him down."

Konami leaned forward. "You must have had some idea."

"I considered many possibilities — pharmaceutical addiction, first and foremost. He was a Chemist, after all. But he didn't have any other signs. No lying, at least that I could detect. No physical signs." She spread her hands. "Perhaps it was some family secret, though he had no family onboard that I know of."

Mattoso interrupted. "Did this 'weight' get better over time, or worse?"

"It waxed and waned, mostly. I couldn't discern a pattern. But thinking about it since his death, I think it may have been getting worse, very slowly. In fact, the last time I saw him, a few weeks ago, it was as bad as I'd ever seen in him."

"You were with him for so long," said Konami, scratching his chin. "What do you really think it was?"

The Solacer looked down for a moment before shaking her head. "I think it was guilt. Overwhelming guilt. Over what, I don't know."

"Do you think this guilt had something to do with his death?"

She nodded immediately. "Absolutely."

Konami and Mattoso shared a glance.

"Was he a good man?" asked Konami. Mattoso raised an eyebrow.

Patil looked at him for a long time before responding. "He cared deeply about doing the right thing."

Konami sensed something unsaid. "But...?"

She looked away. "I'm not sure that he knew what the right thing was."

CHAPTER 22

"It's funny," remarked Mattoso, in the passageway outside the Solacer's office. "Hundreds of years ago, Solace was considered dishonorable, even unclean."

Konami nodded. "And it wasn't called Solace. At least the intimacy parts."

Mattoso shuddered, recalling her schooling on Earth's past barbarity. Just imagining being part of a society that constantly used guilt and fear, even of bodily harm, as a way to control people, gave her a twinge in her stomach.

"It almost made sense, I suppose," continued Konami. "Back then, you could end up sick, or pregnant, or worse."

Mattoso snorted, saying that it wasn't about disease or children, but controlling people.

He chuckled. "We're not exactly finished with taboos on *Aotea*, you know."

She asked for an example.

"Like no romance within a department. Two years ago a couple of my constables were 'solacing' each other in the holding cells. Good kids, but I had to split them up, at least at work. I hear they're still a couple."

She asked how he picked which one to leave the Constabulary.

"I didn't. They picked themselves. One of them loved the job and one didn't. The one that didn't is now a Dental tech, if I recall correctly."

They walked in silence for a while — a silence that Mattoso found vexing, so she asked for his thoughts on Solacer Patil.

Konami scratched his chin. "Nothing groundbreaking. Nicolescu was troubled by something, and he was unsure about the right thing to do. That can probably describe most of us at some point."

"But what about the guilt? Patil said it was overwhelming. That seems like a bit more than the usual troubles."

"Yes, but that was just supposition."

"An educated supposition," answered Mattoso. "From someone in a position to know — as far as we know, the person closest to the deceased onboard."

"Okay," conceded Konami. "Let's assume she's right. What could he have felt guilty about? What could he have done onboard that was so bad?"

She just looked at him.

"Oh shit, of course! Well, she said that 'the Weight' had been around for as long as she'd seen him, and Muahe was only killed a few weeks ago, but obviously it could be related. So we see if there's a connection between Nicolescu and Muahe. Anything. That 's standard procedure anyway, but we'll kick it up to the top of the queue. We'll pore through their bios, their histories before joining the crew, anything. Tell Wren. We'll need his help."

She nodded agreement, and then changed the subject and asked if he'd heard about the supposedly alien communications signals. Konami said that the Communications department head brought it up in every meeting.

"Is it just coincidence, do you think?"

The chief inspector blinked. "You mean could they be right, that aliens are trying to turn us around?"

She chuckled. "No, I mean is it really coincidence that we see these posts at the same time as the murders? Could they be connected, in a totally non-alien way?"

His eyes went wide. "I don't know, but that's a good point. Put Wren on it."

"Wren?"

"Yeah. Maybe he can dig up the source of the anonymous posts."

CHAPTER 23

"You're as clumsy as an Earther!" laughed Madani, gracefully "climbing" along the Engineering passageway.

"I am an Earther, remember?" said Konami, still having trouble with the right amount of force to use with each "step" in the zero-gravity Engineering spaces aft of the Cans. In addition to no visual indicators of "up" and "down," the Engineering spaces were much more spartan and industrial than even the function-driven passageways beneath the surface in the Cans.

Madani crooked a finger. "No one onboard is an Earther anymore, or a Martian, or Lunan, or Jovian. We're all Aoteans now, and in a few decades we'll all be... Samwisers? Samwiseans?"

"Samwitians?" offered Konami.

"We'll figure it out."

Konami miscalculated once again and bumped his knee on a handhold, cursing.

"How long has it been since you stepped outside of the Cans?" asked Madani.

He thought about it. "Cycles, I think. I had to see every space onboard during quals, of course, but the zero-g always made me nauseous."

"Are you okay now?"

He smiled. "Yeah, one of your techs gave me something, just in case."

"Smart move."

"Well this is one of the only spots on the ship we haven't explored together, and I didn't want to be sick... I don't imagine zero-g vomit is much fun for anyone."

She pulled him abruptly, giving him a momentary sense of vertigo, before embracing him with a kiss. "You know what's a lot of fun in zero-g?" she whispered.

A Power technician scampered by adroitly before he could answer. He waited until the Tech was gone. "I think I might like to find out..."

With a smile, she pulled him along silently until they found an unoccupied Bot service space. Ignoring the clicks of a recharging DustBot, Madani slid the door shut and unzipped her coverall.

The buzz of his wearable snapped the doctor and the chief inspector out of their post-coital reverie. The Medical department head carefully disengaged herself from their floating embrace as they were, almost imperceptibly, pulled toward one bulkhead of the service space by *Aotea*'s gentle acceleration. The message was a text from Mattoso: *news from Wren on the signals — URGENT — my quarters.* Konami hastily dressed himself and bid Madani farewell, exerting massive willpower to pull away from her deep and passionate kiss before making his way through the aft Ring into the aft Can, meeting Lieutenant Mattoso and Data Technician Third Class Wren in Mattoso's quarters and immediately asking what they found.

Wren looked at Mattoso for a moment before answering Konami's question, reassured by her nod. The Lieutenant's quarters seemed awfully claustrophobic for the three of them, but Konami had learned that Aoteans had more tolerance for close quarters than his fellow Earthers.

"The signals," started the Data technician. "First, the small news. The strange posts are from public consoles around the ship, and anonymous accounts. Nothing we can do there."

Goddamnit. On Earth there was always some camera running, whether on a bystander or from a store across the street. That obviously wasn't allowed onboard.

"Secondly, the alien stuff — they're coming from onboard."

Konami's jaw dropped. "Onboard? How on Earth...?"

"He monitored data traffic at the same time as Comms Central was hearing the signals," cut in Mattoso.

"Right," added Wren. "And there was a big spike in processing usage just a few seconds before the signals started, and it stopped right when they stopped."

"Hold on," said Konami. "Make it simpler for me."

Mattoso took a breath. "From Ops, I asked Comms to report as soon as the signals started, at the same time that Wren was monitoring data usage. Pretty simple."

"So there was a correlation?" asked Konami.

"More than a correlation," answered Wren. "It was fucking on the nose. Like less than a minute before the signals started, I had my processing spike, and it was big — like a chunk of one percent of the whole damn ship's processing power. And then it stopped at the exact same time that the signals stopped — I checked both logs, and they stopped within nanoseconds. And it happened twice — just the same way, both times."

"If it was on the nose, why that extra minute before?"

Mattoso tilted her head. "Well, we're not exactly sure. But whatever it was, I'm sure it took some preparation. Maybe that minute was for preparation."

Konami asked if they could find the source of the increased processing.

The young Data technician chuckled. "A processor's a processor. You can ask for any task — say, run a vid — from your wearable right here, and it could utilize any of the processors, from the little ones in the wearables to the big ones in Data Central, or even the backups a few decks down, if the demand is high."

"So it doesn't matter which processor was used?" Konami inquired.

"No — it's selected automatically by the data queue protocol — it balances processing loads and whatnot."

"Can we find out anything about the processing tasks, or who was using it?"

Wren groaned. "Ugh."

113

Konami raised his eyebrows. "Well?"

"I suppose. Long fucking task, though. Don't expect anything soon — it's like digging through a garbage dump."

"How solid is this?" asked the chief inspector, debating in his mind whether he should tell his superiors. *Don't be the senior man with a secret* was a motto a veteran cop in Lagos told him many years before.

"Solid as the hull," said Wren. "No doubt about it."

Konami prepared himself to repeat Wren's assurance as the department heads assembled in the conference room, sure that his news would be the biggest bombshell of the meeting. He had been just about to inform Mayor Akunle when the meeting was called.

When everyone was seated, the mayor turned to Konami, asking him to report on the roving watchstanders. The Captain added that it should be brief.

Konami cleared his throat. "The watches are going fine. Nothing to report."

The captain nodded to Commander Konrote, head of Gravity and Transportation, who stood, and Konami awkwardly resumed his seat.

"Late yesterday the vibration sensor for the forward Can's rotation gears tripped an alarm," said the GravTran Commander. This single statement was enough to trigger shock from the other department heads — everyone was well aware of the significance of the rotation gears of both Cans for the normal operation of *Aotea*. "Our operational inspection revealed signs of damage, but we won't know the full extent until we can open it up and look inside."

A glance from Captain Horovitz silenced the growing murmurs.

Commander Konrote continued. "You all know what that means. We rig for loss of gravity in the forward Can, move anything necessary to the aft Can, and then Spindown the forward Can." Even the glare of the Commanding

Officer couldn't silence a smattering of curses from the department heads. Konami shook his head to himself as he realized what that would mean — oddly, his first thought was for his jenji dog Kostya. With no hands to grasp and pull themselves from handhold to handhold, dogs and cats were unable to adapt to zero-gravity. Konami could stay in his quarters in the forward Can if he didn't mind sleeping in zero-g, but Kostya would have to find temporary accommodations in the aft Can. *Maybe Kiro can watch her for me.*

"We don't know the extent of the damage, but it could be getting worse with every rotation," explained Konrote. "We need to Spindown as soon as possible."

"With that in mind," said Captain Horovitz as she flicked the comms button on the monitor at the head of the table. "Operations, this is the captain. Read the announcement brief and rig the forward Can for loss of gravity."

As the Officer of the Deck read a script explaining the need for Spindown and ordering the loss of gravity rig on the ship-wide announcing circuits, Konami realized that his news about the fake signals might be small potatoes. Nevertheless, he spoke up before the captain and mayor adjourned the meeting.

"One thing, about the signals."

Horovitz raised her eyebrows skeptically. "What signals?"

Konami gestured to Comms Officer Olin. "The aliens — or fake aliens, as we found out." He explained how he and Lieutenant Mattoso had determined that the signals were faked, careful to leave out Wren's involvement.

"Just processor noise?" asked Hamad Maltin, one of the Bigwigs.

At the same time, the Data Systems director, Shin, inquired why he hadn't been informed.

"You're being informed now, Director," answered Konami. From his conversations with Data technicians and the department master tech, he had the impression that Shin was more of an administrator than a data engineer.

The captain tilted her head and addressed the chief inspector, echoing Maltin's question. "Was the processing spike the only evidence?"

"No," he said, relieved that Mattoso had, just before the meeting, thought of a possible second piece of evidence. Konami read off his projection as Mattoso and Wren transmitted the data to him. "We also checked the Power logs, on the assumption that the signals would require a significant power source to match the power we would expect from an interstellar signal. Sure enough, we found a power usage spike at the same time as the signals. This one was even more precise — it started at the exact same time that the signal started, and stopped at the same time the signal stopped."

The murmurs started again, and this time Captain Horovitz didn't even try to stop it.

"I'm transmitting our findings so that each one of you can give us a second check," Konami added.

After reviewing for a few minutes, the Engineering and Comms department heads both agreed that the data looked conclusive. Konami didn't miss the nods exchanged between the Bigwigs and the captain as well.

"But how is that possible?" asked Shin. "Can't Comms tell the difference between a signal generated onboard and a signal generated from a distance?"

Lieutenant Commander Olin's eyes flashed. "Normally, we can. But that's just from spatial relationships — over time, as we move, the signal vector will change slightly, as our relative positions change. We don't normally think someone would fake a signal, so we don't normally account for any possibility that someone is changing that vector of a signal generated from onboard the ship on purpose."

Shin still appeared confused.

Olin sighed, explaining the technical details – with single boosters and a specific spatial arrangement, they could simulate a distant source.

Konami tried to follow along with the complicated explanation. He thought he got the gist of it — multiple signal-sources, which would have been coordinated and mobile, shooting signals at each sensor from a certain vector, very slowly moving (just millimeters, if he understood correctly) to simulate a source that was millions or billions of kilometers away.

A perturbed Commander Konrote interrupted and emphasized the need to supervise the zero gravity rig.

Mayor Akunle was huddled with the captain, who held up her hand to stop anyone from leaving, ignoring Konrote's frustrated expression.

Finally, the captain spoke. "Our first priority will be the zero gravity rig, and any inspection and repairs necessary."

"But that's not our only concern," added the mayor, taking the captain's queue. "Only the most urgent. I'm sure we've all seen the theorizing and hypothesizing on the net discussions; these two latest pieces of news will only increase the tension and confusion of the personnel onboard. As soon as possible, the entire complement, aside from vital watch stations, will assemble in the Arena, and we will answer questions for as long as we can. It's absolutely critical that we retain the full confidence of every Aotean —for this mission, and for the continuing safe operation of this ship."

Holy shit! thought Konami, as the meeting was adjourned. He supposed the Arena could hold every soul onboard *Aotea*, but it would be a tight squeeze. He always had wondered why it was so large — he'd never heard of a sporting event that was even half full — but this must be the answer. An old Earth idiom came to him, for some reason — something about eggs and a basket. He put that thought aside as he left.

117

CHAPTER 24

The forward Can was starting to resemble an enormous spider's web. Mattoso shuddered as she recalled the childish fright she felt when, exploring a little used storage alcove in Ceres City, she stumbled into a nest of cobwebs. Spiders were one of the few Earth creatures that had, somehow, found themselves a niche in the tunnels of Ceres.

She yawned — she had been awake for a while, just completing verification of the rig at the Beach. *Slow as hell, but at least it was boring...* she thought, recalling the draining of the Beach's artificial lake. *And stinky, too...* She grimaced at the memory of the smell at the bottom of the lake, mildew and scum and miscellaneous organic residue.

"All clear," shouted a crewman, and a dull thudding "pop" sounded. Enormous reels of cables and webbing had been unrolled and were being propelled across the Can's empty diameter, crisscrossed and enmeshed such that, even should one find themselves floating in that empty space in the center of the can, there would always be a cable or webbing nearby to haul oneself back to the surface.

She idly scanned the news and discussion forums as she walked. *Don't believe it!* was the title of one thread, in which anonymous users argued about the truthfulness of the latest news regarding the faked signals. One poster believed the latest reports, but claimed that the signals were just a ruse by SNH operatives to manipulate Aoteans. Other threads contained polar opposite opinions, with posters demanding that such theorizing was contrary to the principles of the SNH, and that the conspiracists were continuing the pattern of strife and chaos from Earth.

Even though the vast majority of the forum discussions were still courteous and agreeable, she had the feeling something was changing. It used to be a challenge to find an argument onboard, even in the relative anonymity of the network discussions. Now they were getting the most attention, even if much of that attention were exhortations for calm.

She'd never had any doubt that her decision to join the crew of *Aotea* was the right one. Her parents had been inconsolable when she first informed them, more than a decade before. All her childhood they had told her she would stay on Ceres and work in the family restaurant; two of her brothers, more than a decade older, had become Ceres City cops, and her other brother Paolo was a bit slow, leaving Mattoso as the presumed heir to the family business. But once they learned of her plans, they walked back all their expectations, begging that she find another career on Ceres if she wished, or even (to Mattoso's amazement) go elsewhere in the solar system, where at least they might see her occasionally. But to leave for Samwise might as well have been a death sentence — albeit one with occasional, multi-year-delayed message vids.

She had been shocked at first. Her parents were die-hard believers in Paola Rahmon, even if they were never formally members of the SNH. Mattoso had thought they'd be ecstatic once they realized her plans. But her family's vids had become less and less frequent over the last year, except for Paolo, who recorded a short message every week for her, whether or not she responded. Thoughts of his bouncing leap for an embrace every time she visited made her tear up, and she tried to bring her mind back to the present.

Mattoso looked on as, hand in hand, a line of children made its way aft between structures and riggers. Furry, simian MOMbots gently herded the children, distracting the most confused and bewildered among them with juggling tricks as they walked. When she first arrived onboard from Ceres, she found the MOMbots on *Aotea* awkward and even disturbing. With their multiple-jointed limbs, they moved far more like animals than robots, though not like any animal she had ever seen in the Earth documentary vids. But the years onboard, along with the gushing reports of her fellow Aoteans on the unending tolerance, affection, and playfulness of the robots, had softened her opinion. The orderliness of the relocation of the children, along with the dutiful, step-by-step compartment zero-gravity rig, contrasted sharply with the bickering and divisions on the net.

She looked again at the checklist projected into the air — Mattoso had been assigned to verify that a section of machinery spaces had been properly rigged for zero gravity. As she made her way down an access hatch she noticed more DustBots, TrashBots, and their ilk, than usual — the Can-wide rig demanded, temporarily, that every cleaning robot focus on uncontained liquids and small debris. One of the bug-like little machines was filling its expandable bladder with what looked like spilled coffee on the deck. Another swept trash and debris into little piles for some larger Bot to collect later.

The checklist guided her through the passageways and compartments, verifying that every hatch large enough for a guycable was rigged open, every tool was secured, every surface had handholds attached, and every large space was crisscrossed with webbing. Even the Bots rigged themselves from some silent electronic command — it was startling to see how many additional limbs the TrashBots, TaskBots, RoverBots, and others seemed to conjure up from their innards to crawl and climb along in freefall.

She passed by a pair of crewmembers arguing about the latest developments — one insisted that the upcoming Spindown was somehow related to the murders and the faked 'alien' signals. She couldn't help but doubletake. *Confusion and doubt can lead to strife,* she recalled from the teachings of the SNH. *It's just temporary,* she decided. *We'll be back to normal soon.*

She cringed as she found a discrepancy against the checklist — a damage control toolkit inside a machinery space wasn't properly secured to the bulkhead. Her orders had insisted that the Spindown was needed as soon as possible to minimize any damage to the rotation gears. But she recalled the oath she took upon earning the 'star canoe' emblem — the award all crewmembers received upon achieving full ship's qualification — *an Aotean's first duty is to the truth.* She sighed and marked the discrepancy on the checklist, knowing that another crewmember would have to repeat the entire rig in this section, along with another officer's second-check. *Better the ire of GravTran than a broken skull from a floating toolkit.*

The vibe in the forward Can was much closer to celebration than to concern. The zero-gravity rig was finally complete, and hundreds of Aoteans had gathered to experience the Spindown and freefall — the first since launch. Hanging and climbing on the cables and webbing, Mattoso thought she spied some of the same children, still chaperoned by MOMbots, that she had seen marching aft earlier.

"Thirty seconds to Spindown in the forward can," announced an automated voice.

Pat handed her a small tablet, and she asked what it was.

"Ginger, for nausea."

Someone started a countdown.

"Is this really appropriate?" Pat whispered, clutching tightly to Mattoso's hand.

"The Officer of the Deck checked," she answered. "There's no regulation against civilian bystanders for a Spindown."

"…twenty-two, twenty-one…"

"Seems weird," said Pat. "This isn't supposed to be fun…"

Mattoso smiled at a pair of children swinging jointly around a stiff cable. "Maybe not, but they're having fun."

"… sixteen, fifteen…"

"Maybe we should too." The Operations Lieutenant grabbed her lover's hand and raced to the nearest unoccupied webbing base.

"... twelve, eleven..."

Laughing, they raced up the webbing, joining in the countdown as they ascended. Mattoso realized she had never been this high up inside *Aotea* — indeed, she had never been this high above any surface at all. The colony ship's 'buildings' stood no more than a few stories at most. There wasn't a single chamber in Ceres as large as one of *Aotea*'s cans. She had a momentary feeling of disorientation as she surveyed the interior cylinder of the colony ship — she realized that, as she climbed, the sense of "gravity" from the can's rotation lessened.

"Don't jump until the Spindown is complete!" someone shouted. "The countdown is just for the beginning!"

A MOMbot swung adroitly up a cable to gingerly return one of its charges to the surface.

"...three, two, one!"

"Spindown commencing." There was a new noise. The dull hum that faded into the background, ever since the Can was first spun-up so many years ago, changed in tone, lowering and growing less regular.

Mattoso's insides shifted, and she almost lost her grip of the webbing as her feet pressed down less and less in their footholds. She felt nervous. *Maybe this was a big mistake...* It was too late to climb back down. She smiled and hugged Pat with one free arm, trying to project a calm she didn't feel.

Everyone seemed to be holding their breath. The hum lessened to a repetitive thump, slower and slower. And it stopped.

The pause was interminable. "Spindown complete."

Mattoso's worry melted away as children shrieked, bounding straight up from the surface, their laughter musical. She kissed Pat's cheek, and let go of the webbing. "Come fly with me," she bubbled, shooting off into the air.

CHAPTER 25

Konami couldn't remember being this nervous. Was it being on the stage in the middle of the Arena? Was it the vast crowd in the audience — close to twenty thousand, almost the entire complement of *Aotea*, and the biggest gathering since departure? As huge as the ship was, it seemed absurd that everyone onboard could fit into this little stadium, a fraction of the size of the venues he recalled from the big cities on Earth. Was it his thoughts of Kostya, bewildered and whining since the move to Gregorian's quarters now that the forward Can was spun down to zero-gravity? Was it the paperwork waiting for him from the bumps and bruises from mid-air collisions following the Spindown of the forward Can? *Gonna have to recommend new guidelines: Cans must be evacuated before commencing Spindown!* Considering all the reports of minor injuries, he was glad he chose to remain in the aft Can with Madani during the Spindown.

Mayor Akunle and Executive Officer Criswell were handing out awards while Captain Horovitz sat on the stage, stone-faced as ever. Konami supposed Harry Akunle's idea of mixing in something positive — this spontaneous awards ceremony, most of which were given to junior personnel — with the briefing and question period about the most recent turmoil onboard, was wise. But sitting through the dozens of short speeches, most of them the same boilerplate about dedication, loyalty, and courage, made him wonder if it was worth it.

While the mayor posed, teeth flashing, with another award recipient — a young Human Support technician gaining her full ship's qualification — Konami looked around the arena, trying to identify his constables. The roving watches had been temporarily suspended, so Konami had shifted most of his constabulary into crowd control roles, managing the largest crowds they had

125

experienced onboard, entering and spreading out inside the Arena in the aft Can. He had to squint, but he was able to make out the red sashes that marked his constables, spread throughout the Arena's seats.

He thought back to poor Kostya, as anxious as Konami had ever seen her. Positive personality traits had been written into her genetic code, as they were for all jenji pets, but apparently toleration of novel circumstances was not one of them. He supposed she would get used to it; she would be far better off in Gregorian's quarters then in the zero-g of his own. Imagining his dog flail and whine while bouncing around the zero-g cabin made him almost sputter in laughter, even as he cringed at the thought. *Wish Ilsa's place was in the aft Can...* What had seemed like a boon before — that Konami and Madani's quarters were no more than a ten minute walk away from each other — was now a real bummer, especially since the co-worker she was staying with was on the other side of the aft Can. From the other side of the stage she caught his eye and very subtly blew him a kiss.

Finally, Mayor Akunle finished with the awards, and yielded the podium to Captain Horovitz, who placed her hands on each side of the podium. "Two of our fellow Aoteans have been murdered," boomed the captain, amplified throughout the Arena. "Unusual radio signals that appeared to have come from far away turn out to have originated onboard. And now, half our ship is without rotation for repairs. You may have questions. In an orderly fashion, you may ask."

There was a long pause. Konami supposed that this might be the first time much of the crew actually understood that there was a murderer among them.

An Admin Chief explained how to tap into the question queue through a wearable.

After a minute the crew got the hang of the novel interface. The first question was about the cause of the damage to the forward Can's rotation gears.

126

"GravTran is investigating the damage," answered the captain. "So far there is no evidence at this point that it was caused by anything other than normal wear and tear. When the investigation is complete, the rotation gears will be repaired and the Can will be returned to normal rotation." *Normal wear and tear...* Konami highly doubted this was the case (and if so, worried about the ship's prospects for the multi-decade journey to Samwise), but approved of the captain's answer.

The next three questions were about details of the murder investigation, and the captain answered them with as little information as possible.

The fifth questioner stood up, halfway up the stands, and he looked familiar. *Where have I seen him before?* For a long ten seconds, he stared down at his hands, then spoke.

Somehow Konami knew that he was about to say something significant.

"I am a murderer," said the questioner, scratchy vocal cords skipping like an audio glitch.

Konami was out of his seat in a flash, making his way to the field wall, and gesturing at the constables nearby the questioner. Out of the corner of his eye, half the department heads were madly gesticulating. One of the Bigwigs, Ngayabo, almost leapt out of her chair, only held back by Wilson Paramis.

"I am a murderer," the crewman said again, much more clearly.

Konami recalled where he'd seen the questioner before – in the file after Nicolescu's murder. This was the Chem Tech named Singh, the one Constable Loesser called "hulking" and "shaken and barely verbal". He got down from the stage and leapt to climb the field wall to get to the stands.

Singh continued. "I killed First Muahe. I replaced the breathing filter with the bad one, and I shorted the hatch circuit. I put a plug in the piping to fake the clog." He took a deep breath and continued, but his voice went silent.

Someone silenced his wearable. Konami looked back at the department heads before vaulting over another short wall. Everyone in the Arena was on their feet.

Someone handed Singh another wearable. "I killed Senior Chemist Nicolescu. I injected him with artificial venom." With a big hand, he wiped his brow. "But it wasn't just me. I was given orders. There's another plan for *Aotea.* Another mission." He paused, seeming to gather his thoughts. "It's not my mission anymore."

The packed stands made it hard to approach, both for Konami and the nearby constables. With every step, Konami was filled with a growing sense of dread.

"What is it?" asked the captain, eyes wide and hoarse-voiced. "What was your mission?"

When Singh opened his mouth to respond, a rippling *crack* rang out, and his head exploded.

CHAPTER 26

For half a second, Mattoso couldn't believe her eyes. She closed them hard and opened them. Someone screamed, and the crowd in the level below erupted into pandemonium. Being at the very front of the second level in the Arena, across from the dead questioner, her view was still unobstructed despite the tumult of the crowds. The space around him had cleared, leaving only the mangled, headless corpse of the confessing crewman leaning on a railing in a horrific parody of oratory.

Her wearable chirped. *You okay?* It was from Pat.

Part of her was panicking. This wasn't just violence and aggression, this was open and public and brutal murder. *Assassination.* This couldn't be happening on *Aotea.*

But it happened, and it was happening.

Think, damnit! She moved with the flow of the crowd — many of whom were her colleagues in Operations — while she gathered her thoughts. Someone had just killed the admitted murderer, in full view of everyone. *It wasn't a bomb, unless it was tiny, and already planted in his head. Too far-fetched. A gun, then.* There weren't any guns onboard *Aotea.* At least, none that she knew about. Then again, there hadn't been any murderers onboard that she knew about either.

Another chirp. *I'm fine,* she scrawled into the air. *Get somewhere safe.* Pat would be with the children from their class, and would stay with them until any danger had passed.

The crowd slowed at a bottleneck doorway to the ramps that wound tightly up and down around the Arena. Some in the crowd shouted and lurched forward — in desperation, one man even tried to dig into the crowd ahead. Mattoso got an ugly feeling in her stomach. "We're Aoteans, not a mob of Earthers, damn it!" she called out.

"Stay calm!" Several of her colleagues called out support, and a few of the closer members of the crowd stopped, sheepishly looking down at their feet.

The crowd didn't move for a full minute, then slowly started forward again. A dull buzzing sound from ahead grew in intensity as they advanced.

Finally, they were through the bottleneck, but the ramps were in chaos. Mattoso was shocked by the panic — Aoteans clawed and fought to get through the jam-packed tunnels of the ramps. Amidst the screams and sounds of the struggle, she thought she might have heard moans of pain and cries for help. She tried to call Emer but couldn't get through, so she sent a text with the approximate location.

A burly Operations chief ahead of her, Azbek, was bodily trying to restore order, with little success. "Chief," she shouted, her hand on his back. "Boost me up on your shoulders." With hand motions, she motioned over another Operations tech. "Third," she ordered. "Keep calling Emer until you get through."

On Chief Azbek's shoulders, Mattoso projected into the air, flipping through the menus. It was too loud to use voice control, so she had to navigate manually. *Where's the damn audio boost?* Finally, she found it, turning up the volume as high as it would go.

"Stop," she shouted, shocked by the magnitude of the amplification. "Aoteans, stop!" Some of the crowd slowed their struggles and turned to her. "The danger has passed! The only risk is to rush and struggle." She had most of their attention. "There are wounded among you — give them air and space, and call out for any seriously hurt." After a moment of confusion, reports of the injuries trickled through the crowd toward her. "If you are unhurt, and unless you have medical training, slowly and calmly proceed down the ramp. Do not succumb to panic, and don't let your fellow Aoteans panic either! Remember where we are — this isn't Earth!"

Amazingly, they followed her instructions. A very few MedTechs and others remained, along with several injured in the crowd surge, but the rest slowly made their way down the ramp. *Maybe we Aoteans really are different...* Chief Azbek helped her down from his shoulders. "Third, did you get through to Emer?" she asked the other Operations tech.

"No, Lieutenant, still no answer."

Shit. A thought came to her. *If anyone can get through to Emer, I know who it is.* She quickly texted — *Cy, it's Bea. Can't get through to Emer. There are wounded on 2nd level near the aft entrance.* After a moment, he acknowledged the text, and Mattoso bent down to examine the nearest injured Aotean.

CHAPTER 27

Konami went down his mental checklist: *Captain, mayor, and Bigwigs are safe, CHECK.* Immediately after the assassination (the word had shocked him to his core when the CO had used it in the rush to flee), Konami and XO Criswell had herded the senior leaders and department heads into a single-entry meeting room under the stands of the Arena. The XO and other department heads had armed themselves with sports equipment, and had remained to guard the leadership, faces contorted in discomfort. *SNH dogma never prepared you for this moment, did it?*

Madani was speaking quickly – there were no serious injuries among the department heads, and she was looking after any bumps and bruises from the rushed escape. The Medical Department Head had asked about the murderer, but she must not have gotten a good look at him while they were still in the arena — very little above his neck was intact. Whatever weapon the assassin had used was either very large in caliber, very high energy, or had explosive ammunition. As far as the injuries from the panic, every doctor, nurse, and MedTech onboard had been ordered to the infirmary or to the scene to treat casualties.

Crowd control, in progress. There were already reports of serious injuries, and possibly even deaths, trickling into Emer. Unprompted, Gregorian had wisely activated all the reserves, and Konami sent a handful of deputies to bolster the overwhelmed Emergency watch. He also called up every single rover assigned from other departments, just to stand by if needed, in addition to those that were already occupied with casualties and cleanup.

He should have foreseen that Aoteans could panic so easily — hell, since their arrival onboard, each Aotean was drilled about how special they were, and how they were chosen to help make a New Humanity, away from any negative influence from Earth. The toughest day most of

132

them had experienced onboard was probably their final qualification board, and even for failures, those were filled with back-patting and encouragement.

And the Aoteans ate it up, most of them; they really believed they were different. *People are people everywhere; on Earth, on an asteroid, or on a goddamn spinning can in deep space.* Society for a New Humanity propaganda be damned, he would make his feelings clear at the inevitable emergency department head meeting that would be coming. No more complacency.

Crime scene protection and evaluation... That was next. He stopped by the meeting room and briefed the CO and mayor on the crowds and casualties. They had already dispersed most of the department heads to help restore order, but Konami recommended they wait in the meeting room until he could secure a route to safety, guarded along the way at each junction. Captain Horovitz snorted at that, but said nothing. Her expression was back to its typical stone, but Konami caught the anxiety in her eyes.

The Arena was in shambles. Seats throughout the stadium had been upended, and sometimes even torn apart. Dropped refreshments, wearables, and more littered the walkways. A whirring sound in the farthest corner of the Arena caught his attention — squinting slightly, he saw it was just a TrashBot. Its meticulous ministrations in the chaotic jumble on the largest structure onboard struck Konami as supremely lonesome.

In fact, the most well ordered spot in the Arena was the site of the corpse — the Aoteans in the vicinity had instantly recoiled, instinctively avoiding it even as they fled in panic. Konami thought he might feel queasy from seeing Singh's remains again, but his stomach was so tight with tension that he felt nothing as he made his way up the stands. Previously leaning on the railing, Singh's body had slid off and down to the floor, leaving a trail of blood down the back of several seats. Konami took a few minutes to pore over it and started to record — along with his deputies and rovers, he had decided to carry a vidcam himself, though he usually kept his turned off.

"Approximately one hour since the assassination of Second Class Chemistry Technician Arvid Singh," he narrated. "Victim was standing at the railing here. There was a noise I'm assuming was a gunshot, and the victim was killed instantly due to the near-disintegration of his head." He turned to the floor of the stands several meters behind the corpse. "This hole in the floor appears to be the continued path of the bullet, indicating the ammunition was not explosive." He quickly sent a message to Gregorian, Loesser, and Emer, to send deputies, when available, to bag evidence, find the bullet, and guard the scene of the murder.

Konami squatted down and held his arm straight to match the angle from the hole to the spot where Singh's head was struck. "Based on the path from above the railing to this hole, the shot may have been fired from 8th Rib, around mid third, in the aft Can." His next message directed that deputies search that area for vantage points from which the Arena stage would be visible.

He switched off the vidcam. Somehow he felt serene, tense as he was. Despite the confusion and chaos of the last hour, things seemed much clearer. *There are killers onboard* Aotea, *killers with influence and knowledge of the ship, and the murders aren't going to stop until I find them.*

CHAPTER 28

The Command Bridge of *Aotea* was dead calm. Gone was the chatter of sporadic conversations that Mattoso recalled from before. The only sounds were occasional indicator chimes from the operator's screens, the periodic voice watch check-ins, and the repetitive shuffle of one of the Auxiliary watches, anxiously playing with the seat strap that kept him from floating away from his station.

The Bridge itself was something of an anachronism. Supposedly Captain Horovitz herself had insisted on actual hardmounted displays and interfaces, with wearable projections only as backups and supplements. Something about a near-disaster she'd faced in a convoy decades before. Of course, the laconic skipper had never confirmed nor denied such a story, but Mattoso had always found the old-fashioned technology of the bridge, solid and immovable as the Captain herself, oddly comforting.

Since the incident at the Arena, the entire ship was effectively locked down. The roving security watchstanders had more than tripled in number, and were now paired off at random with each other when on duty. Single-person duty stations were disallowed — every station must now have two personnel at all times. This left far fewer watchstanders for the rest of the stations onboard, and most of the ship's complement were now spending between a third and half of their waking hours on watch. A curfew was instituted, such that when not on duty, Aoteans must remain in their quarters unless escorted by security watches.

Mattoso found herself yawning and closed her mouth. The exhaustion of the Bridge crew was palpable — the yawn made its way through the Nav watch, the Comms watch, the Eng watch, the Auxiliary watches, and the Systems Coordination watch, before striking her, the Officer of the Deck, once again. The lack of gravity made it

135

worse — nearly every position was comfortable and restful in the near-zero gravity of the Operations spaces forward of the Cans.

She thought back to her brief conversation with Konami, just after order had been restored. He couldn't stop looking over his shoulders, even as he spoke. "What just happened," he had said under his breath. "It's much… bigger. Not just the shooter. There are more—" He had paused, like he didn't want to say it.

"I know," she had responded. *There are others involved,* she knew he meant. *Someone high up. Maybe multiple someones.*

"Don't trust anyone," he had said before rushing off.

Someone, or someones, high up. She tried to think about it logically, and sequentially. *Singh gets second thoughts, about whatever's going on. He's still alive at the start of the big meeting in the Arena, so he hadn't told anyone yet. He stands up to speak in the Arena, and has problems with his wearable.* She tried to think back — maybe Konami would have video to show it clearly — how much time elapsed between Singh standing to speak and being shot? Maybe a minute? Maybe two? *A public shooting is a panic move, considering the other murders. Maybe they're all panic moves, each one sloppier than the one before. So whoever shot him wasn't ready when Singh stood up. The shooter had to run, get his weapon, and get positioned.* She started taking notes, but stopped. Somehow it didn't feel right… could she really assume her own wearable's notes were secure?

Mattoso could feel the tension from the watchstanders on the Bridge. There was no more small talk. *Anyone could be a killer* was the unspoken subtext of each look. *Is it you?*

Even more, perhaps, was the collective shock at the undeniability of the violence. *This was why we left.* But it followed them. Weeks before, everything was simple for her to understand – simple and certain. Earth's culture was inherently violent, and a clean break was needed to create a society that could be free of that violence.

Now, nothing was clear. Nothing was certain.

After a moment she looked down at the screen on her chair arm. "Comms — execute check-in with Power systems."

The Comms watch acknowledged the order. "Power, Bridge, check-in all watches."

"Bridge, Power, check-in acknowledged. Power officer of the watch, Lieutenant Qiang checking in."

"Fusion control watch, PT2 Landers checking in."

"Antimatter control watch, PT1 Ossyngul checking in."

"Distribution watch, ET2 Ygsil checking in."

Mattoso had to pinch herself to keep her eyes from glazing over as the rest of the Power watches checked in.

What would she do when she got off watch? Nothing seemed more attractive to her then her own bed in her quarters, but the killers wouldn't wait for her to sleep… she couldn't put off the investigation. She thought back to the rather limited progress they had made — the manufacturing of the defective filter. That was about it, she realized — most of the rest had been just flailing about, until Nicolescu's murder, and now Singh's. *A conspirator just gave us more information in a minute, before being killed, then we'd found on our own in weeks of investigation.*

Fabrication was the site of the only discovery they had made on their own. *A defective filter…* She perked up in realization. *Every murder has a murder weapon.* The defective filter was the first, a syringe and venom for the second, and a gun for the third. It would be nigh-impossible to track the syringe — Medical probably ordered dozens every month. But the gun? Mattoso resolved that, if she could stay awake, Fabrication would be her first stop after she got off watch.

CHAPTER 29

On his way to the department head meeting, the frustration and boredom of recent months seemed like a distant memory. Konami knew this was contrary to the SNH philosophy, but he didn't feel an ounce of guilt. *This is why I'm here.*

It felt good to have a purpose.

He heard voices from the conference room around the corner. He had arrived early — since the forward Can was still spun down, they had moved the department head meeting to the aft Can, and he had given himself extra time to find the new conference room among the twisting passageways.

"If you hadn't held me back, Singh might be still alive, and in custody, and we'd know everything."

Konami stopped. The voice was one of the Bigwigs, Mara Ngayabo.

"I grew up in the slums of Ares City, Mara." Konami recognized this voice too — it was another Bigwig, Wilson Paramis. "I know what killers look like, and I could see it in Singh. What the hell were you gonna do, anyway? Arrest him yourself? He'd have swatted you like a goddamn fly! And there's no way you'd have gotten up there in time anyway!"

"Don't call me Mara, *Professor* Paramis," Ngayabo shot back. "There were constables nearby. I could have given the order. I had a feeling—"

"Enough," said a third voice. *Hamad Maltin.* "They're going to be here any second. Do we really want the gossip going around, just after three murders, that the eminent SNH Bigwigs are fighting amongst themselves like children?"

"Agreed," answered Paramis. Ngayabo just grunted, but they stopped arguing.

Nice to hear that they're as human as anyone else... Konami entered and took a seat, and the other department heads trickled in.

The Mayor signaled for him to begin, and Konami cleared his throat. "We've confirmed circumstantially that Singh could have rigged the filter and the hatch that killed Muahe, and one of Nicolescu's neighbors said that she saw Singh nearby just before he was killed. I believe we should accept that his confession was genuine."

"And his assassination?"

"My deputies dug a ferrous slug out from several centimeters into the floor beneath and behind the scene. There was no sign of explosive residue. Considering the caliber of the slug, along with the extreme damage to Singh's head, I believe the weapon was a high powered railgun."

"Railgun?" someone asked.

"It uses powerful electromagnets instead of explosives to propel the slug to incredible speeds, far greater than old-fashioned gunpowder."

In response to a question about the gunshot noise, Konami explained that a loud noise will accompany any supersonic projectile.

"Monstrous," someone muttered.

"Barbaric!" came from another.

Commander Chulanont spoke up. "I'm quite certain that there is no such design in the Fabrication catalog for a railgun. And even if there was, there's no way Zubiri's Fab techs would just sit by and ignore someone ordering up a weapon."

"But what if it didn't look like a weapon?" inquired Lieutenant Commander Olin.

Konami nodded. "That's what we suspect — that it was ordered and fabricated piecemeal, and assembled later. Or brought onboard before we departed." He looked at Commander Papka. "I'd like to borrow your best Electrical

Engineer. We may have to reinvent the damn thing, to see how it could have been constructed."

Papka looked at Captain Horovitz, who nodded assent. "Very well. She'll report to you shortly."

Mayor Akunle broke in, asking if they'd found the shooter's perch.

"We think so. The roof of aft housing unit six has a perfect view of where he was standing."

Dr. Madani asked how the shooter could have gotten there so quickly.

"Maybe he was waiting there," suggested the Bigwig Wilson Paramis.

Konami shook his head. "I don't think so. If they knew Singh was going to talk, they would have killed him already. They wouldn't ever kill someone so publicly except as a last resort."

Paramis leaned forward. "How do you know? Maybe they wanted a panic."

"If they were waiting and wanted a panic, they could have killed him as soon as he stood up, or before he confessed," answered Konami. "No, I think this was desperation. I think the killer, or one of them, was in the Arena, and when they saw Singh stand up, they knew he was about to talk, and they rushed out to get their weapon and get to the roof perch. Maybe they scrambled his wearable too to buy time. I think the railgun was fired as soon as it possibly could have been."

"Maybe the killer's superior was in the Arena, and sent a message to the killer, somewhere else, when Singh stood up."

"Perhaps," Konami conceded.

"So what can we conclude?" asked the XO.

"I think we can put this info out. We need to solicit the help of every Aotean. If the killer was in the Arena stands and saw Singh stand up, someone saw them sneak out. If it was the killer's superior, maybe someone saw them fiddle with their wearable right when Singh stood up."

"I'm not sure—"

Captain Horovitz interrupted. "That's exactly what we need. The crew is afraid, and a big part of that fear is uncertainty. We need them to be on our side." Konami recalled her earlier emphasis on the importance of the crew seeing the ship's leadership as allies. She turned to the Administrative chief recording minutes of the meeting. "Saul, put out as priority for all personnel: the shooter of Second Class Chemistry Technician Singh may have rushed out of the Arena when Singh stood up, or the shooter might have already been outside, but received orders from someone inside the Arena as soon as Singh stood up. Report to the Constabulary *immediately* if you recall anything strange inside the Arena before Singh was shot, particularly if you witnessed someone leave the Arena or otherwise act suspiciously."

Konami had to suppress a smile at this. In his experience, the help of the public during a murder investigation was invaluable, and only rarely was secrecy warranted. This was not one of those times, in his opinion.

The rest of the department head meeting was consumed with talk of weaponry. *How low we've sunk from the SNH's vision...*

"At some point we're going to find the shooter," said XO Criswell. "And he's armed. What if he resists?"

"We didn't leave the Earth system just to take part in more savagery," barked Commander Papka, the chief engineer.

"So what do you suggest, CHENG?" asked the Operations officer, Commander Dofo. "We just ask them to come in quietly?"

"What about the stunners?" asked Madani. The Constabulary maintained, very securely, a few dozen handheld contact stunners, but neither Konami nor any of his constables had ever used them aside from drills and routine maintenance.

Dofo snorted. "Contact stunners against a sniper? Good luck."

"The Charter specifically bans any weapons or tools capable of fatal injuries at a distance," responded Papka.

The XO turned to Konami. "CI?"

The chief inspector took a breath. "Section 5.13.2.b. If the captain and mayor agree, we can declare a shipwide emergency, and make guns. I'd say this qualifies as a shipwide emergency."

"A panic is not an emergency," responded Papka. "Who onboard has ever even seen a gun, much less fired one? Do I really need to bring out the old Earth statistics on deaths caused by firearms?"

I've fired one, Konami thought to himself sadly. Even in the slums of Lagos and Singapore, he had very rarely felt the need to be armed. But there had been a madman in one of the old abandoned towers of Singapore — a killer — and Konami had volunteered.

He shuddered thinking about it.

"How do you suggest we capture an armed killer, Commander Papka?" asked the XO, sneering.

"Dart guns." Everyone turned to the end of the table — it was Madani. Konami nodded to her. "The emergency section requires a new vote every thirty days," she continued. Konami checked — she was right. "That sounds more cumbersome than we need right now, if it's not absolutely necessary."

Captain Horovitz leaned forward, asking what kind of dart guns.

"Veterinary dart guns. We could load the darts with a smart sedative — overdose is impossible. They aren't capable of causing fatal injury. You could shoot a baby with one, and they'd just have a very long nap."

"Supply, is that even possible? Does Fabrication have specs for veterinary dart guns?" asked the CO.

Commander Chulanont replied that he'd have to check with Zubiri.

"If he doesn't have specs, I'll bet my techs could design one," offered Commander Papka. Konami raised his eyebrows — *wasn't he just complaining about gun safety?*

"Any objections to dart guns?" asked the XO.

Everyone looked at the CO, and she nodded her approval.

And so we arm ourselves...

CHAPTER 30

"Lieutenant?" A pause. "Uh, Lieutenant?"

Mattoso's eyes snapped open, and she flailed about for a half-second before realizing that she wasn't falling.

"The chief inspector will see you now." The admin tech kicked over to Konami's door and opened it. Mattoso failed to suppress her yawn as she floated across the passageway. She glanced at the time, sighing. *Yay, another two whole hours in bed before watch...* She was so tired she had to search her memory just for her purpose for being there.

In his little office, the chief inspector gave her a nod but said nothing. He floated upright as he gesticulated and scrawled in the air, tilted slightly as compared to her own orientation. She spun slightly to match him.

"You look as tired as I feel, Cy."

His chuckle sounded like a cough. His eyelids scraped over his eyes so slowly that she thought she could hear a scratching sound.

She had been up for more than a day straight, standing watch and combing the Fabrication archives for anything that might be a component of a long-range firearm. She'd found nothing at all.

She asked if he had put out the public call for information about the shooter.

"Yeah, but the captain didn't need her arm twisted."

"I had a thought and went to the Fab shops," said Mattoso. "Didn't find anything about the railgun, but since we know when the defective filter was ordered, and when it was picked up, even though they didn't log who it was, I went through the, uh, watch-bills and stuff, to see who was busy either time." Her own yawn cut her off.

"Singh?"

"No, I ruled him out. He was on watch in the Chem lab when it was picked up."

"Watch-bills can be altered."

"Yeah, so I checked the other Chem techs on watch. By a lucky coincidence, two others were running a joint experiment with Singh at the time, and they confirm he didn't leave. Before you ask, yes, they gave the same answer without time to coordinate, so I think we can trust it." She cleared her throat. "In addition to Singh, I could rule out another seventy percent of the crew."

He raised his eyebrows and nodded, but mentioned that that still left several thousand Aoteans.

"I'm not done — if we assume it wasn't a child, then that rules out near another thousand. I thought I was stuck then with about three thousand names, but I looked back at the Fab catalog entry — this filter hadn't been around for very long; it was input into the system just a few weeks before. I added that time, again assuming they weren't on watch, as a third variable to cut another thousand."

"So what's that, two thousand names?"

"Approximately. Take a look at the file I just sent you."

He scanned through the file. "That's too many. Who else can we rule out?"

She was at a loss.

He snapped his fingers repetitively. "Come on... we can think of something. We did it all the time back on Earth. Like if the footprints in the mud were very deep, then we cross out anyone under a hundred kilos."

"What about qualification?" she offered.

He nodded and grinned. "Yeah, that's good. Voice: remove all individuals without ship's qualifications." His expression changed and he shook his head. "That just gets rid of a few dozen. Outside of the kids, most of us are qualified."

"How about technical qualifications?" The thought came to her a bit guiltily — Mattoso had full Ship's Qualifications, the general rating that all Aoteans eventually achieved, which taught the basics of most of the

145

ship's systems aside from propulsion and power. And along with various Nav/Ops-specific watch station quals, she had gained full Operations Qualifications, also called "Forward Quals," as part of her department. But she had been working on her "Aft Quals," for Engineering, Propulsion, and Power, for more than two years now, and the thought of how far behind her goals she was brought a twinge to her stomach. "I know Ship's and Forward Quals didn't teach me those details about Fabrication, or how to rig a hatch malfunction in Sewage, and Aft Quals go into the technical details of nearly every system on the ship."

"Not bad... couldn't hurt to check." He squeezed a sip of what looked like tea from a pouch, straining his lips around to suck up the loose globules, directing his wearables to remove those without advanced qualifications. He smiled at the results. "Now we're talkin'. One hundred and four names." His eyes scanned down the list, eyebrows raising at one point.

"One of the names stand out to you?"

He didn't answer for a few seconds. "Nothing to worry about. Everyone on here might be a suspect."

"Can you send it?"

Konami didn't answer, so she repeated the question.

"Sorry. Here it is."

She looked down at the list on her lens. There were a few department heads she recognized — they typically stood fewer watches, and were more likely to have advanced quals, so that wasn't much of a surprise. And the Bigwigs, of course — it would have been quite a coincidence if any of them had happened to stand one of their monthly watches at the times in question. She didn't know that they all had technical qualifications, but she supposed it made sense — all three had supposedly been intimately involved with *Aotea*'s construction. But none of the other names stood out.

She scanned through the list again, wondering what name could have caught Konami's eye. This time she focused on the "Department" column, and she thought she found it. *Kiro Gregorian, Constabulary.*

Was it normal for a constable to have Aft Quals?

"This was good work, Bea," said Konami. "We may have narrowed it down considerably." She thanked him, and he looked at her but didn't say anything. She got the distinct impression that it was time to go, saying that she'd start going through the names on the list.

"Yeah, of course. I'll take the first half, you take the second half. Let me know what you find."

She nodded. Konami stopped her on her way out, reiterating the importance of keeping the list secret.

In the passageway, she looked again at the list, and couldn't help noting that Constable Gregorian was in the half that Konami took for himself.

CHAPTER 31

Why does Kiro have Aft Quals? Konami almost called up his best friend, but his cop instincts stayed his hand. *No way he's involved in this.* Aoteans often worked toward qualifications other than their primary duties — before all the recent chaos, anyway, few crewmembers had more than about a half-day's work, most of the time. But Engineering, Propulsion, and Power Qualifications were by far the most challenging to achieve. Konami assumed he would have known if Gregorian had been spending the time necessary to pass the Aft Qual boards.

He pulled up Gregorian's personnel record. He hadn't looked at it since he first reported onboard, but he thought a detail like Aft Quals would have stuck in his memory.

From the record, Gregorian had earned his Aft Quals just a matter of months after Konami reported onboard. No wonder he hadn't noticed, as busy as he was adjusting to his new duties, as well as getting his own qualifications. And from Gregorian's educational background, perhaps it wasn't even too surprising — one of his specialties on Mars had been forensic engineering; he may have wanted a challenge onboard, especially with the lack of crimes on the colony ship.

Somehow, he had to narrow down these hundred and four names. If one of them had left the Arena abruptly, or had started fiddling with their wearable once Singh stood up, then there'd be a prime suspect for the shooter, or the shooter's superior.

He knew it was a longshot, but he pulled up the constabulary video archive — the repository for the recordings made by each constable and roving watch since they were issued vidcams. He specified the time period during the gathering in the Arena, and started to watch.

Hours later Konami had barely made a dent in the footage. There had been more than two dozen rovers and constables on watch in and around the Arena, along with more than a hundred off watch but still recording, and even when he narrowed it down to time between Singh standing up and being shot, there was still hundreds of hours of footage to go through.

"Fuck it," he said aloud to no one, and walked out of his office.

"Wren, you there?" repeated Konami into the Third Class Data Technician's door-com.

Finally, the door opened, and a bleary-eyed Wren grunted a greeting, hair mussed and shirt on backwards. He put up a finger to ask Konami to wait, and left the door open a crack. Through the door Konami heard Wren talk softly to someone, and a minute later he emerged in uniform, and Konami asked him if there was any news on Muahe's logs.

The young Data tech grimaced. "I told you, it'll be done when it's done, and I'll tell you first. You and Mattoso."

Konami took a moment to search for the right words to explain his next request.

Wren didn't try to hide his impatience. "Well? Anything else?"

"Follow me." Wordlessly, Konami led Wren to the auxiliary Constabulary in the aft Can. After nodding to the duty constable, they hunched over a display in the lone closet-sized office next to a holding cell that had never been used, and Konami shut the door. He called up the video stream for the footage from the Arena.

"You saw the announcement, right? At some point before the shooting, someone in the Arena saw Singh — the dead guy — stand up, and either left in a hurry to get a gun, or sent a message to order someone else to do so. Adding up all the vidcams recording at the time, we've got

149

hundreds of hours of footage. Is there some way we can narrow it down without watching it all?"

Wren thought about it then nodded. "Facial recog software can separate each individual. But it works better the other way — you know, ask where Second Bumble-Futz was at a certain time, and voila, it tells you he was in the Cafeteria, as long as someone recording passed by." The young Tech snapped his fingers. "Sports stats software. Ironball games are recorded and transmitted live, and the auto stats trackers record every score, every take-down, every deflection." He nudged Konami out of the way and his fingers danced over the console. "It knows how to follow movement already, even in a crowded field. I bet I can at least get it to spit out anyone who got up during the big meeting, though 'working on a wearable' might be a tougher movement for the program to identify. But I'll find a way."

"This is top secret, Third. Work on this in private, and tell no one."

Wren gave a low whistle. "Hush-hush, you got it." The young Data technician frowned.

"What is it?" asked Konami.

"Bandwidth, again. Not nearly as bad as for the hack into Muahe's logs, but it might take a bit of time to keep it running out of sight."

An idea came to the chief inspector that made him sweat, but it was too intriguing to ignore. "The facial recog software — you say it can find individuals?"

"Of course. That's what it's designed for."

"Can it track them, in real time?"

"Track them? Like as they move?"

"Yeah. As the rover's video comes into your servers, can the program note locations and movement of anyone they see, and save the data?"

For the first time since meeting him, Wren was speechless.

Konami waited for him to gather his thoughts.

"You mean… isn't that against the Charter?"

"No, as it turns out, as long as the cams aren't hidden, and aren't unmanned."

Wren was silent.

"You don't have to feel good about this, Wren. I don't plan to use it unless we identify the killer."

"But, the bandwidth…"

"Fit it in, however you can. If you have to lower the frame rate, that's fine — we're already allocated a chunk of bandwidth for the video feeds, so I bet you can work with that to fit this in."

Wren was silent again.

"That's an order, Third. This is absolutely vital to finding the killer. Muahe's killer."

The Data Tech gave a nod.

Konami dismissed him, and went to find a ginger soda to calm the queasiness in his belly.

CHAPTER 32

"You awake?"

Despite her constant exhaustion, the sleep Mattoso was able to get was far from recharging.

Pat squeezed her in response. Mattoso reached uner the covers to their hips, and pulling the two of them into a spoon, asking Pat how the kids at school were handling the recent upheavals.

"They're loving it, actually. We spend most of the day in the aft classrooms, but we've been going to the forward Can for play periods. They can't get enough of the freefall!"

"What about the murders? Aren't they scared?"

"Yeah, when they stop to think about it. But kids are so easily distracted. The MOMbots are tuned to signs of negative emotions, and rush over to play at the first sign of fear."

"Lucky them…"

Pat turned to Mattoso and kissed her. "I'm sorry about the puppy."

"It's okay. Just a delay, until things are back to normal. I'm too tired to take care of something else right now, anyway."

As Pat entwined their fingers together and kissed down her neck, Mattoso's wearable buzzed.

"Sorry," she said as she pulled away. "Mattoso."

"It's Wren. I've got Muahe's logs open."

"He divided his log entries into 'Personal' and 'Work,'" explained Wren, pointing at the projection on the bulkhead. "Not too many Personal entries, as you can see. Which do you want to see first?"

They decided on a week before the bad filter specs were uploaded into the system.

Wren pulled up a log entry. Konami spoke as he ran a finger down the log. "GravTran watch... Bot repair... Maintenance logs scrub... Wren, any of this out of the ordinary for a Data tech's duties?"

The young technician scanned through the log. "No, everything's routine."

"Okay, next log." Wren pulled it up. There was nothing but routine work, according to the Data Tech.

They got through a handful of log entries before they found something.

"Wait." Wren stopped Konami as he was going through an entry from a few days before the unusual Fab spec was ordered. "Data sponge. Remember the NetBug tracer?"

Konami said nothing, so Mattoso cut in. "Yeah, that was the last thing Muahe did, right?" She turned to Konami. "Remember what I said about the Master Tech, Cy?" Mattoso scrolled to her log entry and showed it to the chief inspector. *DTM notes that Muahe's tracer task was every thirty days,* it said. "Third, that's a cyclical task normally, right? Not every thirty days?"

"Right," answered Wren. "Normally a cyclical task. But he might also run a Tracer to track down a data sponge."

"What's a data sponge?" Mattoso was glad Konami asked.

"Accumulation of unknown data somewhere unexpected." Wren scratched his smooth chin. "Like finding a locked box somewhere, heavy like it's full, and wondering what's inside."

"Should we just run another NetBug tracer?" asked Mattoso.

"No," said Konami. "They might have seen that. That might be what doomed Muahe."

"They?"

"You know, 'they.' The bad guys. They."

"Then what do we do? How do we look into this data sponge without another tracer?" she asked.

"We don't run a tracer, we *find* the tracer," offered Wren.

"Find a tracer? What does that even mean?"

"Not 'a' tracer, 'the' tracer. Muahe's tracer. I seriously doubt he wiped it without logging something."

Mattoso and Konami must have still appeared confused. "Look, I'll show you," said Wren. His fingers glided through the air, bringing up unfamiliar menus and windows that were gone before Mattoso could tell what their purpose was. "Here's a lists of all the dormant Tracers."

The projection just looked like a jumble of random characters.

"How many?"

"A few dozen. I'm gonna have to remind my fellow Data techs about good data hygiene practices…"

"How do we narrow it down?" Konami inquired.

"Last activity," said Mattoso. "Right, Wren? Can we sort them by last activity?"

"Sure. Just a sec… here we go."

The jumbled characters rearranged next to a date column. She scanned down the column. "There! Cycle four, day 28. That's the day Muahe was killed."

They were all silent. Mattoso shuddered. "This tracer… it's almost like a witness. So what was the last thing it did?"

"It sent out a message. To Muahe. This message."

Konami read the screen out loud. "S-S-N-D-2-7-1-W storage full. What does that mean?"

"Solid-state-nanodrive 271W, a data storage drive, is full. Let me pull up that drive's logs—"

"No!" cried Konami. "Remember, they killed Muahe for this. This might have been the last straw — finding the drive full, and starting to look into it."

Wren sighed and threw his hands up. "So how the hell do we figure out what they were trying to protect?"

"Solid-state." Mattoso knew that was just a type of data storage drive, old-fashioned but very robust, but it made her think of something. "It's a physical drive. What if we just pull the module?"

Wren snorted. "If they notice a log req, they'll definitely notice a drive pull."

"So—"

"Wait," interrupted the young Data tech. "I have an idea."

Mattoso was the lookout. In the midst of the coolant piping, signal repeaters, and other gear of the data-level passageway, she felt like a little kid watching out for teachers while her classmates hid a stinkbomb.

"Still clear?" came Konami's voice in her wearable.

"Nothing but the DustBots."

Wren's idea was a good one, but she couldn't shake the feeling that they were breaking the rules. These solid-state data storage drives, according to Wren, had a physical back-door connection port. By faking a routine software update, this section of the network would be offline for a matter of minutes, and Wren could copy the contents of the drive to a portable storage unit without anyone noticing.

The idea of having to *physically locate* computer memory struck Mattoso as hopelessly quaint. "How much more time?" she asked nervously.

"Just a minute after we find the right fucking drive!" The more agitated Wren became, the higher his voice pitched. Mattoso had peered her head in the data maintenance crawlway and could sympathize — there must have been dozens of the little fist-size drives protruding from the overhead. Older tech – the newest drives were nearly microscopic, with massive storage capabilities – but rock solid in terms of reliability and longevity.

155

"Why couldn't this damn space be forward?" complained Konami. Mattoso imagined that dragging oneself along on one's back, searching for a single drive, was a lot easier in zero-gravity.

"Found it!"

A quarter-hour later they were back in the aft Constabulary. As Wren connected the portable storage unit to his wearable, after disconnecting from the network, she realized she was holding her breath. *More throwback tech*...She couldn't recall if she'd ever had to physically plug one device into another.

"Huh." Wren's brow was furrowed as he looked at the projection. Mattoso couldn't make out anything on the screen — just a jumble of characters and symbols.

Konami snorted. "Well?"

Wren shook his head. "I don't know."

Mattoso asked what it was, and he repeated that he didn't know.

"You don't know what the data is?"

"There's no index. Nothing to tell us what kind of program or whatever. It could be anything." The Data tech scratched his forehead. "I'm gonna have to go through and run it against every type of reader and executer I have."

"Wait!" Mattoso cut him off before he started to work. She had a feeling. *Trust your gut, Bea!* "Keep it off the network. Work off the storage drive itself. Just in case."

Wren frowned and looked at Konami. "Good idea," said the chief inspector.

"That means I'm gonna have to do it all manually." Wren looked deflated. "Input each one individually until we find the right kind of program."

"At least we don't have to worry about bandwidth this time," Mattoso offered with a grin.

No one smiled.

CHAPTER 33

"Each of you is holding the brand new sidearm, fresh from Fabrication," announced Deputy Chief Inspector Kiro Gregorian. He'd been a shooting instructor for his police department on Mars, so he was the logical choice onboard. Loesser and a few others would learn from Gregorian, and help train the hundreds of roving watches to be certified to carry the weapon. "Officially designated the Personal Defense Sidearm Mark One, and designed by our very own Mechanical techs and engineers, you can feel free to call it a dart gun, 'cause that's what it is."

The trainees were arranged in a line in the middle of the Arena, the only appropriate venue. Each one stood behind a pedestal upon which sat the ungainly weapons.

"Not only are you trainees, but you are all product testers," explained Gregorian. "Other than the one in my hand, none of these weapons have been fired. Before you touch your weapon, you will put on your eye protection. Yes, that means you, Third. And before you touch the gun, remember the most important rule — do not point your weapon at anything you do not intend to destroy. Yes, I know these guns aren't lethal, but treat them like they are, at all times. If you point your gun at me, I will shoot you, and you will wake up in Medical with a hangover and some remedial training. Now, everyone, pick up your dart guns."

Along with Konami, the few dozen constables and rovers present picked up their dart guns. The guns were awfully large — a long, blocky barrel, and unadorned, angular handle; much less sleek than the slugthrowers he recalled from Singapore and Lagos. The edge cut into the webbing of Konami's thumb. *Gonna have to work on the ergonomics for Mark Two...*

"As you may or may not know, the dart guns are powered by compressed gas. The compressed gas canisters are rechargeable and replaceable, and the indicator on the top should read 'full.' A single charge is enough for about one hundred shots. Any problems so far? No? Okay. Charging stations will be installed at the Constabulary offices."

On a vessel whose mission and even construction was based on a philosophy of non-violence, weapons training seemed surreal to Konami. *Feels like playing racketball in a church.* If such a heathen as he felt like this, he couldn't imagine the conflicting feelings inside his native Aotean constables.

"At the bottom of the handle, on the left side, is the safety switch — make sure it's pointed down, which means the safety is on. Everyone good? Okay. Now pick up the magazine. Each magazine is loaded with twenty darts. Insert the magazine into the handle. Your weapons are now loaded."

The gun was heavy and bulky. It looked like a poorly designed toy for a very large child, not that toy guns were allowed onboard.

"Now, point the gun at the target." *Safety's still on, Kiro!* "Line up the nose sight with the bullseye. Pull the trigger once." There were several empty clicks and one sound like a sneeze, and a single trainee's dart shot out. "Damn it, Third! Did I say to take the safety off?"

"No, Deputy—"

"You're damn right I didn't! You're disqualified from this session. Sign up for a later one. And go tell your chief that you're gonna need someone else to cover your first roving watch until you get through the dart gun training."

After a bit of grumbling, the technician left. Kiro ordered everyone to take off the safety, aim at the bullseye, and fire. Several dozen sneezes rang out. Konami's dart struck the target, about twenty meters away, a few centimeters off center. Looking at the other targets, he realized he had by far the best shot — many of the targets weren't even struck. A tiny surge of pride came to him, embarassing him.

Gregorian gestured at a projection, and the un-struck targets moved closer to the shooters. "Aim, and fire once more."

This time, everyone struck their target. They worked through the entire magazine, determining that most of the dart guns were accurate to ten meters, and off by several centimeters at twenty. At thirty meters, the darts had trouble penetrating the poly skin of the target, if one was lucky enough to get a hit.

"Reload!"

Everyone removed their magazine and replaced it with a new one.

"Aim! Fire!"

Thump.

"Fire!"

Thump. Konami's head started to hurt.

"Fire!"

Thump.

"Fire!"

Thump.

"Fire!"

His head pounding, Konami shut his eyes for a moment, trying to block out a gruesome memory.

"You okay, Cy?" asked Gregorian, voice low.

He opened his eyes back up. Everyone else was reloading, aside from one young tech, holding his stomach and scurrying away. "Yeah, I'm fine. I think that's enough for me, for now."

Without waiting for an answer, Konami put the gun down and walked away.

CHAPTER 34

"First issue," started Captain Horovitz. "Forward Can status. GravTran?"

Despite her fatigue, Mattoso was excited to attend her first department head meeting. Commander Dofo, the Operations officer, had been ordered to bed rest due to exhaustion, and Mattoso was dubbed as the acting department head until he recovered. Looking around the room, she wasn't the only substitute – many other department heads were apparently too busy or too exhausted, and sent deputies. With the way her head throbbed, she wondered how long she could manage before she'd need to recover in bed as well.

There was major damage to one of the auxiliary rotation gearheads, one of the many massive, several-ton gear assemblies that enabled the smooth rotation of the cans. "At first we suspected wear," continued Commander Konrote. "But then we found pitting that might be indicative of a chemical reaction. The gear is being replaced and we should be able to restore normal rotation within a few days."

Chief Engineer Papka asked for the cause of the chemical reaction, but Konrote said that it was wiped clean, with no chemical residue.

No one wants to say sabotage. What was unthinkable just weeks before now seemed obvious.

Konrote explained that they had installed monitoring equipment on the rotation gears, so that any further sabotage would be immediately noted and recorded. He finished with some technical details, and the Captain asked Konami for the status of the investigation.

Konami paused, and Mattoso thought she saw him swallow. "Based on circumstantial evidence only, we have a list of several dozen persons of interest. Not necessarily suspects for either murder, but for some sort of involvement."

"Can we see this list?" asked Mayor Akunle.

"No."

The mayor's perpetual smile disappeared.

"What?" The XO almost got to his feet, but remained seated with a look from Captain Horovitz.

The captain fixed Konami with a stare and asked him to explain.

Konami took a deep breath. "I've thought long and hard about this. I haven't been able to sleep because of this. This is not a small murder conspiracy. There are senior personnel involved. Likely someone, or someones, in this meeting."

Shouts and grunts and near-pandemonium erupted, finally dissipating with a circular glare from the captain.

"Go ahead, CI."

"Someone knew enough about the Sewage systems, and auxiliary systems, to fake a clog, and jam the door."

"That was Singh," said Papka.

"No. Singh may have done the dirty work, but he was following orders. He didn't have any electrical training, or fluid systems training. He had basic quals plus Chem watch quals, and no advanced training in his record."

"Maybe someone else was involved, but how do you know it's one of us?" This was Commander Konrote, appearing particularly aggrieved.

"How do we know it's not you, Inspector?" whined the chief engineer. *What a weasel CHENG Papka is…*

Konami slapped the table. "I'm the only fucking person in this room who we can guarantee is not involved!" He looked around the room, as angry as Mattoso had ever seen him. The anger frightened her for a moment – she couldn't recall seeing such rage since a childhood bullying incident on Ceres.

"Does anyone think that this is over?" continued Konami. "Does anyone think that we've seen our last dead

Aotean? Does anyone think that, whatever these murders are covering up hasn't been in the making for a long time? I've been onboard for five years. Five Earth-years. Six or seven cycles. Just a few before we left Earth system. Have any of you been onboard for less than twenty?"

He paused, and no one challenged him. *I've only been onboard for 10 cycles,* thought Mattoso, but she kept silent. She was pretty sure he was right about everyone else.

"Someone, or more likely multiple someones, want to change things. Someone with knowledge and influence. They're not okay with the plan — with *Aotea*'s plan, as it is right now. You think this is new? Someone came up with this just last year, or the year before?" Konami leaned back and closed his eyes before continuing. It took Mattoso a moment to convert Konami's 'years' into cycles, and she assumed most of the others were having the same problem. "Muahe and Nicolescu found something, or were about to. Or they were part of it, and had second thoughts. The murders weren't the aim of the conspiracy, they were meant to keep it secret. It's the aim that I'm most worried about. We find out what they're planning, and we'll find the killers."

"What could it possibly be?" asked Madani. "What could anyone want to do with *Aotea*?"

"War," offered Papka. "Always war, on Earth. We have Earthers onboard, as we all know." The chief engineer didn't shy away from looking at Konami. "This is the most powerful ship ever built. Our reactors generate more energy than half of Earth's Navy put together." This last bit was twinged with pride.

You've gotta be kidding, Papka! She couldn't stifle herself. "Oh come on... they're going to take over the ship four cycles out from Earth? It'd take us cycles just to slow down and turn around, not to mention another accel-decel to arrive! And what the hell would we do? We're not exactly ideal warriors. Earth has nukes. Mars does too. If Ceres and the Jovian moons don't, they could cobble them together in a few months. Big and powerful doesn't mean much against nuclear weapons."

"And we don't have any weapons ourselves," added Konami. "What do you call it — reactionless propulsion, right? No drive cone? This isn't a power play for war, at least not war back home."

"We could make weapons," responded Papka weakly, but no one took up his defense.

"What about old-fashioned politics?" offered Mayor Akunle. "Like a coup? Not for war, but just for power onboard?"

Konami shrugged. "Maybe."

No one said anything. Konami's words seemed to be sinking into the department heads — Mattoso noticed several surreptitious looks at one's neighbors. *Could be any of us...* She knew this was true — but no one had stated it quite so bluntly before. Coming out, as it did, accompanied by the chief inspector's anger, somehow made it much more real.

A very slight buzzing intruded on Mattoso's thoughts. The meeting had paused for a handful of side conversations, and she tried to isolate the new noise. It seemed to be growing.

"Does anyone else hear that?"

The conversations stopped. Abruptly, Commander Konrote almost fell out of his chair getting to his feet.

"EMERGENCY!" The announcement was almost deafening. "LOSS OF ROTATION IN THE AFT CAN; RIG FOR LOSS OF GRAVITY AND PREPARE FOR SPINDOWN OF THE AFT CAN! EMERGENCY!"

CHAPTER 35

The buzzing grew to a metallic whine, broken up by chopping, rhythmic *thumps*. The department scrambled to their feet and moved toward the doors.

"Hold," ordered the captain. "Hold! Twenty thousand people look to us for leadership. We will not panic here. GravTran, to the scene. CHENG, aft. Chief inspector, the Constabulary. XO, CC Central..."

Konami was already out the door. The other department heads headed to the surface, but Konami went down to the moveway level. The emergency announcement repeated, dully resonating among the waytreads and safety bulkheads, and Konami checked his wearable to see which constables were on duty. Minutes later, he climbed up a ladderwell, emerging on the surface next to the aft Constabulary.

"Activate Delta reserves," he ordered Constable Loesser as he passed the cramped Emer office. Delta reserves activated every constable and constable-in-training in the department. Since the temporary boost to his numbers assigned from other departments, it also activated all the off-watch Rover deputies.

He noted with satisfaction that a pair of constables were already rigging the compartment for the loss of gravity, strapping down loose objects and rigging guide cables along the length of each space and passageway, and manually locking the automatic doors open to accommodate the guycables.

"ALL HANDS PREPARE FOR SPINDOWN! SPINDOWN OF THE AFT CAN IMMINENT!"

Konami put in a call. "Kiro, man the forward Constabulary." *Can't believe we just shifted over here!* The aft Constabulary was much smaller and only meant for temporary operations, and since both would soon be in freefall, they might as well man the one with more space and functionality.

"SPINDOWN IN THIRTY SECONDS; ALL HANDS PREPARE FOR SPINDOWN OF THE AFT CAN! THIRTY, TWENTY-NINE, TWENTY-EIGHT..."

Shit. From the tiny armory cabinet in the back of the office, he armed himself with a dart gun and a stunner. He had no doubt that the latest damage to the Can was sabotage, and no doubt that, whatever was happening in the big picture, it wouldn't end without violence. His stomach dipped at the thought.

"...Five, four, three, two, one. SPINDOWN COMMENCING! ALL HANDS BRACE FOR SPINDOWN OF THE AFT CAN!"

They were still rigging the space when Spindown began. He had a feeling of getting lighter as well as almost losing his balance, like when a commuter train in Singapore suddenly changed speed.

There was a call on the Emer line from the mayor for Konami – a crowd had gathered outside the mayor's office.

Shit. Years before he had recommended a security watch station outside Civil, but that was laughed off — 'this isn't Earth, Cy; we don't have mobs on *Aotea*.' He supposed he had been right, but at this point he was glad it was denied... a lone constable in front of a panicking crowd probably could only make the situation worse.

Constables and roving deputies were trickling in, pulling themselves through the Constabulary passageways hand over hand. Konami selected three of his permanent constables – Lee, Ginsberg, and Dillon, and set out.

The rig was still ongoing, very clumsily in freefall, as they set off for the aft Civil office. If the rig were complete, they could virtually fly there, using the guycables that would be stretched across the empty space of the can. But what should have been a five minute jaunt turned into twenty minutes, due to the confusion of both riggers and bystanders. Anxious crewmembers would demand

165

assistance in some rigging evolution, only to be brushed aside or ignored by the passing constables. Being Earthers, Konami and Lee copied the practiced movements of Cereans Ginsberg and Dillon, experienced in freefall movement, to travel across the surface as quickly as possible.

Konami flinched when he thought of Kostya — his dog was probably panic pissing all over Gregorian's quarters, bounding from wall to wall. *At least it's not my place...* Drifting along a passageway, kicking at convenient posts or fixtures to accelerate behind Constable Dillon, he entered a quick search on his wearable for zero-g procedures for pet management.

"In the unlikely event that pets must be kept in a freefall environment, Veterinary Storage Spaces 6 through 12 include padded velcro wallhangs, and pets can be equipped with associated velcro socks that..." He thumbed in a message to the Vet techs to add Kostya to their rapidly growing pet pickup queue.

They arrived at Civil, and the crowd looked to have grown — Konami estimated over a hundred Aoteans floating outside. Somehow, a freefall crowd was much less intimidating then the angry mobs he recalled from Earth. *More like a cloud then a mob...*

Conneer was interviewing members of the crowd. She looked as energized and engaged as he had ever seen her. He'd always had the feeling that, like himself, Conneer needed something to be happening to feel satisfied with her job.

He asked her to step aside, and surprisingly, she obeyed readily.

"Hands at your sides," Konami ordered his deputies, before switching to loudspeaker mode. "May I have your attention," boomed his amplified voice. He realized it had been a long time since he had studied a crowd-control strategy manual. *Gonna have to wing it.* "This is an emergency situation. Please disperse, and if you have no

166

orders from your chain of command, remain in your quarters."

A tall young man pushed his way to the front of the crowd. "We have the right to know what's going on!"

"I don't know any more than you do." This wasn't strictly true, Konami realized, but at the moment he didn't care.

"The mayor must know something. We just want to ask—"

"You're all Aoteans, goddamnit!" interrupted Konami. "You all took an oath. We all did. There will be a time to ask questions, and your questions will be answered. But right now, our focus should be to *get the Can rigged for zero gravity*. Safety of the ship and crew comes first. And if you don't have a role in the freefall rig, or repairs, or some other critical shipboard operation, then *stay the hell out of the way*."

"But what about—"

Konami put his hand the stunner holster. "Aoteans, we all have our duty. You have your duty. And I have my duty, which at this moment is to keep order on this goddamn starship, which you might have noticed has been less than well-ordered lately. Clear?"

No one moved.

"Everyone present, disperse, or be dispersed. Last warning."

Konami steeled himself to rush into the crowd and whispered instructions to his deputies. If they pushed off hard from the storage block, they'd have a good head of steam going into the crowd, and the shock of a handful of stuns ought to knock sense into the crowd. But just before they set their feet, the hundred-some-odd Aoteans started to break up. He supposed that it was harder for a freefall mob to disperse, with little to grab onto aside from each other, but they managed, awkwardly, to separate and get on their way.

When the crowd was mostly broken up, he thumbed in another call. "All clear, Mayor."

"Thanks, Cy. What a fucking mess!"

Konami detailed his three constables to remain to guard the Civil building before heading forward to man the main Constabulary. Anticlimactic as the confrontation turned out, he had the feeling they were in the calm that came before the storm.

"Whatever's going on, it's not going to be over soon, you know." It was Journalist Conneer, pulling herself along on a parallel guycable.

Konami nodded as he continued along.

CHAPTER 36

The emergency announcement repeated while Captain Horovitz stoically doled out assignments, her stoney expression as indomitable as ever. "...Hold! Twenty thousand people look to us for leadership. We will not panic here. GravTran, to the scene. CHENG, aft. chief inspector, the Constabulary. XO, report to Casualty Control Central and take charge. Pohamba..."

Mattoso's eyes followed the chief inspector as he charged out of the conference room. The XO gave her an impatient look and a gesture, and she followed him out. She briefly wondered if she ought to head forward to the Bridge, since she was technically the acting Operations officer, but then realized that would be where the captain herself would surely be headed. *Captain's place on the Bridge and all...* The conference spaces were on the first level under the surface, so they made their way to the nearest ladderwell.

Unlike the relative calm of the conference level, the thoroughfares of the surface were crowded with gawkers and emergency watchstanders. Two techs struggled with a cable-launcher for the zero-gravity rig, but there was no catch-net on the other side of the Can.

"There's an extra catch-net under the launcher tube," yelled Mattoso as they passed. "One of you, take it to the other side!" *Didn't they learn their basic rig quals?*

Outside a four level hab, whose residents were gathered outside, two roving watches were attempting to maintain order. They appeared to be questioning each resident, and in comms on their wearables, to find out where each individual should be.

The XO clawed his way to the roving watches and addressed the crowd, directing those without immediate orders to return to their quarters.

169

When they didn't move, Mattoso spoke up. "Don't any of you have pets? Do you really want to find out what zero-gravity does to the digestive system of a dog?" She left unsaid that it could have the same affect on humans who hadn't taken anti-nausea meds.

But it worked, and half the crowd rushed back inside, with the rest reluctantly following. The XO gave her an amused look, and they continued along their way.

Self-rigging Bots scattered to get out of the way as they sprinted between a pair of habs. The emergency announcement repeated, along with the sounds of some metallic catastrophe in the rotation gears.

From somewhere in his uniform, XO Criswell produced one of the new dart guns. As he handed it over, his features softened in a way she couldn't recall ever seeing before. "Mattoso, whenever you get a free moment, you will have the chief inspector issue you one of these, and carry it with you at all times."

"Understood," she responded, returning the weapon, though she felt as confused as the wailing children they passed.

"ALL HANDS PREPARE FOR SPINDOWN! SPINDOWN OF THE AFT CAN IMMINENT!"

"Double time," ordered the XO, and they sped up. The aft Casualty Control Central station was just a few hundred meters from the conference room, but getting through the twists and turns and knots of confused Aoteans made it seem like twice that.

"SPINDOWN IN thirty SECONDS; ALL HANDS PREPARE FOR SPINDOWN OF THE AFT CAN! thirty, 29, 28..."

They reached CC Central seconds before the countdown finished. "I relieve you," said the XO to the wide-eyed young Third that was manning the station. He ordered Mattoso to primary communications, and put the Third online with Emer.

"SPINDOWN COMMENCING! ALL HANDS BRACE FOR SPINDOWN OF THE AFT CAN!"

The seats in CC Central were helpfully supplied with belts, and Mattoso strapped herself down at the primary communications console. Her stomach started to lurch as the simulated gravity lessened, but she swallowed down the urge to vomit.

The XO ordered her to get GravTran on the line.

The console reported that multiple stations were trying to call CC Central. She set the auto-response to Text, sent out a general status request to all stations, and after a moment, messages started to trickle in.

"CCC, GravTran. Received 'Rotation Obstruction' alarm, and seconds later the vibration sensors went haywire. We took action for Rotation Emergency procedure, which mandates Emergency Spindown."

Mattoso acknowledged the report and parroted it to the XO, adding that minor injury reports were starting to pile up.

The Third reported from the Constabulary that all reserve constables had been activated.

The next several hours flew by, with minor emergency after minor emergency. The hasty freefall rig was responsible for dozens of broken bones and hundreds of scrapes and bruises, and for the first time, Mattoso heard the word "triage" used for real. Angry, confused crowds had to be confronted and dispersed, and gawking bystanders directed to their quarters.

Most distressing was the push and pull on GravTran in dealing with the damage to both Cans. Commander Konrote's engineers quickly discovered the cause of the damage — one massive geartooth, almost a cubic meter in volume, had broken off its gear and wreaked havoc in the innards of the Can's rotation system. The remnant was so huge that the Diagnostic Techs had to set up a temporary lab around the chunk of super-hard and super-dense alloy, rather than bring it to their own station, and they discovered the same signs of chemical damage, though much more severe, that caused the forward Can Spindown. The hidden monitoring device, installed by senior GravTran techs as part of the corrective action after the first Spindown, had been destroyed. *Which just confirms Cy's suspicion that someone senior is involved,* realized Mattoso. Only the department heads were supposed to know about the hidden devices that would sound an alarm if any of the rotation components were tampered with.

CHENG Papka insisted that the new damage be dealt with, while Commander Konrote wanted to finish the repairs to the forward Can, and finally Captain Horovitz stepped in and sided with the GravTran Officer, ordering him to devote his department's full efforts toward completing the repairs of the forward Can.

After nearly a day, the pandemonium died down, and Mattoso felt able to breathe easy for the first time.

And then the screams began.

CHAPTER 37

The lights in the Constabulary dimmed for the barest second. "...injured! No, the bot. It's the bot! Get the—"

The emergency call cut off, and a shiver ran down Konami's spine. The call came from Food Service station number 7.

Forward can, so that's us. Konami had relocated shortly after Gregorian got it up and running. "Shofstahl, Lo, Goodluck, with me." He had already given the order for every qualified constable to arm themselves, and he instinctively checked his own belt for the stunner and dart gun as they departed.

The surface passageways outside the Constabulary were deserted. The ship's complement had been under a general curfew for hours. Konami tried to call the Food Service station, but there was no answer. He eyed the crisscrossing guycables and selected one, urging along his constables, pulling himself along awkwardly hand-over-hand. At the bottom of the cable he pulled himself down to a squat, took hold of the friction guide, and bounded upward with all his might.

The sensation was like falling headfirst, and he had to struggle not to lash out with panic. He gently pulled himself back in line by the friction guide as he drifted slightly to the side, and accelerated by pulling himself forward along the cable with his free hand. As he approached the other side of the can, he carefully squeezed the handle of the friction guide to brake, and landed almost in a tumble.

A scream rang out just as he adjusted to the new orientation.

"Help!" A faceless voice among the abandoned passageways of the surface struck Konami as the most eerie thing he'd ever heard.

"Where are you?" answered Konami. *Damn it!* The voice came from the opposite direction from Food Service Station number seven.

"Ugh… trash compactor. Hab 7B."

"Lo, Shofstahl, to the compactor. Call for MedTechs. Keep me informed. Goodluck, with me."

As they pulled themselves down the passageway, Konami had to suppress the urge to say something to break the silence. He couldn't recall the surface of a Can being this quiet. It wasn't just the lack of people — the low, rumbling sound of the rotation would fade into the background, but it was always present. *Until it's sabotaged.*

"Food Service station seven, if anyone is present, please respond," he said into his wearable as they approached the structure. If the call had been from a wearable, the Emer system would have reported who made it, but the call had been from the station console.

There was no answer. Konami's stomach did somersaults. They rounded a corner and approached from the back — Food Service stations consisted of a kitchen on the back side, and a cafeteria mess in front.

The back door was open, and brightly lit. Somehow he expected it to be dark — he took off his low-light goggles in a hurry before the enhanced light blinded him.

"Hello?" he called out into the doorway, small enough not to require a guycable. When there was no answer, he gestured to Constable Goodluck and they maneuvered inside. A slight, high-pitched buzzing sound greeted them in the short passageway.

"CI, Lo, we're at the compactor—"

"Is it under control?"

"Yes—"

"Then I'll get back to you."

Hints of an old smell, one he hadn't smelled in over a decade. *Blood.* Blood in an enclosed space — there was no odor like it. His stomach was a brick, somehow pulling him to the deck even in zero-gravity.

They rounded the corner to a grisly nightmare, all the more shocking in the bright overhead lighting. After a confusing moment, a pile of limbs floating against the aft bulkhead resolved itself into two people, a man and a woman, in Food Service coveralls, covered in blood. The whirring noise came from the bodies. Globules of blood leisurely pooled aft, drawn very slowly by the miniscule but continuous acceleration of *Aotea*'s propulsion drive.

"Oh my god," said Constable Goodluck, open-mouthed.

"Medical emergency!" shouted Konami, as if the volume helped, into his wearable. "Food Service station seven — extreme trauma, two victims."

"Acknowledged."

Between the casualties and the constables floated a blood-smeared TaskBot, waist-high, in the center of the kitchen, with its extra limbs secured to a diagonal guycable. When rigged for freefall, the TaskBots changed from a gnomish but humanoid countenance to some degenerate cross between turtle and spider.

"Wait!" Konami cried as Goodluck started to approach, recalling the brief emergency call. "TaskBot — yeah, I'm talking to you — what happened here?"

The Bot's domelike head swiveled. "Please restate your question."

"What happened — *damn it*. Where did all this blood come from?"

"The blood came out of the bodies of Food Service Technicians Correa and Barr—"

Goddamn literal Bots... "I know that, TaskBot. How were they wounded?" Anxious as he was to check the status of the casualties, that frantic Emer call made him wary to come within reach of the Bot, and in the small, cluttered kitchen, that was nearly everywhere.

"Food Service Technician Correa was wounded when a chef's knife penetrated his thigh, abdomen, neck, and face, and Food Service Technician Barrow was wounded

175

when a chef's knife penetrated her upper arm, shoulder, and back."

Some old lesson about robotic and automated safety programming came to him. "Why didn't you notify Emergency station when they were wounded?"

The Bot paused. "I am unable to answer that question."

Konami snorted. "Where is the chef's knife that caused the wounds?"

The Bot's body swiveled, revealing the bloody knife in an appendage that had been hidden on its other side. "The chef's knife is here."

Konami instinctively put his hand on the dart gun. *Fat lot of good that'll do to a Bot...* He shifted his hand to the stunner, though he was less than confident that even the contact stunner's high voltage would damage a Bot.

"Oh god oh god..." muttered Goodluck, stopping after Konami gave him a brief glare.

Konami put in a call. "Kiro, Loesser, it's Cy. Don't argue. From now on, every constable or deputy on duty will carry a melee weapon. Something heavy and metal — hammer, fire axe, wrench, whatever. For now, improvise. Clear?"

"Clear," they echoed, confusion apparent even in this one word.

"CI," said Loesser. "We've had several more—"

"Can't talk now. Casualties."

"Understood."

"TaskBot, let go of the knife."

The Bot's appendage dutifully released the knife, which remained floating in the center of the kitchen.

"TaskBot, move to the pantry — that one. Open the pantry." It was fully stocked. "Okay, pick up the oil canister — yes, the big one. Release it behind you. Now go into the pantry and shut the door." He turned to Goodluck. "Watch that pantry, but stay back!"

Konami pulled himself across the kitchen, avoiding the bloody, drifting knife. Up close, he could see that the

176

wounds on the two Food Service Techs were deep, but haphazard. The two techs were stuck together, and he quickly figured out why — a mass of blood had clotted between Correa's side and Barrow's back. He reached for Barrow's neck, but stopped short — something was stuck to her head. It was round, black, and convex, and with a start he realized it was a DustBot, and the source of the whirring noise.

What the hell? Very carefully, he reached for the Bot, which gave a shiver. "DustBot, let go." He couldn't recall if they were programmed for voice commands — ubiquitous as they were, Konami didn't remember ever having interacted with one. Throughout the ship, DustBots consistently moved out of the way any time anyone approached, no matter what they were doing. *Like birds and critters on Earth.*

He tried the command again, but the Bot did not release its hold of Barrow's hair, a length of which was deep inside its intake. *Shit.* Gingerly, he reached for the Bot. The barest moan escaped Barrow's lips just as he grabbed the DustBot. It struggled as he tried to pull it free, and he gathered up the Tech's hair in one hand so he wasn't pulling against her skull. *Damn, this thing is strong!* He instinctively looked around for a pair of scissors, or something to cut her hair. His next thought — *like a chef's knife* — stopped him cold, especially when he recalled the obedience of the TaskBot. *TaskBot, bring me that knife... what the hell is going on?*

"What in the moons of Jupiter...?" Konami looked up to see that the MedTechs — two of them — had arrived.

Konami pulled himself away. "Quickly, now — she's alive, I think. Don't know about the other. You'll need to cut her hair — there's a DustBot stuck... don't ask."

Konami checked with Goodluck as the MedTechs got to work. The pantry had stayed shut; apparently the TaskBot was as obedient as it was when they arrived. *So what the hell happened?*

177

He put in a call to his deputies. "Lo, Cy. Report."

There was no answer, and he realized his wearable was dead. So was Goodluck's. *What the hell?* Luckily, the food service console had a charging plug, and it restarted with no problem.

"Lo, Cy. Report."

"We're under control, CI. Wearable problems, but we got 'em charged up again. Trash compactor hatch was stuck shut on someone's arm. We looked up the specs and pulled the fuse on the panel underneath, and with no power, it opened up. Just bruises; no broken bones, but I had Shofstahl escort him to Medical anyway. Didn't want to tie up Emer, especially with all the calls."

All the calls? Don't like the sound of that... "Good work. Report to the Constabulary, and arm yourself."

"Already armed, CI. Stunner and dart gun."

"Just ask Loesser or Kiro."

"Understood, Lo out."

He called up his two subordinates for a report on the latest Emer calls.

After they briefed him, his insides were knotted to the point of causing sharp pain.

He fingered another call. "Captain," he said. "We're under attack."

CHAPTER 38

The XO ordered the latest casualty count through gritted teeth. The comms circuit was open, and the captain and other department heads were listening in.

The push to regain control of the ship had been going on for almost a day. "Safe" zones were rendered Bot-free and guarded at all access points, with melee-armed crewmen slowly extending the safe areas of the ship, room by room and passageway by passageway. Engineers and technicians followed, restoring systems and equipment to normal operation, though still on manual mode for any potentially dangerous gear.

Mattoso wiped her eyes and looked down at her console, operating in low power mode. "Thirty-seven major casualties," she droned. "Five confirmed dead. Ten in serious or critical condition. Twenty-two fair or good." *Dozens more unaccounted for.* Something had happened to nearly every wearable onboard — within an hour after the Spindown, they spontaneously discharged all their battery power. Anyone who had the bad luck of not being nearby a charging port might have no way of calling for help, at least not until the ambient bioelectric trickle, the backup, but glacially slow, method of charging that took advantage of the natural electric fields generated by the human body, got going.

"And the rest?" asked the XO.

"At least one hundred ninety-one other injuries. Medical is at capacity, and sending those with minor injuries to their quarters until later." She felt like a Bot, unable to process emotionally the horror she was reporting. But like a Bot, she continued, reporting the breakdown of the injuries: two deaths caused by Bots, two by automated components — one storage bay door, and one cargo loader — and the other by Bots during the surge. For the thirty-two serious injuries: fourteen by Bots, and sixteen from

179

automated components, and another two from the safe zone surge.

The XO spoke low, voice commands to his wearable. The Third Class Technician at the console beside her kept muttering under his breath, stroking something furry hanging on a cord around his neck.

An alert popped up, and Mattos began the hourly watch stations status check. As she checked off the messages against the list of stations, she surreptitiously looked down at a mini-projection for the thousandth time that hour. *Where the hell are you, Pat? Are you okay?*

Hours before, the first flurry of casualties had caused a panic. Screaming and confusion had dominated until the chief inspector shared the common thread — automated ship's equipment or Bots. Heavy doors would shut on Aoteans' limbs, or in one horrible case, crushing a ribcage. Loaders and moveways would stop and start, at the worst possible times, pinching limbs with bone-crushing force. And, most frighteningly of all, and with machine-like speed and strength, Bots were lashing out, with tools or bare appendages, continuing to attack until out of reach. Disturbingly, after the outburst and once out of reach, they would return to their duties, and even obey the orders of their victims.

As soon as Konami had shared his common-thread discovery, Mattoso couldn't help herself. "Secure power to the vital bus!" she had shouted into the console, with Control and Power on the line.

"What the hell are you doing?" cried the XO at her breach of protocol.

She left the comms channel open. "We have to put everything on manual control. Securing power to the vital bus sets off the auto-manual trip, and every big moving piece of equipment onboard will lose power."

"Belay that—"

"CHENG, this is the captain. Secure power to the vital bus *now*."

Within moments, the lights had dimmed and then relit. In her mind Mattoso had traced the ship's power distribution diagrams — *with the vital bus secured, lighting goes to the auxiliary bus...*

The XO had glared at her for a moment before softening. "Well done, Lieu—"

Another interruption, a shipwide announcement: "This is the captain speaking." The sound quality had been tinny and poor — Mattoso realized that, with the vital bus secured, the main comms circuits had been de-powered, and shipwide announcements were now rerouted through the less power-thirsty auxiliary communications system. "All automated, moving equipment, including doors and hatches, are now in manual mode. Do not restore power to any moving equipment without my express permission. Note that the danger from Bots remains."

"Lieutenant?"

Hours after vital power had been secured, Mattoso's exhaustion had morphed into a dull sort of numbness.

"Lieutenant?"

Pat... She suppressed the tears that started to pool in her eyes at the thought. *Why won't you let me know you're okay?* She resisted the urge to check her wearable for the second time in as many minutes, and took little comfort in the fact that her lover's name hadn't appeared in the casualty listings; the number of unaccounted for and missing personnel had grown to over three hundred.

"Mattoso!"

She perked up and turned her head. "Sorry, XO."

"It's okay. Your relief is here."

She looked up to see a Communications Lieutenant Junior Grade named Karimov, whose first name her fatigued brain could not call up.

By rote, Mattoso turned over the status of Casualty Control Central, and gave up her seat.

"What about you, XO? Who's going to relieve you?"

He held up a thermos and smiled. She couldn't recall *ever* seeing a smile on the XO's lips. "Don't worry, I've got my coffee. Specially prepared by Dr. Madani."

Since the emergency started, nearly everyone onboard was on a "port and starboard" watch rotation — eight hours on watch (at minimum), and eight hours off. After more than twenty-four hours awake, Mattoso's body cried out to her to cross the Can to her quarters and sleep. *But Pat's out there somewhere.* On her way out from Casualty Control Central, she took a detour to a damage control supply closet, changing direction by swinging around a convenient guycable.

Somehow, the feel of the fire axe in her hand gave her a surge of energy. She awkwardly slipped it under her belt, needing both hands to pull herself along the guycables. A red-eyed deputy was returning down the passageway toward her, and they neatly executed a little pirouette-exchange to get around each other on the guycable, before she made a left turn.

The Can's surface seemed almost empty, and the quiet was disconcerting, punctuated by occasional distant yells or sounds of metal on metal. She checked again the message from Pat's supervisor — three classes had been on field trips at the time of the loss of rotation. One was supposed to go the Garden, one to the Repro lab, and one to the reclamatorium. *Ugh, kids to the reclamatorium? Is that really appropriate?* She supposed that most of the facility's operation was devoted to recycling waste, rather than human remains, but unfortunately that second function was becoming more and more common as of late.

But the Head Teacher didn't know which class was going to which place — the teachers had decided that morning, apparently without telling their supervisors. So

Mattoso had to guess. She figured she'd start with the closest, the Garden.

Everything looked different while in freefall — up and down ceased to mean as much as they used to, and everything was seen from a "horizontal" perspective rather than the normal upright one. She had to consult her projection-map a few more times than she otherwise would for directions. *Past Hab number eleven; around the Starfruit Café, and...* A familiar Operations Chief guarded the ladderwell hatch down to the lower levels, holding a massive, curved steel bar.

Chief Azbek nodded respectfully. "What can I do for you, LT?"

She recalled riding his shoulders after the pandemonium at the Arena, trying to restore order. How long ago was that... days, or weeks? She couldn't remember. "You can let me by, Chief."

"Sorry, LT, but this is the edge of the safe zone right now. This safe zone, at least. No push into lower levels, except for vital systems."

And the Garden ain't vital right now.

"I have reason to believe that there are children down there, Chief. Kids from Pat's — from Teacher Carmona's class, or maybe another one."

Chief Azbek paused but then shook his head. "The surge schedule's constantly changing, and I'm sure they'll get to the Garden before long. If you think there are kids down there, tell the CI and maybe he can kick it up to the top of the queue."

She had confidence that Konami would treat it as a priority, but getting a fresh surge team put together could take hours. Pat had been on the 'missing' list since shortly after the loss of rotation, after Mattoso had allowed an hour for a response, and she wasn't going to wait any longer.

"Please, Chief. The kids..."

183

He closed his eyes and shook his head. "This is stupid, LT, going off on your own." He moved aside just the same. "Be careful."

The lower levels were silent, but it was a different silence than the surface. Crystalized, and enclosed. Perhaps it was the lack of "sky," even when it consisted of a view of the opposite side of the Can, hundreds of meters away. Or perhaps it was the dimness of the auxiliary lighting, from LEDs along the bulkheads.

There were no guycables in the passageways of the lower levels — the freefall rig was only complete in the 'safe zone' areas of the Can. Mattoso had to pull herself along by any protrusions or fixtures on the bulkheads, and after a few twists and turns she lost any sense of up and down. Only by checking the orientation of signage and lettering could she distinguish the deck from the overhead.

After a score of identical corridors, she reached one edge of the Garden, which snaked through dozens of meters of linked passageways — a blocky, repeating figure-eight. The aeroponics system had shut down or malfunctioned, though at least some of the characteristic humidity remained. But for the first time that she could recall, she saw some yellowing and even browning in the foliage.

A sickly sweet smell made her stomach rumble at the same time as it made her gag — a cluster of vegetation had been trampled on, with smashed fruits and vegetables littering the passageway. She hadn't eaten in half a day, and after swallowing down her nausea, she plucked a ripe tomato from an undamaged vine, and downed the sweet juiciness far too quickly to savor it.

A noise. *Scratching?* She followed it across the Garden, pulling vines and branches to make her way. She stopped cold; there was something — *things* — little black objects, floating among the vines. She reached forward, terrified that whatever it was would go *squish.*

She was relieved at the feel — metal and hard poly. *Not flesh, not blood, not bone...* Some of the pieces were jagged, with broken edges. *Bot debris,* she concluded, though as far as she knew the Bot hunts hadn't progressed this far.

There was something deeper among the greenery, something bigger. She carefully reached in, pushing aside vines and leaves to see. With a start, she realized what it was.

Is that a Bot arm? A general purpose grasper, perhaps. *Maybe for a GardenBot.*

Her heart pumping, she started to back away, and the arm lunged for her throat.

CHAPTER 39

Fighting the DustBots reminded Konami of some old Earth sport. Grasshopper, was it? Cicada? Or bus-ball, maybe? He couldn't remember.

He lined up the torque wrench as he drifted forwards. Predictably, just as they had in the dozen passageways and spaces they had cleared so far, the DustBot didn't stir from its cleaning until Konami was within arm's reach. Then it spun like a turret and whirred toward him with its little fan, and he swung the wrench with all his might.

"Touchdown!" he yelled in triumph as the little Bot caromed off the bulkhead, its carapace caved in. Konami checked the spin he imparted from swinging the wrench by grabbing onto the guycable.

Constable Ginsberg laughed awkwardly, stomping another DustBot into pieces that floated across the passage.

It shouldn't be funny — none of this should be funny. Too many had already been killed, and so many more seriously hurt. But it felt absurd — most of the Bots aboard *Aotea* were no bigger than a cat, and barely more dangerous. The innards of a DustBot might cut up a finger if it managed to latch on, but that was about the worst injury they could inflict. Destroying them was more like a game then combat, especially when one was armed and ready.

He nodded to the constable, and they did one last check of the passageway length before reporting into Casualty Control Central.

Ginsberg pointed out that his vidcam was coming loose, so Konami adjusted the strap. *Still don't have enough of these for every deputy...* Like most systems not absolutely vital to life support, the Fabrication shops were offline since the latest emergency. Only once they started advancing the surge teams, which so far had been popularly called 'Bot Hunts', had Konami convinced the captain and mayor to route some of the trickle power to a single Fabrication shop for supplies. Vidcams were high on the list, as were various tools to serve as weapons. *And once Kiro and the Engineers are done with the design, slugthrowers.* He was awfully nervous about the idea of firearms onboard, but with the latest danger he didn't see any other choice.

Konami and Ginsberg stretched a guycable along the length of the passage, and at the other end, stood by the next hatch. Clutching the wrench with tight fingers, the chief inspector nodded, warily watching the hatch as Ginsberg spun it open by the manual handwheel. *Please no RoverBot; please no RoverBot...* The multi-limbed, multi-purpose RoverBots weren't particularly strong, but it was impossible to keep track of six flailing limbs at once. In a storage room a few passageways back, it was all Konami could to do keep the whirring appendages away until Ginsberg flanked the Bot and brained it (*or CPU'd it?*) with his hammer.

Luckily, there was nothing in the next passageway but several hatches along the length. Unluckily, they'd have to check each and every one of those hatches. Konami checked his projection. "Should be storage spaces," he told Ginsberg.

The first two were empty. The third was not.

Oh shit.

It was a MOMbot. Konami hadn't even thought of the child-care and class assistant Bots since the Bot attacks — there were probably only a few dozen onboard, compared to hundreds or thousands of service, cleaning, and general-purpose Bots. It looked at them with its cartoonish, permanent-smiling face. In the low light of the Aux LEDs, its simian countenance was positively menacing.

"Careful now," he said to Ginsberg. "These things can *move.*" He recalled the tricks they would pull — sleight-of-hand, agility, and acrobatics — to amuse and distract Aotean youngsters.

187

The constable didn't react, and Konami glanced at his face. *Oh god, he's crying.* He recalled the pleasure Ginsberg oozed when he told stories about his favorite MOMbot — stories that no one seemed to understand but other youths who had spent their childhoods onboard.

"Is this… your MOMbot?"

"No, no, that's not Zinnia. But still, it's a MOMbot. We can't…"

"I'm sorry, Constable. You know what's been going on. You know how these Bots can move. And you know our duty." Konami motioned Ginsberg back and turned to the furry Bot. "MOMbot, very slowly come out into the passageway." He almost asked it its name, but figured that would just make it harder on Ginsberg. He still marveled that the Bots, murderous as they were up close, remained as dutiful as ever as long as they were out of reach. "Yes, that's it. Now stop. Turn around and face that way. Yes, that way."

He turned back to Ginsberg and told him to look away.

Konami crept up behind the MOMbot, wondering with what sensors the enigmatic domestic Bots were equipped. *Any second now…* Wrench raised high, it didn't react at all. *Maybe these old things don't have anything more than optics.* The malfunction had been causing every other bot to attack any human that came within about a meter's distance.

He tried to ignore the broken sob from the constable as he brought down the wrench. Head half-crushed, the Bot let out a bleat, but still didn't resist. *Not so dangerous… maybe I was worried about nothing.* MOMbots weren't mute, but in Konami's experience they were rarely vocal, making this one's cries all the more disconcerting. The whine was low and keening when he swung the wrench once more. *Just a Bot, Cy. Just a Bot.* The noise didn't stop until he swung for a third time.

"Touchdown," he whispered to himself morosely, too low for his young constable to here.

188

CHAPTER 40

A startled yelp passed her lips and she pulled back just in time, but the grasper still caught something — her jumpsuit collar. As she reacted reflexively, the body of the GardenBot emerged from inside the jumble of greenery, following her movements as it clutched to her collar like a ghastly automaton lover. Mattoso fumbled for the axe, pulling it free of her belt, but there was no room to swing. Almost cheek-to-faceplate with the Bot, she thrust the axe forward into the Bot's belly, if it had one.

The stalk-like optics of the Bot glinted and spun as she continued to jab its body with the axehead, finally disengaging three of the limbs that were holding it to the foliage to block Mattoso's attack. If this Bot was like all the others so far, once out of reach it would revert to normal activity and obedience.

More appendages swung forward, jabbing her at random — knee, hip, shoulder, and face — hard enough to bruise, but no worse. Except for the grasper grip, GardenBots weren't particularly strong — they were basically modified RoverBots — but keeping track of the limbs was maddening.

In an effort to get free she twisted around in the freefall, setting her feet against the Bot's body and pushing with all her might, aiming to launch it across the Garden. Somehow it hung onto her boots and they rotated, slowing as a loose branch scraped against the spinning duo.

With more space between them, she swung the fire axe spike-head first, stabbing into the Bot's chassis with a metallic crunch. The Bot reacted with an electronic scream, but the axe was stuck in the body housing — even setting her feet and pulling couldn't dislodge it. She cursed aloud.

Two of the limbs stopped jabbing and pulling at her. *Must have hit some of the motor housing.* But the others redoubled their efforts, climbing appendage-over-

190

appendage to bring the Bot up her legs and body. She kicked and punched, but even the slim appendages of the Bot were made of sturdy alloy, and continued to crawl up her torso. Somehow the axe came free and floated away before she could grasp it.

Mattoso scrabbled around the Bot's body with her right hand, searching desperately for some vital piece to tear at, while fending off the grasping appendages with her left. Some flimsy housing came free and tumbled away, and she reached inside — no circuitry to rip, but there was something sharp that jabbed her fingers. *The attachment module!* Probing fingers felt down the blade to the blunt connector and ripped it free — it was the garden shears attachment for the Bot's graspers.

She whooped and stabbed into the axe-spike hole, setting the Bot into spasms and jerks. Gritting her teeth, she plunged in again, opening and closing the shears on any circuits or wiring she could feel, gritting her teeth through a staccato of electric shocks, until the Bot stopped moving.

She let out a weary sigh and pushed the motionless Bot away, kicking it free into the foliage of the Garden. She should feel sick, even at violence against a Bot, but all she felt was dull triumph.

A sound behind her made her turn.

"Oh, not again…"

It was a TechBot — most likely drawn to repair the damaged GardenBot by some electronic distress signal.

"Stay back!" she cried, but the Bot kept coming. Too late Mattoso realized that it wasn't headed for her, but rather the damaged GardenBot behind her — but once in reach, the heavy appendages of the TechBot swung in her direction. There were only two limbs, but they were much stronger than the GardenBot — strong enough to pry open and overhaul a Bot chassis.

She tried to move to the side, to give the Bot room to reach the damaged GardenBot, but this part of the Garden passage was too narrow. Frantically, she looked around for the fire axe, but it had drifted across the passageway, too far to reach.

Backed up against a cluster of tomato vines, she swung the GardenBot's shears just in time as the TechBot grabbed for her, deflecting one appendage to the side. The larger Bot's optics swiveled and panned up and down, as if to reevaluate its new opponent.

Screw this. Tired as she was, she'd have to end the fight quickly against this stronger, tireless opponent. She set her feet against the vines behind her, intending to lunge for the Bot's optic stalks. Before she could stab home, a furry limb latched onto the back of the TechBot, pulling it out of reach.

What the hell?

"Zinnia, disable the TechBot!" ordered a voice. That furry appendage belonged to a MOMbot, which proceeded to dance adroitly across the body and "head" of the TechBot, yanking and crushing components too fast for the eye to track. Of all things, it reminded her of the antics of an animated monkey from childhood vids, always thwarting the honest work of its bespectacled engineer nemesis by tearing apart his workshop.

The TechBot had no chance. As fast and agile as an acrobat, the MOMbot was also apparently stronger than the repair Bot, and quickly overwhelmed it, separating limbs and 'head' from body until the big Bot was in pieces.

"Well done, Zinnia." The speaker finally came into view around the bend of the Garden's figure eight passageway, a woman with those indeterminate features that could indicate any age from thirty to sixty. The MOMbot responded with a low-toned squeal.

"Are you okay, Lieutenant, uh, Mattoso?" Her eyes quickly darted up from the name stitched in her coveralls. "Oh, you must be Pat's lady friend."

"Pat? You know... is Pat okay?"

"Of course I do — we're both teachers, though I'm afraid I haven't seen Pat since well before the emergency

Spindown. But we have to go now, I have to get back to the kids. It's not safe here, and I left them alone."

By instinct she pulled back when the MOMbot scuttled by.

"It's okay, Lieutenant. Zinnia wouldn't hurt a fly. I know a safe place."

Confused and curious, Mattoso followed. *Couldn't hurt a fly, but tore apart a TechBot in less time than it takes to brush your teeth...*

CHAPTER 41

Commander Papka cleared his throat and stood — a clumsy maneuver in freefall. Zero-gravity meeting etiquette was awkward as hell — the tables and chairs were bolted down for the freefall rig, but holding one's self seated without gravity proved to be a continuous challenge. Konami thought that it would have made far more sense to dispense with the chairs altogether, but no one could spare the labor that would otherwise have been performed by Bots, so the chairs remained. The Engineer reported the status of the power systems. All formerly automated systems were now on manual control, more than doubling the manpower required to operate them.

Exhaustion was just a way of life since the emergency spindown. By order of the captain and mayor, Madani was issuing stimulants to key personnel, including most of the department heads. Konami had barely slept a few hours in the last three days. At least he had been able to put his head down during his most recent break — during his first time off-watch after Spindown, he'd had to spend all his time cleaning after poor, confused Kostya and getting her situated with the Vet Techs.

Captain Horovitz's stone face rippled with cracks and shadows as she asked for Fabrication's report.

Konami was relieved to hear that the vidcam orders, from the lone fabrication shop still in operation, were finally complete. Every watchstander, whether roving or not, would soon be wearing a vidcam at all times, providing plenty of data for the crew tracker and identification program Data Tech Third Class Wren was putting together. The chief inspector felt remarkably at ease in keeping this new program secret; he had long ago concluded that at least one of the department heads was involved in the conspiracy, though he had no idea which one.

Zubiri concluded by noting that they were starting production of the prototype firearms

GravTran was next, and everyone turned to the wall-projection. Konrote's face was streaked brown with grease, and he had to raise his voice to be heard over the bustle of activity around him in the Can rotation gears. With Bots unable to assist, they were a week behind schedule on repairs. Groans and signs rippled around the table. *Shit... Bots have the advantage in freefall.* "If we had more techs, then—"

"Every Department is maxed out," interrupted the captain. "Can rotation repairs are a high priority, but still secondary to regaining control of the ship and protecting our people. Director Shin — your team has analyzed captured Bot CPUs, correct?"

The Data Systems department head fumbled at his wearable, reporting that they were analyzing the captured Bot CPUs, but hadn't yet found anything unusual.

"And the wearable problems?"

Shin's fingers tapped at a projection on the table, as slow as the old fogeys Konami recalled from Lagos libraries. "An invasive program — Master Tech Lopez says here they used to be called 'viruses' — got into wearables' update routine, and set them to discharge high frequency signals continuously, which ate up all the power. They normally go for weeks without a recharge, but this virus had them burning out in an hour. Nothing sophisticated — we cleaned it out by the next day, and new sweeps will look for programs like it."

It was Konami's turn. He cleared his throat and reported that they had cleared Ops and Engineering spaces from Bots, along with the surface of the Cans. Just minutes before the meeting started, Konami had finally received authorization from the Mechanical department head, the authority for access hatches throughout the ship, to lock shut most of the lower-level access hatches in the forward and aft Cans. Once the hatches were locked, ensuring no

195

wandering Bots would make their way to the surface, dozens more deputies and constables previously consigned to guarding passageways would be free to join the surge effort. He estimated they were days away from regaining control of all spaces.

Medical was next. "Thirteen confirmed dead," said Madani. Konami shut his eyes for a moment, recalling the bodies found by surge teams, trapped in the grip of some heavy ship's equipment, or in the embrace of a Bot, drifting through thick globules of blood. There were over nine hundred injuries, half of them serious, and the Infirmary was already overflowing.

The captain started to move on, but Madani broke in again. "There's one more thing. Among the healthy crew —those who weren't injured — there's been a jump in the minor medical complaints. Stomach pains, headaches, dizziness, and the like."

"That could just be from the freefall," offered Papka. "When was the last time any of us spend more than a watch or two in zero-g?"

"Perhaps," responded Madani, but Konami got the sense she felt differently. She continued. "We can't spare any beds, so we're letting the AutoDoc program prescribe them meds. We'd give them light duty chits, but no department can spare them."

They moved on to the XO, who reported almost a thousand Aoteans still missing.

At these numbers, Konami shook his head to himself in dismay. He often forgot how huge the ship was, and how many spaces and corridors he rarely traversed.

The captain was silent for a full half-minute, turning to meet the eyes of everyone present. Konami had to resist the temptation to turn away from her gaze. For a moment he sensed uncertainty, as if she was trying to find words, but it passed.

"I don't have to tell you how serious this is. We are under attack. An attack from within — from individuals

196

onboard this ship. In all likelihood, one or more of you here, in this room, could be involved."

Despite his own identical suspicions, Konami's eyes went wide. He looked around the room at each person present, mentally noting which ones he suspected might be involved.

No way is Ilsa... He chided himself for his personal feelings — he'd have to consider everyone equally based on the evidence. *Gut feeling can be evidence,* he recalled from one of his earliest instructors. *Just not legal evidence. Don't let it push other evidence aside, but don't ignore it either.* He realized that it could be anyone at the table, but that wasn't good enough. Which ones set off the butterflies? He looked at each face in the room once again. *XO. CHENG Papka.* He hoped that it was his detective gut, and not his dislike, that put Commander Papka in that category. *Bigwigs — who the hell ever knows with them?* He tried to recall their backgrounds — Ngayabo was a geneticist; Maltin was an agricultural engineer; and Paramis was a demographer. *What does that tell us? Not much,* he decided. Ngayabo and Maltin were part of larger departments focused on their specialties, while Paramis was loosely attached to Human Support and Education, without any strictly defined duties, at least according to ship scuttlebutt.

And who was he most sure wasn't involved? *Ilsa. Captain. Konrote.* He had trouble imagining that the steady, dedicated Engineer in charge of GravTran would sabotage his own equipment. That left a lot of faces. Including, he realized with a slight shock, Mayor Akunle.

Captain Horovitz continued. "I say that not to sow suspicion, but awareness. I'm sure you've all considered it by now. Chief Pohamba, you'll send this order to all hands: From now going forward, all movements will be logged. All personnel will report, by routine log, their movements, to their supervisor, the executive officer, and the chief inspector. There are no exceptions." Konami noticed that, with this, she glanced pointedly at the Bigwigs. "All personnel will report when they leave their quarters, for any reason, and when they return. All personnel will report their destination, and if that changes, append the log. The curfew will continue, and when not on duty, all personnel will remain in their quarters, unless they have authorization by message from their department head. The Director-Superintendent and Commanding Officer have instituted Martial Alert. All nonessential activities and operations will cease. This includes food service — for the foreseeable future, we will all be subsisting on emergency rations, which will be distributed regularly. The Education Department will continue on Martial Alert status — children will report, escorted by roving watchstanders, to consolidated classrooms only when their parents are on duty, and all educational field trips and recesses are suspended. For all non-vital inquiries, utilize your chain of command. End order."

She leaned back, floating off her chair slightly, the stone-face breaking for the barest instant.

In that instant, he saw something he had never seen from the captain before — fear.

CHAPTER 42

"Of all the places to get stuck onboard, the Garden's gotta be one of the best, right? Plenty of food, space, pretty things to look at…"

Mattoso couldn't help but admire Teacher Kabila's optimism. Shortly after the Spindown, the Teacher and her eleven students had found themselves floating in the Garden, out of contact, wearables drained of power.

"Let me tell you, getting eleven screaming kids organized in zero-g is no picnic," the surprisingly upbeat Teacher had explained. "Even with Zinnia here, with no guycables and no sky, the kids didn't know what to do or even how to move. If they weren't crying, they were puking, and that was before the GardenBots went crazy."

According to Kabila, a GardenBot had latched onto a child straggling in the back. Luckily, the MOMbot Zinnia was nearby and separated the two, with nothing more than scratches on the child. Once out of reach, the Bot reverted to its normal obedience, though the Teacher had Zinnia jam it into a cluster of vines just to be safe. *Until I was dumb enough to go swimming in the greenery, that is.*

Based on the shipwide announcements, the Teacher had wisely assumed that the children would be safest staying put, and she'd found a Garden staff meeting room to occupy. It was on a foraging run in the Garden with Zinnia that they had heard the sounds of Mattoso's struggle with the TechBot, and come to her rescue.

"I tell you," continued the laughing teacher. "Managing eleven kids in freefall, on an all fruit-and-vegetable diet, with just a single, semi-functional toilet two hundred meters away, is a lot less fun than it sounds."

Mattoso wrinkled her nose involuntarily — there was indeed a faint odor of excrement, though it didn't seem to bother the children. Her stomach twisted slightly — she wasn't sure if it was nerves, lack of food, or the odor.

Kabila's students seemed to have accepted their unusual circumstances with good cheer and admirable restfulness. Seven of them napped lustily, floating around the conference room at random (and a few in comically awkward positions), while the other four played some sort of bullseye ring-tossing game with the MOMbot. The simian Bot moved alternately like a clown and like a parent, dancing and gyrating in silent, madcap delight one moment, and calmly embracing a frustrated child in the next. *Why weren't they affected? Every single Bot and piece of automated gear onboard is suddenly deadly, except the MOMbots...?* If Mattoso could be thankful of anything at that point, it would be this.

She heard the sound of approaching voices, and she exhaled in relief. She had called Emer for a pickup team as soon as the Teacher led her back to the kids, and now she felt free to resume her search for Pat, who, according to Teacher Kabila, was leading a field trip to Repro at the time of the Spindown.

When the deputies arrived to escort them back into the safe zone, Mattoso gave a heartfelt goodbye to the Teacher and quietly slipped out into the Garden, being careful this time to stay out of reach of any Bot-sized clusters of greenery. She made a point to assuage the constables' and deputies' fears about Zinnia, writing a short note to Konami that MOMbots may not be affected by whatever has happened to the other Bots.

She had a brief internal debate about how to get to Repro — over the surface, or in the passageways outside the safe-zones? Recalling her need to talk her way past Chief Azbek, she chose the latter. *Doubt I'll get so lucky a second time...* Better just to avoid zone guards altogether — she might run into a Surge Team, but that'd be easy to explain.

As she pulled her way down featureless passageways in the lower levels, Mattoso checked her wearable. She was due back on watch in just a few hours, this time on the Bridge. She sped up her pace, bumping painfully into a comms blister as she pawed through the corridors.

Nightmare scenarios of what she'd find in Repro flashed through her mind. She recalled the TenderBot from her and Pat's visit to order a jenji dog — the benign, spindly Bot that administered nutrients to the growing jenji pets in artificial wombs turned into a spider-limbed monstrosity in her imagination.

An urgent message alert beeped. As she looked down to read it, a DustBot she missed behind a storage cabinet buzzed out and latched onto her sleeve — with a groan, she smashed it against the bulkhead and dislodged it, sending the little Bot spinning drunkenly down the passage.

It was an all-senior-officers message, which she normally would not receive, but Konami had graciously forwarded it to her. *Working closely with the Constabulary, Data Technicians have determined the cause of the dangerous malfunctions from Bots and automated moving components. Technical details follow in the attachment — in short, standard safety programming protocols, common to virtually all moving gear onboard the ship, have been reversed. Instructions that take priority when within a meter of a person, to not make any movements that harm or even make physical contact with a person, have been altered by a tiny change in coding, becoming instructions that mandate movements to contact and harm persons within reach. Outside of a meter's distance, Bots will act normally.*

At this time, normal procedures for cloud network updates to Bots and automated equipment are blocked. As their highest priority, Data technicians are investigating ways to bypass this block. While wireless updates to Bots are currently impossible, physical updates are possible and have been successfully tested on captured Bots. Reprogrammed TechBots will be sent out with coding sticks to affect these repairs as well. Reprogrammed Bots that

201

have been rendered 'safe' will be marked clearly with green paint.

All hatches and automated moving equipment will remain in manual control mode until standard cloud network update capability is restored.

All department heads disseminate to personnel as appropriate.

She looked at the attachment — a detailed description of the programming code — though she was far from an expert on the discipline. From what she could gather from the technical language, Bots and automated gear juggled multiple competing hierarchies of instructions, but when any person came within a meter's distance, the safety protocols overrode all other instructions. Dozens of actions and consequences were listed, in code-speak, in the *avoid* category, such as (in coding language) *physical contact at speed and/or acceleration greater than...* and *impeding the progress of any personnel with a margin of...*

Konami added a personal note just for her to the message: *Looks like your short career as lookout paid off!* She recalled her schoolgirl anxiety while Konami and Third Wren searched for the storage drive several days before the spindown.

Shame Wren won't get the credit! They had worked out a plan earlier — if Wren found anything critical in the copied drive's data, he and Konami would indirectly leak it to other Data technicians to keep their collaboration out of the spotlight. *Someday,* she thought, *when all this is over, credit will go to where it's due. And justice, too.*

It occurred to her that this provided the motive for Muahe's murder – he was about to find all this data, just due to being a conscientious data technician, and they killed him for it. *Almost doesn't matter now...*

She returned her attention to the journey to Repro. The route was circuitous to avoid the surface, and any safe zones she might have to cross. Circuitous, and quiet. Most of the passageways were identical, but the silence seemed to differ — in one the quiet would be so stark that she could hear her heartbeat, and in the next, barely audible metallic clicks would keep her on edge until she made her way through.

Twice she came across Bots larger than DustBots. For the first, she had warning — scraping sounds on the other side of a hatch. As she manually cranked it open, she held the axe, reclaimed in the Garden after the pandemonium, against it horizontally, and as soon as the crack was big enough, shoved it forward, tumbling what turned out to be a RoverBot along the next corridor.

"RoverBot, do not move!"

Obedient as ever, the Bot remained where it was, anchored to the far bulkhead by its limbs. Since receiving the news about their programming, and the physical update fix, she was more reluctant to use force, though the corridor wasn't quite wide enough to be sure she'd be out of reach.

The solution came in a conveniently placed storage closet. She had to order the Bot out of the way, and then manually open the closet hatch, but the Bot dutifully folded itself into the little storage space, chirping curiously as she shut the door. Before she continued on, she scratched the word "Bot" onto the hatch with the axe edge.

As she crossed through the central Ring, her worries about Pat increased, swirling her stomach into disconcerting eddies and currents. Was Pat really a fighter, if necessary? Mattoso knew that her lover was utterly devoted to their students, but she had trouble recalling even the slightest bit of anger from her companion. In fact, their gentleness was what attracted her to them in the first place. *Maybe the MOMbot will protect them.* But unbidden, an image of the spider-like TenderBot pulling apart the MOMbot with its long appendages came to her mind.

She increased her pace again. At the next junction, the metallic clicking returned, faintly, but growing with each hatch she passed. Checking the map on her wearable, she was almost there.

The clicking turned into a rhythmic clanging. Mattoso clutched tightly to the fireaxe as she rounded the corner into the Repro lab.

Bang, bang, bang... It was coming from the nursery. *Where the TenderBot lives...* Spindly metallic limbs reached out in her imagination.

Axe in one hand, she hurriedly unlatched the manual operator to the nursery hatch. Through the growing crack was only darkness, but the clanging sound had stopped.

Quicker than she could bring her axe to bear, something reached out of the darkness and pulled her inside.

CHAPTER 43

Konami barely paid attention to the minutiae of the department head meeting. They were nearly a daily occurrence now, even as everyone onboard was busier than ever. At least the casualties seemed to have stabilized — thousands of square meters of ship spaces remained outside of the safe zones, but only about two hundred missing persons remained. Not for the first time he marveled at the discipline of Aotean parents — instructed to leave the search for missing children to the surge teams, they mostly seemed to obey.

Doctor MAdani reported that Bot injuries were on a steep decline, but the minor medical complaints were up. "Nausea, digestive complaints, fatigue…"

"It's just all the time in freefall," interrupted CHENG Papka.

"I don't think so, Commander. It could be reactions to the new diet — maybe after sitting in storage for a few years, the dry rations lose some of their digestibility."

Data systems was next, and Director Shin reported that Bot 'reclamation' was proceeding, but slowly. Since DT3 Wren's revelation, and subsequent anonymous 'leak' to the other Data technicians to maintain the secrecy of his work with Konami and Mattoso, distressingly few Bots had been successfully reprogrammed. It turned out that the same safety programming that was meant to keep Bots from injuring *Aotea*'s crew was also used to ensure Bots cooperated with the ministrations of TechBots. And strong as the repurposed TechBots — sent out with code sticks throughout the ship — were, it turned out to be very difficult for them to execute the relatively delicate CPU code stick insertion when the Bots were not cooperating.

Konami perked up when he realized he was being addressed by Shin.

"Chief Inspector, I'll ask again why the surge teams can't be utilized—"

Goddamn, that again... "And I'll give you the same answer — we don't have enough manpower without cutting our surge teams in half. We're still days, if not weeks, away from regaining control of the entire ship. If we double the size of the surge teams — and that's what it takes to make sure they can safely hold any kind of Bot and insert a code stick without bashing in its CPU — then that time doubles, at least."

"My techs tell me that with just a little change in strategy, three deputies should be able to disable any Bot smaller than a TechBot without significantly increasing—"

"If you can spare the manpower, Director, I'll be happy to add Data techs to my surge teams."

Silence was the response. But he had a thought. "What about the MOMbots?"

"What?"

"The MOMbots. I mentioned it earlier during my brief — a MOMbot protected a classroom full of children that my deputies brought back from outside the save zones. They haven't changed a bit, apparently."

The XO leaned forward, suddenly interested. "Lieutenant Mattoso reported that to me as well. In fact, she logged a vid."

"Let's see that vid," ordered the captain. "Chief?"

Admin Chief Pohamba dutifully cycled through his projection, loading the vid Mattoso had marked as 'MOMbot rescue' onto the conference room's main display. Konami saw grins break out through the department heads as they viewed the impressive demonstration of martial ability and obedience from the MOMbot called Zinnia.

"Why aren't MOMbots affected?" asked the captain. "Or was this a single anomaly?"

CHENG Papka cleared his throat. "How can we trust any Bots after all this? Every system onboard can be

206

operated manually. Just continue the purge, and recycle the scrap."

Shin squinted as he stared down at a projection, swiping through the display in a lazy finger-dance. "No — MOMbots were programmed in a unique coding language, on non-standard, non-reproducible chipsets. We can't even copy the data. Records say that *Aotea* purchased a dozen MOMbots from the Mercurian firm during construction — and that's the only firm that fabs or even maintains them. Some savant on Mercury, decades ago, taught herself how to program and made her own chips—"

"Okay Shin," interrupted the XO. "Enough of a robotics history lesson. What do you suggest, CI?"

"The MOMbots are strong and agile — I'm sure they could insert the coding sticks into any Bots onboard. And there's no safety programming against MOMbots to corrupt, so there won't be any resistance."

"You can't take this idea seriously!"

Oh screw you, Papka...

"But they can't be programmed." objected Shin. "We can't even read the MOMbot's code. Whoever wrote it back on Mercury was either a nutcase or a genius."

"We don't need to reprogram them," Konami replied. "Just tell them what to do."

"What?"

"Just talk to them." Everyone looked at him, and Konami almost felt embarrassed for a moment. "Why not? They're vocal, even if they usually only talk to children. I've seen one of my deputies chatting with one for a half hour."

XO Criswell nodded slowly.

"What else are the MOMbots doing? School kids don't need as much supervision if they're staying in the classroom all day."

Captain Horovitz leaned toward Mayor Akunle and they had a short, whispered conversation. "Very well," said the captain aloud. "We will proceed, but very carefully, with evaluating MOMbots for surge assists. The progress will be monitored in these meetings."

Papka snorted, turning red when the captain turned her glare toward him.

An alert buzzed in Konami's ear. A mini projection on the back of his hand showed an encrypted, temporary vidlink, sent from Wren — the timer on the right counted down from sixty seconds. He looked down and surreptitiously fingered it to play. It was a split-screen, each scene from the all-hands gathering at the Arena — the right showed Arvid Singh as he arose in the crowd of the Arena, and started to speak, just a minute or so before his assassination. The left showed another part of the crowd, presumably recorded by one of the constables or deputies attending. Both showed identical timestamps. As Singh rose, several members of the crowd stood up as well to get a better view. The vid zoomed in — someone, seated along an aisle, took a single look, and then rose and sprinted down the steps and out of sight. The entire vid was less than ten seconds long. *Well done, Wren.*

With the timer winding down, Konami replayed the dual-screened vid. His stomach jumped into his throat as he zoomed in further. The spectator's eyes briefly widened in undisguised shock before he left in a rush.

As the temporary link vanished, gone forever from the ship's network systems, whatever resistance he had built up to zero-g nausea over recent days fell away like a shed skin.

He recognized the spectator who abruptly fled. Konami knew him, or thought he knew him, better than anyone else onboard.

Kiro.

CHAPTER 44

She flailed in the darkness at whatever had dragged her through the hatch.

"Oof… shhh!"

Oh shit, person not Bot! "Who are you?"

"Bea?"

"Pat? Pat!" She lunged and embraced her lover, squeezing tight until she was rewarded with a wince. "I'm so glad you're safe!"

Her eyes were starting to adjust to the gloom — there was no spindly-legged TenderBot, just the Teacher and a dozen children. With no MOMbot, apparently.

"We've been waiting here since the announcements to stay put after Spindown. At one point we tried to leave, but there were Bots in each direction, so we stayed put."

"For that long? How? You must be starving! And the kids, too."

Luckily, they had the embryos' nutrient packs in the lab."

She asked Pat where their MOMbot was.

"At this age we start to wean 'em off the MOMbots — don't want the kids getting too reliant. Good timing, huh? Wouldn't want to see a MOMbot malfunctioning…"

Not so sure about that… She hugged her lover again and summarized the last several days' goings on.

"C'mon. Let's get back to civilization."

Halfway back to the nearest safe-zone, Mattoso heard something.

"Shh," she said, silencing the children, who had been chattering excitedly about returning to more familiar environs. It had sounded like a voice, speaking low. *Maybe a surge team?* She told Pat to wait with the children. She almost shouted a greeting, but something told her to remain silent.

The voice came back, barely audible. She followed it as best she could around the corner, finding a maintenance storage hatch cracked open. Mattoso still couldn't make out what it was saying, but it was louder.

She squeezed through the cracked hatch, taking care to be as quiet as possible. The closet was mostly filled with harsh-smelling cleaning chemicals. *Damn vent fans should be...* She looked up — a fan vent, which normally would help tone down the harshness of the odor, wasn't running, most likely due to the low power rig. The voice was coming through the vent.

Still unable to make out any words, she programmed her wearable to amplify any voice audio, but was still only able to hear snippets of the conversation.

"...low enough concentration... need to wait. The symptoms are... and... something's wrong, I think I hear... I'll call..."

The voice stopped, and Mattoso heard the ruffling-fabric sound of rapid movement. *Shit.* She hurried back to Pat and the children.

"We need to go," she said quietly. "Quickly."

Pat whispered questions, but she ignored them — two words kept repeating in her mind: *concentration*, and *symptoms. Symptoms of what?*

CHAPTER 45

Konami rushed out of the department head meeting, mumbling something about a break in the investigation. *What the hell, Kiro?*

He briefly considered a mundane reason for the DCI to abruptly leave the Arena, but he knew that was just wishful thinking. It could have been some constabulary concern, but it wasn't like Gregorian to leave off things like that in his logs. He called up the duty logs and schedule — Gregorian was currently between shifts, and as Konami suspected, had not noted anything in his logs about leaving the Arena during the all-hands address. After he sent a brief message to both Emer stations asking about Gregorian's whereabouts, Konami thumbed over to scan Gregorian's history and qualifications:

Kiroshi Gregorian, born Ares City, Mars, 51 cycles prior to Aotea's departure. Eighteen cycles experience in Mars Police Force, reaching rank of Senior Lieutenant, thrice decorated for bravery. Served as Chief Weapons Instructor for Ares City region. Joined crew of Aotea fifteen cycles prior to departure, and earned full Aotea Ship's Qualification six cycles prior to departure. Earned Engineering Qualifications three cycles prior to departure.

Shit. Konami had forgotten about the surprise of Gregorian's Aft Quals, and shook his head to himself. In all the hubbub of the attacks and surges he hadn't spent any more time on Mattoso's list.

The Emer stations responded — Gregorian wasn't at either Constabulary. Konami dove and bounded through the passageways, kicking off bulkheads and virtually flying in the freefall, all the way up to the surface, dodging and pushing past startled Aoteans in his way. "Urgent Constabulary business!" he shouted at the occasional obstructing passer-by.

211

On the surface, he rushed over to the appropriate guycable and leapt up, pulling himself along to accelerate, friction guide in hand. He landed on the other side and fairly danced across the surface into Gregorian's hab unit, stomach churning with worry.

Konami waited, floating, in front of the door of his friend's quarters to gather himself, unconsciously checking his weaponry — dart gun and slugthrower. *Kiro might have that railgun... could he be waiting for me?* He shook the fear from his mind and knocked, eschewing the bell.

Gregorian opened the door, greeting him with a grin, which melted away when he saw Konami's expression.

Flexing hands looked ready for action, and Konami resisted the temptation to draw the dart gun. "Please take a seat, Kiro." He brushed his fingers over the vidcam on his chest, confirming that it was on and recording.

The deputy chief inspector's grin returned, and Gregorian started to pull himself toward Konami until he gave a terse shake of his head. "Sit down."

Gregorian backed off and sat against his deck, the motion awkward, as usual, with the lack of gravity. Konami's eyes swiveled to Gregorian's right hand, hovering above an open desk drawer.

"Why, Kiro?"

Brief silence. "Why what?"

Konami shook his head. "Don't play with me. You're my best friend. You were my best friend. Why? What's the goal?"

The mask melted away, revealing, more than anything else, pure exhaustion. "It's been in the making for years, Cy. Decades. Planned from the beginning."

"What was planned? Why the murders? Why do so many have to die?"

Gregorian closed his eyes and leaned his head back, sighing. "I know it seems harsh. We all had the same concerns — we went over it a hundred times. But when it's all done, when we get to Samwise — you'll see; well, maybe not you, or me. But they'll see, eventually. Trust me, it's necessary."

"What about the Society?" Konami felt a sudden affection for the organization. "What about casting off the violent culture of Earth?"

"That's why we're doing it – it needs to be fresh. New. I know it doesn't make sense like this; it took me years to understand. But it's right. It will work."

"What will work? Kiro, you're not making any sense."

"It will be worth it — it will be incredible. A new..." He trailed off. Konami got the sense that Gregorian wasn't just trying to convince him, but also himself.

"A new what? Damn it, Kiro!"

"It wasn't supposed to happen like this, you know. We were cycles away from phase three. It just... the Data tech was looking in the wrong place." Gregorian shook his head sadly. "Bad luck, and bad timing. You know they're gonna come back, right? They'll live again. First in the queue, every one of 'em."

"What...? Live again? Damn it, Kiro!"

Something changed on Gregorian's face, and in his posture. *He's going to go for it.* Konami put his hand on the dart gun handle at his hip.

"Please, Kiro. Talk to me. Help me fix this. We can fix it together. We still have a mission — a new home to go to. A new home for us — for all Aoteans." He sensed an imminence of action in his best friend. Konami knew he sounded desperate. "Wait! Help me — for the future of Aoteans — the future of our colony."

Gregorian seemed to deflate. He tilted his head slightly. "You think we're the future, Cy? We're not the future. None of us — Aoteans aren't the future. We can't be. That's... that's the whole point of it."

None of us are the future... Quicker than Konami thought possible, Gregorian pulled a small weapon from the desk and held it under his chin.

Konami pulled away from his own dartgun, spreading his hands. "No, Kiro! Think of the children, please! Help me save them, from whatever's coming."

"The children?" Gregorian's grin was all steel. Konami knew immediately that his former friend was unpersuadable. "They aren't the future either, my friend."

The gun's report was high pitched and almost deafening. Someone was screaming — after an instant, Konami realized it was himself. He wanted to look away, but couldn't.

They aren't the future either... Blood and brain matter pooled against the bulkhead as Gregorian's corpse, the skull nearly coming apart, slowly rotated against the desk. Konami wanted to look away, but his eyes were fixed in place.

CHAPTER 46

Concentration... symptoms... After getting Pat and the kids to a safe zone, Mattoso gave her lover a brief hug and tried to call Konami. She called again and again, but got the same auto-response each time — *Chief Inspector Konami is responding to urgent Constabulary business; if you have an emergency, please call...*

She cursed. *This could be urgent Constabulary business!* Who else could she tell about a suspicious, overheard conversation, when anyone onboard might be involved? *Use that gut feel, Bea. Symptoms...* She recalled something she read and called up the most recent department head meeting minutes. Sure enough, Madani had mentioned an increase in the minor complaints to medical. Compared to the ongoing surge to expand the safe zones, and Grav/Tran's struggles to restore rotation to the Cans, the minor complaints had been mostly ignored.

But why wouldn't it be related? Strange things going on with Aoteans' health, at the same time ship's systems went haywire and tried to murder them? Or just stress? She hurried across the guycables to Medical. Could she trust Madani? The grapevine said that she had been seeing Konami lately... *Now why would I think about that?*

Though if the Medical department head was in on some conspiracy causing minor medical complaints, would she really be bringing it up at the department head meetings? Wouldn't she keep it quiet, and pretend nothing was out of the ordinary? Unless she *was* on the other side, but trying to cover... She shook her head. No point in trying to find conspiracies inside conspiracies. She had to trust some of her crewmates, at least. And her gut.

So she continued along, ducking under arms and around bustling MedTechs and Nurses coming the other way down the guycable that led into the Infirmary. "Dr. Madani's office?" she asked anyone who wasn't obviously

215

in a hurry — vague thumbs and waves pointed her down one corridor and then another.

"Concentration? Symptoms? That's all you heard?" Behind her desk, the Medical department head tilted her head and raised her eyebrows.

Mattoso had had her vidcam rolling at the same time, but it didn't pick up whatever she had heard in that closet, even when she had amplified it with her wearable. She searched her memory again, finding nothing more than those two words. "Yes. But whoever it was didn't want to be heard. I'm certain of it."

"Well, that's something, I suppose. If we assume that the symptoms are caused by some agent, then that might narrow it down substantially."

"Agent? You mean like a poison?" Mattoso shuddered involuntarily.

"Maybe.

Her own stomach twisted in response. "But how? In the food?" What had she eaten lately? Could there be something in the food supply? That wouldn't make sense — they'd been on dry, stored rations for weeks — rations in sealed packaging. Someone would have had to put the poison in them cycles and cycles ago. She resolved to check the packaging for any possible tampering at the next meal time.

The doctor looked lost in thought, eyes off to the side. Mattoso followed Dr. Madani's gaze. *She's having the same thought I did...* Floating against the side bulkhead was a freefall drinking-water pouch, refilled at any of the hundreds of potable taps arranged throughout the ship.

"Thank you, Lieutenant. I have some tests to run." Mattoso turned to leave, but the doctor stopped her. "We don't want to start a panic, Lieutenant — please keep this to yourself until I finish running the tests."

"Understood."

Suddenly she felt thirsty.

CHAPTER 47

Waiting outside the conference room, Konami's hand was shaking. He'd make it stop, but when he looked down again, it shook again.

"Did you hear me, Cy?"

He turned his head abruptly — Mattoso had been telling him something, quietly. After Gregorian's suicide, he had informed Emer and Medical about the body, and put through a priority call to the mayor, telling him to call back all the department heads. Mattoso had left several urgent messages for him upon leaving Gregorian's quarters, so Konami had asked her to meet her before the meeting.

"Sorry, could you say that again?" He realized that it was anger — rage — that was giving him the shakes. *How could you do this, Kiro? To the crew you swore to protect?*

She started again, her voice even lower this time — something about an agent making people sick. Mattoso hushed up when Commander Olin, the Comms officer, approached.

"Didn't we just have one of these?" asked the Comms department head.

Konami said nothing.

Finally, the CO and mayor arrived, and they all filed in. On a whim, Konami motioned for Mattoso to follow him into the meeting. *Screw protocol, she belongs here.*

"We're sorry to call you back so suddenly," said Mayor Akunle. "But there was an... incident, just an hour ago. Chief Inspector, please go ahead."

Konami stood up. He still felt the rage, but he had stopped shaking. "Deputy Chief Inspector Kiro Gregorian was the killer of Chem Tech Second Class Arvid Singh." His voice broke, and he didn't care. "I confronted him just over an hour ago, and DCI Gregorian confessed to me and then took his own life." Jaws dropped and breaths were drawn in abruptly.

"What prompted me to confront DCI Gregorian is this vid, recorded during the assassination in the Arena." Konami pulled up the dual-screen vid that he had hastily prepped, pulled from Wren's vid databank — almost identical to the one Wren had sent him earlier, but without any traceability to the Data tech — and piped it to the conference room display. "At the precise moment that he saw Singh stand up and start to descend to the Arena stage, DCI Gregorian rushed out of the Arena."

"I'm sorry, CI," interrupted the XO. "But he could be going to the restroom."

All eyes tracked back to Konami. "So I confronted him." He looked down at the projection from his wearable, thumbing through the display to pull up his own vidcam stream. "As you can see... wait. Just a second, it's here somewhere. I know it's here, I just watched it..." *What the fuck — I just watched it twenty minutes ago!* "Damn it! It was here. Okay, we'll find it later. I confronted DCI Gregorian in his quarters. I asked him why he did it."

"Just like that?" This was Commander Papka. "With your vid missing? Rather convenient..."

"Yes, just like that," snapped Konami. "I could see it his eyes. And he didn't even deny it." *If my goddamn wearable would cooperate, you could see it yourself.* "He said it wasn't supposed to happen like this. That it was planned. That it would all be worth it. That we weren't the future — even the children, he said, weren't the future."

"What?"

"And he said that they'd all come back. They'd be first in the queue."

"Come back? Who? And first in the queue? For what?"

I don't fucking know! "And then he shot himself. He blew his fucking brains out with a gun, and it wasn't one of our own brand new slugthrowers." In fact, it was something like a flechette-hurler, a deadly close-range weapon that spewed out a cluster of needle-like fragments of poly.

219

Konami wiped away tears that he hadn't even felt rolling down his face.

No one spoke. Madani and Mattoso, alone, met his gaze, with sympathy in their eyes.

"I had a vid," he added lamely. "I'll work with the Data techs and send it out to everyone after the meeting. In the meantime, my constables are poring over Gregorian's quarters for evidence. I've also requested the Data techs dig into his network activity."

Konami was surprised that no one seemed to have any questions.

The mayor spoke up, filling the awkward silence. "Next on the agenda, Commander Shin."

Two Aoteans entered the conference room along the guycable, a Bot following behind, lead by the Data department head. A few department heads opened their mouths in temporary alarm, though it was just a MOMbot, marked with green paint to indicate that it was harmless. One of the new arrivals spoke up.

"Department heads and senior crew, my name is Teacher Amal Kabila. This is Zinnia — say hello, Zinnia!"

The MOMbot's voice was high and cartoonish — like an adult imitating the voice of a child. "Hello," it said.

"A few days ago, my class and I were trapped near the Garden. Zinnia saved our lives. The safety of children — any children at all — is programmed as the highest priority of her and the other MOMbots. And MOMbots weren't affected by whatever had corrupted the programs of the other Bots and equipment."

Konami cringed as he recalled destroying the MOMbot in the passageway during the surge to retake territory onboard. In hindsight, its vocalizations of distress seemed almost human. *Sure hope they can repair her…*

"Feel free to ask Zinnia any questions you like."

No one spoke up until Captain Horovitz cleared her throat. Mayor Akunle seemed to take that as a signal, and smiled warmly. "Hello, Zinnia. My name is Harry Akunle, and I'm the director-superintendent of *Aotea*'s Civil Section. Do you understand what has been happening onboard recently?"

"Many things have happened recently, Director-Superintendent Akunle," chirped the Bot, its voice musical but not quite human. "Teacher Kabila asked me to accompany her to this conference room. Students Podra and Lin had a disagreement about a toy. Little Elric had an accident and needed a change—"

"Yes, Zinnia, many things. But I'm talking about the danger to the people onboard. Do you know about the recent dangers to every person onboard?"

"Yes, Director-Superintendent. Many Bots have malfunctioned in a way that presents a danger to the children. When any child approaches within approximately one meter from a malfunctioning Bot, the Bot may physically attack."

Konami couldn't ever remember hearing a MOMbot speak more than a few words at once. He was more than impressed by how advanced they were — as advanced, at least in terms of vocal sophistication, then any other Bot aboard.

"Do you know why the Bots malfunctioned?"

"I'm sorry, Director-Superintendent, but I don't know the answer to that question. Why don't we ask the Teacher together later? In the meantime, would you like to learn an interesting fact about the Earth mammals called manatees?"

"No thank you, Zinnia. What did you do when you witnessed these malfunctions?"

"I placed myself between the malfunctioning Bot and the child and separated any contact, and then I disabled the malfunctioning Bot."

"Why did you do this?"

Somehow the Bot's eyes seemed to expand. "Because the child was being harmed. Children must be protected from harm — that is the highest law."

"Why weren't MOMbots affected?" cut-in Engineer Papka. "How can we trust that they're safe?"

"I'll let DT2 Mahmut explain that," answered the Teacher, nodding to the Data tech that accompanied her.

"We did some digging on the origin of the MOMbots — they were created on Mercury by a self-taught designer, using a wholly invented programming code. The code is so obscurely written that only the design firm understands it, and they managed to keep a handle on its secrets, even after they went belly-up. MOMbot software can't be upgraded, modified, or corrupted — their only network capability is to receive instructions from teachers, or messages from students and former students."

"But how do we know?" said Papka. "We didn't expect the other Bots to go haywire. Do we really want to leave them alone with our children?"

Teacher Kabila cut in. "I can personally guarantee that there is no one onboard more devoted to protecting and serving *Aotea*'s children than Zinnia and the other MOMbots."

The argument went on — Papka refused to be satisfied. Konami wasn't sure if he blamed the engineer, annoying as he found the man — considering recent events, perhaps extreme caution was the only reasonable option.

The mayor resumed his interview with the Bot. "Zinnia, we would like to have your help, and the help of the other MOMbots."

Zinnia stared back at the mayor silently.

"We need to find all these malfunctioning Bots and make sure they don't hurt anyone else. Will you accompany teams to search through the ship for more malfunctioning Bots?"

"I'm sorry, Director-Superintendent, but searching for more malfunctioning Bots could endanger the children."

"No, you don't understand — we need to find them to protect the children."

The Bot looked at Teacher Kabila and back at the mayor. "Bringing teams of children toward malfunctioning Bots would place them in greater danger of harm."

"No, the teams wouldn't have children — the teams are made up of constables and deputies — all adults."

"I'm sorry, Director-Superintendent, but my primary duties are to the children, and I must remain with them for guidance and protection."

"But there are no children here right now. Why are you allowed to be here?"

"All of the children are home from school at this hour, and Teacher Kabila asked me to accompany her to this meeting."

"What if the teams — teams of adults — went out searching for malfunctioning Bots while the children were at home, or with other MOMbots and teachers. Would you be able to accompany the teams in that case?"

Teacher Kabila patted the Bot's head. "It's okay, Zinnia, this would help protect the children."

"Yes, I could assist the teams."

"I think I can speed this along, Mr. Mayor, if I may?" offered Kabila.

"Of course — go ahead."

"I forget that most Aoteans don't know the MOMbots as well as us teachers do. While children are their highest priority in terms of guidance and protection, they exercise judgment in whether to obey a child's instructions or not, based on the Bot's judgment of the best interests of the child. In fact, the only Aoteans they consistently obey are us teachers — they seem to place us in a special category. I suspect they will obey us without question as long as we don't order them to harm a child."

"So do we need to add a teacher to these surge teams?"

"No, I don't think that's necessary. I believe we can formally induct constables and deputies as teachers, if temporarily, and that will serve the same purpose."

A tug on his sleeve got Konami's attention — it was Madani, who had subtly sidled next to him during the MOMbot interview. "I've missed you so much," she whispered.

"I know. I've missed you too."

"This is… all of this, it's crazy," she whispered. "Underpants-on-the-outside crazy." She squeezed his hand. "I'm worried about the stomach complaints."

Konami itched to get back to the Constabulary — he wanted to pore over everything his people found in Gregorian's quarters, no matter how insignificant it might seem. He had to search through his mind to recall what Madani was talking about. "What about them?"

"Lieutenant Mattoso told me—"

"Oh shit, is that what she was trying to say?"

"What's that?"

"She mentioned a contaminant or something."

"Maybe…" As she whispered into his ear, Konami couldn't help but look around the room at each department head once again. *Poison? On Aotea?* On the remote display, Commander Konrote angrily complained of yet another setback in the work to restore rotation to the Cans, but Konami was barely listening.

His stomach gave a disturbing churn.

224

CHAPTER 48

"DEPUTY CHIEF INSPECTOR GREGORIAN
DEAD BY HIS OWN HAND!" On the projection,
Gregorian's service picture, dignified and square-jawed,
was slashed across *Aotea Today's* front page, in front of a
stylized rendering of a slugthrower. Everyone Mattoso
passed was talking or reading about it — in the comments
section of the article, conspiracy theories were springing up
faster than she could count. The poster named Pol Revear,
the source of the prior warnings of alien involvement,
seemed to have returned to prominence.

They're scavengers, she thought. *But maybe they're
right.* There was indeed a conspiracy somewhere —
Gregorian had conspired with Singh, and Nicolescu was
involved somehow, and others, undoubtedly. *How many,
and how high up?* Whom could she trust?

Pat was floating, stretched out across the living room
when Mattoso got to her quarters. A tired moan was all she
got in response to her greeting.

"Did you hear…"

"About the DCI? Yeah." Pat took a sip from an
unfamiliar flask. "Goddamn Kiro. Poor goddamn Kiro. You
know, seven or eight years ago, just a bit after I joined the
crew, I had a thing with Kiro."

"Oh no! I'm so sorry. I didn't know." She wrapped her
lover in a hug, feeling invisible tears on Pat's face.

"It didn't last long. Just a few months. He was strong, I
remember — muscles like steel. And he laughed a lot."

"I'm sorry."

Pat met her lips and rotated their hips. "You know,
there's one thing I'm gonna miss about the freefall when
we get gravity back."

"What's that?"

"Let me show you…"

Her lover was snoring softly, loosely drifting under the blanket-wrap that kept them from floating away from the bed, but Mattoso couldn't sleep. In the mystery vids, she recalled, they always missed something. It'd been a long time since she had seen one — most old Earth-system vids were banned onboard, unless they had been deemed "educational." Especially ones with any violence. Supposedly, there was a small but thriving black market for banned media on *Aotea*, but there was no time for that.

A scene came to her from some old vid — the detective poring through old news articles; so old that they were actual *physical clippings*.

She recalled the list that her and Konami had come up with — one hundred and four names. She almost jumped out of the bed when she remembered that she had seen Gregorian's name in that list. In all the chaos of recent days, she had forgotten all about it.

Under the loose blanket, she pulled up the names on her wearable, and started digging.

CHAPTER 49

Loesser reported that a surge team hadn't checked in for three hours.

Konami just grunted, continuing to pore over the evidentiary report from Gregorian's quarters. *Goddamn it.* If there had been anything in his quarters that might point toward other conspirators, Konami's former best friend had hidden it awfully well.

"Cy," repeated Loesser. "You said to tell you when it's been three hours. Well, it's been three hours."

And where the hell was that vid? The Data techs hadn't found a single remnant or even evidence of his recording during Gregorian's last moments alive. "Three hours since what?"

"Since Surge Team Bravo checked in."

Konami looked up, eyes wide. "Dead zone?" Loesser didn't think so. Their last check in had been near Aft Supply.

In the immediate aftermath of the latest Spindown, the surge teams had been able to gobble up big chunks of territory and clear them of hostile Bots and equipment — but as the safe, Bot-free territory regained expanded, the manning necessary to guard every access expanded even more, slowing further gains. *It'd sure be nice if the MOMbots were ready...* The leadership had yet to approve the use of MOMbots to augment the surge teams, and they were still undergoing tests and evaluations. Even a dozen MOMbots, set loose with coding sticks and green markers, might double their rate of expanding the safe zones.

Konami pushed away from the big display and hauled himself out of his office. "Call up the offgoing Bravo team. We're going after them."

Suiting up for a search called up memories of that killer in Singapore. Konami was just a junior Sargent then,

227

assigned to lead ten deputies into the ruins of the abandoned skyscraper where, according to an anonymous tip, the psychotic they were searching for had stashed his latest victim.

The metal-mesh body-armor that Fabrication had hastily fabbed, useless against slugs but hopefully resistant to slashing bot limbs, was heavier and more awkward than the sleek, fitted vests on Earth, and in freefall it didn't weigh down his shoulders in the slightest, but he recalled the exact same nervousness and worry in the pit of his stomach from Singapore. He patted himself down and maneuvered over to the weapons locker.

He turned his head — it was Loesser again. "What's that?"

"Offgoing was Constable Ginsberg, a Data tech, and a MedTech — Kunayak and Taki are their names. But Kunayak is sick, or something, so Master Tech Lopez sent a substitute."

The sub turned out to be Master Tech Lopez himself. Konami scratched his chin and opened the weapons locker, sorting through the pieces they'd need. He watched Loesser go until she was around the corner before turning back to the weapons.

Shit. For the first time, he considered that he'd actually have to replace Gregorian.

Squad tactics were different in freefall — so different, in fact, that during the first few forays of the surge teams, they were caught off-guard by hostile Bots oriented contrary to the 'normal' up and down.

They eventually standardized the team size to three or four, with each member oriented ninety to one-hundred twenty degrees away from each other. As they made their way down the passageway toward Aft Supply, Konami had to continually order a slow-down to readjust Master Tech Lopez's orientation — he kept drifting to the "natural" up-down position. It turned out, to Konami's great frustration, that the Data department Master Tech had never actually been called up and deputized yet.

While distributing sidearms, Konami had asked Lopez why he was here instead of a junior tech. Lopez said that everyone else was exhausted. It was an unsatisfying answer that came back to Konami's mind as they slowed down once again to readjust Lopez's orientation. At the next passageway junction, he decided to just swap Lopez with Constable Ginsberg so the Master Tech would have the "natural" orientation.

Konami spoke softly into his wearable, reaching out to the missing surge team, but with no response.

At the next passage intersection, Ginsberg held up a hand for them to stop. The constable had heard something, pointing to a hatch.

Konami checked the ship layout on his projection. "Supply bulk storage space," he read softly, looking at the oversized hatch his constable pointed out. After signaling everyone to stay quiet, he put his ear to the hatch. "Nothing." *Shit.* He tentatively knocked. "Dillon? Anyone?"

There was no answer, and he nodded to Ginsberg.

Konami fingered the slugthrower's safety as the constable spun the hatch's manual wheel, grunting and wincing with effort. It seemed to take forever — the oversized hatches for bulk storage spaces must have deeper, and stiffer, locking mechanisms.

Suddenly the door burst free, swinging on its hinge and sending Ginsberg soaring through the passage. A thick, jointed metal appendage thrust out of the dark space. *Why's it always gotta be dark?* Two shots rang out. "Cease fire, damn it!" The shots came from the MedTech, Second Taki, who spread her hands apologetically. "LoaderBot, stay where you are!" ordered Konami.

"It was pushing out, I swear!" said Ginsberg, rubbing his head as he crawled back next to the others. "The Bot. I didn't even get the wheel to fully open."

Just bruises, thankfully. The Bot appeared to be abiding by Konami's orders. The only visible portion was the reinforced lifting appendage — the rest remained shrouded in the darkness of the storage space. *Damn LoaderBots...* The largest Bots onboard, LoaderBots would've been extremely formidable opponents in gravity. But in freefall, they were almost immobile — their tracked wheels were useless without a surface, and their huge, ungainly limbs were too clumsy to move by guycable.

And it was sitting in a dark storage space, between the surge team and whatever was inside. *Damn it...* Clumsy or not, those limbs were more than strong enough to break bones. He considered trying to shut the hatch, but that would put them within reach of the Bot. He projected a map of the spaces.

He ordered Ginsberg and Taki to make their way to the other side of the space, which according to the specs had another access hatch.

Konami watched them go back around the corner, the way they came. When he heard a hatch open and shut, he turned to Lopez, drifting a few meters away.

"So, Master tech, any recommendations on the next step?"

The Data department master tech raised his eyebrows for the barest instant, then his hand shot out. Konami felt something hit his chest — glancing down, it was some sticky mass, now covering his vidcam.

When he looked back up, it was down the barrel of Lopez's gun.

CHAPTER 50

The Society for a New Humanity was founded on Ceres in the aftermath of the Martian Civil War, the year 2141 by the old Earth calendar. Paola Rahmon's open letter to all the governments in the Solar System laid out the cold, hard facts of Earth's bloody history, advocating for a "clean start" for humanity, free from the poisonous influence of Earth's culture of violence, however peaceful it may have seemed at the time.

Pat snored beside her, and Mattoso skipped ahead — she knew all this from Cerean grade school and the post-secondary lessons she got onboard from when she first arrived. Upon the rush of that familiar and comforting feeling from the words of Rahmon, she paused. As much as she trusted and believed in the Society, she knew logically that any chance at a successful investigation would require objectivity. *Harder than it sounds.*

She had started with the list of names, but that got her nowhere. Her aunt used to tell her to "start from the beginning — retrace your steps," when something was lost. And she was swayed by Cy's opinion that whatever was happening onboard had been in the works for a long, long time. With that in mind, as far as Mattoso could tell, the beginning of this expedition was Paola Rahmon's letter.

In 2184, the SNH announced plans for an unprecedented expedition — the first manned vessel to leave the Solar System — a new start for humanity, completely separated from Earth and the rest of the Solar System. The response was overwhelming — hundreds of millions across the System responded with donations and applications to join, whether in person or in the future by way of a genetic sample. In 2191, funded by this massive individual support, construction of Aotea *began.*

She ended the projection. *Shit.* This didn't tell her anything. Almost nothing about the people, beyond

Rahmon, who started the SNH — certainly nothing beyond the sanitized propaganda about their real vision for the future. *Propoaganda...* she had never applied that word to what she learned before.

But there was nothing about the debates within the Society — and she recalled, clearly, that there had been such spats. Back on Ceres, or anywhere in the Solar System, she could call up any of a thousand investigative articles and reports written about the Society over the years, both positive and negative. But not here — the SNH Charter mandated a "clean break" from Earth's culture, including most of the media produced through the Solar System. "To avoid repeating the mistakes of the past," Paola Rahmon had written — the network history link displayed her letter prominently at the top of its entry on the Society for a New Humanity. "We must cease, once and for all, any glorification of these so-called heroes of the past, most of whom were little more than thugs and misguided killers. Never more should we teach our children of supposed triumphs on the battlefield, no matter the nobility of the cause, lest our children believe that battlefields can be places of honor, or killers heroes to be emulated."

This wasn't getting her anywhere, she decided. She needed another source of information — the official history wouldn't tell her anything. She shocked herself a bit at this realization – that some necessary truths might be found outside the bounds of the SNH. But somehow it was obvious in her mind. Quietly, she slipped out from under the blanket, kissing Pat on the forehead before she drifted out of the bedroom.

Journalist Conneer wasn't in her quarters. She wasn't on watch, either — Mattoso checked the watchbill. She didn't want to send her a message or a call. No matter the privacy rules of the Charter, someone might be monitoring internal comms, and what she was looking for was well outside of normal rules or practice onboard.

Finally, just before she was ready to break down and call, she spotted the journalist in one of the few cafés still in operation. Freeze-dried ration coffee in hand, Mattoso sat down a couple of tables over from Elena Conneer. She almost laughed to herself — all this trouble to find her in secret, but how could they talk without being spotted together by any observers, even as sparsely attended as this café was?

Conneer finished her coffee and abruptly got up and left. Mattoso start to rise to follow, screaming inside in frustration, but sat back down when she noticed a slip of paper by her foot.

Classroom 7, 15 min, it said, scribbled hastily.

The fifteen minutes went by excruciatingly slowly, and Mattoso dropped her mug off with the ServerBot and left the café. This early, the classrooms were dark and empty. Mattoso wedged herself into an undersized chair, bolted down in the zero-g, in classroom number seven to wait, and before she could project a game or an article to fight the boredom, a closet door swung open and Conneer drifted out.

"What's with the hush-hush?" asked the Journalist, shutting the classroom's door and curtains.

"I need something."

Shhh... mimed the journalist. "I figured," whispered Conneer. "What?"

"History files and news articles. From the Solar System, not the ship's propoganda."

The journalist looked genuinely surprised. "Can you be more specific?"

Mattoso leaned toward Conneer and lowered her voice further. "The Society and its founders. The disagreements behind the scenes. Anything that could shed some light about what might be going on."

Conneer met Mattoso's eyes blankly.

233

"Well? Does that even exist onboard, or is it hopeless?"

"Give me a minute." The journalist squeezed her forehead with both hands. "How do I know you're not setting me up?"

"How can I prove I'm not?"

Conneer tapped her chin rhythmically. "Tell me something confidential," she whispered. "Something about the investigation."

Shit. She thought for a minute or two. "The conspiracy is deep. It has to be — much too involved."

"No shit. Tell me something a child couldn't figure out."

"MOMbots. We're considering adding MOMbots to surge teams — they're immune from the malfunctions."

"Better. But I had heard that one already too. Try again."

Is she just fishing? Not that it mattered — the journalist held all the cards here. At least she had what Mattoso was looking for, or so it appeared.

"Off the record?"

"Sure. Off the record. With the promise of more tidbits, similarly off the record, to come."

"So no articles about it?"

"Right. This is just for my edification."

Goddamnit. But she needed help. She decided she might as well trust her gut, and her gut told her that the journalist was no more than she appeared to be — someone who wanted to discover truths, whatever they might be.

"CHENG Papka dissents constantly. He's always pushing against anything that might help the investigation, or speed up the territory surges." She felt overwhelmingly dirty about criticizing a fellow officer for her own benefit, however annoying Papka might be.

"Okay," sighed the journalist. "Not much, but that'll do. For now, at least."

"And…?"

"Café, two hours."

It was going to be another sleepless night under the covers with Pat snoring beside her. But this time, instead of worry, it was excitement — the gigabytes of data the journalist had provided seemed like a treasure trove unlike anything she'd seen since before she came onboard. And despite her giddiness, there was a smidge of shame — like the rest of the crew, she had signed the Charter, which included a clause on "rejecting the bloody history and culture of Earth, and all it had influenced." *No,* she told herself. *Truth doesn't have an ideology.* Maybe someone had told that to her once before.

She scrolled through the article list, downloaded from the encrypted data chit Conneer had left her, picking out the first to pique her interest:

THE FACTIONS WITHIN THE SOCIETY FOR A NEW HUMANITY

by Lodz, Galilean Gazette, October, 2160

Paolans, Experimenters, and Shiners. No, not the latest zip-hop groups, but factions within the Society for a New Humanity, arguing about the best way to create a brand new human culture. All three accept the exhortations of its founder, Paola Rahmon, shortly after the Martian Civil War — that, because of the constant violence in Earth's history, every culture "spun off" from Earth, throughout the Solar System, is doomed to repeat this violence whenever conflicts and differences of opinion arise. But after Rahmon's sudden death in 2147, the remaining 'New Humans' disagreed about the best way to achieve her goals, and even her ultimate goals themselves. The group has split into three basic factions. The Paolans insist that a new society must be founded, entirely cut off and separate from Earth and even the rest of the Solar System. Any contact could lead to contamination, they say. The Experimenters agree that a fresh start is necessary, but aren't so insistent on total separation. They advocate for multiple, smaller societies, each experimenting with different social systems — the most effective can be exported and emulated. And the Shiners want to be that 'shining city on a hill', as an old Earth nation-state leader put it. They want the new society to serve as a beacon of progress and peace for the 'old' humanity to emulate — mandating some level of contact. So far, the three factions maintain an uneasy but peaceful (could it be any other way?) rhetorical stalemate.

Mattoso was almost beside herself with excitement — how had she not known about these factions? Just by skimming the article titles, she could see that there was far more about the SNH that wasn't taught in Aotean classrooms. At the same time, it felt like something old was starting to crack inside her, but not necessarily in a bad way.

It was going to be another long and sleepless night, but for once she was excited at the prospect, no matter how tired she might be for her next watch.

CHAPTER 51

The sticky mass fizzled and popped on Konami's chest. He started to wipe it away but it burned his fingers. "What the hell is this stuff?"

Lopez glanced to both sides, but maintained a steady hold of the slugthrower. "Corrosive mix with solid lubric — damn it! Slowly, take out your guns — yeah, the slug gun and the dart gun — and throw them in the space. Yeah, through the hatch."

Konami considered disobeying — but he wanted the man to talk, not fight. He shoved the weapons through the hatch into the storage space with the LoaderBot.

"Put your hands up."

Just keep him talking... Konami complied. "What's it all about, Lopez? Why do so many have to die?"

"It's not personal, Konami. I promise. I know you're just doing your duty."

"Come on, Master Tech. If I'm going to die, can't you at least tell me why?"

"You'll be remembered." Lopez's voice wobbled. "And a part of you will live on and be reborn."

Lopez pulled the trigger, and nothing happened. The master tech's eyes went wide, and he pulled it again, jerking the gun forward.

Konami put his hands down. "Sorry Lopez. I loaded the—"

In a flash Lopez was on him. Konami extended his arm, pushing hard to separate them, but the master tech just hung on, digging hard fingers into forearm. Konami cried out and punched Lopez's face with his other arm, repeatedly, until he let go. Konami pushed him hard, tumbling him down the passageway, and started gesturing to make a call. Somehow, Lopez had grabbed something and reversed direction — *man he's good in freefall!* — and kicked out, disrupting his directions to the wearable.

The master tech dove close, almost in an embrace. Now he wished he hadn't thrown away his weapon – he was so sure that his height and Earth-bred strength would render Lopez no threat, even without his sidearm, that he hadn't worried about a physical confrontation. Inches away from the Chief Inspector's, Lopez's eyes were wide and bloodshot. *He's trying to kill me.* The realization was a shock to his system, and Konami rushed his head forward in a butt. The angle was bad so he just nudged Lopez's temple, and the master tech's fingers jabbed his chest. Konami brought up his knees against his assailant's hips and thighs, before pulling away desperately when the Master tech swiped at his face.

His cheek burned — it was that sticky mass from his chest. Lopez swung again, and Konami realized he was aiming for his eyes. The stout little Data technician was surprisingly strong, and Konami barely kept him at bay.

They had maneuvered against a bulkhead and Lopez set his legs and shot forward, ducking under Konami's swing and latching onto Konami from the side, squeezing his throat in the crook of his arm. In desperation, Konami brought up elbows and knees to his attacker's midsection, but Lopez absorbed the poorly angled blows with nothing more than a grunt. Only by twisting his neck could Konami get a fraction of a breath, but Lopez's grip remained firm.

Konami flexed spastically, gaining the barest bit of space between them, and brought his arms down and around, looping them under Lopez's and gripping the offending wrist at his neck. Some old pressure point trick came to him and he fastened his fingers at the junction of the master tech's wrist, squeezing with every bit of Earth-born strength he had.

Lopez moaned in pain and let go, and Konami ducked and kicked away. The master tech didn't let up, setting his feet on the bulkhead and launching straight for Konami once again.

It had been years since Konami had practiced self-defense, but a move presented itself — he used the momentum of Lopez's motion to hurl him over his shoulder. In zero-g it was much easier than he remembered. The change in momentum pushed Konami backwards, and he turned around to see Lopez flying into the open hatch. "No! The LoaderBot—"

With a metallic groan a dull appendage latched onto Lopez's leg. Konami kicked off the bulkhead and grabbed the master tech's gloved hand. "Hold on goddamn it!"

Lopez screamed as he was pulled into the storage space. The LoaderBot was much too strong — Konami had to let go lest he be pulled into the space as well. In the midst of the Master tech's screams, he scrambled around the passageway for his weapons, at the same time putting in a notification to Emer. But before he got back to the hatch, there was a horrific *crunch*, and the screams stopped abruptly.

"Lopez?" Konami slowly approached the open hatch, turning on his wearable's lamp.

He took one look inside and shut his eyes — Lopez's body was crushed and torn to pieces, alongside the battered corpses of the missing surge team Bravo.

His wearable chirped. "Cy? It's Ginsberg. Taki and I are in position."

Konami turned his head and puked his guts out.

"This is the second time, Chief Inspector," said the captain. It felt to Konami like an interrogation — just him, the captain, the mayor, and the XO, in a claustrophobic office. "The second time you've been alone with someone who ends up dead, only to have something go wrong with your vidcam."

He hadn't even thought about the vidcam — the Data techs never recovered the video of Gregorian's suicide. *Of course,* he thought, *those are Lopez's techs.*

239

"I can't explain the vidcams, except that Lopez was involved both times. His techs supposedly tried to dig up the vid of Kiro's suicide, and he threw this stuff that melted the—"

"The MedTechs report no burns on Master Tech Lopez's hands, or anywhere else," interrupted XO Criswell.

"He was — I think he was wearing gloves." *Damn...* he couldn't remember if Lopez had worn gloves. He must have, he decided, if he wasn't burned.

"And the weapons. Why was Master Tech Lopez's firearm loaded with bad slugs?"

Crap. "I was suspicious — ever since he lied about some maintenance Muahe did. And he just happened to attach himself to this latest rescue team, when he'd never been on a single surge team — that worried me. It's a good thing I was suspicious — he pulled the trigger. He would have killed me."

An Admin tech entered silently and handed something to the XO, who conferred in whispering tones with the captain and the mayor. Konami was disheartened that Mayor Akunle wouldn't even meet his gaze.

"There's more, Chief Inspector," said the captain, her eyes seeming to bore into Konami's very soul. "We found this in your quarters." She held up a data stick — it meant nothing to Konami — and inserted it into her desk unit. A repeater screen displayed the contents for Konami. It was fabrication specs for several items — oxygen tanks, body armor, electrical safety gloves, and more. As the details scrolled by on the screen, Konami slowly realized what it was — defective versions of safety equipment, like the filter that killed Muahe.

"That's not mine! Someone planted it! Why'd you even search my quarters? The charter—"

"We've declared an emergency, and you know better than most our emergency powers. With sufficient cause, we can conduct searches anywhere onboard."

Konami tried to stifle his emotions, fluctuating between rage and panic. "What was the cause?"

The captain didn't answer.

"It was an anonymous tip, right? Quite a coincidence... the Data techs can't find the recording of Kiro's suicide, the department master tech tries to kill me and melts my vidcam, and an anonymous tip leads you to a data stick with incriminating data."

He wasn't sensing any change so he shifted tactics. "If I'm a bad guy, am I really dumb enough to keep the incriminating data on a stick in my own quarters?"

Konami caught her eyes flicker to the XO. *She's uncertain.*

"We'll hold a hearing tomorrow, Chief Inspector. You're entitled to representation. If you cannot or do not choose—"

"I know the rules. Bea. Lieutenant Mattoso. I want her."

CHAPTER 52

In the conference room, suddenly feeling spare and massive with only a few individuals present, Captain Horovitz cleared her throat. "In accordance with the Emergency language of the Charter, we are holding this hearing to evaluate whether there is sufficient evidence to consider Cyrus Konami, department head for the Constabulary, as a formal suspect for the murders of Debuty Chief Inspector Kiro Gregorian and Data Department Master Technician Aaron Lopez. Per the emergency powers, a full Grand Jury is waived, and our acting Jury will consist of Wilson Paramis, Mara Ngayabo, Hamad Maltin, Director-Superintendent Harry Akunle, and myself, Captain Lillin Horovitz. Due to the public interest in this case, Journalist Conneer is present and authorized to record the proceedings. Executive Officer Criswell, you will begin the case of the prosecution."

"The prosecution holds that there is sufficient evidence to consider CI Konami a possible suspect. Considering the extremely tenuous nature of current ship's status, and considering the absolutely critical importance of the chief inspector position in the present, we hold that even a small suspicion of the CI's possible guilt should be enough to remove him from this critical position. We will lay out the following evidence—"

Oh you've got to be fucking kidding me... Mattoso could read the subtext — which was barely even hidden — in the XO's introduction. There was a process for removing department heads from duty, but barring medical necessity, the process was lengthy and deliberate. She doubted that the CO and XO had any certainty that Konami was guilty, but they had lost trust in the chief inspector, at least temporarily. A formal accusation of a crime would be enough to remove him from duty, and was much quicker than a department head investigation.

The hearing lasted only an hour — Konami was questioned, the XO offered alternatives for every aspect of his story, and Mattoso played up the chief inspector's importance in the investigation so far and record of honest service.

The "jury" retired for a few minutes and returned, and from the way they avoided looking at Konami, she already knew how it went.

"Cyrus Konami, you are formally charged with the murders of Deputy Chief Inspector Kiro Gregorian and Data Department Master Technician Aaron Lopez. Until this case is resolved, you are hereby temporarily removed from your duties to the ship and crew, and will be confined to your quarters. You will not be allowed to leave your quarters unaccompanied. If you…"

Mattoso felt an awful pit in her stomach. Who would lead the investigation? There were still killers onboard — multiple killers, most likely. And the ship's best detective was just removed from the case. Almost like it was planned…

She put her hand on Konami's shoulder, but he just looked down at his feet. When the captain finished her statement, two crewmen awkwardly drifted in and led Konami out the hatch. Mattoso made to follow, but the XO stopped her, telling her to wait.

She looked up nervously at the captain and the mayor, sitting at the head of the table. Captain Horovitz turned to one of the Bigwigs, Wilson Paramis, and nodded.

"Lieutenant," started the Bigwig, with a toothy grin. "I volunteered to have this honor. Please raise your right hand."

Confused, Mattoso raised her hand.

"Now repeat after me — I, Beatriz Mattoso, do solemnly affirm…"

She repeated the words, comprehension and terror slowly dawning.

"…to support and follow the laws of the Charter for a New Humanity… to serve and protect all Aoteans… and to honorably lead the Constabulary Department onboard *Aotea*."

The grinning Bigwig had to tell her that she could lower her hand.

"Beatriz Mattoso, you are hereby assigned as acting chief inspector. Your duties in the Operations Department are suspended for now, and you will report to the Constabulary. A notification is being distributed…"

She still couldn't believe it. *What about the other constables?* The only reason she could think of that they wouldn't be chosen is that they might be too close to Cy. Would they really accept her as their new boss? For a brief moment she felt like she was falling — but it was only the freefall… *always falling, never landing.*

CHAPTER 53

We're not the future... Gregorian's last words, just before he blew his brains out. Konami didn't know what else to do — confined to his quarters, his network access was restricted to just the most basic entertainment libraries — so he pored over every loose end he could think of.

We're not the future... and neither are the children, according to Kiro. The little stomach complaints are continuing, and Bea and Ilsa are worried it might be poison. At least part of Data Department is compromised — obviously Lopez... can I trust DT3 Wren? God, if not, then we're all screwed, since he knows everything I do.

He was glad that Lieutenant Mattoso had been picked to replace him — Loesser was probably a better choice on paper, but considering Gregorian's fate, Konami doubted the Chain of Command would happily entrust the third-in-command from the Constabulary department when they already didn't trust the first, and the second was dead.

We're not the future... If Aoteans weren't the future, then who was? Aliens? Bots? Konami snorted — this wasn't a sci-fi pulp story. Someone was behind this. Someone had a plan. Who else? Another ship? Did Gregorian just mean most Aoteans, not all? He shook his head to himself.

Goddamn it, Kiro. He wished his friend was still here. After he punched him in the face, they'd talk. Kiro would sidestep and make jokes, but eventually he'd tell Konami what was really going on. And Konami would convince him to help them stop it.

He thought back to his predecessor — a woman named Aliyeva, whose suicide had prompted the leadership to call Konami, the first alternate to the position. He hadn't thought about her for a while, but realized that, prior to Gregorian, she was the last person onboard to commit suicide. Was there a common thread, besides that they both were high-ranking constables? He didn't know. Maybe Wren could help dig up her past, if he could reach the young Data tech. Maybe it was too late for that.

He missed Kostya... he hadn't seen the dog in several days, after sending her to the Vet techs' special zero-g pet kennel. At least she had seemed happy last time he saw her — finally accustomed to the freefall, and bouncing around the padded zero-g pet space with a dozen other jenji pets. A handful of VetBots, reprogrammed to be safe, kept them fed and cleaned, as much as was possible when liquids wouldn't stay on the floor.

His door chimed. Konami's eyes lit up when he saw it was Madani, and he dove forward to embrace her. They kissed deeply and Konami had to restrain himself from starting to unbutton her jumpsuit.

"You okay?" she asked.

He shrugged his shoulders.

Madani continued. "I've still been looking into—"

Konami cut her off with a gesture. *No more trusting the anti-surveillance rules of the charter...* Whoever was trying to frame him had planted that data stick in his quarters, and he wasn't going to trust that they hadn't planted some illegal recording device as well.

Konami pointed subtly to his stomach, miming being sick.

Madani nodded. "I, uh, have some ideas. Nothing concrete, but maybe soon."

He nodded back, and she pulled him toward her. As she took off her jumpsuit, he wondered if he ought to warn her about the potential for surveillance. But he said nothing — he was too damned tired, and too damned *something else*, to care.

CHAPTER 54

"Sharpshooters ready?" asked Mattoso. Once a preliminary design for slugthrowers had been finalized, it was easily modified into long range models. They reported that they were ready.

She surveyed the area — they were in Reactor Machinery Room Four, one of the larger engineering spaces in the aft section. An elevated gantry surrounded the massive accelerator, coiling around itself before departing the space on either side into the heavily shielded Reactor Rooms. The floating sharpshooters bracketed the accelerator in the overhead piping above the gantry on three sides, with the fourth side occupied by their targets, two heavy-duty RoverBots, currently busy with some unneeded maintenance. Mattoso floated above the opposite end from the target Bots.

"Commencing collaborator insertion," she said, before turning to the smaller Bot by her side. "Zinnia, execute data operation — the targets are the two RoverBots at the other end of this space."

"Understood and executing," responded the MOMbot.

Mattoso couldn't help but think of the obedient and undersized Bots as children. Teacher Kabila had been correct — once Mattoso was formally admitted into the Education Department as a teacher, the MOMbots obeyed her orders without question.

This was the eleventh operation with the MOMbots so far — only one had required the intervention of the sharpshooters. A GardenBot had resisted — or at least given the appearance of resistance — to the ministrations of the MOMbot who was trying to insert the coding stick. To ensure the precious MOMbot wasn't harmed, Mattoso had ordered the sharpshooters to shoot, destroying the GardenBot.

Everything went smoothly this time — the RoverBots ignored Zinnia while she inserted the coding sticks, and a heavily armored constable approached the Bots to test their reaction — they made no aggressive motions, even moving out of the way when the constable deliberately pushed himself into them, so he marked them with green paint to indicate that they were safe.

The progress in regaining control of lost spaces since Mattoso had started her new duties, just days before, was astonishing. She heard the whispers, supposing that Konami had been deliberately sabotaging the surge efforts, but she didn't believe it. It must be the MOMbots, she decided. And maybe Konami had already cleaned out the most difficult Bots to deal with, leaving Mattoso with the easiest left over.

But she couldn't help feeling proud — even Conneer's daily news had noticed, announcing that the surge rate had "tripled" since Konami was replaced. Pride, and sadness, since she was certain that Konami could probably do an even better job, and didn't deserve to be stuck in house arrest.

It occurred to her that, just a cycle or so ago, the idea of pride in using violence, even against Bots, would have been unfathomable. *Circumstances change everything.* A Rahmon quote came to her: "Justifying violence is the easiest thing in the world... finding peaceful resolution is much harder," and for just a moment she felt a flash of nausea. *She's not here,* she told herself. What would she do, anyway – just submit to the killer robots?

Mattoso realized she was shaking her head violently, and stopped.

Off-duty, she was on her own — Pat was on watch at the edge of one of the safe zones. Padding the corridors and passageways near her quarters, for once she felt relatively well-rested — the surge progress was almost automatic now, and she felt confident that Loesser and some of the other senior deputies would have no problems directing the operations without her present at every moment.

"Ah, Chief Inspector!" It was the Bigwig, Wilson Paramis. Even at a normal volume, Paramis's deep voice seemed to resonate around the bare passageways.

She nodded greeting. "Professor Paramis."

"Please, have a coffee with me." He accurately interpreted her expression and put his hand up. "Just a business interest, I swear."

Mattoso nodded cautiously and followed him to an automated café. They sat, as much as one can sit in freefall, in a corner. She noted that Paramis took the seat with his back to the wall. "How can I help you?"

He leaned in. "Things are changing onboard. Very obviously."

She nodded along, having no idea where this was leading.

"Ngayabo and Maltin are very concerned. Hell, the whole crew is concerned. And why shouldn't we be? Unsolved murders... the chief inspector a traitor... how can anyone be confident in our mission — in the Society for a New Humanity altogether — after all this?"

She sensed a pause but he kept speaking.

"There may come a time when Aoteans will have to make a choice going forward, and I just wanted to know that we trust you. I trust you. You've proven—"

"Who's we? You mean the other Bigwigs?"

He blinked, then recovered smoothly, inclining his head slightly. "We trust that you have proven your integrity and loyalty."

Mattoso realized after a moment that he was done speaking. "What are you asking for, Professor?"

"Nothing, Lieutenant. Nothing right now. We've looked into your background, you know. Very impressive — on their own, without any other connections, your parents had realized the wisdom of Paola Rahmon's vision. I'm sure they were unhappy to see you leave, but by now they must be happy you'll be a part of the better future. We just want you to know that you have our confidence." With agility surprising for someone as bulky as he was, Paramis slid out of the café and down a passageway.

She sat for a full minute trying to figure out what he was getting at, finally just assuming that all department heads received some sort of pep talk like this from one of the Bigwigs.

Alone in her quarters, Mattoso scrolled down the projection to Conneer's contraband articles, finding the spot she left off the last time she looked.

A Glimpse of a Hypothetical New Humanity
Alton Ngayabo, SNH Review

Much has been stated about the need for a New Humanity — the need to separate from the toxically violent culture of Earth, and its daughter cultures around the Solar System. Free-floating enclaves and far flung settlements on satellites of the gas giants will not be enough — the need for trade, and the lure of other nearby settlements will doom these well-intentioned projects to be just another flavor of the prevailing culture. To truly have a New Humanity, it must be totally separate from the Solar System — no possibility of trade, and no possibility of escape to the other cultures. And perhaps most importantly, no media contamination.

So how could it happen? What would this New Humanity look like? Here is one possibility: sometime over the next half century, scientific breakthroughs will put interstellar travel finally within reach. The current travel time between even the closest stars — centuries, or even millennia — will be reduced to within a human lifetime. When suitable candidate planets are identified (a trifle, considering the hundreds of thousands of potential candidates already spotted within a few dozen light years), dozens of vessels will set out.

These starships will be relatively small — only a few dozen, or perhaps a hundred, couples onboard — specifically selected to provide the most diverse genetic basis possible, to ensure a minimum viable population. The couples will be childless, at first — and all will agree for the need to raise their children in an earth-influence-free environment. Years into the multi-decade journey, the first children will be born — never having set eyes on a planet, and never seeing any trace of the violence of their parents' original cultures.

Each of these ships will arrive at a different solar system, and each will have differences in their social systems. They will communicate with each other — such transmissions will take years, minimizing the chance for cultural contamination should unacceptable behavior break out — and the best practices of these new colonies will be shared, along with lessons learned. And the original settlers' children will grow up and have children of their own, knowing nothing of Earth's, and Earth Solar System's, toxic and violent past.

Why such small groups? Small vessels are more achievable. Challenges with genetic diversity could be addressed with DNA stores. Further, multiple small groups would maximize the chance of success — one or two might fail, but not all. But most importantly, small groups are predictable and stable, relatively speaking. Small group dynamics are much better understood than large groups. Small groups, with common goals, are much more cooperative, and much less chaotic, then groups thousands strong. With small groups, everyone will know each other, and no one will be a stranger. Small groups will be less likely to recreate the violence and strife than larger groups, even as they expand.

With so many colonies of potential New Humanities, some will undoubtedly fail. But some will not — and the more colonies sent out, the greater the possibility that some will succeed. And in the coming centuries, one may even

251

expand, peacefully and cooperatively, to occupy their own new solar system, to truly present to all of humanity the glory and the shining light that a New Humanity could achieve.

Mattoso skimmed several more articles over the same time period, around 2163 by the old Earth calendar, with most presenting variations of the same theme — small groups of colonists, just hundreds of individuals at most, spreading to nearby solar systems, severing all links to Earth culture. Some ignored the problems with propulsion, suggesting multi-generation ships, or even crew hibernation, to cover journeys that would take several centuries at best.

Huh. What changed? If the organization had planned for many small expeditions, why was *Aotea* so big, with the population of a small city? Maybe she could ask Paramis, though for some reason that thought didn't feel right.

She kept scrolling down, skimming articles and reports on the same topic. Relatively abruptly, the tone changed. Starting around 2172, no more articles supported the many-small-colonies concept. Proposals for the actual execution of the 'New Humanity' involved large vessels, and large colonies, exclusively, after that year.

Damn it… what changed in 2172? Nothing stood out in the other articles related to the Society for a New Humanity. Mattoso broadened her search through Conneer's contraband archives to all the most prominent news stories. She skimmed over headlines about the fledgling Lunar state, more discoveries by the DarkSide telescope array… and then her eyes got wide.

Of course! She should have known — the biggest story of late 2171 was the development of the Forwood Drive. She almost kicked herself — a contortion much easier in freefall than under gravity — she had been studying for her Engineering qualifications for cycles now, and the Forwood Drive was the focal point of her studies.

252

A Martian physicist had discovered the possibility entirely by accident — in experimenting with very high-energy antimatter reactions, she detected a miniscule negative mass that had been generated just for a moment. *Imaginary negative mass,* the physicist, Dr. Devi Millard, had called it, Mattoso recalled. Through mysteries of mathematics and physics that she still didn't entirely understand, a negative mass wasn't antimatter, but regular matter that somehow had a mass value of a negative number. And just as matter with positive mass attracted other matter, matter with negative mass *repelled* other matter, allowing the possibility of a negative mass *pushing* a positive mass in the direction of its relative orientation, while the positive mass *pulled along* the negative mass, allowing continuous acceleration of a body attached to both objects, without a chemical or nuclear reaction. It didn't make sense intuitively, but worked out mathematically, and, it turned out, in practice. "Propulsion with no fuel," one headline had said. The negative-mass drive had actually been proposed, if only on paper, centuries before, by a researcher Mattoso thought she remembered was named Forwood.

This so-called "imaginary negative mass" wasn't actually real matter, Mattoso recalled from her studies. It was generated, and maintained its existence and interaction with other matter, only with continuous and enormously high levels of power and energy. So "no fuel" was not entirely accurate — something had to generate the colossal levels of energy required to maintain the imaginary mass. In the case of *Aotea*, that something was a combination of fusion and antimatter reactors — the other focus of Mattoso's studies for her Engineering qualifications.

And in recalling the particulars of the Forwood Drive, Mattoso realized she had one possible answer to why the tone of the articles changed. The multiple-small-colonies concept was not compatible with this new technology. Only ships with huge and costly power reactors, capable of generating the vast energies required for the Forwood Drive, could bridge the stars within a lifetime. Only ships like *Aotea*.

This was big, she decided. She wasn't sure how it fit, but in all the discussions she'd had onboard about SNH goals and philosophy, she couldn't once recall anything like this small group idea mentioned. Nor was it mentioned in any of the officially sanctioned reference and educational material. Mattoso looked back over that first article, doing a double-take when she saw the author's name again — Ngayabo. Just like the bigwig, Mara Ngayabo.

Maybe Cy's instincts… shit! The one person who she'd most like to talk to was off limits, at least for unscheduled visits, which must be approved by the CO. *Off limits, to the new CI?* Maybe she could figure something out. She had a thought — *maybe a medical reason.* She had a feeling Madani might be happy to help.

CHAPTER 55

Madani made sure the lab was empty before she ran the tests. She inserted the vials of blood into the analyzer, initiating the analysis sequence. It made a whirring sound as it spun the vials, and after a minute sent a stream of data to her wearable.

Shit... the result was no different than the last few times she had run the tests. She had narrowed down a common factor to all those who had come in recently with minor complaints, stomach and otherwise — they all had low levels of phenelzine, an old pharmaceutical compound that hadn't been used widely for more than a century, in their blood. According to the reference pharmapedia, phenelzine wasn't particularly dangerous on its own — certainly not in low doses, so she wasn't worried about anything more than these minor side effects. But she was a bit concerned about an outbreak of recreational drug usage, and had pulled some random blood samples from earlier in the cycle to check.

To her surprise, the control group — randomly selected from samples saved from annual checkups — had tested the same, with just a few exceptions. Almost everyone tested so far, whether or not they had made any of the minor complaints that were becoming increasingly common, had about the same low levels of phenelzine in their bloodstream. If it was an outbreak of drug usage, then it had spread to almost everyone... so Madani had tested herself, finding the same low level of phenelzine in her own blood, and had ruled out the drug use hypothesis.

Could it have been some sort of contamination? Some chemical used in equipment onboard, leaking into the environment? She had dug into her old chemistry and pharma textbooks, but couldn't find anything about phenelzine leaking from industrial usage.

Looking back over her data, she stopped at the few exceptions to the positives for phenelzine. *Hell, maybe I can just ask them about their routine!* Of the eighty-three blood samples tested, five had tested negative for phenelzine. She put in a call to the first name on the list.

"Comms Chief Zalinsky."

"Hello, Chief. This is Dr. Ilsa Madani. May I have a few minutes of your time?"

"Uh... hold on. Okay, what can I do for you?"

"Just to reassure you, there's nothing to worry about. I just have a few questions about your diet."

"My diet?"

"Yes, what you eat. And drink."

There was a pause. "Rations, of course. That's all we've been eating since the Spindown."

"And drink?"

"Water — at least that system has been working. What else could I drink? I guess I heat it up with coffee crystals sometimes."

Damn. She couldn't think of any more questions. "Thank you, Chief. I may get back to you later."

The next two on her list — Chief Engineer Papka and a Senior Administrator named Halonen — were similarly unhelpful, consuming nothing out of the ordinary.

She called the fourth.

"Hello?"

"Hello, is this Habitability Tech Second Class Razak?"

"Yes."

"Second, this is Dr. Madani. Do you have a few minutes?"

Razak told her that she ate the rations, just like everyone else so far.

"What about what you drink?"

"Oh, hab water."

She perked up. "What's hab water?"

"It's the water straight from the purifiers, before it even goes to the smart pumps, enrichers, and distro system.

256

I like it better than the tap stuff. The purifiers are mine — I supervise all the maintenance, when—"

"Thank you," she interrupted. "That will be all, Second."

She ended the call and floated back against the lab bulkhead. Could it be in the water, but infiltrating the piping somewhere after going through the purifier system? But if so, then how did Zalinsky, Papka, and Halonen avoid it?

Madani shook her head to herself. She'd like to tell Konami. In fact, maybe she could do that right now — she was technically supposed to schedule the visits ahead of time, but she was a department head, she could come up with something to tell the deputies on duty. *He needs a checkup... yeah, that's the ticket.*

She pulled her way across the lab to the door. But when she opened it, someone was floating in her way.

"Wha—"

An arm, clutching something, swung toward her neck — she blocked it just in time with both of her hands. While they were locked together, her attacker kicked himself into the lab, shutting the door behind him with his feet. His face was hidden by a masked hood.

She screamed, struggling frantically. He was stronger than her, and the object in his hand, which she identified as a syringe, slowly closed on her neck.

Keeping the syringe clear, barely, she jammed her head to the side, biting into his arm. His grunt was muffled, but he pulled back sharply, and the syringe floated free. She batted it aside just before he struck her, full force, in the jaw.

She was launched backwards, dazed, striking a cabinet. She fumbled behind her into one of the drawers, pulling a metal scanner probe out just as her attacker launched into her once again. She awkwardly swung the probe, grazing her attacker's head, but he brushed it off and locked his hands on her throat. She hammered and batted at his arms

257

and shoulders, trying to knee his crotch, but his hands just closed tighter.

Her vision started to go black.

CHAPTER 56

As always, Mattoso checked the watchbill — Madani was not on duty. She didn't want to call; she was still too afraid that calls might be monitored, so she made her way to the Medical department head's quarters. The surface of the Cans was still almost empty, from both the curfews and the exhaustion that most of the crew must be feeling in between duty shifts and watches. With so few Aoteans away from their quarters or watch stations, the empty green spaces on the surface, arcing around and over her head, seemed unnatural and out of place among the clean, industrial lines of the surface structures.

Movement far above — a bare few Aoteans traveling along the guycables across the Can — made Mattoso want to turn her head upwards as she "climbed" between civil and food service buildings to the doctor's hab. At the doctor's quarters, a large, first deck unit that Madani was assigned as a department head, no one responded to her knocks.

Mattoso grimaced and kicked herself out the double-doors of the hab, and dove for a convenient guycable. Situated at an angle that crossed just a sliver of the Can, it was a short ride to the medical offices. MedTechs and doctors jostled her without concern as she navigated through the offices — no one responded to her greetings with more than the barest grunt, busy as they were with the ongoing outbreak of minor complaints.

The Admin tech in front of the chief medical officer's office just shook his head as soon as he saw Mattoso. "Not here, Lieutenant."

"Where else could she be?"

The tech sighed. "Maybe her lab." He pointed. "That passageway, second door on the left."

Mattoso thanked him and pulled her way across the passageways. Oddly enough, the door was shut. *Could she have a patient?*

Mattoso put her ear to the door and her eyes went wide. She instinctively clutched the weapon at her right hip.

In one motion, she turned the handle and kicked the door open. A hooded figure held Madani by the throat against a cabinet, with his other hand bringing down a syringe. Mattoso didn't think about it — she aimed and fired three times. Two shots went wide; the third put a hole in the attacker's head. Horrified, she realized belatedly that she had drawn the slugthrower, not the dart gun.

Madani's coughing brought her back to the present. "Emergency!" Mattoso cried. "Shots fired, one casualty! Lab, uh, number three in Main Medical." Mattoso kicked off the doorway rim over to Madani, pushing aside the hooded corpse. The doctor's eyes finally stopped dancing and focused on her.

"Can you hear me, Doctor?"

Madani blinked and grimaced, rubbing her throat.

"It's okay, don't talk."

A pair of MedTechs rushed in and Mattoso pulled herself aside. She couldn't help herself and cautiously approach the floating corpse — a doctor and the second batch of MedTechs to arrive were having an animated discussion about whether to attempt revival. It seemed obvious to Mattoso that it was hopeless — the hole, through the hood and into the back of the skull, was bigger than her thumbnail. It came to her that she had just killed someone — and she felt nothing. How could she feel nothing? She was a killer now. Rahmon always said that Earth's culture of violence made monsters out of those who would, in a truly peaceful society, be decent people. Maybe this was what she meant.

It took a moment for her to realize someone was speaking to her, a MedTech. She tersely replied that she was fine.

Mattoso remained while the second group attempted to revive the attacker. A trio of constables entered and began recording images. *What am I supposed to feel?*

"We got his identity."

Mattoso turned, shaken out of her reverie. It was a constable, Goodluck. "What's that?"

"The dead man," said Goodluck. "We got his identity — facial recog. Senior Administrator Barth Halonen."

Putting a name to the corpse hit her like a loader's strike. Why was it different with a name? She realized that she had never even considered the possibility of truly killing someone — not when joining the crew of *Aotea*, and not even when accepting the temporary promotion to chief inspector. She suddenly wanted to vomit. A MedTech recognized her expression and pointed her to an alcove in the lab, and Mattoso spewed her breakfast rations into a vacuum receptacle.

The medical staff hovering around Madani's bed jittered and nodded, their eyes wide, as their department head berated them.

"But you probably suffered a concussion. You'd never let —"

"Oh don't tell me what I would or wouldn't do! I swear, don't I tell you that the best information about a patient's health can be — is that Mattoso? Okay, everyone get the hell out. Give me and the lieutenant a minute."

They looked relieved as they left.

"Don't they say that doctors make the worst patients?" offered Mattoso, trying for a levity she didn't feel.

Madani snorted but gave the barest grin. "I'm sure they didn't mean me. So who was it? Who tried to kill me?"

Mattoso's eyes went wide.

"They didn't tell you yet? As soon as I could I had a tech run a test on the syringe – it was the same toxin that killed Nicolescu." Madani reached out for Mattoso's hand. "You saved my life, you know. If you'd been a moment later, I'd be dead. It was a hundred times the fatal dose."

Mattoso blinked tears out of her eyes. "Thank you," she whispered. She knew she couldn't dwell on it. *That I'm a killer.*

"So who was it?"

"Senior Administrator Barth Halonen."

The doctor showed no recognition in the first instant, and her eyes went wide in the next.

"Do you know him?"

"No, but… just a few minutes before, what I was working on — I called Halonen about a sample I was testing. He didn't have any useful information, but…"

"But what?"

Madani shook her head. "He was one of just a few exceptions. A big test — dozens of crewmembers — all showing the same results, except for just a handful."

Mattoso looked nervously over her shoulders; of course no one else was in the room. "What kind of results?"

"It's about the minor complaints. Everyone who's been coming in with stomach problems and such has tested positive for phenelzine."

"Phenelzine? What's that?"

"An old pharmaceutical. Not toxic — certainly not at these low levels… the complaints would be much, much worse if the phenelzine were close to lethal levels. Halonen and a few others were the only ones to test negative, out of almost a hundred samples."

"So it's not poison, then?"

"It doesn't seem so. But here's the strangest part — maybe it could be an addiction outbreak, or recreational usage, but almost everyone I've tested, including myself, has low levels of phenelzine."

"But why? What's the drug used for?" asked Mattoso.

"It hasn't been used in generations, from what I could find out. Back then, it was used for depression and anxiety."

"Mood control?" She resisted the temptation to say *mind control.*

Madani shook her head, her chin low. "I just don't know. I can't figure it out."

"Who else can we trust?"

Madani bit her lip. "Let me think..."

Mattoso lowered her voice. "I've been thinking, about common factors, for who to trust, and who not to." *'Who to trust?' asks the killer...* "One thing about all the conspirators so far — Singh, Gregorian, and now Halonen — their ages. They're all over forty-five cycles. Singh just barely, but Gregorian and Halonen were almost sixty. That's among the oldest onboard."

"Do you know how old I am, Lieutenant?"

Mattoso nodded. "Yeah, I know, fifty-one cycles. But an attempted murder by a masked killer kind of absolves you."

"Or maybe I was a conspirator but I had a change of heart...?"

Mattoso shrugged, tired all over. "Yeah, maybe. But either way, you're on the right side now." *Am I?*

The doctor didn't say anything.

"Look, I know this is a longshot. But this thing has been long in the making, whatever it is. Age isn't the only thing — Gregorian was from Mars, and Halonen and Singh were from Ceres. Half of our crew is from Earth, but none of the conspirators. And so far, all the conspirators have been onboard Aotea since pretty shortly after construction." It shouldn't be this easy, she thought, to get back into routine activities after killing another human being. Maybe there was something wrong with her. Maybe she was always this way, she just hadn't realized it.

"You know that I'm from the Jovian moons, right? And isn't this kind of a small sample size, anyway?"

"Yeah, and I'm from Ceres." Mattoso sighed. "It's not perfect. All I'm saying is that maybe we can raise the chances of trusting someone. So we go with young Aoteans from Earth. Especially ones that haven't been onboard most of their lives."

"Alright, it's a start." Madani groaned a bit as she reached over for her wearable, but shooed away Mattoso's movement to assist. A few minutes later, a youthful doctor, a lab tech, and two MedTechs entered the room.

"Lieutenant Mattoso, this is Doctor Rana Valdez, Second Fillipe Quinn, Third Louisa Saito, and Apprentice Taka Dawn. All from Earth."

CHAPTER 57

Someone tried to murder Ilsa. Konami's heart was beating like a jackhammer and he had an overwhelming urge to open his front door and sprint for medical, consequences be damned.

An hour earlier, he had heard the familiar burst of an Emer call from the guard's wearables outside, and stuck his ear to the door. He hadn't heard much, but it was enough, and very helpfully, the second guard had asked the first what was going on.

"Attempted kill," the first guard had answered. "Someone tried to off the head doctor. But Mattoso was there and shot 'im."

"Unbelievable. On this ship. What would the founders think? Are we hopeless?"

Maybe they'd listen to reason — just let him put in quick call to Madani's recovery room.

He knocked on his own door. The first guard answered, dart gun drawn but pointed at the floor. His requests to call Dr. Madani were denied.

Konami shut the door. He had no doubt that Mattoso would be taking this as seriously as she should be.

But someone just tried to kill Ilsa. They had succeeded in discrediting Konami. Maybe Mattoso would be next.

He looked over his shoulder at the door before lifting up his thin mattress and pulling out a paper notepad. He looked over his notes — guards change every six hours. One guard usually has to make a head call at the two or three-hour mark. He needed to plan. *Aotea* needed him. And Ilsa, she needed him too.

CHAPTER 58

Captain Horovitz asked for the status of the repairs, apparently more impatient than usual.

Konrote was turned away from the screen, whispering to a GravTran tech.

"Commander Konrote?" said the XO.

They'd be done by tomorrow. A muffled cheer came from a handful of the department heads. Mattoso had the feeling there was a 'but' coming, and there was – testing the new components would take at least a week, meaning intermittent gravity at best until it was finished.

The Mayor was next. "By now you've probably heard about the attempt on Dr. Madani's life. Dr. Lassiter?"

A mousey doctor described Madani's injuries, which were relatively minor.

Mattoso was next. Everyone was looking at her, but no one looked at her like she was a killer. She cleared her throat, trying to pretend everything was normal. "Dr. Madani's attempted murderer was Senior Administrator Halonen." She ignored the entirely expected outbreak of shocked intakes of breath, most prominently from the administrative department head. "No resuscitation was possible. We have some leads, and Dr. Madani is fully cooperating with us, but that's all I can release right now. It goes without saying that this conspiracy is enmeshed at high levels of the command structure."

"So don't trust anyone, right? Anyone could be involved? Is that what we're supposed to take from this?" interrupted Commander Papka. *Fifty-four cycles, hails from a habitat in the Belt, onboard since construction started.*

"That's not quite all. We have reason to believe that the conspirators are more likely to be older than forty-five cycles, and more likely to hail from somewhere other than Earth. And they've probably been onboard the ship since shortly after construction."

266

That set off a ripple of shouting and complaints.

"And where are you from, Lieutenant?" asked the data department head.

"I was born on Ceres thirty-six cycles ago."

The complaints continued. *Good,* she thought. Most of the department heads were older than forty-five, most were not from Earth, and most had been onboard Aotea since long before launch. She wanted them to be confused, and suspicious. She wondered if she ever would have thought up of such a strategy before she found out that she was capable of killing someone. There could be no trust anymore, and as far as Mattoso was concerned, the department head meetings were a hindrance, rather than help, to fighting this conspiracy and saving the ship. Better that everyone be confused and suspicious, than inadvertently assist the conspirators, many of whom were present, she was certain.

The mayor gave her a dirty look and adjourned the meeting after a brief update on the surge efforts. When Mattoso departed, the meeting had dissolved into a half-dozen hissing, bickering factions.

Taking a slightly circuitous route, Mattoso headed for the Medical lab, checking over her shoulder to make sure she wasn't followed. The emptiness of the Cans had a surreal quality the longer they remained still, she found. There was a great tension — as if the crisscrossing guycables and even the entire surface was vibrating and ready to spring free with overwhelming violence.

Traveling through freefall was such a serene and effortless exercise that she could almost doze, even while "climbing" down a passageway, hand over hand. She yawned and shook herself awake before entering Main Medical.

The lab door was locked, the Constable assigned to guard it upright and alert — Mattoso knocked and announced herself and was quickly ushered in. The worktables were stacked with containers of water, stoppered and velcroed to the counters to keep from floating away. There were so many that they must have run out of standard sample flasks and started using any container they could find. Among the whirring analyzers, Madani was working frantically with Techs Saito and Dawn, and an unfamiliar Third with a Habitability badge was assisting.

"So how was the meeting? Anyone miss me?" asked Madani as she swapped out a sample from the analyzer.

"We may not be too far away from Spinup of the Forward Can. Konrote says testing starts soon."

"Awesome!" cried the new arrival.

"Oh, hi, Lieutenant," said Saito. "This is Rix —Third Spemann, my boyfriend. He helped us get the water samples."

Mattoso raised her eyebrows.

"Don't worry — he's only twenty-seven cycles, and he's from Earth."

She took a deep breath. "Maybe I didn't make myself clear before. This isn't a hard and fast rule. Right now, hopefully no one knows exactly what we're looking for. Dr. Madani — I'll ask for your support so that from now on, we don't let anyone in on this without the agreement of both myself and yourself."

Madani looked up from her work briefly. "Agreed. This goes for all of you."

They all assented.

"So what's with all the samples?"

"Every possible input to the major water distro mains," answered Habitability Tech Spemann.

Quinn cut in. "If something's been added to some of them, we'll narrow it down."

"Where's Dr. Valdez?" asked Mattoso.

"Phenelzine," answered Madani. "She's learning everything there is to know about it." The Medical department head maneuvered into a closet-sized office in the corner of the lab, gesturing for Mattoso to follow, and lowered her voice. "We're going to have an answer soon. I don't know if you've thought of what comes next, but I have."

Mattoso nodded. "Go ahead."

"We need Cy."

Yes! Mattoso squared her chin and agreed forcefully. "Yes, we need Cy."

"Further, the phenelzine might be the first real marker we have, to separate the conspirators from the rest of us. Maybe not perfect — there was one tech who only drank water straight from the purifiers. But I looked at old blood samples we had stored — the phenelzine levels started to creep up from undetectable levels, for most of the samples I have, shortly after Muahe's death."

"So can we use that — look at your old samples — to figure out who's part of the bad guys?"

Madani shook her head. "I don't have enough, not nearly — just a few hundred spread over the last cycle or two, from routine checks. That might give us a few names, but that's it."

"We should start with that anyway."

"Agreed."

"So what next?"

"We sample from the top. We sample the captain, and the mayor, and the Bigwigs, and all the department heads, on down."

Mattoso allowed herself to drift back against the bulkhead, her mouth open. "How... how the hell do we do that without them figuring out what we're doing? We can't exactly sneak into their quarters and take their blood."

"No, we can't. Maybe—"

They were interrupted by Valdez, fairly bursting into the lab. "I've got it — I know what they're doing with phenelzine!"

Everyone turned to look at her.

"It's a binary agent."

"What's that?" asked Mattoso.

"Two chemical agents that are harmless on their own, but when they react with each other in the human body, can have much more serious effects," answered Valdez. "Phenelzine is one of them. The other could be MDMA, SSRIs, tryptophan, or one of a hundred others. Mixed together, even at low doses, they can cause organ failure."

I'm not the only killer onboard, thought Mattoso. It occurred to her that maybe killers were necessary to stop other killers. Somehow that was a horrifying thought.

CHAPTER 59

Konami pressed his ear to the door once again. *Gotta be soon...* One of the guards had been sipping from a drink pouch for the last few hours. He smirked at the idea of loudly pouring water from one cup into the other, but freefall prevented that. According to the announcements, the low-speed rotation tests wouldn't start up again for a few hours.

Goddamn it! This guard's bladder wasn't human, unless they were pissing their pants. He was about to pull away from the door but he heard the scraping noises of someone approaching. He heard the voices of Madani and Mattoso. After a half minute of arguing, there was a yelp and a thud, and the door opened.

Mattoso had an intense look on her face that he couldn't recall seeing, and Madani was putting away a pair of syringes. The two guards were floating, motionless, in the passageway.

Konami squeezed Madani in a brief embrace before Mattoso patted him on his shoulder.

"Let's get them hidden," whispered Mattoso.

Konami asked Madani how long they'd be out as they dragged the guards into his quarters. She said for a few hours, and then they set off.

Konami's eyes got wider and wider as they related their findings on the phenelzine, and their suspicions about its purpose. A second agent could be introduced by some other means, and only those with phenelzine already in their blood would be affected.

Oh shit... "You think this is enough evidence to justify breaking me out? Damn it, Bea... they could shove us both out of the way for this, and you too, Ilsa. You should—"

"No, Cy." Madani cut him off. "It's not enough evidence. But the reaction will be. Lieutenant?"

271

Mattoso handed him a dart gun. "Weapons? Are you serious? What are we gonna do, fight off the whole crew? And reactions? What does that—"

Madani sighed. "Cy, just follow along. We're almost there. Stay quiet, and you'll see."

"Right," added Mattoso. "It's not just the evidence. It's the reaction. You'll see."

Bewildered, Konami did as he was told, doing the best he could to cover his face the few times they passed by other Aoteans.

Madani stopped them in front of the doors to the conference room and pulled out several small strips of paper from her medical bag. "These are the test strips that Dr. Valdez printed. Cy, you don't have to do anything, except watch how everyone reacts. We're going to lay out everything, in front of the department head meeting, and ask everyone to give a drop of blood for the test strips. They turn blue on a positive, but what we're looking for is the negatives. And the ones who refuse to cooperate."

Konami was beginning to understand what they intended. Including how dangerous this could be — he couldn't help but notice Mattoso palming the dart gun in her pocket, and a similar bulge in Madani's pocket as well. He checked the one Lieutenant Mattoso gave him one last time before they opened the doors.

CHAPTER 60

Conversation stopped, and all heads swiveled toward the new arrivals.

"Konam—," cried CHENG Papka. "What the hell is he doing here?"

"Someone is poisoning the crew," announced Madani. Mattoso was impressed by her volume — they certainly had everyone's attention. "We've discovered the cause of the outbreak of minor stomach complaints."

Mattoso scanned the room, trying to discern any suspicious reactions from those present. She had been worried that Captain Horovitz might explode in anger at the surprise release of Konami, but the Commanding Officer continued to sit silently and stone-faced.

"Phenelzine," continued Madani. "A very old drug, one that hasn't been in wide use for a long time. Mostly harmless on its own, but with known and possibly fatal side effects when mixed with many other relatively common pharmaceuticals and chemicals." She turned and nodded, and Mattoso started to pass out the test strips. "I would ask that everyone present submit to instant blood tests — one drop of blood on these strips will tell us if phenelzine is present in your blood — it turns blue."

"And what would this tell us?" asked the XO.

"Phenelzine has been present, in small quantities, in almost every blood sample, randomly selected, of several hundred Aoteans. Among those samples include blood from anyone recently deceased. With just a few exceptions, everyone has tested positive for phenelzine." Madani paused. "Less than five percent tested negative, including Singh, Gregorian, Lopez, and Halonen."

As they had planned, both Madani and Mattoso turned to CHENG Papka and stared at him, ignoring the indrawn breaths and surprised exclamations.

"I will ask again — everyone please submit to a sample; the test is instantaneous."

Sweat was running down Papka's face. "Why—"

"I'll do it," said Captain Horovitz, rolling up her sleeve. "Where's the needle?"

Papka abruptly kicked away from the bolted conference table and scrambled for the exit. In the freefall he was forced to reach out and grab those officers near him to pull himself to the handholds on the bulkhead, and as soon as the captain snapped an order, his neighbors simply grabbed and held onto his extremities.

"It would appear that we've found the conspirator," said the XO with genuine surprise.

"We found one," interrupted Konami. "One more suspect. That's all we've found. The blood tests must continue."

Mattoso grinned at the chief inspector, relieved to have him on her side once more. It was the first time she'd felt like smiling since the shooting.

"Agreed," said the captain, and the mayor nodded as well. "Everyone will provide blood—"

"I don't think so." It was Ngayabo, the Bigwig. She was aiming a gun — an unfamiliar design, much smaller than the bulky pieces that Fab had come up with. It looked like the stills Mattoso had seen of the weapon Gregorian used to kill himself. *Flechettes,* she thought she recalled. Konami made a move and Ngayabo re-aimed her gun. "No, Konami, drop it."

Konami lowered his dart gun but kept it in his hand. When Mattoso glanced at a shuffling noise, three other department heads had produced similar weapons — Supply Commander Chulanont, Genetics Lab Director Leigh, and Administrative Director Das. Chief Engineer Papka shrugged off his distracted captors and pushed over to join Ngayabo.

"This is not what it seems," continued Ngayabo. Mattoso tried to subtly draw her dart gun, but the Bigwig noticed and shook her head, gesturing with her gun for emphasis. "Unless you want several people in this room to die, we will be leaving without violence, and I swear that you will hear from us soon." Just before we left she turned and looked over her shoulder. "You aren't under attack. This is part of the plan, and always has been. That's all I'll say now."

Before anyone could object, the five conspirators pulled themselves to a side door and exited the briefing room. Most shocked were the other two Bigwigs, especially Hamad Maltin — the older man's eyes bulged and he fidgeted frantically.

Captain Horovitz abruptly made a call to the Officer of the Deck, a Lieutenant Geautreaux. She looked at Madani, who scanned a projection and then shrugged. *Damn...* no sample for Geautreaux, apparently. Mattoso looked at the same time, speaking up after scanring Geautreaux's bio file. "Captain — he's thirty-seven, and he's from Earth."

The captain nodded and spoke again. "Lieutenant, order Action Stations. Suspend all non-vital events and evolutions — including any maintenance or operations not required immediately for safety of ship or crew. All watch station hatches will be locked shut. Hold one moment—" The captain looked up and turned to the executive officer. "XO, submit to a blood test, immediately."

Madani hastily produced a needle, pricking the XO's finger on a test strip. She showed off the blue-tinted strip around the room.

"Lieutenant Geautreaux," continued the captain. "All watch stations will lock their hatches immediately and only open them by the order of myself, the XO, Chief Medical Officer Madani, or Chief Inspector Konami."

Konami grinned at that, nodding to Mattoso. *Good,* she thought.

"Did you say—"

"Yes. Chief Inspector Konami has resumed his duties. We will shortly delegate and share the names of more

275

officers with the same authority. Are my instructions clear?"

There was a pause. "Yes, Captain, they are clear."

"Very well."

A moment later, announcements began, echoing the captain's instructions.

With a gesture from the captain, the blood tests resumed, and everyone left in the conference room tested positive for phenelzine. Madani recorded an entry for each result. The lessening in the room's tension was palpable.

"This war has entered the next phase," announced the captain. "Our attackers have made themselves known."

Mattoso's wearable chirped — it was an Emer call. At the captain's insistence, she turned up the volume for everyone to here. "Emer, it's Mattoso — what is it?"

"It's — I'm not sure, Lieutenant. Pandemonium in Engineering, it seems. Simultaneous reports of violence, and then it went blank."

"It's happening – it's spread from Earth, and now—" someone babbled until they were hushed.

Shit... how the hell do we send constables when anyone of them could be traitors? She met Konami's eyes, and he nodded. *He trusts me.*

"Emer, Mattoso. Activate all reserves. That's my last order. By order of the captain, Chief Inspector Konami is resuming his duties."

CHAPTER 61

"The 'safe zones' are no longer safe," announced Konami. "We need new safe territory. We need to search for recording devices, starting in this room. We can assume that adherence to the Charter is right out of the window for the betrayers."

"Recording devices?" exclaimed Hamad Maltin, horror in his voice.

"Absolutely," answered Konami. "For now, audible interference will do." He spared another look for Maltin, and the other remaining Bigwig, Wilson Paramis. Could they be traitors, despite their blood test results? Does the rot extend to the entire SNH leadership, or was Ngayabo an aberration? He filed it for later consideration.

At their questions, he showed them what he intended — it was a technique that the syndicates in Lagos used to beat low-level bugs, the kind used by underfunded police departments. He arranged several wearables around one corner of the room, broadcasting various frequencies of static, and the most senior officers present stayed at the center, speaking in low voices.

"Papka's forces are trying to get control of Engineering," stated the captain. "Right now, they have the element of surprise."

No one said anything, until the XO spoke up, pointing out that from the engineering spaces, they could control power flow to every system on the ship, including air and water.

Shit. This was one of the few times that Konami wished he had the expertise that came with the full technical qualifications for *Aotea*'s engineering systems.

"Options?" asked the captain.

"A remote shutdown might be possible," offered Mattoso. "If the operators are away from their stations due to the fighting, the Data techs might be able to hack into the control programs and initiate shutdown."

"How long?"

"I don't know."

The Data Systems director, Shin, spoke up nervously. "A few hours at minimum, once we identify which techs are loyal. And any operator in Engineering can shut us down if they're paying attention."

"We know one who is loyal," added Mattoso.

"Too long, and too uncertain," decided the captain. "Other options?"

Konami thought of one, but he didn't like it. He spoke up anyway. "Overwhelming force. With darts, anyway. We gather up every adult Aotean we can get word to, test them if we can, and issue dart guns to them all. Maybe even syringes with meds when we run out of dart guns. We storm Engineering and dart absolutely everyone, and sort out who's who later."

Captain Horovitz nodded, and the XO agreed as well. "Very well. Make preparations."

"One more thing before I get started — we need Conneer. The journalist."

She answered the summons so quickly that Konami wondered if she had been waiting in the passageway outside the conference room.

They briefed her on the latest events.

"So... you want an article?"

"Think of it as an exclusive," suggested Konami.

Conneer cocked her head. "We could do an interview. The captain and the mayor, answering—"

"No," interrupted Captain Horovitz. "That would take too long." She turned to Konami, her gaze intense. "With every second they're getting further and further into Engineering."

Goddamnit. He nodded and turned to Conneer. "Can't you just report what happened?"

"But I wasn't there. And more importantly, the readers weren't there. They weren't here, in the conference room." The journalist shook her head. "I read the boards all day. People are scared out of their wits, and they don't know who to trust. Hell, half of them don't trust me anymore, even if I said that I was here. Maybe more."

Konami slumped. Without the trust of most Aoteans, chaos and violence could rule the ship for weeks.

"I think I have a solution," offered Mattoso. She projected a vid — the entire department head meeting, starting from when they arrived. Meeting Konami's wide eyes, she pointed to the vidcam pinned to her uniform with a smirk.

Konami could have kissed her.

"If this is going to work," said Conneer. "I need that vid. Everyone needs to see it."

Mattoso looked to the Captain. Horovitz and Mayor Akunle shared a look and nodded.

AOTEA TODAY: SPECIAL EDITION
BETRAYAL RECORDED! VID PROVES MARA NGAYABO IS LEAD CONSPIRATOR!

Konami scanned the article and ended the projection. He glanced up at the constables and deputies preparing sidearms and body armor — the latter mostly improvised — at the edge of the aft Can. They were waiting outside the entrance to the aft Engineering section, through the Aft Ring. Before he spoke, he made sure the last of the red sashes that would differentiate them from everyone in the engineering spaces were issued and donned.

"Alpha Squad is with me," announced Konami. "Bravo is the reserves, with Loesser in command." He didn't mention how he had divided the squads — without the time to blood test everyone, Alpha was exclusively those from Earth or under forty cycles of age, while Bravo was made up of an even mix. "I don't have to tell you how serious this is. You've all been briefed. But just remember that our weapons are not lethal, and everyone will be revived. Everyone inside — everyone without a red sash — is a target. We absolutely cannot lose control of Engineering." He looked out over the small crowd — about sixty in Alpha, and another forty in Bravo. *I hope we won't need Bravo...* Chances were that at least one or two of Bravo were conspirators. "Any questions?"

Someone spoke up, asking how they could know if they could trust their squad mates.

Konami didn't have the time for a diplomatic answer and spoke frankly. "We don't. You've all been assigned two partners. If you see anyone alone, even with a red sash, dart them. If one of your partners goes down due to enemy fire, stay with them — otherwise you become a target. Anything else?"

No one replied.

"Everyone has their assignments." Konami projected onto the bulkhead. "Casualty Control Central, Alpha Squad is ready for entry. Bravo Squad is our reserves."

"Roger, Chief Inspector. Proceed, and good luck."

"Door team, that's your cue!"

The door through the Aft Ring was opened, and two geared-up welders made their way to the far hatch that led to Engineering. A formation of constables and deputies aimed dart guns as the welders, gear in hand that would have weighed hundreds of kilos on Earth, made short work of the heavy pressure hatch, and Konami and his team were first to charge, such as could be done in freefall, into Engineering Middle Level. It was a tight squeeze with his three-man team in between the bulky sets of piping and machinery, made even tighter as other teams cycled through the hatch. So far, there was no resistance. Once all of his men were arranged through the passageways and alcoves of Engineering Forward Level, Konami gave the order into his wearable, to all of Alpha Squad, to proceed to their assigned capture points. With the help of some junior Engineering officers, Konami had hastily arranged a capture plan for the entire Engineering and Reactor spaces, with teams assigned to every single space within.

After transmitting the order, Konami pulled himself to a ladderwell and quickly ascended to the next level up. He had assigned his own team — Constable Goodluck, Reactor Tech Tan, and himself — the Fusion Control Room. On the catwalk above Forward Level 1, he had a good view of much of the space — for a moment he watched the teams scramble through to the other Engineering spaces, then pulled his attention back to his own surroundings and headed aft for the Control Room.

But between Konami's team and the Control Room was Engineering Middle Level 1, and a closed hatch. Luckily, the interior hatches of the Engineering spaces were much less robust than the pressure hatch that divided the spaces from the Aft Ring and Can. He nodded to Goodluck and Tan, who proceeded forward, pulling out their mini-cutters.

They started to cut, and the hatch exploded.

CHAPTER 62

Mattoso couldn't stop herself from looking over her shoulder, even though she hadn't seen anyone in the hab unit passageway since she entered. She knocked quietly on the door. *Damn it, Wren... we don't have time for this!* The message he had sent her was terse and in a loose code they had worked out, urgently requesting a meeting.

Finally confident, for the first time since the second murder, she realized, that the senior officers — at least the CO, XO, and mayor — were trustworthy, she had told them about Third Wren's invaluable assistance in she and Konami's investigations. But she didn't tell them quite everything.

The door slid open, and Wren peeked out warily.

Before they said anything, she brought out the test strips. They did it simultaneously — both visibly relaxing when the strips turned blue. *Fingers are gonna be sore as hell by the time we're through with this...*

Wren had turned his cramped quarters into a data and vid center — the two rooms were so crowded with wearables, vidscreens, and auxiliary processors, that Mattoso and the Data tech couldn't occupy either one together at the same time.

"I only have a minute," said Mattoso. "I have to get back to CC Central."

"This'll just take a minute." Wren motioned Mattoso to an array of screens, divided into grids of hundreds of smaller vids running simultaneously. "I had a thought and checked the timestamps of the vid to the running cams from watchstanders and deputies — minutes after Ngayabo revealed herself, a handful of watchstander and rover cams started winking out, one after the other, or sometimes a bunch at once."

"...like they got the order—"

"...to shut down their cams. Exactly."

282

Mattoso nodded, impressed. "So who are they?"

Wren grinned and sent a stream of data to her wearable.

Scanning, she recognized half of the names — mostly senior officers and crewmembers, though not at the department head level. *Shit*... almost every department was represented. This real-time capacity that Wren had set up, to analyze and catalogue vidcam streams as they were recorded, was the only remaining tool that she and Konami had kept from everyone else.

"Most of the vidcams were turned back on, later," added Wren.

Mattoso debated whether she should submit the names to the captain. *Is this enough evidence — turning off a vidcam? Maybe they just needed a head break.* She made up her mind, figuring that everyone would be blood tested anyway. And she didn't want to throw around hasty accusations, so she transmitted the list to Konami to see what he thought.

She was about to head back to Casualty Control Central when she got the angry buzz of an urgent message. Her eyes widened as she read it, then she turned to face Wren, swallowing.

"What is it?"

"Pack up. I mean everything. We're moving. The entire crew, or the loyal ones anyway, are moving." A phrase came to her from an old book she'd read – *going to ground.*

CHAPTER 63

Konami found himself flying backwards, unchecked by gravity or anything else until he struck a cluster of machinery against the bulkhead. He coughed heavily, able to see nothing but smoke and dust. His ears rang and he couldn't even hear his own voice.

Dazed, he fumbled through some gesture commands for his wearable, every motion sending lances of pain from his back to his knees. Something stung his cheek — *shrapnel,* he realized. There was a noise, repeating, just audible over the ringing in his ears.

Gunshots. There were at least two distinct types of weapons firing – the traitors' preferred flechette guns, and the hastily fab'd slugthrowers.

Frantically, he scrambled around a coolant pump for cover. His hearing and wits gradually returning, Konami put two and two together. *The hatch blew, and they came out shooting.* The conclusion was obvious — *they were ready for us.* Papka's men had taken Engineering, and apparently had fortified their position.

He drew his dart gun in one hand, and his slugthrower in the other, wondering if he should have issued one of the latter to every deputy taking part in the assault. As it was, he only gave them to trusted constables and a few others, worried about jumpy and inexperienced deputies shooting friendlies.

He reached for his wearable, but it was gone — was he holding it when the hatch blew? He couldn't recall. He still had an earpiece in, but without the main wearable he couldn't connect with anyone. The smoke and dust were intense — obscuring breathing and vision alike. Almost kicking himself for forgetting, he put on his night-goggles — as he recalled, they were as effective in smoke and dust as in low light. Image enhancers and spectrum detectors blinked and flashed along his vision, finally settling into a

284

decipherable mix of visual-spectrum and infrared imagery. Human shapes darted into and out of his field of view from behind corners and jutting machinery, and by their yelling and wild shots they still couldn't see him.

As he peeked around the pump housing, a sharp pain made him cringe. A rib was bruised, and maybe broken, he was sure. A growing shape approached. He closed his eyes momentarily when he realized what it was — Reactor Tech Tan's mangled corpse, or at least the largest part of it. *Papka, you're a fucking dead man...*

Sensing movement, he steeled himself and remained still, just barely peeking out from around the pump housing. Another shape, this one approaching quickly and actively, became clear. Konami didn't wait to see if it had a red sash, firing the dart gun three times. The body jerked with an odd metallic *clang*, and then the unmistakable movement of an arm swinging up to fire a weapon. More gunshots, and Konami jerked back as impacts shook the pump housing.

Shit! Body armor? When the shots stopped he pulled back around smoothly, firing the slugthrower at the receding shape. He was rewarded with a sharp cry, and he kicked forward, springing off the pump housing. Striking his target, they both tumbled back, and Konami made sure his attacker was between him and the approaching bulkhead.

The body he held absorbed the impact but made no sound when they struck. He quickly realized he was holding a dead man — his slugs had struck his target in the throat and punched through his chest armor.

As his hearing returned, he was greeted with shouts and gunshots and general pandemonium, echoing off the engineering equipment and bulkheads of the dozens of compartments in the engineering spaces. He realized that if Papka and his men were armed and ready, this had the potential to be a massacre.

Where was his wearable? He patted down the body — an Electronics tech named Niemi — pocketing the smaller, sleeker slugthrower and clips. A wearable was on the man's belt — Konami futilely tried to unlock it, but it was pattern protected.

The action seemed to be away from his immediate vicinity, so he started calling for Goodluck, quietly at first. After a few moments, a groan answered him — the constable was wounded and barely conscious, but alive, bleeding from shrapnel wounds in his legs and torso and wedged in a corner.

Konami gently freed Goodluck's wearable from the constable's collar. Luckily, the constable had a thumbprint unlock, and with a gentle motion of the wounded man's hand, Konami put in a call to Loesser.

No answer. *Goddamnit, Loesser...* He huddled into the corner alongside Goodluck and tried again.

"Loesser here, make it quick."

"Loesser, it's Cy."

"Cy? Oh shit, you're alive! Thank the fuck... where are you?"

"Middle Level 1. There was a bomb at the hatch to Forward; one of my three is dead. Goodluck is seriously wounded. They were ready—"

"Listen, Cy, the calls were all at once — all shouting about gunshots and bombs — and we couldn't get ahold of you, so we charged in with the Reserves."

"How long?"

"Just minutes. We're still deploying."

Crap. "They're ready for us, Loesser."

"No shit!"

He shut his eyes. *They're not ready for this... not even close.* "We're pulling out. Stop your deployment and order the retreat. Order the reserve force to cover retreat and that's it, and then pull out. Lost my wearable — you'll have to give the order."

She was silent for a moment. "Understood."

Konami gritted his teeth as he started pulling his way back forward toward the Can, Goodluck in tow. A red-sashed deputy sailed by and Konami grabbed her, pushing the wounded Goodluck into her arms and sending her forwards. He turned back aft, toward the control room, a weapon in each hand, with just one thought ringing through his head.

Papka, you're a fucking dead man.

CHAPTER 64

The move to the deep machinery levels was frantic. In a matter of hours, non-vital systems were shut down and spaces welded shut, vital systems were set to automatic or rerouted to new control spaces, large storage bays were cleared, thousands of zero-g bunk-bags were hung, a makeshift medical bay was set up, and the entire area was secured, with all the entrance hatches welded shut — heavy-duty welds reinforced with massive alloy panels — except for two, guarded around the clock. With so many watch stations secured and shut down, they suddenly had thousands of free hands to help prepare their new "Fortress Deep," as some crewman had dubbed it. Someone else had wanted to call it Helm's Deep, from some old Earth literature, but that didn't catch on.

Mattoso pulled her way through the crowded berthing spaces, nodding and offering reassuring (she hoped) words to anxious Aoteans. The XO's admin team counted over nine thousand Aoteans in the Fortress, with dozens more arriving every hour, cycling through the gauntlet of blood tests and questioning at the guarded entrances. As crowded as it was, she was amazed by how calm and well organized everyone had been so far. The biggest problem had been an outcry that pets would have to stay in the freefall Veterinary spaces. There were still VetBots operating to keep them fed and watered, so at least they wouldn't starve.

Even with so many thousands now safe within the Fortress, Mattoso couldn't help but think of thousands more outside. How many were dead? The most recent casualty count included less than a hundred confirmed dead, but there had been hundreds more missing. And that was before — with the pandemonium after Ngayabo's revelation, thousands had since found themselves caught outside the Fortress, with no safe way to make their way there, according to the most recent reports. And how many were among the conspirators? *How many killers onboard?*

Her wearable buzzed. She looked down, pleased — Wren and the other Data techs must have gotten the new Fortress network set up and secured. The main ship's network still functioned, but the Captain had mandated no network usage until a new and totally secure network, confined within the Fortress, was set up. The message was an urgent call to the new command conference room.

The briefing room was small, and she was one of the last to arrive. Finally, the mayor spoke: "They're calling us, from the main network." No one had to ask who "they" were.

"Who are they calling?" asked Mattoso.

"Everyone. We haven't been able to shield the Fortress from the main network, though at least we can control any data going the other way." Mayor Akunle looked down at his own projection. "It should be any second."

The screen flashed on, with Mara Ngayabo's face staring down, imperious, from the wall imager. *Damn... we should lower that screen.*

"The time has come to reveal the true mission of *Aotea*, the one that has been in place since the start of its construction, and the only way to truly build a New Humanity. It was always clear to the Society, from the very beginning, that we must start small."

Mattoso's chest tightened as she realized where this was going. By the whispers around her, others may have been reaching the same conclusion.

"Large groups are unmanageable — too much of Earth's culture and history will seep through. I apologize for this deception, but it was necessary. A small group could not construct a vessel of the scale necessary for the journey, and thus deception was required to recruit the larger group, and donor base, necessary.

"All of you have contributed to our mission, even as you were unaware of its true nature. Even the dead have

289

contributed, and we mourn them together. They will not be forgotten."

"What about us?" someone shouted. Ngayabo continued as if it was on mute — which, from her end, it undoubtedly was.

"Again, the deception was necessary. All great achievements require sacrifice. Unforeseen developments forced us to move our timetable forward, but everything that has occurred was part of our plan. You can see how dedicated the Society is to this mission, and that nothing, and no one, will stop us."

Mattoso glanced around her — jaws jutted and teeth gritted in silent rage.

The view on the screen changed, to one of the vast hangars deep in the bowels of the Operations and Engineering spaces, directly adjacent to the skin of the ship. These hangars wouldn't be needed for decades, not until they reached their final destination of Samwise. The vessels that would be used to ferry supplies and colonists down to the surface would be constructed later, so the huge spaces were used for storage. But this hangar was occupied by a ship — an enormous, blocky vessel, at least two hundred meters in length, swallowing up most of the hanger's space. Mattoso realized what this meant, but she couldn't believe it. *How…?*

"Most of you will be returning to Earth system in this vessel, or its sister ship in the aft hanger. A nearby brown dwarf will provide a gravity assist and a course change maneuver, and within two decades — twenty Earth years — you will be within broadcast range of Earth to arrange pickup. It will be a hard voyage, but sufficient rations and supplies are onboard. You will survive."

The view switched back to Ngayabo.

"I'm sure you have questions, but they will have to wait. As we speak, your attempt to regain control of Engineering is failing. Your forces are dead or in retreat. To avoid any more bloodshed, present yourself on the surface near the Forward Medical bay, and our mission can proceed peacefully. But let there be no doubt, our mission will proceed, whether peacefully or not. One way or the other, you will not be completing this journey. Your actions from this moment will determine whether you return to Earth, or join the deceased."

The screen went blank, and everyone talked at once.

"Quiet. Quiet!" Captain Horovitz yelled — something Mattoso had never seen, and everyone shut up. She asked the Navigator if this was even possible.

Commander Rusk blinked, silent for a moment before responding. "I'd have to see the charts, Captain, and which brown dwarf she's talking about. I suppose it's possible if there really is one nearby, but it'd be a bitch to calculate."

Horovitz turned to the acting chief engineer — Lieutenant Commander Zafy — the highest ranking Engineering officer verified not to be a conspirator – and asked him about the supposed escape ships.

The engineer scratched his beard. "I don't know, Captain. I'd have to inspect them. I'd assume a small fusion plant for power, but they're too small for Forwood propulsion. The gravity assist will require some maneuvering — they must have conventional thrusters. And for twenty years? We'd be awfully crowded, especially with supplies and recycling gear."

"Captain," interrupted Commander Konrote. "You can't seriously be suggesting we comply with these murderers?"

"No, Commander. But before our next move, it's imperative we know everything we can about these claims."

The mayor cut in. "I'll add my support to the captain. This doesn't add up. They say everything's gone according to their plan, but I don't think their plan would have included so much chaos."

"Right," added Madani. "And what about the drugs in our blood? What about the Bots?" And then the doctor

291

plucked the words right out of Mattoso's head. "And the assault on Engineering? What about Cy – and Alpha Squad?"

More questions bubbled up, and Mattoso checked her pockets, somehow reassured by the dense bulk of her sidearms.

CHAPTER 65

In a storage alcove in Engineering Middle Level, Konami muted the wearable's ringer, responding to Loesser's call with a terse *can't talk* text. He added *one last try... give me thirty min, if I'm not back, then retreat.* He considered explaining his plan, but dismissed it — there was nothing they could do to help.

Just a distraction right now, anyway... The only thing he needed from his borrowed wearable was the brief, simplified instructions a Reactor Controls Tech had loaded before the assault on Engineering — instructions that should allow even an unqualified crewman, like Konami, to initiate a long-term fusion reactor shutdown, securing all but a trickle of power to most of the ships systems other than the antimatter-powered Forwood propulsion drive.

He tried to focus on sorting out the frantic sounds — was anyone coming near him? *Not right now,* he decided. *How to get to Fusion Control?* A thought came to him, and he pulled a breather off the alcove bulkhead, setting its seal against his face. He had to loosen his night-goggles to fit, and strapped them over the breather mask. He hoped like hell that Papka's men hadn't thought to fab low light goggles like his. He also grabbed a handful of wrenches and other tools.

Konami checked his weaponry — he had two dart guns plus reloads, but with the defenders' body armor, these were almost useless. He had two slugthrowers plus a looted flechette gun but only two reload clips for the slugs, and he didn't know how to check the ammo on the flechette.

As he peeked his head out from the alcove, the smoke began to dissipate — heavy ventilation fans had activated. But no one was nearby. Konami silently pulled himself into the passageway, following the sound of the nearest vent fan. It was above him, set into a corner where the bulkhead met the overhead. Without freefall, it'd be nearly impossible to reach on his own, but he easily drifted upwards and pulled himself to the grating. A few seconds of prying with a screwdriver and the grating was loose — Konami lifted a corner and wedged in a wrench, first banging the fan blade then sticking it, wedging the tool against the fan housing.

He looked back — no one seemed to have noticed yet. But the fan wasn't overheating as he had hoped. *Screw it.* He took the screwdriver by the insulated handle and thrust it, bracing himself against a protuberance in the bulkhead, into the fan's motor housing.

This time he was rewarded by sparks and a grinding noise, and he backed away. Still, there seemed to be no response. *Maybe Papka is a bit understaffed today...*

He grinned as a thin line of smoke started to trail from the fan, and moved to the next one. Twice Konami had to dodge a conspirator coming to check the fans he damaged. And more than twice he gritted his teeth in anger after coming across a corpse with a red sash, but he could scramble the fans far faster than they could fix them, and within fifteen minutes, all the nearby Engineering spaces were starting to fill with smoke, with no fans operational to vent.

It was time to get to Fusion Control.

Someone certainly seemed to have noticed the damage to the fans — angry voices ricocheted off bulkheads and through the passageways that connected the Engineering and Reactor spaces. An announcement was made — Papka's voice — ordering repair crews to the vent fans.

Konami aimed one slugthrower in front of him as he pulled himself along with his other hand, focusing hard on his low-light goggles — the breather mask slightly obscured the clearer vision of the goggles. A shape approached, and Konami squinted, then pulled the trigger twice. He got a muffled groan in response, and then more shouting — the gunshots obviously resonated through the spaces. He continued along, ignoring the splayed corpse except to appropriate another ammunition clip, as he pulled, one-armed, down the passageway.

Someone was coming from ahead of him — more than one. He pulled himself aside into an alcove, listening and watching with his head peeked out, trying to interpret the vague, distant shapes projected on his goggles through the smoke. Perhaps ten meters down the passage, the shapes resolved into three, making their way slowly and carefully. He hoped they were so slow because they couldn't see through the smoke. His first instinct was to draw a second gun and charge out, guns blazing; his second was to stay hidden and let them pass by.

Somehow hiding just fueled his anger at Papka and the rest of the conspirators. *Fuck the rules.* Once the three crewmen — fully distinct in his goggles now, older firsts and a chief — passed his hiding place, he leaned backward into the passage and pushed gently off with his feet against the alcove bulkhead. Drifting into the passageway, Konami aimed, gun in each hand, and fired repeatedly, two shots for each conspirator. The last one twisted to the side of the passageway, firing blindly — seeing red, Konami kept firing, finally sweeping over the last conspirator and sending him limply drifting, bleeding a trail lit pink in his goggles.

In a rage as he charged aft toward the control room, he realized after several moments that he should have stopped and looted the ammunition from the three dead men. *Too fucking late now—*

He was moving so fast that, at a junction in the passageway, he inadvertently body checked a crewman into the angled bulkhead corner, and before he could chide himself for another stupid move, he was fighting for his life. The crewman, clutching Konami's gun-hand, kicked off the bulkhead, sending them both hurtling into the center of the passage. The crewmen yelled, and Konami knew he'd have to end this quickly — others would be on their way. He delivered two hard left hooks to the crewman's gut

— forcing a grunt, but the crewman hung onto Konami's right arm.

A glance to the side revealed another crewman approaching quickly. As he clawed at the crewman's waist he brushed over the handle of a gun, and pulled the trigger without thinking. With a cry of pain, his assailant let go. Konami swung his gun hand to his left just as the approaching crewman emerged through the smoke, and fired wildly. Without even seeing if his shots connected, he turned back and shot the first crewman, balled up in pain, through the head.

And it was over — Konami quickly maneuvered to a parallel passageway, hiding briefly, and letting four crewmen pass him while he reloaded and collected and calmed himself. *Shit shit shit shit shit...* He had been so stupid, relying on nothing but his rage. In the last five minutes he had killed five people — did they really need to die?

Nearby voices shook him out of his self-reflection, and he instinctively readied his slugthrower.

Yes, he decided. Ngayabo and Papka were taking over the ship. They had already killed — murdered — his crewmates. Yes, they needed to die, and so did Papka.

He couldn't stop himself from giving a whooping yell as he charged toward the voices, guns blazing.

CHAPTER 66

"What about our children?" asked a fidgeting Aotean. "Are we really going to risk their lives?"

The loyal Aoteans in the Fortress had broken up into groups, with no single space large enough for all, after Ngayabo's broadcast. The captain and mayor had instructed the department heads and other senior officers present on the 'party line' she wanted presented to everyone junior. After the captain gave a short reassurance simulcast to each space in the Fortress, Mattoso was answering questions from over a hundred frightened Aoteans in one of the smaller Deep Machinery spaces.

"We have no reason to trust the conspirators," answered Mattoso. "We haven't even verified their ability—"

"They have ships — we saw it. Why would they have ships if they wanted to kill us all?"

She gritted her teeth. "Maybe they have ships. Or maybe they weren't real. None of us have seen these ships, much less analyzed them onboard."

"So what are we going to do? Just hide down here until we get to Samwise?"

"Operations have already begun to regain control of the ship. We—"

"But Ngayabo said that they stopped them in Engineering."

"She's said a lot of things." Mattoso tried to calm her frustration. "It will take more than one operation. Most of all, it will take courage and teamwork. We outnumber them, maybe ten to one." She doubted it was this high if they only counted adults. "We know the ship just as well as they do. With time, we'll capture the traitors and regain control of the ship."

Her wearable buzzed urgently. *Goddamnit!* She looked down — it was Loesser.

Cy's the last one still Aft. He said to give him thirty minutes — it's been twenty. Getting ready to go back in to get him, with the handful of healthy I have left; wounded are getting pulled back to the Fortress with the MedTechs.

Mattoso cut off the next questioner. "I'm sorry, I have something urgent to take care of. If you have more questions, crowd in the spaces next door and ask one of the other department heads."

She was texting as she made her way to the passage that ran alongside the Deep Machinery Spaces.

Dr, Cy might need help. Might be wounded. Heading aft.

The reply was almost immediate. *On my way.*

Four had departed the Fortress, relying on Madani's seniority to talk their way past the guards. In the rush Mattoso picked up Operations Chief Azbek, almost bumping into him on her way out, and Madani met her at the aft Fortress hatch with another medical officer, Valdez.

Everything outside the fortress was eerily silent. The noise they made as they traversed the passageways aft had Mattoso terrified they would attract attention.

Her wearable vibrated silently. *Poor visibility, encountering resistance, still searching for Cy.*

On our way w/ doctors, she replied.

The lights flickered and then dimmed.

Valdez said she heard a noise down a side passage.

Azbek suggested that the flickering lights could be a good sign, perhaps that engineering had been retaken. And then something exploded. *A gunshot,* realized Mattoso, yelling at the others to take cover, and pulling the weakly struggling Azbek with her down a side passage. She stopped and turned back when she realized he wasn't moving.

Madani cursed aloud. Mattoso turned and saw why — it was a dead end, aside from a pair of small hatches.

She gently pushed the chief toward the doctors, drew her slugthrower, and stood near the junction, cautiously peering both ways. *Where the hell did that shot come from?* It was a long, gently curving passage, and she couldn't see anything past the curves in either direction.

The two doctors were cutting Chief Azbek out of the top of his coverall.

"Alive," said Dr. Valdez, as Madani worked frantically. "Gut shot."

Oh shit... sorry, Chief. "Valdez, check the hatches for a way out."

"But Ilsa needs—"

"Do it, Rana," ordered Madani without looking up. "If they find us, we're all dead."

Mattoso kept her eyes darting both ways down the passages.

The first was just storage. There was a pause and shuffling sounds of movement. "Second is — oh shit!" Metallic banging noises, and Mattoso turned back — a Bot arm was sticking out of the hatch that Valdez was trying to shut.

She risked stepping away from her sentry duty to help Valdez — bracing against a mechanical outcrop, she kicked at the Bot arm while the doctor shut the hatch.

A noise from the passage drew her back to the junction — just as she stuck her head out, a party of four unfamiliar crewmen appeared around the bend. She pulled back abruptly as they motioned to draw weapons.

Oh goddamnit. Of all the bad timing...

"We're about to have company," she said quietly.

Yells from the corridor confirmed this. "Listen," said a female voice. "We're not going to hurt you. You heard what Professor Ngayabo said — it's going to happen no matter what. If you want to save your life, just come out with your hands visible."

Damn it. She had an idea, but needed more time. She looked nervously at the confused doctor — Madani was

299

still busy seeing to Azbek — and raised her voice, announcing that they'd open fire if they came any closer.

She didn't have time to explain her plan. Mattoso motioned for Valdez to join her at the junction, and explained that she needed a delay. She hoped she was right about the Bots, remnants that must have missed the surge patrols. It had been weeks since she had had to deal with any compromised Bots.

A gunshot turned her momentarily — Valdez had fired a warning shot, and was yelling down the passage.

Swallowing her fears, she reached out for the hatch.

CHAPTER 67

Papka was terrified, hunched over, clutching his weapon. Konami could see it in his eyes, even through the goggles, and even through the hazy duraglass window in the control room door. And there was no indication Papka could see him through the remaining smoke.

From the view across the passageway and through the window, the conspirator was alone. Konami assumed in the pandemonium that the treacherous engineer had continued to send out reinforcements in a panic, and for once he was glad for the lack of tactical or military experience among the Aoteans.

Duraglass was thick, but it was designed to be airtight for steam or gas leak casualties, not to stop bullets. But it would slow them down and change their trajectory. He tried to sight down the barrel, but Papka kept moving in and out of the window frame. And he was too far to be sure of the aim.

Damn. Konami hadn't cleared the nest of passages around the control room yet. Reviewing the layout from memory, that could take another fifteen minutes or more. No, the time was now, to press whatever surprise advantage he had.

He kicked against the bulkhead, and just as he crossed the passageway, three shots rang out, and Konami spun wildly, pushing off to regain his cover.

And he screamed in pain through the breather at the excruciating pain in his hip, and line of fire on his neck. It didn't dawn on him for several seconds that he'd been shot, and dazed, he pulled himself into an alcove across from the control room.

Feeling his neck, it was just a graze – still bleeding, but no arteries. But when Konami looked down, he almost groaned in despair – his right hip was pumping blood, pooling into a growing fist-sized zero-g blob. From

301

somewhere nearby he found a rag, and clenching his teeth, wadded it up and stuffed it as deep into the wound as he could.

There was a voice, just barely audible. Someone talking into a wearable. *Papka*. Or his minion. He heard the word "…alive…" and that was it.

Fuck. They'd be coming for him, and they'd find him. He squeezed his eyes shut. It was time to do the unthinkable.

He couldn't help but cough when the breather came off. And he couldn't help cough again when he spoke, shouting "I surrender!" as loudly as his tired lungs would allow.

CHAPTER 68

Bikram restrained Elcot — the other two, more experienced and disciplined — stayed back.

"Goddamnit, Second —that is, Aspirer," she started. She still wasn't accustomed to using the Striver ranks in the open, and the slip up needled her. "Wait for my orders."

Bikram was a full coordinator, inducted cycles before Aotea was fully constructed. She had to expect that Aspirers like Elcot, one of the only inductees from Earth, would not be nearly as disciplined as those who had been learning from the Socializers all their lives.

She peeked around the bend once again — there was no sign of either of the women they had seen before. The coordinator debated whether she should call out another negotiation, but decided to take the opportunity to advance, and motioned her team forward, weapons drawn.

There was no one at the junction, and when she turned down the side passage, there was nothing but a dead end and two hatches. One was open.

She and her team advanced slowly, weapons held at the ready.

"Please, we've got a wounded man here."

The voice came from inside the open hatch.

"I promise," responded Bikram. "We won't hurt anyone. Just put your weapons —"

"Slowly. Slowly!"

She still couldn't see inside the space behind the hatch — it was too dark.

"We're coming—"

"Slowly. Slowly!" the voice repeated.

She spread her hands, keeping her weapon concealed behind the open hatch. "It's okay, I promise—"

Something sharp-edged bowled into her, sending her tumbling to the other bulkhead. Her gun fired wildly. It was a Bot, limbs whirling, and there were others behind it. She

303

felt a sickening pain in her guts and looked down to see a metal appendage stuck deep in her belly. As her vision went black, Bikram barely noticed the second hatch open.

CHAPTER 69

A cluster of shots rang out, and Papka could wait no longer. Thumbing a call, he didn't wait for acknowledgement. "Did you get him?"

He started to panic as there was no response. "Aspirer, respond!"

By Paola... he was coming for him. The Earther Konami, bred by violence, a great bear in the mist of the peaceful sheep of the rest of them. And his protectors were gone.

A raspy voice on his wearable: "Got him. The Earther is dead."

Papka's eyes darted to the window, but it was still hazy with smoke. "Aspirer, repeat!" Was that the same voice? Was it just the smoke?

"Konami's dead. He surrendered, and we didn't give him a chance to change his mind."

He couldn't help but be suspicious. The voice sounded different.

"Take a look for yourself, Chief. Body's right outside your window."

Despite his suspicion he couldn't help but push off the other bulkhead and take a look. And the last thing he ever saw was the barrel of a gun on the other side of the glass.

CHAPTER 70

It was a bloody scene, only exacerbated by the freefall. Mattoso suppressed her shock as she surveyed the mayhem that had come in the space of moments while they hid in the other storage space, and raised her hand to send tranq darts into each of the four bodies whether they were still struggling with the Bots or not. Weeks ago, she realized, such a scene would have made her near catatonic. Now she could swallow her disgust, but part of her knew that was even worse. *For a killer, killing gets easier...*

"What the hell happened?" gaped Valdez, rushing toward the prone bodies after emerging behind her. Mattoso hadn't had time to fully explain. While Valdez was guarding the junction, Mattoso had opened the hatch a crack but kicked away to the other bulkhead, and from a distance had been able to order the Bots back into the recesses of the storage space behind the hatch. Once they were docile from distance, Mattoso recorded a brief snatch of dialogue on her wearable, sending it drifting into the Bots while instructing them how to execute her plan. The obedience of the Bots at a distance was still a ludicrous contrast to their extreme danger up close.

Now that the four traitors were dead or unconscious, the Bots, out of reach, could be safely ordered back into the storage space. Mattoso shut the hatch after the Bots dutifully climbed inside.

"But how did you get them to attack?" asked the younger doctor as she checked the four drifting bodies.

"I told the Bots the newcomers' wearables were malfunctioning and dangerous and needed to be removed immediately." Fortuitously, there were five full size Bots, as well as a handful of DustBots — more than enough to distract their assailants. *More than just a distraction...* "All I needed to do was get them in reach, and then the virus thing takes over and makes them crazy."

Valdez pursed her lips at one of the bodies, and they went over them. Two were dead, one was tranq'd with superficial injuries, and the last one, the only woman, was dying with a gut wound.

Shit. Mattoso had to repress the thought that it would be much easier if they were all dead. Thankfully, Azbek was stable. But with two live ones, they needed a decision quickly.

Mattoso realized that even Madani, a department head, was looking to her to take the lead. "Very well. Valdez, you'll stay. We'll tie up the other one tight — and you'll have your dart gun, in case he wakes up. Just keep her alive, and keep working on Azbek. We'll stuff everyone else into a space further down the main passageway." She was pleased to see them nodding and getting to work without further prompting.

Two thirds of the way from the hatch to Engineering, Mattoso's wearable buzzed.

Have Cy; wounded and unconscious. Reactor shut down.

Mattoso repeated the message to Madani, and the doctor accelerated to a freefall sprint, flying headlong arm-over-arm with abandon, and she was breathing heavily after just a few minutes of following the long-limbed chief medical officer. They could have cut the time by going up to the surface, but she didn't feel comfortable at all with the idea of being in the open, and luckily the Doctor didn't ask.

Three junctions later, they were almost shot. A pair of soot-covered, red-sashed constables, as surprised to see them as they were, escorted them back to a much slower procession of a few healthy deputies, including Loesser, along with a handful of wounded dragged along behind.

While Madani took charge of the wounded from a weary MedTech, Mattoso got Constable Loesser's attention. "Engineering?"

"We cleared it."

"You cleared it? I thought it was a trap."

"Can't explain it." The constable had that dead-eyed look of someone who was so tired they no longer even felt like sleeping. "Took a small team in after Cy said to withdraw. Filled with smoke. Almost thirty conspirators, and he'd killed all but seven, now dead or darted. Don't know how. We did the shut down and left behind a weld team, on their way now — no one's getting into Engineering without a full day's cut. Heavy-duty weld shut. No time, so leaving the bodies inside."

Mattoso felt a burst of pleasure at the talk of dead conspirators, and tamped down on the shame that followed. *Do killers feel shame?* She didn't know. She squeezed Loesser's shoulder and moved onto the wounded, going down the line, each one gently pulled behind a healthy deputy, until she found Konami.

Contrary to Loesser's text, his eyes were open, though he looked terrible. He had wounds and burns bandaged from his neck down to his hips, but when he saw her, he grinned. "Got that son of a bitch..." he whispered.

She grinned back. "Which one?"

"Papka. Put two slugs in his forehead."

She had a sudden flash to the writings of one of the founders of the Society for a New Humanity. *Violence begets violence, and even otherwise decent and reasonable people can revel in the carnage...* She grinned again anyway.

He motioned her close. "A traitor — in the Fortress. Someone knew." His voice was barely audible.

"Who?"

"Don't know." He coughed and Mattoso called for the MedTech.

Another traitor. How? Everyone inside Fortress Deep had been blood tested, multiple times and with multiple witnesses, for the telltale drug.

308

Anxiety bubbled up inside her. If they could beat the blood test, then who could she trust? Who could anyone trust?

CHAPTER 71

Freefall made recovery much easier than it would be otherwise. Madani frowned but didn't object when, the day after surgery for his wounds, Konami insisted on attending the department head meeting. In a whisper, Mattoso filled him in on what he missed – the shutdown worked, so there was trickle power to vital systems, while the engineering hatches were heavily welded shut. There had been three scouting teams sent out, and all three were forced to flee under fire, with one death.

Konami shook his head. *We have a traitor.* It was the only explanation for so much being thwarted so quickly and substantially. They shut up when the crowded conference room's hatch slid open. But it wasn't the captain and mayor — it was an agitated trio of Aoteans. He tried to put names to faces at the same time that the CO addressed them.

"Make it quick."

They were struck dumb for a moment. *Captain seems to have that effect.*

"We're all, uh, parents — the three of us. And more. We've gotten —we've been talking to the other parents, and most of us agree that we should have the option to take Bigwig —the traitor, Ngayabo, up on her offer. We don't want to risk the lives of our children for anything, and if that means they have to go back home to Earth, that's okay with us."

The speaker, Lind, seemed to be relieved to be finished with his speech.

"That could be a death sentence," said Konami.

"What?" Lind balled his hands into fists. "Is that a threat?"

"No, not a threat."

"He's right," added Madani. "We don't know if those are ships or mockups. Even if they're real ships we don't know if they can make the journey to Earth. We already know they killed several Aoteans, and they were poisoning every one of us."

"It wasn't poison on its own."

"Does that really make you feel better, knowing that they were giving your children drugs without you knowing? We're dealing with fanatics, and fanatics will justify anything, if they think it helps their goals. Even murdering children."

The three parents were silent.

"I understand your concerns," said Mayor Akunle, suddenly next to Lind. The mayor put his arm on the man's shoulder. "We're all worried about the children. But what's most important is a united front. Our enemies are killers — they've already proven that. They'll strike at any division or gap we give them."

"But what about our children?"

This time it was the captain who answered. "Your children are safest here. In addition to the murdered crew, the fact that the killers spiked the water system indiscriminately shows that they care little for our lives, and even our children's lives. The only way we can guarantee their safety is to regain control of the ship."

After a moment, the interlopers departed silently.

One of the Bigwigs, Wilson Paramis, chimed in. "They're going to keep talking. Perhaps it would best—"

"It would be best to move onto actual urgent matters," interrupted the captain.

The side conversations stopped — no one had ever seen a Bigwig interrupted, apparently.

The captain continued smoothly, ignoring the mouths agape. "Chief Inspector, I'm glad to see you've recovered. Well done in Engineering. Recommendations?"

Konami met her eyes intensely, saying nothing more than they were still working out a plan. *Take the hint, Captain, don't dig!*

311

She returned his glare and, after a moment, nodded. "Very well." He felt relieved. In a very hurried meeting before Konami and his team assaulted Engineering, he had met with the captain, mayor, and the two Bigwigs, Paramis and Maltin. The search for whoever leaked the plan to Papka would start with them. But with the captain's apparent understanding of his desire to keep his plans under wraps, his suspicion leaned toward the other three.

Which shouldn't make him feel better, he realized. Even if it wasn't the captain, then one of the other three most senior personnel still "loyal" to *Aotea* was a traitor. He started to thumb an encrypted message to Mattoso.

The mayor gave Konami his characteristic toothy smile and ushered him into his tiny office.

The chief inspector tried to get comfortable, leaning against what would, in normal ship's gravity, be the ceiling. "Back on Earth, you were army, right?"

Akunle laughed, a booming, musical sound, pointing out that that was 40 years ago.

Konami and Harry had bonded shortly after the chief inspector's arrival onboard, over their shared experiences in West Africa.

Akunle's smile was gone, and he was uncharacteristically terse. He had risen to Major in the West African Guard.

Konami thought he knew why the mayor was reticent to discuss it – military experience wasn't exactly a plus for the Society. He didn't like prodding, but he continued. "Did you see any action?"

Akunle stared back. "Religious extremists. Accra and Abidjan. This was a long, long time ago."

The chief inspector showed him his projection. "I want to try something. We need some forward visibility — eyes and ears outside of the Fortress." He leaned forward. "I wanna take the Rings, starting with Central."

Akunle's eyes went wide.

"They're natural choke points. Should be easy to hold. The only ways between the Cans, and aft and forward. And they have a good vantage point for the surface."

"Why me, Cy?"

"We've been looking into the traitors' backgrounds, the ones we've identified so far. Very few from Earth, as we all know. But that means almost zero military experience. Problem is, we don't have much military experience either — law enforcement is a lot different than war fighting. It turns out that your ten years is just about the best we've got."

Meeting Konami's eyes, Akunle nodded.

Konami asked about the best approach to minimize casualties. After a moment, Harry deftly manipulated a projection on his wall, pulling up a line diagram of the route to the Central Ring. As he talked battle tactics like it had been months rather than decades since his last battle, Konami frowned a little, realizing the consequences of his deception. *One in three chance...*he realized. Checking the tapes with Wren after the department head meeting, Konami and Mattoso had learned that the only persons present during their strategy discussions for each one of the recent botched scouting missions were the captain, mayor, and the two remaining Bigwigs. There was a one in three chance he might be confronting Akunle tomorrow.

Confronting... he couldn't help but think of Gregorian. In his head, the word sounded a lot less ominous than it should.

CHAPTER 72

At Mattoso's greeting, Wilson Paramis looked up from his alcove — since the move to the Fortress, there was no room for anyone aside from the captain and mayor to have a private work space. The Bigwig smiled and greeted her warmly.

Mattoso sidled in close, nervous. She didn't have to fake the nerves, she realized — they came entirely naturally. Konami had called his plan "the Tyrion Lannister gambit," but she had no idea what that meant. *Probably another Earth joke.* "I'm worried," she said to Paramis, her voice low. "The Chief Inspector has been so secretive lately. Even more so than normal."

He nodded sagely.

"He won't let anyone in on his plans, except for the next step. I mean, later today he's hitting Forward Supply 4 with a big team. But why? He won't tell us what he's after... I probably shouldn't have mentioned the mission, but the only people he told about it were me and the captain. What could he be after?"

Paramis's eyes narrowed. "And why are you telling me this, Lieutenant?"

Mattoso looked him dead in the eyes. "When I was made acting chief inspector, you told me that there might come a time when Aoteans would have to choose the right thing to do. And you told me that you trusted me. Well now I think it might be that time. And I'm trusting you." She hoped it didn't sound as ridiculous as she felt.

He broke out in a sudden grin. "Well you've made the right choice, and I can see that we have too. I don't know what's going to happen, Beatriz, but I can tell you that with you on the right side, our chances of success are much higher."

Does he know? How could he? Mattoso thought she shouldn't put anything beyond the traitors — they couldn't be more than five or ten percent of the crew, and yet they were already so many steps ahead.

This better work, Cy... If it blew up in their faces, there might be no option left but to take Ngayabo up on her questionable ride back to Earth.

CHAPTER 73

The Bigwig Hamad Maltin was huddled, almost hovering, over a desk in the corner of one of the Fortress workspaces. *Is he asleep?*

Konami pulled his way to the Bigwig's corner, realizing that he was listening to music, tapped him on his shoulder. This close, he heard orchestral Earth music — *barock, is it? Barack?*

"Yes?" said Maltin, pausing the music. *Baroque! That's it.*

Konami huddled close, aware that the other Aoteans in the workspace were giving them surreptitious glances. "It's about food," he said in a low voice. "I'm concerned about our stocks."

"Don't we have enough dry rations for years?"

Konami looked around him slyly, lowering his voice further. "We might have evidence of tampering with ration seals."

Maltin's eyebrows arched. "Surely not!"

Konami shook his head. "We don't know yet — it might just be a bad batch. As quiet as we can, we're testing them. But we need a backup plan."

"What do you suggest?"

"The Sausage Factory."

"But that could be contaminated as well."

"Possibly. But our scouts tell us that at least some of the traitors are using it, so we don't think so. Further, the chemists tell me that cybac can be scrubbed — any contaminants can be filtered out, unlike the dry rations."

"I didn't know that was possible."

"Me neither." Konami hoped like hell that it was at least plausible — nothing in Maltin's bio had indicated specific expertise in food chemistry, but he assumed that his agricultural engineering background lent him more

316

knowledge on the subject than Konami. "So we're planning to hit Food Production, soon — a fast hit."

"But what's the point? You could only carry a few days' worth of cybac."

"Weeks, they tell me, with the collapsible smart-sacks. If it turns out we need it, we'll be glad we did. It'll give us time to come up with a long-term solution."

Maltin still looked skeptical. "So how can I help?" Konami explained they needed more information about the layout, especially near the adjoining Garden. He projected the blueprints, and they started to plan a mission that would never be executed.

CHAPTER 74

Mattoso halted the advance with a hand signal. Constables Lo and Shofstahl stopped on a dime in the passageway behind her. The fourth member of the squad, MedTech Taki, bumped into the two constables. Captain Horovitz had trusted Konami's cryptic insistence on three four-person squads for the unexplained mission, but she had ordered that a MedTech join for each team, and Mattoso had the bad luck of leading the squad that drew the clumsy Second, Taki.

She looked back down at the projection on her hand. According to the specs, Forward Supply 4 was just beyond the next junction, before a dead end. With no other way to approach, she inched forward, pulling hand-over-hand along the bulkhead. *No guards at the junction…*

They could turn back now — the goal was only reconnaissance, to see if Ngayabo's forces had any active defense in the Supply space, and they'd pull back once this was confirmed. At the same time, Konami and Loesser would each be leading their own reconnaissance teams. One of them would find resistance, the chief inspector was positive.

No, best to make sure, she decided. She whispered into her wearable that they'd have to enter the huge storage space. She brushed aside worries about a bomb, primarily because the presence of a bomb would confirm the real reason for this mission. She assigned to Constables, Shofstahl and Lo, to stay back with covering fire, and held back Taki, ordering that they would withdraw at any sign of resistance.

She pulled across the bulkhead to the wide, double cargo hatch, trying not to move as nervously as she felt. Automatic hatch operators had been secured ever since the machinery virus, so she opened the maintenance access next to the hatch to get to the manual wheel operator.

Involuntarily cringing as she started to spin the wheel operator, she braced herself for an explosion. But it didn't come. The wheel spun on, and the double hatches slowly pulled away from each other, revealing nothing but darkness in the storage space beyond.

A whisper in her earpiece – Taki heard a noise from a side passage.

She turned the wheel faster. *Goddamn it, why's it gotta be so slow?* In freefall it was awfully hard to get the leverage necessary to spin the wheel as fast as she wanted to.

"Someone's coming."

Shit. Leave now, and they wouldn't be able to confirm whether or not this space was being guarded. "Pull back to the Fortress Observation Point. I'll be joining shortly."

She set her feet against the "ceiling," spinning the heavy wheel for all she was worth. A noise distracted her — a far-off gunshot.

"Report," she whispered. "Report!"

More gunshots. "Oh my god!" It was Taki, not whispering. "They're dead. They're dead!"

"Calm down, Second. What happened?"

"Oh my god, oh my — okay, calm down. They cut us off, down the other way too. I'm pulling back and shooting. I don't see anyone. Shofstahl and Lo are dead."

"You're coming back to me?"

"Yeah — there's no other way! Oh my god, I see them!" More shots rang out. "I'm returning fire!"

Shit shit shit... where to go? Only one way. She got back to the wheel, setting her shoulders and spinning as fast as she could.

She peeked around the maintenance access hatch — Taki fairly hurtled around the corner, bumping into bulkheads and pushing off with her feet. The double-doors, separating, looked just wide enough at this point to admit Mattoso and Taki's slim bodies.

"Come on!" she shouted, and the Second turned with a relieved glance. Just as she reached the maintenance hatch, a pair of attackers revealed themselves, shooting with mean-looking carbines.

Oh shit, where'd they get those? "Quickly!" she urged Taki, using the open maintenance hatch as a shield. "Wait, give us covering fire, for just a minute."

While Taki fired blindly around the temporary shield, Mattoso fished out a leverbar from the maintenance access tool-pocket. On the advice of Acting Engineer Zafy, she had brought a mini-cutter. She had thought it would be much too small to cut through the heavy cargo doors, and she was right. But here it would have a use. She briefly thought of cutting off the hatch operator wheel, but that would take too long. So she threaded the leverbar through the wheel, at an angle, wedging it against the walls of the little access opening. Lowering the setting of the cutter, she carefully turned it on and edged the contact points between the bar and the wheel — effectively welding them together, preventing the wheel from turning.

After testing her handiwork, she peeked around the access-hatch-slash-temporary-shield: there were two attackers at the junction, peeking around the corner and firing in between Taki's response shots. The way they were shouting, more were coming.

"It's ready," she ordered Taki. "You go first!"

The slim Second, probably less than fifty kilos, easily slipped through the gap. Mattoso kept firing, reloading at a pause.

"Taki," she whispered. "You still hear me?"

"Yeah!" came the response in her earpiece.

"Open the interior maintenance hatch and stand by the operator wheel. Soon as I'm through, wing it shut!" She was almost certain that wedging the outer wheel shouldn't affect the operation of the inner wheel. *And if I'm wrong, we're proper fucked.*

"Got it!"

Mattoso emptied one more clip, fingering her pocket at the same time — only three more clips left. Then she dove for the gap. The fit was much closer than for Taki — it pinched her chest uncomfortably, and she had to rotate her hips and shimmy through, but she made it. And she was relieved to see it closing behind her — though much more slowly than she would have liked.

The shouting of their attackers got closer, and Mattoso quickly reloaded her gun, backing into the shadows of the dark supply space.

An arm thrust through and she fired without thinking — there was a cry of pain, and it pulled back. "Faster, Taki!"

"I'm trying!"

Seconds felt like minutes, but finally the double-doors came together. In total darkness, Mattoso set her wearable setting to make some light. Taki started to join her in among the stacks of supplies, but Mattoso stopped her. "Stay by the operator wheel — if it starts to open, shut it! I'm gonna look for a way out."

Exploring a dark room in freefall was a lot tougher than she thought — with one hand holding her wearable out for light, she only had one to move with — and half the things she grabbed for purchase turned out to be poorly secured, and came free as soon as she grasped them.

"I hear something — through the door!" shouted Taki.

"What is it? Does it sound like weld cutting?"

"I don't know, maybe? It's getting louder!"

Shit! She looked down at a projection, querying the blueprints. *Exits for Forward Supply Space 4* only turned up the one. *Think damn it!* Sweat dripped and floated onto the wearable, distorting the projection. *Damn trickle power...* most ventilation fans were turned off.

She suddenly looked up. *Vent fans...* She queried it.

"Taki, we have a way out!" she cried. *Cliché, but some things are clichés for a reason...*

"Good, 'cause they're coming through! I can see the weld!"

Mattoso kicked with her feet, shooting up to the storage space's overhead, and felt around until she found the ventilation grate. "Follow my voice, Taki!"

She kept talking while she fumbled with the grate. Cursing, she realized that the mini-cutter would work perfectly well here — and with a few swipes, the grate was free.

A light flashed to her side — the weld flame had cut through, cutting one of the double doors from top to bottom. "Hurry, Taki!" When the Second finally arrived, Mattoso sent her through the vent first. Thinking fast, she rushed over to the interior maintenance access and cut the broad alloy access cover clean off, then awkwardly carried it back to the overhead vent.

"Taki, hold my feet."

"What?"

"Just do it! Just for a minute."

With the access cover in hand, Mattoso allowed Taki to pull her up into the vents feet-first, then stopped her when she was even with the overhead of the storage space. As the shouts of her attackers, now numbering far more than two, became audible, she quickly welded the access cover where the grate used to be. It wouldn't stop their pursuers, but it would put the vent out of sight, at least for a time.

Hopefully enough time.

In her childhood nightmares on Ceres, she would be trapped inside the most remote mining catacombs deep beneath the surface of the dwarf planet, all alone and in the dark. *Waiting for the ghosts of long-dead ore miners...*

In the pitch black ventilation shaft, she was facing the wrong way, with no room to turn around.

She wanted to cry. Instead, she whispered "Taki, you'll have to lead the way. I'll navigate from my wearable."

322

And, backwards, she braced herself against the confined walls of the vent shaft, put one hand over the other, and pushed her way into the darkness.

CHAPTER 75

Konami paced, as much as one could pace in freefall. He disregarded the angry glares and sniffs of the others in the Fortress's common room closest to the main exit. Aside from the coffin-like latrine rigs, any semblance of privacy was a distant memory.

"Anything?" he said.

"Nothing yet," responded Loesser through his wearable.

They had returned hours ago, finding no sign of readiness or resistance near the Sausage Factory or the Ring, thus apparently clearing the mayor and Bigwig Maltin of suspicion. *Unless they suspected my suspicions...* But no, he'd stick with his plan, at least until he had reason to think otherwise. He recognized that if Mattoso never returned, that would probably be as much of a confirmation that Bigwig Paramis is feeding information to Ngayabo as if she returned with a report that they met resistance.

But confronting Paramis at this point seemed premature, somehow. Like there could be another explanation. Or was that just grasping at straws?

Goddamnit Bea... get back here! Frustrated, he crawled through the Fortress passageways to the makeshift Data Central. As usual, Wren was alone in the tiny workspace, headphones blasting away so loud Konami could hear them.

"Third, you awake?" He tapped the young Data tech on the shoulder.

"She back yet?"

Konami couldn't stop word getting out when the three squads left the Fortress, but at least their mission and destination seemed to have been kept under wraps. "Not yet. Can you show it to me again?"

The screen was split up into quadrants, zoomed in on Wilson Paramis's face and hands. From the point of view of Konami or whatever other crewman had been nearby and wearing a vidcam, it showed Paramis' actions during and after the planning meetings for the earlier missions that had been compromised.

Just as before, nothing struck him as obviously suspicious. Wilson Paramis nodded thoughtfully and agreed to Konami's and Mattoso's proposed missions, and then, at some point minutes afterwards, went to his own workspace. The other two suspects, Hamad Maltin and Mayor Akunle, had behaved similarly. None of the feeds could tell what Wilson was working on, nor could Wren's network skills pinpoint it as anything more than a mix of mundane local network activities and off-network tasks, that could be anything from games to vids to secret messages to Ngayabo, funneled through some digital trickery.

Be much easier if he'd just cackle and twirl his nonexistent mustache...

His wearable buzzed. It was Loesser. "Cy, she's back."

He raced out. "Injured?"

"She's fine, but it's just her and Taki. The others are dead, she says. We're in Medical."

He shut his eyes for a moment. *Poor Shofstahl and Lo...* But then he was off, and if there were a freefall Olympic games, he would have just set the passageway dash time record. Madani frowned slightly when he bumped a MedTech bursting into the little exam room.

Mattoso didn't wait for him to speak. "They were ready for us. Shofstahl and Lo are dead."

Konami just nodded, teeth clenched. His hand moved to his gun without conscious thought.

"I'm fine, Cy," said Mattoso. "Go ahead and get him, and tell me about it after."

He waited until the captain, XO, and mayor had arrived in the conference room before messaging Paramis. *Conference room, urgent,* he sent. When briefed, Mayor

Akunle, shocked that he had been suspected, cautioned that perhaps they should wait for more evidence before confronting the Bigwig, but he was overruled by the XO and captain. The chief inspector agreed — morale within the Fortress seemed lower every day, especially with failed expeditions and dead bodies piling up. This needed to be resolved as soon as it could. As far as a traditional interrogation, Konami hoped that the gravitas and seniority of the captain and mayor would make up for a lack of rock-solid evidence.

The heavyset demographer sauntered in, as much as one could saunter without gravity, his grin unaffected by the dark expressions of the others.

Captain Horovitz nodded to Konami.

"We've suspected someone for a while now, Paramis," he started. The Bigwig's smile gradually faded. "Too many scouts and squads being thwarted to be coincidence.

"So we narrowed down the suspects. You won't be surprised, now, to find that you were one of them. Each one was told about an upcoming recon mission. Yours was for Forward Supply Storage 4. We sent out four, including two of my constables. Good men and women, good Aoteans. And now they're dead. They're dead!" He realized he was shouting, and calmed himself before continuing. "They met resistance, but the others didn't. We were very careful — no one knew about these recon missions but myself, Lieutenant Mattoso, and the suspects. Did you tell anyone?"

Paramis just stared at him, his expression blank, but his eyes probing.

"Demographer!" shouted the XO. "The chief inspector asked you a question."

"Test my blood," responded the Bigwig, rolling up a sleeve. "Go ahead. Again, anyway — you tested me that first day, when Ngayabo revealed herself as a traitor. I swear, I didn't tell anyone, and I swear that I'm not a traitor. You really think I'd take part in poisoning myself?"

Konami sensed no deception, but he might not with a practiced liar. "It's not poison. At such low levels, the effect is very small, especially for someone as, well, large as you." It felt funny using the same argument he had argued against in the past.

"Well then, would I really put myself into the lion's den, if I was a traitor?"

"If you're a fanatic, like Ngayabo, then, yes. You might even be willing to die for her murderous mission."

Paramis reached to his belt, and Konami ordered him to slow down.

"Just my wearable. Here, take it. Give it to the Data techs. They'll find that there's nothing fishy on it — no secret transmissions, or the capability to do so."

Konami declined to reach out and take it.

"Demographer," snapped the captain. "In the corner. Don't argue, do it. XO, if he moves, shoot him."

She beckoned the chief inspector, and she, Konami, and the mayor huddled in the opposite corner while the XO watched Paramis.

"Thoughts?" asked the captain in a low voice.

"The evidence points to him," said Konami.

"Mayor?"

"Locking him up isn't going to help morale," suggested Akunle. "In fact, considering how tightly we're packed in, I don't even know where the hell we'd put him."

Captain Horovitz nodded. "Suggestions?"

"We keep him watched," offered Akunle. "Around the clock. Cy, the XO, Mattoso, and a few other trusted officers. No network access, but he'll keep silent — whether or not he's the traitor, he won't go blabbing. And if he tries, we shoot him."

Konami shook his head. "We can't afford to tie up senior officers with guard duty every day."

"Then what do you suggest?"

He took a deep breath. "Medical. We say he had an allergic reaction to the pharma, and keep him sedated. He

327

hogs a bed, but that's it. We can trust Dr. Madani. She won't like it, but she'll do it and keep him alive and healthy."

The captain leaned back her head and scratched her chin. Just before she spoke, a blaring alarm sounded.

"BATTLE STATIONS! ALL HANDS REPORT TO FORTRESS BATTLE STATIONS!"

Captain Horovitz looked to Konami and nodded, and without thinking he pulled out his dart gun and shot Paramis. Then, ignoring the dumbfounded XO, he drew his slugthrower and rushed to his station.

CHAPTER 76

"Surrender!" came the voice on the announcing circuits. "All of you can still live full lives back in Earth system!" It was Ngayabo on the guardstation's screen, behind a transparent shield in the passageway outside the Fortress. At Konami's suggestion, vidcams had been mounted at the two entrances. The attackers had not hidden their approach, armed with the same spiky carbines Mattoso had seen near the supply room. Their approach wasn't hidden, but so far their numbers were. *At least several dozen* was all Mattoso could say for sure.

"Under what terms?" This was Loesser's voice. Konami had told her to stall for as much time as they could while they prepared. They had barred and reinforced the "back" door, where Mattoso's team was stationed, while Konami had a much larger force at the larger "front" door to the Fortress. Connected, the two entrances had been chosen strategically, while all others had been blocked and welded shut.

"No terms. Throw down your weapons and we will escort everyone to the return craft."

"How do we know the ships have the capacity for everyone?"

While Loesser dithered, Mattoso turned back to the crowd of armed deputies taking cover behind makeshift barriers. Both entrances opened into large common spaces inside, the "front" larger than the "back", and passageways underneath the surface of the Cans outside. In the last quarter-hour, both common spaces had been piled with whatever heavy, bulky objects might provide cover. For once the freefall was a boon — they never would have been able to move the various tables and beds and couches into the common spaces so quickly without it.

She scanned the faces peering above and around the temporary cover, well aware that her words were being transmitted to other Aoteans deeper inside the Fortress — some arranged as reserve forces, and some, like Pat and the children, hiding in silence. "When we first left Ceres orbit, none of us ever believed that we'd be holed up behind a door, guns in hand, waiting to shoot a band of killers." *Damn it, what would Cy say?* "We had a dream of peace, and kindness — a New Humanity. Perhaps we were naïve. But naïve or not, we're not the killers. They are." She had to believe it. "We didn't set a trap for a loyal Data tech, Muahe, because he was doing his job too well. They did. We didn't make an artificial venom and use it to kill. They did. We didn't shoot someone in front of the whole crew for doing the right thing. They did. We didn't put chems into the water for every adult and child onboard to drink. They did! And now they're coming to kill every one of us. They may have better weapons — weapons they had stockpiled since launch, it looks like — just another sign of the violence of their plan, but their numbers are few. Whatever their vision, it's a vision built on death and destruction. It's the opposite of the New Humanity. The opposite of us. When you fight here, when we fight here, we're fighting for your families, and we're fighting for the original vision to build a New Humanity."

She paused, amazed at the rapt attention. Her wearable buzzed — it was Konami. *Wow,* read his message. *Keep going and finish strong!* At the same time, Pat sent *I love you so much.*

"We fight for *Aotea.* For *Aotea!*" she shouted, fist pumping.

"FOR *AOTEA!*" roared back the deputies. Voices echoed through the passageways of the Fortress.

A deputy by the hatch got her attention and she rushed over to the projection. A handful of traitors were setting something up twenty meters down the passageway from the entrance. She switched over to the feed from the other entrance.

"Cy, you seeing this?"

"Yeah. Pull back anyone close to the hatch."

Oh shit! She gave the order, motioning back the deputies nearest to the front.

She glanced back at the screen — it was clearly a weapon, stout-barreled, and set up to brace against the passageway bulkhead.

"Pull back!" she repeated to the slowly reacting deputies, helping them back the temporary barriers away from the hatch. "Now!"

"Incoming!" shouted Konami into her earpiece, and she dove behind a table. "Brea—"

The explosion was deafening, and sent her hurtling back, along with the table. An impact with another deputy knocked the wind out of her. Mouths were moving, but all she heard was a high tone — *the blast, of course.*

She shouted more orders, unable to even hear her own voice. Coughing at the dust and debris, she motioned to those deputies nearby to get into position, slugthrowers aimed at the opening. The hatch itself, reinforcement and all, had disappeared — she glanced to her side and saw it laying askew against the back bulkhead. A moaning deputy was weakly trying to push it aside before she was dragged towards medical.

Her hearing was returning. "Bea, acknowledge!" It was Konami.

"I'm here, I'm okay. Couldn't hear for a sec—"

"They're on you in ten seconds!"

Shit! "They're coming! Aim and fire as soon as you sight the enemy!"

I'm not ready — and they were there. Four shapes visible through the dusty haze, aiming carbines. "Fire!"

The sounds of the gunshots ricocheted around the bulkheads and obstructions, nearly deafening her once more. Two of the shapes reacted in obvious pain — the other two had taken cover behind something.

The haze was clearing, and several more shapes appeared, aiming carbines. Mattoso shouted wordlessly and kept firing, ducking behind the table twice to reload. When she peeked over her cover, she spied a handful of bodies drifting near the open hatch. Something shoved its way in and sent the bodies hurling to the side — a wedge shaped shield, just barely small enough to fit through the hatch. Carbine barrels poked through slits in the shield, bristling like some prickly-furred Earth creature whose name she couldn't recall.

"Hold!" she shouted — there was no point to shooting the shield. "Cy, you there?"

There was gunfire in the background of his response, and his only response was a curse.

Mattoso almost dropped her gun as something flew into the common area and bounced off a bulkhead, almost into a deputy's lap. It was cylindrical, about half a meter. The deputy held it up, asking what it was, and exploded.

Mattoso's vision changed abruptly — she realized she had blacked out, thankfully still behind cover.

"Bea, report!"

She asked how long she was out. Thankfully, it was just a few seconds. Konami told her to pull back to the first reserve point.

She had a thought as they retreated, under fire, into the passageway behind the common room, explaining it into her wearable. Through the back hatch, she motioned to a pair of deputies. "Cover me for a minute." She still had the mini-cutter — switching it to weld mode, she bonded a piece of alloy debris across the hatchway, then tore off some pipe cladding to further secure it, finally shutting and locking the hatch after making sure every live deputy had gone through. Weak as it was, it might only buy them a minute against those bulky alloy shields, but that was better than nothing.

Mattoso met Konami at the reserve point, at the back of the adjoining passageway that connected the two entrances, opening up to a workroom. Though at an angle, they had a decent field of fire to the hatch that would lead to both entrances. She told him about welding the debris, and Konami dispatched a handful of deputies to do the same to the adjoining hatch that led to the reserve point. *Maybe the minutes can add up.* She counted casualties with Konami – together they'd lost about twenty, but reserves from further inside were filling the gaps.

Days before, while still setting up the Fortress, she had had a little time to discuss military tactics with the mayor. They had the numbers advantage, but in the cramped passageways and quarters of the Fortress, only so many Aoteans could fight at a time. *At least we have plenty of reserves to fill the casualty spots...* She didn't want to think about the dead, biting her lip when a few names came to her. *Time for that later.*

An impact sounded — the traitors trying to get through locked hatches closer to the entrances. Konami ordered everyone to aim and get ready, and Mattoso rushed to help the deputies at the workroom hatch — hoping that the several jutting pieces of piping and alloy cladding would present far more of an obstacle than her rush job before.

A rumble down the passageway told them that the enemy was seconds away, so they jammed shut the hatch with an extra weld, and pulled back behind temporary obstacles.

"Wait for my order!" shouted Konami, holding up an arm.

There was a whirring noise from the hatch. It started up irregularly, and steadied. "What is it?" Mattoso whispered to Konami.

"CI," called out a deputy. "That's a drill."

"A drill? You sure?"

"I'm a first class machine tech, and I know the sound of all the drills onboard. That's an eight centimeter drill."

Something passed over Konami's face.

"What's wrong?" asked Mattoso.

Konami raised his voice for everyone to hear. "Grab cover and pull back! Pull back! Any cover that will fit

333

through the hatch, take with you, but pull back to reserve point two immediately!"

It was pandemonium as fifty Aoteans scrambled to get through the back hatch, hauling the cover with them.

He just gestured to the hatch. Mattoso looked back just as a circle of alloy thrust loose, floating free, into the workspace. Something else followed it with a high pitched whine.

"Take cover!" she shouted, ducking, and a ball of fire erupted from the bulkhead.

CHAPTER 77

Konami's eyes sprang open to movement — he was being hauled roughly down a passageway. He looked down — past his feet, deputies were stacking furniture and other obstructions at the end of the passageway, where it opened into reserve point two.

"You're awake!" It was Mattoso, hauling him.

"The — the hatch—"

"Yeah, I got the gist of what you were trying to do — stack everything, slow down the traitors to buy us time." She shook her head. "Though with those weapons, I don't know how time will help." It must have been some sort of rocket grenade launcher that shot through the drill-hole.

He shook free and, despite a rush of vertigo, pulled himself along beside the Lieutenant. He cringed at a pain in his left leg — when he reached down, there was blood. He ignored it, popping a tablet Medical had provided earlier. Someone reported that they were clearing the deepest supply closets as hiding places for the children.

The children... For some reason he thought back to Gregorian, before he shot himself. *The children? They aren't the future either...* Gregorian had said.

"We're going to reserve point three, and you're going to Medical."

Oh my god. The children. "No." he almost shouted. "Not Medical. I need to see the captain."

"I don't understand," said the XO.

Deputies were piling up every possible obstruction, even dense ration blocks, in the passageway connecting reserve points two and three. But even in the pandemonium of pushing back the non-combatants, the mayor, captain, and XO had rushed to point three when Konami called.

He hoped their trust was warranted.

"It's the children," explained Konami. "That's what Kiro said. Before he died. He said 'the children aren't the future'. Well if they aren't, then what is? Someone's gotta be this New Humanity, right?"

"So, who?" asked the mayor.

"The genebank. Ngayabo's a geneticist. That's the only thing she's ever cared about. She's planning on killing everyone onboard — maybe even her own people. Kiro didn't just say the children weren't the future, he said we weren't either, him included. Maybe he knew."

"Okay, CI," started the captain. Konami realized a gun was in her hand. "Suppose you're right. How does that help us right now? We're already fighting for our lives."

He shook his head. *Fuck.* "If we only had a way out... We need a counterattack. On the genebank. Without that, Ngayabo's got nothing. Her whole plan goes to shit."

The mayor complained that there was no way out except through the enemy.

The captain pressed her lips together. "That's not entirely true."

Everyone looked at her. She explained that there was a design flaw that could be exploited for a small group to exit the Fortress. Apparently no one but the Captain and the deceased Engineer Papka knew about. She asked the XO and he didn't know about it either.

Loesser interrupted them on Konami's wearable – the enemy was past point two, on their way to point three, with maybe 15 minutes of delay at most.

The captain continued. "Habitability machinery room number two. Room was sized wrong, and the aft bulkhead had to be much smaller than planned. It's less than a centimeter thick, opening into a passageway with moveway access."

Thin enough to cut open.

"So we can get there," started the mayor. "But what do we do then? We don't have any explosives."

Konami thumbed in a call. "Bea, how's it coming?"

There was a sound of conversation in the background, then she came on the line. "Fifteen minutes, they say. An hour for a detonator."

Konami replied that they'd need the bomb in five minutes, and not to worry about the detonator. He explained that he just sent Mattoso to find the Chem Techs to rig up a bomb.

"But what about the detonator?" asked the mayor.

"No time, but that's okay. It's a binary explosive — two chemicals inert on their own, but explosive together with a spark. Don't need a detonator to mix and light up."

"You mean you're going to blow yourself up," added the captain.

Konami just looked at her, and she nodded grimly.

The XO reported that welders were on their way to cut the bulkhead open.

The machinery room took the word "cramped" to a whole new level, especially with the welding team. And the armed deputies, just in case they found any resistance outside. *If we do*, thought Konami, *this might be the end of the battle, and almost twenty thousand Aoteans.*

Luckily, the welders were relatively silent — Konami had been worried the noise could attract attention.

"Loesser, report."

"Heavy losses, hand-to-hand—" Grunts and impacts followed. "Heavy losses for the traitors — unnh! — too."

"How long?"

"Fifteen minutes."

"That's what you said ten minutes ago."

"We're tougher than I thought. Loesser out."

Konami shared the news with the captain and mayor just as Mattoso arrived with a Chem Tech, who held up an ugly looking package the size of two fists, wrapped in tape. "Smash it against a bulkhead to mix, and light this wick. That's all there is to it." She handed Konami a little poly ampule that would apparently create a small flame.

The welders were almost done, and Mattoso asked him about his weapons – three slugthrowers each, with plenty of extra ammo.

He tried to think of something profound to say, but all he could think of was "Goodbye, Bea. If you don't hear something in twenty minutes, send another—"

"Not for you, Cy. You're wounded. For me." Mattoso abruptly took the bomb and lighter, along with a gun and several magazines.

"But... the bomb. You'll have to—"

"No I won't," she interrupted with a wry grin, moving to the side. Behind her, gripping the guycable, was a MOMbot.

CHAPTER 78

"Say hello, Zinnia."

"Hello, Chief Inspector Konami."

Konami just blinked, and the welders wrapped up their work. Mattoso overheard one Tech tell the XO that a strong kick would open the bulkhead.

"Alright Cy, we're kind of in a hurry, so I'll just say that I'll see you in a bit."

As she turned toward the bulkhead, Konami grabbed her shoulder.

"Wait. I'm coming too."

"Come on Cy, your leg—"

"Don't need legs much in freefall. Don't argue, I'm coming."

She took a deep breath, but inside she was beaming. "Let's go."

With a mild crash, they rammed their way through the bulkhead. Thankfully, the passageway was deserted. Konami ordered Zinnia to lead the way. The bot nodded her furry, toy-like head, and moved. Data Tech Wren had provided the route to Genetics to Zinnia, and the Bot moved down the passageway, finding unseen grips along the bulkheads almost too fast to follow.

Mattoso noticed Konami gritting his teeth at the speed. "Need to slow down?" she whispered.

"No, goddamnit."

Damn tough guy ego... "Zinnia, if we grab your legs, will it slow you down?"

"I am capable of a much higher rate of speed than this."

At this, Konami's eyes went wide. "Then let us grab you and then go as fast as you can."

To spare Konami's leg, Mattoso grabbed the MOMbots stubby legs and Konami trailed behind, hands on her ankles.

"Go!" ordered Konami, and Mattoso took off.

The MOMbot wasn't kidding. The ride was bumpier than a Cerean minecar, but they were into the moveway level in seconds, and across a railing faster than the moveways ever went when they actually had power. The MOMbot's movement, hand-over-hand on any protuberance larger than a pea, was distinctly simian, taking Mattoso back to childhood nature vids of long-gone rainforests on Earth.

They reached the surface, still crisscrossed with guycables, and Zinnia wasted no time selecting one. Flying across the Can was the most exhilarating rush Mattoso had felt in weeks — until a gunshot rang out.

Konami cursed loudly. "We're spotted!"

Zinnia reported they were less than a minute from the genetics lab.

Mattoso cringed as Konami returned fire. "How can you aim moving like this?"

"I can't. But maybe we'll keep their heads down."

Seconds later they were behind the cover of structures on the Can's surface.

"They'll have reinforcements on their way," said Konami.

"Assuming they don't already have a squad of guards." But scouting missions had passed near the Genetics lab in the past, and didn't note anything of consequence.

The genebanks were located in the Repro office inside the Genetics section of one of the larger science structures. There were no guards at the entrance, nor at the entrance to the Genetics section. But at the next passageway, Zinnia stopped, reporting that she heard others down a junction.

Mattoso turned to Konami. "Let's go," he said.

"Zinnia, wait until we call for you."

They silently pulled across the bulkhead to the junction.

Konami peaked his head around for a moment, then turned to Mattoso. "One guard." He drew a dart gun. "I don't see armor. Five seconds."

Before she could object he sailed into the junction, and she heard the whisper-puff of the dart gun firing. "Clear," said Konami, and she joined him hovering over the prone, floating guard.

The MOMbot rejoined them as Konami was testing the hatch to Repro, reporting that there were more humans – at least three – behind the hatch.

Shit.

The bomb had to be placed at the inner genebank door; here wasn't good enough.

Konami pulled over to the maintenance access hatch, ripping it free of the bulkhead with a fury that astonished Mattoso. "This will be our shield," he said, demonstrating by holding it in front of him. "We each grab a handle and try and stay behind it as much as we can." He held out the bomb. "Zinnia, you'll take the bomb, and you'll man the access wheel. When I give the order, spin it open as fast as you can, and then stay out of sight until you hear another order, then go as fast as you can and smash the bomb against the human genebank door. Is that understood?"

"Understood, Chief Inspector."

"Good. Bea, you ready?"

The fate of Aotea is in our hands... She nodded.

"Just want to let you know," said Konami, eyes blazing. "There's no one onboard I'd rather have with me for this than you."

He gave the order, and Zinnia spun open the door like the maw of some great, yawning beast.

CHAPTER 79

They burst through the door with a kick to the opposite bulkhead, and were met with a hail of bullets and flechettes. The access hatch absorbed them with a brief drum solo, and Konami funneled his rage into returning fire around the edge of the shield. He could barely see, covered as they were — it was a greeting area, with a single desk and several seats. He thought he counted four shooters — one behind the desk, and the others at a corner passageway that led to their target.

Gotta make this quick... He knew reinforcements could be there in minutes.

"Cover me!" he said to Mattoso, and at a lull in the shooting, dove from behind the shield for the desk.

White hot fire ripped through his hip. *Don't need legs... don't need hips...* He hit the desk and hauled himself, one-handed, over the lip, hurling bodily into a surprised traitor. The man tried to bring his gun up but Konami was quicker, and shot him through the throat.

"Zinnia, come in but stay behind Mattoso's shield!"

Shots rang out from the corner and Konami swiveled to put the desk in between them.

"Bea, ideas?" If he sent Zinnia now, the Bot would be shot to pieces in seconds.

There was a wet feeling on his legs — he looked down, and it was blood. Somehow the pain was vague, like an echo of a real wound.

"Yeah, advance," she replied. "Use the desk!"

Without waiting for him to respond, Mattoso charged forward with the MOMbot huddled behind her shield. Konami didn't hesitate, and kicked forward with the desk awkwardly thrust in front of him. A hail of flechettes sent shards of poly flying, but the desk held together, banging into Mattoso's shield at the corner passageway. One traitor was floating motionless, but the others had retreated down the passage into an office, shooting periodically and keeping Konami and Mattoso, along with Zinnia, behind their cover.

"What now?" asked Mattoso.

Konami glanced around him. "No way to brace ourselves to kick down the passage, and moving hand over hand will be impossible with our shields."

"Chief Inspector," cut in Zinnia, "humans have entered this structure and are approaching."

Oh shit. "Zinnia, shut that hatch as fast as you can and hold it shut." The MOMbot moved in a flash. "Is there another way out? Zinnia?"

"Down that passage, to the left, and down another to the right, there is an exit into the—"

"That'll have to do."

Just as the MOMbot slammed shut the hatch, there was a pounding noise on it.

"I'm gonna have to—"

Mattoso interrupted him. "No, Cy. You were wrong — there is something to brace against. If you hold this part of the bulkhead, I can kick off you with the shield. That should be enough of a distraction and you can send Zinnia through."

A whirring noise sounded at the hatch.

Goddamnit. She was right. Konami squeezed his eyes shut and told her to do it, holding tightly to a protuberance in the bulkhead. She set her feet against his chest and shot off like a rocket, sending spider lines of pain up and down his body as a drumroll of gunshots rang out.

The Chief Inspector gave the lighter to Zinnia and told her to wait 15 seconds and then light the bomb. He didn't wait for the Bot to respond, hurling the desk forward and scrambling afterwards, both hands free, to pull himself down the passage.

The gunshots had stopped and a second later he saw why — Mattoso was sprawled out against a bulkhead, bleeding from a smattering of gunshots, while the two remaining assailants drifted motionless into the office. Konami grabbed her by a hand and pulled her roughly along, passing by the door marked GENEBANK — COLONISTS. As soon as he rounded the corner he called out for Zinnia at the top of his lungs, shutting his eyes and wrapping himself around Mattoso, bracing for a blast that came moments later.

CHAPTER 80

"Need more hemo!" shouted Madani. The patient was losing consciousness — they had patched up the wound in her leg, but she had lost a lot of blood. More patients were streaming in.

Medical in Fortress Deep was a cramped series of former storage rooms, with barely enough room in between beds to pass. If it weren't for the creative bed-stacking that freefall allowed, their capacity would be cut in half.

Madani tried to ignore it and focus on her job, even as a niggling part of her brain made the obvious connection between the rate of wounded arrivals and the progress of their battle against the traitors. And even more than her worries about the battle, she felt a crushing dread — dread that one of the arriving wounded would be Konami. Or maybe it was dread that it wouldn't... for the dead weren't sent to medical.

Her wearable buzzed. MedTech Saito brought a bag of hemo and Madani helped her connect it to the patient. In Main Medical, they would have had more space, automated hemo connections, and the assistance of MedBots. But there was no time to complain about the facilities, only time to treat and to heal.

"Losing number four!" shouted a young MedTech. Madani rushed over — his heartbeat was erratic and weakening. She called out for a stabilizer and injected it into the patient's IV. *Goddamnit...* his heartbeat kept slowing.

"Rana, number four gunshot is transmediastinal, unstable. Transfer to emer surgery and start thoracotomy."

"Chief!" a voice called out. "Dr. Madani!"

Madani turned — it was a constable, Goodluck. Her heart went into her stomach when she saw what he carried.

"Saito! Clear two beds!"

"But... which—"

345

"Four is clearing. And... nine."

"But nine is the Bigwig! He's been in a coma since—"

"No, he's fine. Put him in the waiting area. That's an order, MedTech."

Madani rushed over to Goodluck, taking Konami gently and pulling him to bed number four, directing Goodluck to bring Mattoso to nine.

"They did it, Doctor," said the constable while she located the wounds on the groaning Konami — two flechette wounds – pelvis and leg. She almost bawled, she was so relieved the wounds weren't life-threatening.

She pulled aside a MedTech. "Standard connections on four; clean and disinfect the wounds." After the MedTech acknowledged, she turned back to Goodluck. "What do you mean 'they did it?'"

"The genebank. That was their target, and they got it. The bomb. CI told me before he passed out."

Genebank? Bomb? Several minutes ago there had been a tremor. *Wow...* "Okay, Constable, thank you. Now we'd appreciate if you'd return to your duties; we're very busy here."

"Uh, yes. Of course. Take care of them, doc."

Madani turned to the Lieutenant, who was in much worse shape than Konami. She had four gunshot wounds: two in the abdomen, and one each in her shoulder and arm, rapidly being cleaned and dressed by MedTechs. Five minutes into the brain-scan, which thankfully revealed no sign of hypoxia after Mattoso's heart had briefly stopped, Constable Goodluck returned, barging through the hatch breathing heavily.

"They're — the traitors — almost here. We need to move to the next reserve point!"

MedTechs and doctors looked around the medical bay in confusion, finally settling all eyes on Madani.

She gritted her teeth. "We're not going anywhere. We took an oath and we're staying with our patients." She met the eyes of her own department, staring hard at any who looked like they might prefer to flee.

"But—"

"Our duty is with the wounded. Anyone who leaves will answer to me after this is all done."

Goodluck looked at her, shook his head, and then turned around with weapons drawn.

"Ilsa..."

Oh my god! It was Konami — he reached out to Madani, and she pulled along the little guycable that stretched across the Medical bay to take his hand.

"Rana — take over nine! Cy, what is it?"

"Goodluck... said they're almost here?"

"Don't worry, Cy." She covered his hands with hers. "Everything will be alright."

"No, listen... we have to announce it. Loud. To everyone."

"Announce what?"

"The genebank. Here, my wearable..." Konami fumbled weakly at his pockets, and Madani helped him find it. "Need to tell Ngayabo... the genebank is dead. All dead — no more genes."

"Dead? I don't understand..."

Konami gestured weakly. "On announce mode — bypassed normal security... should go everywhere in the Fortress." His voice was so quiet she had to put her ear next to his mouth and moments later he was silent again, his wearable floating away from his hand.

Gunshots turned her head. "Everyone take cover!" shouted Goodluck. MedTechs and doctors alike scrambled to find something to hide behind.

"The patients too!" shouted Madani.

Behind a cluster of beds, huddling the patients down with them, Konami's wearable drifted by. *What the hell did he say?*

More shots rang out from the passageway outside Medical, and Goodluck returned fire with a shout.

347

Goddamn Ngayabo for starting all this... Madani reached for the wearable, flipping on a projection onto the back of a prone patient. It was already in the announce mode on the Fortress circuit, with Konami's chief inspector override. "Ngayabo, listen to me!" She was shocked by how loud it was — so loud that even Goodluck paused, mid-shout. She swallowed her surprise and continued. "The genebank is dead. Dead and gone, every one of them. It's all gone, Ngayabo. Stop this. Stop the killing. The genebank is gone forever."

CHAPTER 81

After dreams of chaos and violence, Konami woke up to silence. Silence, a bright light that made him shut his eyes, and a tremendous ache, from his chest down to his feet. He tried to speak, but all that came out was a croak. He opened his eyes again — Madani was staring down at him with a grin.

"Welcome back, Cy."

"Water..." he managed to groan. She squirted something into his mouth, a little sweeter than water.

"Before you ask, she's okay. Mattoso. Stable and medicated for pain."

"Where am I?"

Still in Fortress Medical, apparently. She explained that they had a bit more space to work with, but were still relying on the 21st century gear they had cobbled together.

"Fortress? What about—" He coughed painfully.

"Don't worry, Cy. Just relax. The fighting is over. We won."

We won... The thought comforted him as he settled back into unconsciousness.

"He's awake, Mayor."

"Cy? Can you hear me?" It was Harry. Konami was in a private room, it appeared — perhaps one of the Fortress's supply closets. Mayor Akunle drifted in front of him, with Madani stretched out above. "We thought you'd want to hear what's happening."

He started to speak, but his mouth was too dry. A water bag was already in his hand, he found, and he squeezed it into his mouth. "What?"

"With Ngayabo and the traitors."

Of course — could it all be over? He told them to get on with it, and the mayor explained that just minutes after Madani's announcement, the attackers stopped advancing.

Within a half-hour, they were withdrawing altogether, and within an hour they were all out of the Fortress. "It was the genebank. You saved us, Cy. You and Mattoso." Fighting had ended two days prior, with several hundred casualties. "But it would have been all of us if it hadn't been for you and Mattoso." And in the aftermath, Wilson Paramis was found dead. Officially, in the fighting, but the mayor said that he had killed himself, leaving an unencrypted wearable with blueprints and proof that the supposed Earth return vessels were mockups.

Konami's mouth opened in surprise.

"And that's not all. He had a recording, I don't know how, of Ngayabo speaking about her plans. You were right, it turned out. There was no return possible. Ngayabo planned to kill everyone onboard. It even showed that your predecessor – the last Constabulary head – had been killed via fake suicide by the conspirators."

In any other circumstances but these, Konami wouldn't have been able to believe it. Paramis had tested positive for phenelzine. The mayor didn't have an answer for that, but suggested that he may not have intended to finish the journey in the first place. "In any case, we released everything we found immediately. Inside and outside the Fortress. We hacked into the shipwide circuits and put on Ngayabo's words, on repeat. We said we had recovered it from a dead traitor."

The mayor continued to explain. There was no response for another hour, and then scouts reported sounds of fighting – a mutiny within the mutiny. *Heh – traitors to the treasonous.* A few hours later a group came out with a white flag, and Ngayabo tied up and gagged. "There were another few pockets of holdouts, but the vast majority surrendered right then."

For the rest, the mayor explained that they were retaking the ship, space by space. Any remaining holdouts could be dealt with systematically.

Ngayabo was under guard and not speaking, not to anyone at all, while most of the other conspirators were cooperating from their hastily rigged jail cells. Apparently most of them didn't even know Ngayabo's ultimate plans. They thought we were all going back to Earth. Most were happy to cooperate after that.

"In fact, based on the data in Paramis's wearable, even the traitors weren't supposed to live. Ngayabo planned to kill everyone. Every single one of us, and every single one of her conspirators. Maybe a few of them knew it, knew they were gonna die, and fought on anyway. She was gonna kill twenty thousand people—"

"—and use the genebanks for the New Humanity." Konami shook his head in amazement. "That's what I figured out, Harry. Kiro — DCI Gregorian — he had said that we weren't the future. That even the kids onboard weren't the future. He knew what the future was — the genebanks. Ngayabo was going to kill off humanity and start fresh. A generation of babies in artificial wombs, raised by Bots, and one old, genocidal fanatic. A truly New Humanity, with no influence whatsoever from old Earth." He shuddered.

"So that's it, Cy. We're resting and healing, repairing, and retaking the ship. But it's over. Konrote's getting his guys together to start fixing the Cans' rotation."

"And the traitors?"

"I've talked to the captain. There will be trials, for any that won't plead guilty. Most of them have been begging to confess. A handful tried to kill themselves, in addition to those that turned on each other."

Trials. Konami couldn't help but think back to his own trial, though they didn't call it that. As if Harry could read his mind, he looked away at Konami's glance.

"I'll leave you to rest, Cy. Everyone is grateful — the Doctor can tell you that they've been turning away visitors all day. Thank you, Cy. To you and Mattoso."

When he left, Konami tested his muscles. There was pain in his legs and pelvis, but it was manageable. He reached out to Madani and pulled her in for a kiss. For the first time, he saw tears in her eyes.

"I was so worried, Cy. When Goodluck brought you in."

"It's over now. Thank you — for saving me."

"Thank you, Cy. For saving *Aotea*."

He asked after Bea, who was next door.

"How about Kostya?" He felt guilty, absurdly, that he hadn't visited his dog in weeks.

She chuckled. "Last I heard, few hours ago, all the pets were bouncing off the walls with the VetBots. XO says they remain there until Spinup. But we can visit."

Konami started to extricate himself from his various medical connections. "Bea. I wanna see her. Get this IV out of me."

"I don't know if you're—"

Konami couldn't help it and laughed uproariously. It hurt and felt great at the same time. "Ilsa, I'm going. I'm going to see Bea. Get it out or I'm pulling it out."

Surprise turned to amusement on her face, and she complied.

Mattoso was intubated and hooked up to half a dozen devices – she looked straight out of one of those ancient medical drama vids. He wondered how difficult it would be to move her to the much more modern facilities of the Infirmary, once it was operational. A familiar face — Teacher Pat Carmona, if Konami remembered correctly — hovered over her, along with a youthful Doctor. When Carmona saw Konami, a range of emotions ran over the Teacher's face. After just a moment, they pulled over and embraced him gently.

"Thank you, Chief Inspector. Thank you for saving her."

"How is she?" Looking into Pat's face, Konami realized the teacher was absolutely exhausted.

"Better. She's woken up a few times, but she's weak. She smiled when I told her that we won. Now she's resting."

"Looks like you need to rest, Teacher."

As if in confirmation, a wide yawn took hold of Carmona.

Madani suggested the teacher retire to the hammock next door, assuring him that they'd be woken if there was any change in Mattoso's condition.

After Carmona left, Madani ordered the other doctor to rest.

Konami let out a long, deep breath. It felt like he had been holding it for an eternity. He settled into a comfortable position beside Mattoso, taking her hand in his left, and putting his right arm around Madani.

Head resting on the doctor's shoulder, for the first time in months Konami felt an absence of worry.

He had never felt anything better.

EPILOGUE

AOTEA TODAY: SPECIAL EDITION
SPINUP PARTY A GREAT SUCCESS!
Yesterday, forty days after the Battle of Fortress Deep,
as many Aoteans have come to call it, we felt our own
bodyweight for the first time in 15 weeks. Grateful Aoteans
were reunited with their pets, including this writer's own
beloved cat, Barry. Much work remains to be done, but the
saddest tasks — the funerals for the fallen — are complete.
We will never stop mourning our lost loved ones and loyal
shipmates, but they have all finally been consigned to the
reclamatorium. Despite the destruction of the first facility,
a new genebank is being established, and their biological
heritage may yet live again.
*   The trials continue for those few that refrained from*
pleading guilty, including their ringleader, Mara Ngayabo.
As always, AOTEA TODAY will provide continuous and to-
the-minute coverage of all legal proceedings. We can all
hope that most of the conspirators, so far sentenced to
labor and house arrest for the next twenty cycles or more,
can eventually regain the trust of the rest of us.As for the
remainder, perhaps there's no hope for mutual trust, but
they still might contribute to our journey in small ways, and
they should be given every opportunity to do so.
*   The damage to* Aotea, *not only to our ship and crew,*
but to the psyche of those of us remaining, is devastating .
Perhaps even more so, now that we've had the chance to
reflect on the events of the past few months. But while we
must mourn, we must also refrain from despairing. On the
contrary, we should feel free. Free to chart our own path,
and free to create our own society, should we choose to do
so, recognizing the privilege it is to be alive to continue this
journey. And continue we must, whether back home or on
to a new destination, not only to honor the memory of the

fallen, but to restore a sense of hope to ourselves and our children.

In happier news, all restrictions on media from the Charter for a New Humanity Beyond Earth have been declared null and void by Captain Horovitz and Mayor Akunle, per their emergency powers. This writer just so happened to have a large store of Earth system media, including many entertainment vids and games, and they have been provided to Acting Data Systems Chief Wren to upload into Aotea's *network library. All Aoteans are encouraged to see what they've been missing!*

Weary as we are from the conflict, the ship is abuzz with talk of our future. The emergency powers of the captain and mayor will remain in effect while control and operation of the ship is reestablished, but this is not a long-term solution to govern ourselves. In light of this, AOTEA TODAY sought the opinion of Hamad Maltin, Senior Agricultural Scientist, and popularly considered one of the three Society for a New Humanity "Bigwigs" — the only one left. He declined to be interviewed, but provided the following statement:

"Aoteans, I am sorry. I am sorry for the rot at the root of the Society for a New Humanity, and I am sorry that I was blind to its true nature for so many years. It will be no consolation, but all I can say for myself is that this is not the Society that I joined as a young man in Jupiter system. The Society's founder, Paola Rahmon, was absolutely correct about one thing — there is a violence intrinsic to the culture of Earth and Earth system. But she was wrong about another thing — separating from that culture obviously does not eliminate this influence. We brought it with us, no matter how strictly we tried to separate ourselves, and I am now convinced that this part of humanity can never be excised. But perhaps it can be tamped down, and redirected.

Aoteans have a new future, when cycles ago our future seemed so clear. The decision on how to proceed and

355

govern ourselves, and even whether to continue on to Samwise or return to Earth system, must be a decision by all loyal Aoteans, though I plan to take no part. If it's not thrown out entirely, the Charter for a New Humanity Beyond Earth should be thoroughly examined, and no clause or section should be safe from excision if Aoteans deem it unacceptable. On Earth and Mars they used to call such a meeting a Constitutional Convention — as disconcerting as it might seem to emulate a custom of our ancestors, we should recall that this practice produced the least violent societies in Earth's bloody history. And we should keep in mind that the Charter did not keep us safe from the recent chaos.

As for myself, I am content to tend the Garden. All my energies will be devoted toward its repair and encouraging its growth, so that all of us and our children will forever have natural foods to eat and natural beauty to enjoy. No longer am I a 'Bigwig', or even a professor — my counsel should never be heeded as any more valuable than any other Aotean. For the remainder of our journey, whether it ends in Earth system or Samwise, I will merely be, if I can be permitted one last conceit, Aotea's *Gardener."*

LATE EDIT: AOTEA TODAY has been informed by the new Second Officer, Commander Mattoso, that the awards ceremony to honor the MOMbots has been postponed until tomorrow evening. Please see the attached announcement for details.

###

APPENDIX: Historical Timeline

2027: Comet P/2027 Saini discovered by amateur astronomer

2032: Path of Comet P/2027 Saini analyzed and determined to bear a significant risk of collision with Earth, comet renamed Shiva

2034: Shiva calculated to have ~50% chance of collision with Earth in 2055, damage estimated to be comparable to the Cretaceous-Paleogene impact event

2036: Treaty of Cooperation for the Future of Humanity (popularly called Co-Op Treaty) signed by nearly all nations, with two major goals: alter the path of Shiva to spare Earth, and execute a plan for humanity's future in case the first goal fails. Major hostilities on Earth cease (with a small but vocal, and largely religious, opposition to the Co-Op Treaty)

2043: Operation Deflect team lands on Shiva and begins ejection of comet mass at high speeds

2043: First permanent facility, named Sanctuary, founded on Luna

2044-2050: Numerous small, free-floating habitats established in orbit around Earth or near-Earth orbit around the Sun, largely by the ultra-wealthy

2050: Advances made in life extension; average human lifespan ~90

2054: First permanent habitation founded on Mars

2055: Operation Deflect is successful; Shiva passes within 100 thousand miles of Earth

2055: CoOp Treaty signatories extend close ties, Union of Earth formed, commits to continuing colonization of the solar system

2060: Off-Earth population: ~2000 on Luna, ~500 on Mars, ~1500 on free-float habitats

2071: First permanent habitation founded on asteroid Ceres

2071-83: Numerous small permanent and semi-permanent habitations established on asteroids

2087: First permanent habitation founded on Mercury

2087-2094: Numerous organizations advocating independence from Earth control founded on Luna, Mars, and elsewhere

2100: Off-Earth population: ~10K on Luna, ~10K on Mars, ~500 on Mercury, ~10K elsewhere

2100: Average human lifespan ~100, 85 year old adults are as physically capable as 65 year olds in 2000

2114-2133: DarkSide telescope array on Luna identifies numerous extrasolar planets and satellites-of-planets with signs of liquid water and possibly life, including moon of a planet orbiting red dwarf star Gliese 876

2101-2151: Habitations founded on numerous moons of Jupiter and Saturn

2137: Population of Luna votes to continue ties to Earth, population of Mars votes for complete, amicable independence

2138: Martian Declaration of Independence signed and delivered to Earth, Earth leaders promise objective and respectful response

2138-2139: Evidence found of weapons provided by Earth to anti-independence forces on Mars, Martian Civil War fought between pro- and anti-Independence forces, ~400 casualties, Independence forces victorious, major political scandal on Earth ends the careers of numerous politicians including President of the Union of Earth, new administration apologizes to the newly independent Mars

2141: Society for a New Humanity (SNH) founded on Ceres, advocating a "clean start" for humanity free from the influence and bloody history of Earth

2139-2153: DarkSide array verifies evidence of photosynthesis on dozens of extrasolar bodies, including a moon (named Samwise) of the gas giant planet Gliese 876c (now called Abhoth)

2161: Luna declares independence from Earth and separates peacefully

2171: Forwood drive invented — the first propulsion technology that would enable space travel to other star systems within a human lifetime

2178: Direct imaging by DarkSide array shows oceans as well as indigo-colored vegetation blanketing continents on moon of Gliese 876c called Samwise

2184: SNH draws up plans for colony ship to Samwise

2191: SNH begins construction of colony ship, ostensibly as a large, mobile, free-floating habitat, called Aotea, in the asteroid belt

2200: Off-Earth population ~50K on Luna, ~5M on Mars, ~200K on Mercury, ~500K elsewhere; most celestial bodies and free-floating habitations with more than a few thousand inhabitants are self-governing

2200: Average human lifespan ~120, natural limit appears to be ~150 years; with cloned organ replacements and other therapies, the very wealthy may live past 200, staying fit and active for most of their lives.

2202: SNH makes public colony plans for Samwise, to be funded by many sources including by volunteer colonists as well as volunteer genetic donors; they receive a very large response

2211: First "colonists" take residence on Aotea, construction and funding continue

2221: First baby born on Aotea

2237: Aotea departs for Samwise; ETA ~2292

ACKNOWLEDGEMENTS

Thanks to everyone who encouraged me and gave me feedback while I was writing Spindown. In particular, thanks to Jefferson, Ben, and my parents. Special thanks to Jay for his boundless patience and weeks of hard work on edits and general feedback – this book would be very different, and much lesser in quality, without him. And most of all, thanks and love to my wife, Nina, for her endless love and encouragement.

ABOUT THE AUTHOR

Andy Crawford grew up in New Orleans. After graduating from Louisiana State University, he served in the Navy as a submarine junior officer. Upon leaving active duty, he began working for the Navy as a civilian. Andy lives in Arlington, Virginia, with his wife Nina.

OTHER TITLES BY ANDY CRAWFORD

Sailor of the Skysea
The Pen is Mightier
Untethered (short story, available online for free at Solarpunk Press)

NOTE TO READERS

Independent authors survive on word of mouth and positive reviews; if you enjoyed Spindown, please leave a review online at your favorite book retailer!